KAREN CAMPBELL

After The Fire

HODDER

First published in Great Britain in 2009 by Hodder & Stoughton
An Hachette Livre UK company

First published in paperback in 2009

4

Copyright © Karen Campbell 2009

A CIP catalogue record for this title is available from the British Library

ISBN 978 0 340 93562 0

Typeset in Plantin Light by Hewer Text UK Ltd, Edinburgh

Printed and bound by CPI Group (UK) Ltd, Croydon, CR0 4YY

Hodder & Stoughton policy is to use papers that are natural, renewable
and recyclable products and made from wood grown in sustainable
forests. The logging and manufacturing processes are expected to
conform to the environmental regulations of the country of origin.

Hodder & Stoughton Ltd
338 Euston Road
London NW1 3BH

www.hodder.co.uk

A major theme of this novel is finding out who you can turn to when you really need help, and I'm very grateful to the following people:

Jennifer, Agnes, Linda and Tom, for lunches, laughs and lots of encouragement (and a bit of food poisoning too); my brilliant agent Lisa Moylett; my exceptional editor Suzie Dooré; Leni, Karen, Bob, Jack and everyone else at Hodder for doing a wonderful job; Ian Watson at Studio Scotland for treating me to food and photos; Sharon Murphy at Glasgow City Council for benefits advice; Garry yet again for his detective's insight and appalling jokes; Ross, for reading early versions and saying nice things; Willy for still being there for his ex-students; Griz, Maureen, Ailsa, Alison, Ann and Heather for editorial advice and friendship; Roy, for his courage and candour – which had a huge impact on this book; and all my family for their support and interest in my writing.

And, as always, my deepest thanks to my husband Dougie and my girls Eidann and Ciorstan, whose advice, patience, enthusiasm and love mean everything.

For Eidann, my little fiery one.

The First

Noises of voices. A woman crying. He was taken downstairs and put in a holding cell. If they spoke to him, he wasn't aware. Not until the door clanged shut and he realised this wasn't the waiting room. Beneath the street, beneath contempt. No longer in the light.

Jamie was surprised that he cared. Cath had yelled out in the courtroom and he wanted to get to her. See that she was okay she was his wife for God's sake he had to check on her and he was taken down here, encased in metal, ensconced in stone. Panting like a rabid dog. The bench was clammy; no that was his fingers. The bench was cold and it filtered through his good suit trousers like the onset of death, yet, strangely, the coldness calmed him. He wasn't going to lose it, not here, in Glasgow High, where he'd only given evidence the once, at that murder trial for that old Polish boy, when he knew there were cells down here, of course he knew that, where else would they keep the scum, but had never seen them. Up so close, and getting closer all the time. *Blow away the badness*. In through the nose, out through the mouth. Stare straight ahead, but don't look.

He couldn't help it. Graffiti etched the walls, stiff angry letters carved by keys and buckles and he thought of tally marks in *Robinson Crusoe*, marking off days, then weeks, then months and, as his lungs constricted, he thought of a girl who had no more days and his shoulders slumped as it poured on him again, and he became glad to be there. Faraway noises played like waves in the distance. He closed his eyes and drifted.

An echo of steel, more bangs, another key-turn, very near. Jamie jumped up, like to attention, in case they were coming for him. It was the macer. He stood at the door, but didn't enter.

'Mr Worth. His Lordship has sent me down to see you.' The macer lowered his voice slightly. 'He wants to apologise for your conviction, and to advise you and your QC to appeal.'

Jamie nodded. 'Okay. Thanks.' Trite words, but they were all he could think of. Did this usually happen, that a judge sent a special envoy to the cells?

'The evidence that was presented has not been disproved,' the macer continued. 'He wants you to think carefully about that. Do you understand?'

Did he understand what? That there was evidence, that this was a trial? That he was guilty? Jamie screwed up his eyes, trying to think, to hear above the crashing in his head.

'Yes.' A reflex response, a politeness that was expected.

The macer nodded. 'Good luck, son.'

Oh, Jesus Christ, Mother Mary and all the saints. Jamie swallowed as the door shut. Don't anyone start being nice. Please God, I can't take niceness.

Footsteps. Brisker. The courts inspector. 'We're taking you to Barlinnie. Quickly, before the snappers get down here.'

This was it. It was really happening. Rage flared, fused with terror. Rage was good. His heart frenzied on his ribs, but he wouldn't lose control. He was trained to work under pressure – Jesus, these pat phrases – what was wrong with him? Was this how soldiers hyped themselves up before they went to war?

No photographers outside. No crowds throwing eggs and insults. No people at all. He travelled alone, a single cop in the van beside him, another behind the wheel. Not for him the usual civilian security guys. He was *special*. Was that it then, his final polis sendoff? No white gloves or saluting. The cop beside him was silent. Just a young boy. Was he embarrassed; disdainful; sorry? Would he regale his mates at piece break with tales of the green-white murderer, who looked like he would hurl every time they swung a corner? Was he averting his eyes from the corpse, thanking God it wasn't him? Would he go home that night and hold his girlfriend; her perfume tasting like incense? Fucksake. Hold her, man.

It was a small van, one-way windows, and Jamie could see out the back as they rumbled along. See grey houses, grey sky. See the big gates shutting as they passed through the prison walls. Every time he'd been there before, to drop off a prisoner or pick up a colleague, he'd known they were opening again. Not this time.

The driver banged the door. 'Right boys, that's us.' Jamie got out first, and the young cop followed. Automatically, he took Jamie by the arm. The driver shook his head. 'Just leave it Norrie, eh?' Single file, they passed through a narrow door and entered a tight passageway. At the end of the passage, a counter. The driver handed a plastic folder of paperwork to the warder behind the desk. 'James Worth, Glasgow High. Convicted of murder.'

The warder flicked through the folder. 'Thanks guys. We'll take it from here.'

One light touch on his shoulder, and the two cops passed back into the world, leaving him in this one. Wordlessly, the warder took Jamie through a gate and straight down into hell. Bodies growling, glowering, spitting. Circling the holding area like buzzards wheeling over roadkill. An immense wall of sound and hatred, all whipping at him.

'Aye, Worth. Nae luck,' said the warder. 'Think they smell pig – jungle drums have been beating.'

Prisoners, walking around, sniffing at his flesh. They could smell his flesh above the all-pervading stench of pish. The entire holding area reeked of human waste and filth. The odours stuck, smarting in his craw, coating his gullet with slimy vapours. Dante's *Inferno*, towering in babbling Bedlam. Welcome to the Bar-L. Along one wall, a row of wooden cubicles, like the toilets at his primary school. Our Lady of the Annunciation. Pray for our souls. Each cubicle had a blackboard on the outside of the door. Names chalked, white on grey. Mulligan, Forsythe. Hamilton, Gillespie. Pray for our souls. *Worth*.

'Name?' Another desk, another warder. Jamie was sure he recognised him.

'James Worth. James Anthony Worth.'

'Date of birth?'

'Fifteenth of the third.'

'Status?'

'Pardon?'

'Pardon *sir*.'

'I mean, I don't understand.'

The warder stared at him.

'I don't understand, sir.'

'What-is-your-status? Moron, imbecile, remand, what?'

'Oh. Life.'

'Life, eh? You're the murderer, aren't you?'

'Yes.'

'Yes what?'

'Yes sir.'

'Tsk, tsk Worth. Killing wee girls. Now, that's just no very public spirited is it?'

Did they know? Surely they didn't realise he was a cop?

The warder shook his head. 'And you an officer of the law too. What is society coming to, eh?'

An illusory hope fled his body like a soul.

'Right, in the dog box, Worth.'

'What?'

'In.'

The warder shoved him forward. Another level, the seventh circle, reserved for murderers. When the wooden door snibbed shut, a new blackness descended. Invisible, thick air dirtying his skin. His eyes gradually measured his new, smudged surroundings. The cubicle was about a metre by a metre square, a single plank serving as a bench. He sat in the middle, trying not to brush his good suit against the walls, which were crusted with shite and nose pickings, smeared with phlegm and misspelled obscenities. An archaeology of those who had come before him, their animal leavings pasted all around.

They left him there for about fifteen minutes, long enough for the dog boxes on either side to fill up. It began quietly, a kind of low hissing, a tapping that became a hammering. Beating fists in stereo surround, wild voices promising: 'We'll have you. See the night, Fuckcop. You're dead. You're fucking dead.' The prison officers must have heard too, for he could make out their voices above the din. *Name. Wilson, sir.* The occasional *Quieten it down now.*

Was the girl somewhere like this; crouched in a filmy netherworld where shades jeered and cackled? Her face was relaxed above the bloody breast. He remembered that. From her neck up, she could have been staring at the stars, joining dots in constellations. It had been a very clear night. Summer-crisp like apples, smells of bonfire from his gun.

Cath couldn't see the difference between Purgatory and Hell. Proddies just had up or down, no middle ground of limblessness, full of unchristened babes and unfinished business. When he'd tried to explain, he'd started to believe it again, fighting his corner the more Cath scoffed. Arguing right through dinner and two bottles of wine and that was what he loved about her. She could twist his brain and stretch his intellect, then twine it back with a who-cares smile. Less and less now, when wet-arse wails and sticky fingers interrupted, and tired words became a precious commodity, but from time to time it sparked, that challenge of why he loved her. Would she remember to put the alarm on? Take the key out the back door? Maybe someone would stay with her tonight. Cath would hate that.

When the door opened, his eyes snapped back from blurry. The room had become surreal, he'd drawn his mind up inside himself, listened like it was all on telly, and now the channel had changed.

'Out.'

An unknown thumb jabbed upwards. He stood, felt his leg cramp, and followed this new warder.

'Okay, Worth. While you're here, you'll be treated as a remand prisoner. You'll be kept in the hospital wing for your own protection, and you'll not be required to work.'

They were walking down another corridor now, each few paces punctuated by a sliding bolt or a clanking chain. 'First thing is to get you showered and changed. And the good news is, you get the whole place to yourself. Don't want someone taking a razor to your bits, do we?'

The toilet block was primitive. Gristle-white, brick-shaped tiles, four or five urinals, the same number of toilet cubicles and just three showers. An even stronger stink of urine, which made him want to vomit. Yellow scum frothed around the central drainage holes on the swimming floor. This couldn't be where he was meant to wash.

'Take off your clothes.'

There was nowhere to hang his suit. The warder watched him looking. Jamie took off his jacket, then his shirt and tie, folding the garments over his right forearm. When he reached to untie his shoelace, the silk tie slipped and landed in a viscous puddle.

'Here,' said the warder. 'Gie them to me.'

Jamie passed him the clothes, then the shoes and socks. They all went in a black bin bag. Next, would be his trousers, then his. Then his. He clung on to his trousers. God, he played rugby, he wasn't some daft laddie worried his dick was too wee. But neither was he a specimen in a bell jar, or a baboon flashing his proud pink arse to the gawkers at the zoo. He turned sideways, so only his haunch was on show, slipped out of his pants and trousers in a oner.

'Right, in you get.'

The warder pressed a silver button and the shower spurted reluctant, tepid water. He gave Jamie a cube of carbolic soap. Another school smell.

'Gie yourself a good scrub, cos the doctor'll want to examine you.'

Jamie's buttocks tensed. 'How d'you mean?'

'How d'you think I mean? Now, hurry it up in there. There's a whole team outside waiting for a wash. We don't all get the luxury of a private bathroom you know.'

Of course, he'd showered that morning. In his own house, with Imperial Leather and Daniel's sponge and Eilidh's Barbies dripping damp hair down the sides of the bath. And slippers waiting by the radiator. As he washed what felt like pumice grit into his body, he stood on stained, cracked tiles, absorbing the filth by osmosis. The water stopped before he'd finished rinsing.

'Right, out and dry yourself.'

A square of grey cloth was hanging over the partition. No bigger than a dish towel and absorbent as tinfoil. Still, he rubbed and patted, stalling in his stall.

'The doctor will see you now.'

Was this a wind-up?

'What will I put on?'

The warder nodded at his rag. 'Your towel.'

Jamie tried to wrap the towel around his waist. Far too small, and he was forced to pin it with his fingers either side of his groin, like some ridiculous apron. Aware his arse was mincing open to the world, he splashed after the warder and into the medical room. No introductions, just some rough instructions and even rougher hands. 'Open your mouth.' 'Let me see your ears.' 'You take drugs?'

'No. No, I don't.'

'Not yet, eh?'

'Not ever.'

'Any STDs?'

'Pardon?'

'Clap, crabs—'

'No. No way.'

'Not yet, eh?'

The warder sniggered.

'Bend over.'

'Doctor – I'm a . . .'

The doctor paused, sheathed index finger half extended. 'Yes?'

'I mean, I don't have anything . . .'

'That's what they all say, Mr Worth. Bend over please.'

The warder moved forward. 'Arse up, Worth. C'mon, we've seen it all before.'

Once, Jamie had searched a middle-aged man. He'd been done for shoplifting, and the arresting officer was convinced he'd put some tins down his trousers. Jamie had been bar officer that afternoon, and they'd taken him into the detention room. Asked him to unzip his trousers, and he'd started crying.

'Wider, Worth.'

First his buttocks, stretched apart. A moment of utter, open shame. Then a finger rammed up his anus, forcing the stink of prison deep inside, removing him of dignity so thoroughly it was almost pure. His splayed legs began to tremble and he knew he would fall.

'Right, that's you. Clean as a whistle.'

The doctor snapped off his glove and turned away. Before the warder could reach him, just one long lunge, his dick swinging free, and Jamie could seize the baldy bastard round the throat, send his skull cascading on the basin, smashing to the soft-boiled inside to see how clean it was.

Or he could bow his head and wait.

'Okay Worth. Let's get you togged up.' Flat, firm, no hint of apology. Jamie was nothing to this man, or the one before, or the one before that. He was nothing.

The warder still held his towel. Naked, Jamie followed him to the next dim-lit room, where piles of clothing lay shelved and on the floor. Prisoners were doling out shirts and shoes to other prisoners.

'See the trusties for your gear.'

'Sorry?'

'The trus*ees* – trusted prisoners, know? Once you've proved to us you can be a good boy, we let you do special jobs around the place,' he smirked. 'Like give out scants and that. Now, shift your arse. We've no got all day.' He nodded to another warder, who shouted 'Clear!' Those prisoners that hadn't yet got all their clothes were ushered into a side room, one guard standing in front of the door.

The warder nudged Jamie. 'See the service you're getting here Worth? Like when the Queen goes to Harrods. Now, get your gear and get a bloody move-on. This personal treatment crap is throwing my schedule tae pot.'

The first table was covered in trousers. 'Size?' asked the trustee.

'Thirty-four inch waist.'

'Here you go, pal.' The trustee lifted a folded pair and passed them over. Scratchy, brownish-grey wool, they irritated the moment he slung them over his arm. Another table, a heap of red polo shirts. Without speaking, a second trustee reached down to the floor and pulled a dirty shirt from the pile.

Jamie folded his arms. 'I want a clean one.'

The trustee winked at Jamie's dick and grinned. 'Big man, eh?' Then he lowered his voice, so only Jamie could hear. 'Aye, we'll see who the big man is when I take your wife up the arse. D'you know I'm getting out next week?'

Jamie tried to block out the words. He'd heard worse from neds at the football, it meant nothing, but the shaking was uncontrollable, rising from belly to back of the throat. A low creaking, thick out of his mouth. 'Not if I fucking kill you, you're no.'

The trustee laughed. 'You and whose army? You're no a fucking polis now.' Then he leaned forward and hissed, 'Fuck off and die, pigshit.'

Jamie looked towards the nearest warder, who stared fixedly ahead. Hands trembling, he took the shirt and moved on. Shoes, socks, then underpants. Again, the pants were from the dirty pile. Stained and slittered in yellow and brown.

'I'm no taking them.'

'Tough shit,' sniffed the last trustee.

'Excuse me,' Jamie called to the warder. Again, he was ignored. 'Ho, excuse me.'

At once, the warder was in his face, one fist against Jamie's chin. 'Don't you ever "Ho!" me again, you cocky bastard.'

'Look, I'm sorry, but I canny wear these.' Jamie pointed at the filthy underpants.

'Then you'll wear fuck all.'

It was as quick as they could get the prisoners through; they didn't care. Prison officers stood by and did nothing as Jamie pulled the trousers past his naked thighs and watched them fall back down to his ankles. They were at least four or five sizes too big – chosen especially for him, he realised, as the sniggers swelled around the room. A great joke to dress the prize pig. He tried tying the waistband of the trousers in a knot, but the material and his fingers, like his audience, were all too thick. Instead, he dressed his top half, put on his too-tight shoes, then lifted the trousers over his bare arse and held them up with his hands. Once the trousers were fully on, he saw these too were soiled. Shuffle through to the next room, where he was given two folded blankets.

A uniform pushed him forward.

'Where am I going now?'

Same warder who'd taken him to the showers. 'You're being taken up to a holding cell. Up near the hospital ward.'

They walked across an open courtyard, where sky and walls merged in greasy bands of grey. Through a gate, another door and up a flight of tinny stairs. Unlike the dog box, this cell was a decent size. The door grated shut, and he was alone again. Maybe this was where he would spend the night.

Jamie opened the blankets out, and immediately retched. Nothing inside them but wet, fresh shit. He laid the blankets on the floor, as far away as he could. At work, he'd been in plenty of filthy houses; some where your feet would stick to the carpet as you came in; some with no carpet at all, the weans running around wearing vests and a dummy they shared with the dog. So you'd do your business, warn, arrest, report, whatever. And then you could come home, slough off the slime and fall into a clean white bed. The stench of these blankets crept through the cell, and he found his breath catching in his throat, like the air was thickening and crawling away and he was moving down a narrow tunnel, then the tunnel was a throat, his throat, and it was swallowing him. Each gulp pressing further, closer, acid laps of bile.

Someone rattled the door. 'You decent?'

'What?' Jamie rubbed his eyes.

A cheery, red-faced officer unlocked the door. 'Didny want you squatting on the chanty, pal.' He passed Jamie a list of names. 'You the cop eh?'

'I was a cop.'

'Here, take a look at these arseholes and tell me if you've had any dealings with any of them.'

Jamie ran his finger down the list. '*Wheeler*. Aye I've jailed him, and . . . naw . . . aye, and him. Oh.' His finger rested beside *Meek, Michael*. So this was where poor Michelle ended up.

'Him. I know him from a doss on my old beat.'

The prison officer took back the list. 'Well, in that case, you'll no be able to associate with any of them. You'll need to be kept in a cell on your own, so you will. No great loss anyway, pal. Shower of shite up here, so they are.' He smiled. 'C'mon and I'll take you through. Pick up your blankets. You've missed dinner, but I'll see if I can get something sorted for you.'

'I don't want anything.'

Jamie hesitated beside the blankets. He didn't want to touch them again, but maybe if he showed this man . . . maybe this man was alright. He followed the warder down another corridor, each step taking him further into the labyrinth, further from his life. All the vertical, stabbing stripes of bars and gates and doors narrowing his vision, leaving no option but to plod in the gaps that remained.

'Well, I'll see what there is anyway. Right, number twelve – far enough away from the real heidbangers.' The officer unlocked the cell door. 'In you go. Dinner's at three, by the way. I know, daft time, eh? And you'll need to take your meals in here. Breakfast 6.30 a.m., lunch is 11, and after your dinner, you'll maybe get a cup of tea around seven, but that's it. Lights out at 10 p.m., so if I were you, I'd go to the crapper first. Either that, or you shite in the dark.'

Jamie laid his blankets on the floor.

'Excuse me. Is there any chance I can change these?'

'Sorry pal, it's only me and another guy on the day. It'll have to wait. I'll away and get someone to bring you your dinner though.'

'Christ, would you just listen? I don't want your fucking dinner. I don't want to eat food the colour of shite in a cell full of shite in a prison full of shite.'

'Well, fuck you then, buddy.'

The door slammed shut. A grey door, with a grille and no handle. An oblong slice forged to block his exit. Somewhere else, men worked in great heat to bond sheets of metal taken from ore in rock. They shaped the metal into solid doors, then went home for their tea. And this door would be his window, all the time he was here. His picture frame, his TV set, his thing to look at. For there was nothing else. Glazed brick walls. A high-up window, arched like a bread oven. Grey bed-frame. Solid, no bits on which to cut or hang or gouge. Locker, a wooden table thing and the toilet bowl. It would have been white at one time. Now it was stained brown, inside and out, a constant belch of urine pumping like pot-pourri.

He sat on the edge of the bed and watched his hands tremble.

'Mr Worth?'

He looked up. A red mouth at the open hatch. 'Mr Worth? Hi. I'm Moira Agnew. Can I come in?' A key scraped, and a woman opened his door. Middle-aged-portly, in navy slacks. One plump hand extended. 'As I said, Moira. Pleased to meet you, Mr Worth.'

'Hi.'

'I'm a prison welfare officer.'

Her face was pink and round, topped by bouncy brown hair. A healthy, happy do-gooder in sensible black brogues. 'I'm just here to check that everything's okay for you. Got everything you need, understand the regulations, that sort of thing.'

'And check I'm not going to top myself?'

'And, are you?'

'No.'

She sat on the bed beside him. 'I know how hard this must be, Mr Worth. I understand your, um position.'

'That I'm a murderer?'

'That you're a police officer. This must be an unbelievable reversal for you, and we're here to support you through that.'

If she patted his knee, he'd break her fingers.

'There's a whole team here that can help you. You can get access to the prison social workers, we have a psychologist available if required, help for your family—'

'You leave my family alone.' After what that trustee had said, he couldn't bear it . . . he couldn't bear them even breathing this foul air.

'You've a wife, don't you? And little ones? You know that, as you're on remand, you're allowed a visit every day, Monday to Friday?'

'No. I don't want my kids coming here.'

She clucked her teeth. 'No, no, that's fine. But, if you did want a visit, you'll have to book it in advance, okay?'

'I don't want a bloody visit.'

'I understand. Well, is there anything I can help you with at the moment?' She was wearing some kind of talcy perfume. Must go through gallons of the stuff every day, working in this cesspit. And still it would never be enough. He heard his voice, far off, very weedy. 'Can you change my blankets, please?'

'Of course. Are they too thin?'

Jamie leaned forward and opened up the blankets.

She peered down, then flung her head back as she realised what the lumps were. 'Oh, God. That's disgusting. Did they . . . were they like this when you got them?'

'What do you think?'

'And your clothes? What about your clothes?

'Well,' Jamie tugged at his waistband, 'I could do with some trousers that fit me. And a clean shirt. And some underpants.'

'They didn't give you underwear?'

'Well, they did, but I think it was someone else's. Bit like the blankets.'

Moira stood up. 'I'll be having words with the receiving staff.'

'Mrs Agnew. Please. Just get me clean stuff.' He tried to smile at her. 'I don't want to make some issue about this. Just let me keep my head down and get on with it, okay?'

'Yes, of course.' She smiled back. 'Food. What about food? You've missed dinner. Let me send up some food.'

'I don't wa—'

A hand on his arm. 'You have to eat. I insist. Did you eat this morning?'

When was this morning? In that other world, when he'd given up on sleep and got out of bed in the dark and made Cath tea and tiptoed back upstairs, counting her breaths by the rise and fall. Lying on her breast, kneading its softness all around and wishing he was inside her. When she'd stirred and moved so her nipple was at his mouth and his sucking tongue had woken her. When they'd clung and cried and whispered and felt sick.

'No. I don't think so.'

'So, you'll take some dinner? Mr Worth? Your wife would want you to eat.'

She locked the door and left him to his silence. Only it wasn't silent. It was never silent in this place. Bangs and clangs, clattering feet and clamouring voices. Keys, keys, fucking keys. And the buzz of the light above him. Others would decide when to flick the switch, and he would have to wait upon their whim, trying to ignore it as the droning nibbled at his eardrum, nibbled on his brain. To speak, eat and breathe. That was it, those were his only choices in here.

Another key churn, another prison officer. Another trustee, holding a plastic plate. On it, some brownish gloop and a piece of bread.

Jamie folded his arms, the way Daniel did when presented with broccoli. 'I don't want that.'

'Fucksake,' said the trustee. 'I've brang it all the way up fae the kitchens.'

'I want a fresh plate.' Jamie nodded at the trolley behind the man. 'From there. Let me see you dish it out.'

The trustee looked at the prison officer, who nodded.

'Fucksake.' He scraped the plate into the bin bag hanging from the trolley rail.

'And a fresh plate,' said Jamie.

'You taking the piss?'

'Just do it,' said the prison officer. 'You've clean ones down the bottom.'

'Jesus Christ,' he sighed, bending down to pull out a new plate. 'Right sir. The day we have a choice a Irish Stew. Done it special like, for you. I arrest you – geddit? Naw? Anyway, it's stew or macaroni cheese.'

'Macaroni.'

The trustee dolloped on a scoop of macaroni, added some bread, and poured him a cup of tea from the urn. 'Does sir take milk and sugar by the way?'

'Just milk.' Jamie took the cup and the food.

'S'a pleasure.' The trustee sooked some saliva around his mouth, churning it between teeth and tongue. 'D'you like it frothy?'

'Right Speedy, that'll do you.' The prison officer pushed the trustee back towards the trolley and relocked the cell door.

Saliva, urine, no doubt he'd get them all served up in time. At least they knew he knew it.

Lights out came at some point, and he'd forgotten to go to the toilet. He took off his new trousers and cleaner shirt and lay on top of the bed. So tired, drifting off, then cracking back, alert. Afraid. Repeating the sequence, each time more exhausted, more awake. Deliberately not thinking, just looking at the door. Any time his eyes grew heavy, the hatch would clang, eyes would scan him. Three times every hour. Suicide watch. They had him on suicide watch. Twenty minutes, tick the box.

He tried walking up and down. Up and down to tire him out, pace upon pace upon tiny, turny pace, outlining the size and the breadth of the cell. A single cell that would never split and multiply, that would surely contract and grate inwards, crushing him like in the James Bond films. Then he'd lie on the bed and try again. Try so hard.

The new blankets stank of piss, or maybe it was him. Maybe he'd peed himself and just hadn't noticed. Keys turning two corridors away. Quiet noise, white noise. Coming from outside. Hissing tinny batters, clattering and wailing. Banshee low, growing, growling. Howling louder, words spewing. A wall of noise, rising, higher, voices screaming. *Fuckpig. Fuckpig. Fuckpig Worth. Polis bastard. You're fucking deid.*

One clear shriek. *Your arse is mine, ya fuckpig hoor.*

The hospital wing faced another cell block, looking on to it across a small courtyard. 'A' Hall. It was the prisoners in 'A' Hall. Rattling their cups against railings and chanting his name.

All that way, and he'd only been in limbo.

BEFORE

Somewhere, a girl is wearing an anorak in her bedroom. It is cold, yes, but she is used to that. Windows that hiss and drip with weather, newsprint-papered boards uneven and damp. When she was wee, she made a carpet out of rags – bags stolen from the Barnardo's shop. Folk left their stuff outside, at night. If they cared that much they'd have waited till the morning, taken it in properly. A girl at school had made a rag-rug for her Barbie House, and brought it in for show and tell. Talked them through the stages, just as she'd seen it on Blue Peter.

It wasn't difficult to copy. Same technique, just bigger rags. Quick too, she made it in a couple of days. Smoothed it flat on her floor and used it as a countryside. The green tufts were hills and grass, blue was a river. A play world for her hanky dolls. She made these too, with strips of ripped paper hankies. For a lady, you kept the bulk of the hanky, just tore a thin strip off the length, keeping it joined at the top. If you held the hanky in your fist, and let the loose strip drape over the back of your hand; that was the lady's hair. For a man, a simple twist of the point of two corners made a head. One more twist halfway down for the waist, then a tear up the bottom half to make two legs. (The ladies had no legs, just floating, ghostly gowns.) Easily scrunched and discarded, no one would know they were there.

Her brother had set fire to the rug. One flare of a match, dropped careless. Deliberate. And he'd made her watch. When her father returned from wherever he'd spent the day, she was beaten for the mess.

1

Death and life; two states, one being. Finite, absolute, infinite, three in one. A turn, a step, a stop, a start, then one is none. And is all. If he'd not been such a hard man. If he'd waited for the van, used his head instead of his hands. Good wee cop, Billy Wong, that's what they were all saying. Nodding and sighing, launching a volley of anecdotes. *D'you mind the time . . . ?* Spinning thin ropes to bind them in their grief; some slim connection to Billy.

'A quiet officer, much respected by his colleagues. He kept himself to himself. Family was very important to him.'

Was it? Jamie Worth leaned his head sideways, to see through the gap between shoulders. Boys in blue at the back, round, silent faces down the front. A mother, sister, brother. A father who was not there. Friends or family tiered behind. Across the aisle from Billy's mother, the Chief Constable sat with his hands spread on his kneecaps, balancing the weight of the scrambled egg braid that silvered his hat. Rows more men and women behind, caps on knees, necks high. Only the pall bearers were to wear white gloves, but Jamie had his on too. If he'd to wear them when Princess bloody Anne came visiting, he'd wear them for wee China. That's what they called him, after a while. Ma wee China. *M'on ma wee China. It's your turn to get the breakfasts. Haw China – pass the bloody ball. Right, China – this one's yours.*

Billy never drank, and rarely came on shift nights out. Demon at the football though, and he was a natural at winding up the neds. Something about his look, the lack of register, the smoothness, drove them wild. Sweating resentment from their pustules and pores. How many times had Billy heard it? 'Who the fuck d'*you* think you're talking tae?' It was the *you* that set him apart, and Jamie was no better than the rest. They could have had a shift night out somewhere other than the pub.

The crematorium was very blank, an apology of all things to all people. White walls, red curtain and a mobile cross that could be whisked in or out like a weather vane. It surprised Jamie that Billy was Christian. He'd never thought, never asked. Why would you? Jamie had chosen to join the procession, rather than come straight here, even though it meant going all the way into town to come back out. The hearse had left Billy's parents' house, then driven by Stewart Street, where a convoy of cars joined the end. Took twenty minutes of slow sad driving, with bike cops blocking junctions en route. As the cortège passed, each biker stood to attention, saluting this boy they never knew.

Billy's family had asked for Delibes. 'From *Lakme*', it said on the order of service, was one of Billy's favourite pieces of music. Jamie could see folk looking, eyebrows raised as first violins, or a reedy clarinet maybe, then a trilling soprano ached from hidden speakers, swelling, swelling, swelling – ah. A familiar aria swooping. That bit: it was the tune off the British Airways ad. Voices melding, then a split into two overlapping cascades and down again, dragging them to the uplift where voice became pain and beauty and life; a pause in the moment before the plunge, then your heart was left up high behind. The music reverberated in his chest, even as it faded.

Now every time Jamie saw that bloody advert on the telly, he would smell lilies and salt. The family were to have a private ceremony when the polis left. No purvey, no handshakes – they'd shared Billy enough. Some daft bint was sobbing quiet and steady; that Maureen from Two Group who'd a line from the doctor to stop her doing nightshift. Being ushered out, setting a couple of probationers off. They were all filing out now.

'Coming to the pub?' whispered Alex beside him. 'I need a bloody pint.'

'Nah, you're alright. I'm going to head. Things to do.'

He'd thought she'd be there. Out of anyone, Anna Cameron had been a friend to Billy Wong. She'd pushed him for his CID aide, complained to the boss about his sergeant, the lack of supervision Billy was getting. It was rumoured that Anna got Billy through his promotion tickets. Even when she'd left the division, she'd kept in touch; sending Billy reading lists, articles from *Police Review*. Cut away the pith and pretence and that was why Jamie had passed time with Billy; because of his link to Anna. Through Billy, he could hear her name, chart her progress. He could feel her holding the paper she'd cut out, that then rested in his hand, picture her tongue poked from one side as she snipped around edges, pale skim of hair catching a jaw that was sharp, tracing a scoop to lips that were soft. Once, he fancied the gloss sheet about domestic violence procedures was scented, and that he could see her thumbprint on the thick black letters in the title. Tiny crumbs of her skin and moisture pressed into *'BEHIND CLOSED DOORS'*.

Three years was a long time and, like all lusts, it had dissolved slowly with the ebb and flow of days, smoothing rough edges, dulling the shape. Then a frisson would rip his groin and the beat would quicken and he'd be there again, making love to his wife and seeing Anna's face. Luminous, hard-set, with veins like fine marble. Even now, at the funeral. No, before. Soon as he knew the date and time he'd thought *She'll be there*. Gone for a haircut, bulled his shoes and thought *She'll be there*. Stood for the coffin and half turned his head and thought *She'll be there*. Bowed his head in prayer and wondered if he could feel the heat of her gaze on his neck as she watched him. Now his veins were fizzed flat and he wanted to sleep.

But Jamie had to go to work. The final stages of all the training that would turn him into an authorised firearms officer. Only a handful in the force. Plenty of cops would run a mile before they'd pick up a gun. Yet, like Billy, armed only with bare flesh and bravado, they'd challenge a knifeman. When he and Cath had talked, before he put his application in, they agreed it was safer than anything else in the police, if you thought about it. The poor beatman was the one to turn up unprepared, knock on the door for a domestic and get blown away by an unexpected shotgun. Or have his flesh cleaved by a machete. At least a firearms officer knew what he was getting into. They wouldn't call you in unless there was already the suspicion of guns, then you'd have all your cordons and procedures giving you some breathing space. Plus it felt good. To be part of an elite, a justified swagger announcing your arrival at police stations near and far. And it would cheer him up, since no bugger had promoted him yet.

When he was sixteen, a mate of Jamie's had joined the navy. Stirred with a mix of patriotic pride and no future giros, Ricky had enlisted to see the world, learn a trade and get some sex. Poor sod had been seasick from day one. Whenever he came back home though, he'd be full of himself – the places he'd seen, girls he'd shagged. He walked funny on dry land, and said he found it hard to sleep without the drone of engines. The local birds swooned over him; fat wee Ricky with an inch of hair and a face full of acne. Then one time, after a six-month tour, he came back and stayed at his mum's the whole two weeks. Wouldn't speak to anyone. On his last day at home, he fell down the stairs and broke his ankle. That bought him a few more weeks cloistered and off work. Then Jamie heard that he'd put in his tickets and was training to be a butcher.

He'd always thought Ricky had been injured out, till he met him two weeks ago in Morrison's. He'd gone over to get his mum some messages and there was Ricky Nelson, slapping fat red hands behind the cold meat counter. They'd arranged to go for a drink. A catch-up pint became a bottle of confessionals and, unplugged, Ricky had glugged out the story of being sent to the Congo. How they'd come across a lifeboat from an African cargo ship, crammed with desperate refugees who'd deliberately been set adrift. The boat had been on the open seas for days; Ricky had to pick the bloated bodies of women and children from the bilge. He seemed angry when he was telling Jamie. Almost as if he'd really thought the Navy was one long cruise; like they'd cheated him by showing him blood.

Jamie was older, wiser.

Cath had understood why he wanted to pick up a gun. Well, she'd never said she didn't. It helped that she'd been in the job, and he could do away with preamble and context when they talked. He liked their easy knowledge of one another's lives. For a long time though, Cath's face had slipped to dull resentment whenever he mentioned work. Their elastic bonds had brittled and frayed, and he'd thought she was jealous. Then Daniel was born and it seemed to jolt her back to life. She never knew about Anna, thank God. For all it had been. One angry, lost penetration.

The firing range was quite close to the crematorium. Concealed from the road, cut off by several fields, the only features to discern its purpose were skeins of barbed wire and two big no entry signs. The car tyres crunched and slid on the dirt track as Jamie drew up beside a long concrete building. Only two other vehicles there, which meant he was on his own. Rest of the course must have headed. He wondered if they'd all passed this once-in-a-lifetime, no second chances, 'if you fail, you're oot' final shoot. Envied them the buzzed relaxed elation they'd all be feeling right now, while his stomach was plunging like a gibbet-neck. It was the smell that did it, that burn of acrid cordite drawn on the wind, slicing through his *Top Gun* gung-ho and making him think of death.

Before he'd ever touched a gun, he knew he'd be good. A John Wayne sharpshooter with a Glasgow swagger. Then, Jesus Christ, he pulled the trigger for the first time and near shat himself as a hundred cannons exploded in his face and his eardrums screamed in supplication. He'd jumped back, gun lurching into the air, and was struck on the back of the head by an instructor. 'Keep bloody still! Do *not* flail that firearm about. You don't move until I say so. Understand?'

In the pause while they awaited their second instruction, Jamie's mind was set. He would put the weapon down now and back away. The awesome, boyish rush that someone would trust him with a gun had crystallised to cold fear. With his hand, with the one index finger that still pulsated from the force of what it had done, he could tear through limb and bone.

'Jamie, you heard the man. Stop bloody jooking about like that. That you feart of the big nasty bang bang? Or d'you need a slash or something?'

Wee Jinky Robertson in the booth next to him started pissing himself, at least until the next round, when the white-hot casing of a cartridge had come flying out the breech and landed down the back of Jinky's overalls. Ha bloody ha. Jinky was bound to have passed. Every shoot he'd done, there was a neat tight cluster around the target's heart.

Jamie opened the boot, took out his huge canvas kitbag. A smell of dung slid through harsh gunpowder. If he crapped himself every time he fired, what about the poor sheep and cows over-by? Animals outnumbered people here, green farmland surrounding the range, studded with white fluff and brown flanks. Trapped in dyked fields, their animal calm broken daily by unknown bombardment, more often, yet less regular than the thrill of a tractor dragging hay, or the pain of a zealous shear or branding iron. God. Would you look at the udders on that one? Hanging stretched like a massive veined hernia, teats scraping off the ground. Just waiting. His shoulders tightened.

Imagine that every day. Waiting for the blessed relief of a milking machine, every day of your life until they'd bled you dry. And having to do it because you'd no other choice. A quiet lowering rolled across the fields. Maybe they built up an immunity, a placid acceptance of their lot, that let them switch off to all but the twist and tear of grass across tongue.

He took a long, slow breath, hefted his bag, and went inside. The office was like a Portakabin, fake wood cladding cocooning the place in drab. 'Afternoon, sergeant.'

His instructor lowered his tabloid. Stark black headline yelling *Death Cop Off Scot Free.* 'Right Jamie, it's yourself. How'd it go?'

'Good turnout.'

'Poor wee bastard.' He folded his paper. 'Did he have any kids?'

'Don't think he'd even had a girlfriend yet.'

'Canny win, can you?' The sergeant tapped the newspaper. 'There's that poor sod found not guilty, and the papers still want to lynch him. Mind, the cop in Nottingham that shot that loony? And there's wee Billy, scythed in two just for being there. Aye, you're damned if you do . . .'

The sergeant stood, took the kettle from the unit behind him. 'Hope they cut the fucker a new arsehole in jail. Tea?'

'No thanks. Aye well, I think he's planning on a nice long stay at Carstairs Hospital instead. That's what his lawyer's pushing for. Says he was unstable and the polis provoked him.'

'Provoked him to carry a machete and wave it round a shopping centre did they? Aye, right.' Kettle filled, the sergeant turned off the tap. 'Anyway, you sure you're fit then?'

'Aye. Just let me get my gear sorted.'

Jamie carried the kitbag into the adjoining office that served as briefing room, changing room, refreshment room and debriefing room. Unzipped the canvas, pulled out a crumpled set of overalls. The legs were wide enough to wear over his trousers, but these were his good ones. Two hours he'd spent last night, pressing a cotton hanky over blue twill, holding down the iron until the creases were rigid and the hanky crisped. Even after sitting in the car and the crematorium, the single line down the centre of his leg was sharp and sure. If he hung them up now, he'd get by using them for court without having to iron them again. So he took the trousers off and folded them over the back of a chair. The overalls smelled fousty. He should have washed them last night – been wearing them for two weeks solid. You could brush off the grass and mud, but BO was BO.

A webbing belt gave the shapeless cloth a waist, until he strapped on his body armour and became the Michelin man once more. Vest tight against his chest, plates pressing down on lungs and shoulders. He changed his shoes for boots, and lifted a Kevlar helmet from the locker. It looked like a German helmet, smooth beetle-black across his skull. No visor, but it made his head feel still and heavy, like blinkers on a horse. And amplified the rising haste of the pulse at his temple, pushing the thud back into his head. If he failed this shoot, that was it. Didn't matter how well he'd performed over the last fortnight, if you weren't good enough the first time, then, the philosophy was, you never would be.

The sergeant was in the corridor, unlocking the grille of the armoury, then the metal cabinet beyond. Spread before Jamie was a span of smooth black fingers, all pointing at the sky. Each gun elegantly long, with a tiny curved trigger claw beneath the breech. They didn't use handguns any more; everyone learned on Heckler & Kochs. Five point five six carbines, halfway between a rifle and a semi-automatic. Cath had freaked when he told her that, had visions of him drilling holes commando style, until he explained. 'It just means they reload themselves via exhaust gases.'

'Jamie, speak to me like I'm an idiot, eh? Like you normally do.'

'Okay. When a bullet is fired, it makes an explosion, right? And that explosion releases gases from the barrel. The force just draws the next bullet from the magazine. See? Simple.'

'So, it's a machine gun?'

'No. Are you not listening to me? They're all converted to single shot use. So I have to pull the trigger each time.' He'd assumed the voice of his ponderous lecturer. '*Every shot must be measured and accountable.*' Smoothed her forehead with a kiss. 'Don't worry. I'm not going to turn into Rambo or something.'

He loved that face she made, when her lip crept behind her upper teeth.

The sergeant lifted an H & K, then locked the cabinet door. Ratcheted the breech open, looked inside the barrel. 'Clear.' He handed the gun to Jamie. 'Clear?'

'Clear.' Jamie snapped the lever shut. He wouldn't load the ammunition until he was on the range. Inspector Hart came through from the back office, carrying a magazine and a small white box. 'Right Jamie. We'll no bother with the briefing room since you're all on your lonesome, alright? It's nothing complicated. Ready?'

'Yes Inspector.' Gums all sticky. He wished he'd had that tea.

'Okay. You'll be firing from a distance of thirty metres. Standing. The target will turn towards you for one second, and you'll fire one aimed shot on each occasion, for five occasions. You will then drop to the kneeling position, when the target will turn towards you for three seconds, and you will fire three aimed shots for a further five occasions. Are you clear on that?'

'Yes, sir.'

Hart handed Jamie the magazine and the open box. Twenty-five brass bullets, wedged inside a polystyrene tray. The magazine was like a big metal PEZ dispenser, grooved on top where the bullets went. Jamie took a handful. Pushed one in at a time, waiting until the platform dropped down, deposited its contents, and rose to receive the next one.

'Remember, I'm looking for at least ninety per cent. Make each one count, right?'

Jamie ran a hand along the smooth cold firmness of the carbine, weighing it either side, flexing up his fingers on the linseed coated air. He took a yellow duster from the storage box and flicked the metal free of dust. Not delaying; preparing.

The sergeant called from the door. 'Right then, Worth-less. That's us ready.'

'Way to psyche him up, Liam. You're no worthless the day, son, are you?'

Jamie put the magazine in his overall pocket. 'No, Inspector. Not today. Just call me hotshot.' He smiled, so they'd know it was all front.

Three men walking like it was an execution. All the heaviness and heat of his gear made Jamie separate. Senses clingfilmed: eyes shielded by goggles, ears padded with foamed rubber protectors, the only living softness was his brain. Centring limbs, moving one before the other, a RoboCop encased in lead.

A line of booths marked the entrance to the range. Open to the air, each booth was sectioned by a high wooden wall, like starting gates for horses, tunnelling vision in one straight line down the range, ending at the massive sandbank that would absorb the flak. A fold-down table bisected the air at chest height. On to this table, Jamie laid his carbine, and removed the magazine from his pocket. Once more, he proved the weapon, pulling back the lever to open up the breech.

The instruction came from behind. 'Insert magazine.'

He clipped it in place; a simple alchemy set in motion. Still pointing the carbine down towards the sandbank, Jamie raised the table-top like a bar counter and walked onto the range. There was a line drawn at the thirty metres mark, and he shuffled his toes to touch its edge.

'Weapon pointing down range. Make ready.'

He cocked the weapon, pulling back the lever then releasing it to draw the first bullet from the magazine.

'Weapon at high port.'

Held it across the breadth of his chest, like a soldier standing at ease. The dung was stronger here, a strange, sweet sourness. In through the nose, out through the mouth. *Blow away the badness, blow away the badness* – it was a game he played with his little girl. Worked a treat on bruised knees and bad dreams.

'The target turning towards you is your signal to shoot.'

Sometimes it was an angry soldier, coming at you with a gun. Other times, a guy with shoulder-length hair. Black outline on white background, with an oval around its guts. Shoulders, torso, groin, all the major organs ring-fenced off. To hit outside this oval was to fail.

He could still miss. Could fire at the seagulls and apologise for his nerves. But the sin of pride glowed small and hard and bright as eyes. The gun was over two feet long. He raised it in one damp motion, tucking the butt firmly in his right shoulder to cushion the recoil. His left hand supported the muzzle; down near the 'business end', as Jinky called it. Right index finger sliding to the trigger, smooth as honey.

There was a hangnail on his finger, a tiny tear of skin that nipped in the air. He looked at his hand and saw wee fists, white and clenched into a little boy's thighs. Thighs that teetered above a concrete path, dimpled flesh framing fresh scratches on his knees, where he'd scrabbled up the bricks. The top of the wall had a curved pediment with some kind of glaze that made it slippy. His mother down below, reaching out her arms and tutting. *C'mon son. It's easy!*

Her teeth had lipstick on them, and she was looking round as she laughed. Someone was shouting for Dee Dee, though her name was Doris. *C'mon now James.* She sounded shriller. *Don't be a big baby.* Sore knees crouched over stubby feet – he was wearing socks and sandals. Squatting on the wall, his Batman cape flapping in his eyes. A dip in the pit of his stomach as he launched himself off, and saw her moving further away.

Through the sights, Jamie focused on the red electrodot. Whatever this pointed to was where the bullet would strike. A whip of air and the target flipped. It was the soldier, mouth gaping in eternal roar. Red dot on his heart, a little flickering pulse. Tasting metal, Jamie's finger moved. Always a steady squeeze, the slowness calming.

After the pause, the press. Then the bloody loud bang. A tiny, involuntary lurch back from yellow-white flash, from grey-white smoke. Tasting all the colours of an eggy, sickly summertime. Seeing a hole tear through the target's knee. *Shite*. Ears buzzing through the defenders, he controlled the urge to flee. He wanted this. Wanted it wanted it wanted it. Took a second to steady himself as the target turned sideways. Breathed and aimed once more. Bent his finger, and punctured the soldier's gut. The target flinched, turned away, turned back. And on he fired. Dead on. Again and again, till his finger was bruised, each time hitting the mark. Instinct aimed his eyes, and he was flying. On his knees now, for the grand finale. Nothing but the flip and the press and the wetness above his eyes. In one. *Blow away.* In two. *Blow away.* Five clear hits around the heart. Still, not thumping. Stop.

'Hold your fire.'

Square on, daylight stabbing through the target. A peppering of pellets around the soldier's groin, his chest, his lungs. *Behold, what I have done.* There was a burning in Jamie's belly, like he needed to pee, but faster, like stirring sex. Not a pleasant feeling at all, and he stretched up on his toes to be rid of it.

'Make safe.' The sergeant's voice was closer now, just behind Jamie's head. Jamie lowered the gun and unclipped the magazine. 'Magazine out. Safety catch on.' His words were heavy echoes inside his ear protectors. He peered inside the barrel of the gun. Primed his on-fire index finger and poked it inside. 'Clear – visual and physical.'

The sergeant tapped him on the shoulder. 'Okay, Worthless, that's you. Hand me the carbine.'

The H & K wobbled slightly as Jamie passed it over. Heavier than his muscles remembered. Inspector Hart was making his way down to the bottom of the range, to count up the holes – a progress clouded by Jamie's goggles. Tight tension of elastic eased from his scalp, catching on the ear defenders, so it all came off in one tangled mass; sight and sound restored.

'Well I make that ninety-five per cent,' Hart shouted. 'Just the one off, that yin that skelped his knee.'

The sergeant dunted Jamie's shoulder. 'Good man, Jamie. Now, clean up the brass and get those holes taped.'

From maestro to bin-raker, in one stiff stoop. He'd done it. He'd bloody done it. Jamie bent his back, resisting the urge to punch the air. Instead, he kicked about in the grass, trying to find the spent cartridge cases. Not for ecological reasons, or to account for each shot, but so the brass casings could be melted down for scrap. When his pockets were filled, he returned to the firing booth, to be handed two rolls of tape. One strip had black dots, the other white, each dot a self-adhesive circle, the size of a ten-pence piece.

When he'd completed his very first shoot, Jamie thought they were taking the piss. 'We've no really to plug up the holes on the target, have we?' he'd laughed.

His instructor didn't share his amusement. 'How? D'you think the pluggy-up fairy comes to visit when we've all gone home?'

'No, but we get new targets, don't we?'

'Aye, when these have got more holes than hardboard, we do. Now get plugging.'

It seemed further than thirty metres; walking it slow in flappy overalls and weighted vest. Five minutes ago, if he'd stood on this patch of scrubby grass, an inch of tapered steel would have snarled through his skin, bursting open first his veins, then the calcium density of bone, plunging through an organ or a limb to erupt its way out, leaving far more mess than it did with its neat knock of arrival. But the air was bucolic once more, soft and safe and stinky. *He'd done it.*

Inspector Hart waved at him from beside the target. 'Well done, Constable Worth. A near perfect display of marksmanship. Away in and we'll get your card marked.'

There are men in the living room, several, one with a high-pitched laugh, dry and wheezy like hyenas needing the dampness of blood. If she'd been quicker, she could have dodged out the front door before they came, but clinking glass sounds, some fuck yous ya cunt *and a roar, tell her the hall is off limits too. She pulls her anorak across her budded breasts, and turns out the bulb. The voices seem louder in the dark, even when her too-small hood is muffling the din. Little boy kneels at the foot of the bed. A heel of song kicks her from another life, about some wee diddy with a hood on his dressing gown. She peels a single layer of skin from her bottom lip, and crunches it slowly between her incisors.*

When she used to go to school, she prayed that one day a teacher would see her. Would see her real face in amongst the scummy tide, and pluck her out, hang her up to dry. She would listen to the girls talk – of boyfriends and sleepovers and dads who drove them into town, and her vertebrae would take the shape of walls and corners. If they smiled over, she'd walk away.

Her brow aches for soft hands, her body aches for love. And her eyes ache for tears that might moisten them. It is dawn, and the house is very quiet. Maybe today.

'I telt you, I havny got it, man.' Her brother's voice comes, nasal and vile. 'Nae cash till Thursday, me.'

The retort is mumbled, quieter. Then her brother laughs. 'Away you tae fuck.'

'Get the wean to do it,' shouts another voice.

Her brain snaps rigid, then it is easier to go dull. She swallows and swallows and finds she has bent her thumb way into her palm. Footsteps, then the door slams open. 'Ho – you up yet?' Her brother drags the single stained sheet from her head, and thumps her in the back. 'Right get up now, you lazy cow.' She curls onto the edge of the bed, raises first her body then her eyes.

'Gie the man a look at your fanny.'

2

'Upeehtum mum. Upee TUM!'

Daniel's face was thick with snot, his fleshy bow legs damp and pink where the pee had rained.

'In a minute. Wait a wee minute.'

Eilidh's head butted Cath's stomach as she leaned the child forward to reach her bum. 'You'll have to start doing this for yourself, madam. What happens when you need a poo at school?'

'Won't need.'

'Oh yes you will.' Cath stretched over for another bit of toilet paper. 'You'll be there all day, you know. It's not like nursery.'

'Won't go.'

'You won't go to school, or you won't go to the toilet?'

At last, the paper wiped clear.

'Won't go nothing. Shut your geggie, Dan-pants.'

Cath felt a leg lurch out under her side, heard a squeal as Daniel slipped. 'MAA-MEE! MAA-MEE!'

She slapped Eilidh's bare thigh. 'Don't you dare kick your brother, you naughty girl.'

Eilidh started wailing, high above the yells of her brother and the rush of water from the bath tap. 'You hurted me. You're a bad mummy.'

'And you're a bad girl. Now get down and wash your hands. With soap.' Cath ignored Eilidh's snivels, and reached for Daniel, who was slithering in the damp of the floor; his T-shirt now as wet as his pants had been. Eilidh had been dry at eighteen months and here was this one, still spurting forth at two past. Even when he did make it to the toilet in time, like his father, he rarely aimed straight.

Firearms officer – that was a bloody joke. They should come and score Jamie around the lavvy pan.

Eilidh flushed the loo, stuck out her tongue and ran from the room. Half of Cath wanted to smack her again, the other half wanted to kiss her angry cheeks. Crackly, cuddly Eilidh – 'passionate' was how her nursery teacher described her. 'Bloody-minded' was a better phrase. 'Just like your mother,' Jamie would say, as Eilidh flounced past in one of her huffs.

Cath put Daniel in the bath and swirled the water round with her fingers. Big, big day today. Daniel had big-boy Tumble Tots, where the mummies didn't have to stay, and Eilidh was being shown around the big school, in anticipation of entering primary one after summer. Eilidh would be one of the youngest, her winter birthday just making the cut-off. When Eilidh was a baby, if Cath had to be up and out by 10 a.m., she'd have needed an insomniac rooster, two nannies, a butler and a chauffeur to get her ready. With two kids, somehow, she'd developed 'a routine'. A concept she'd long resisted, largely because it originated from her mother-in-law. Cath's children would never be inhibited by timetables and restraints. Their days would be organic, creative, muddled, free, lonely, pointless, empty, suicidal. Their mother would douse her head in foaming bath bubbles, forgetting to surface, wishing it were gas. She would end up in hospital, then recuperating at home, welcoming strangers from the village in which they lived. All lacklustre women like herself, who talked of tiredness and *EastEnders* and created a reverse mentoring system, where they broke her down into submission, to be just as bland as them.

Only they weren't, these women who became Cath's friends. Of a sort. Not friends perhaps, but fellow travellers. They were bank clerks, and nurses, and graphic designers and teachers. United only by spreading public legs and pushing forth the future. None of whom thought they were 'this'. Even her friend Philippa. Cath had looked on in wonder the first time Philippa swept in to the community hall: pregnant with attitude and pushing two more in a double buggy, her little girl Skylar toddling behind. The effect was compounded when another mum whispered in pitying awe: *It's twins you know,* nodding at Philippa's magnificent belly. Three-quarters of an hour in her billowing presence, and Cath still couldn't see why it was so important to Philippa to grow her own fruit, to make her own jam, to go on her own homemade bread. Then, as weeks went by, Cath realised Philippa was 'the one' they'd all been talking about. It had even been in the papers. *Local TV news reporter leaves pregnant wife for young researcher.* And the researcher's name was Donald.

So, the intrigue of 'Mums and Toddlers' crept in, surreptitiously welcoming her, feeding her biscuits like a crumb trail, then expecting her to get there early to do tea duty. They even had a committee, which they inveigled her on to, then someone mentioned Happy Clappy – apparently it was never too early to get them into music, and of course Tumble Tots, and Little Ducklings at the swimming pool – no, it was okay, they did an aquanatal class at the same time. Before Daniel was even born then, Cath and Eilidh had their routine. Of course, it was only a temporary one; this wasn't who she was, this frump in leggings that got excited over fundraising for a new chute. But it passed the time, and got them out and she damn well wasn't going to stop just because some new baby had decided to put in an appearance. And she hadn't. No mornings spent in front of the telly with breasts on tap for little Daniel. Where Eilidh had received exclusive rights of access, Daniel got five minutes either side, a quick burp, and a sniff to see if the nappy would last the morning. Disposables, of course.

'One two three, hup. That's it, wee boy. Out you come.'

Breakfast TV that morning was hammering mothers for their flagrant abuse of disposables. Not the manufacturers who created them to biodegrade in a thousand years, nor the councils for having inadequate recycling facilities, nor the government for the dearth of affordable childcare that might remove the need to seize anything that cut corners and saved time. No, it was dirty, slatternly women, with their scant regard for the environment, their deliberate pollution of the water their children would drink. Add that to the wanton binning of tampons and sanitary towels, and it was clear that women of childbearing age were single-handedly responsible for the rotten mulching of God's green earth. Philippa's solemn face returned to chide her. *Back to boiling rags.* But not this morning.

Cath put Daniel on her lap, rubbed him with the towel, then pulled a Pampers from the opened packet. Daniel screwed up his face as Cath taped up the nappy. 'Tough luck matey. I'm not having you weeing all over Tumble Tots' trampoline.'

'Wan poo-pahns.'

'No. No more pull pants. We'll try again tomorrow honey, okay?'

He began to wail, tugging at the disposable. 'Poo-pahns.'

Eilidh's head popped around the bathroom door. 'Yeah, you are a poo-pants. Jobbie-Danny poo-pants.'

'Eilidh, stop that. Now why don't you go and be a big girl and help Danny boy pick some new trousers eh?'

'Don want – okay.' She smiled, held out her hand for her brother's chubby fist. 'C'mon Danil.'

Cath ran the cold tap and splashed water to her face. Too late, she remembered that was the unwashed hand that had wiped up pee, not the one she'd used to bathe him. Ach well, maybe the urine would give her an acid peel, and reveal the skin of a twenty-year-old. All that trickling water was having an effect. Cath unzipped her trousers, and perched on the loo. 'C'mon you two,' she called. 'We need to go.'

'Comin Mummy,' Eilidh shouted back. Chuckling, she led Daniel into the room. He was wearing a denim skirt, soft-frilled with gingham, and a matching cowboy hat. 'He's a little cowgirl, Mummy. Look!'

'Cowgil,' agreed Daniel proudly.

'Och Eilidh, c'mon. Mummy doesn't have time this morning.'

Eilidh scowled. 'But he's pretty. Why can't Danil wear a skirt?'

'Because.'

Cath, still midstream on the loo, upended Daniel and wheeched off the skirt. One tiny, flailing hand caught at her pubic hair. 'Ow. Bad boy, Daniel.' He liked to pull hair. Any hair would do. No place for modesty in this world where the lowest common denominator was the benchmark of every day. Food goes in your mouth, poo comes out your bum. Anything else was a bonus; or a mystery to be interrogated.

'Because why?' said Eilidh.

'Because boys don't, that's why.'

'But I can wear trousers.'

'I know honey. That's why it's better being a girl.'

'Nee wee-wee Mama.' Daniel was grabbing at the nappy again.

'Mummy. He needs his potty.'

'Well, I can't . . . Och, just do it in the nappy, Daniel. We haven't got time.'

'Weeeeee,' he screamed. 'Weeeeee.' The sound of a piglet being castrated.

'Okay, okay.' Cath peeled back the tapes. 'Down you get then. Where is it Eilidh? D'you know where his potty is?'

'S'in the hall.' Eilidh was squeezing toothpaste on the window-sill.

'Eilidh! Stop that at once, you dirty girl.'

She smoothed the paste out across the tiles. 'But ah'm *cleanin.* S'not dirty, it's white.'

'Just stop it, right.' Cath stood and pulled up her pants and trousers.

'Now wash your hands Mummy.'

'I'm going to, I'm going to, if you get out the way.' She nudged past her daughter and twisted the tap.

'*With soap* Mummy.'

'Yes dear. With soap.'

'Mama,' screeched Daniel from the hall. 'Ah done a poo!'

'Oh, well done, Danny. Clever boy. Now just wait there and Mummy'll—'

'Loo Mama. Ah done a poo!'

Cath turned from the sink. A shiny, oozing turd was nestling in her son's cupped hands. She screamed, flung it from his grasp and straight into the bath, where it slid majestically down white porcelain. Skid marks followed like chains on a launching ship, welcomed to the water with a slow plash, then a plop. The three of them watched the turd bob beside Daniel's Mickey Mouse sponge. Eilidh peered up close to the edge of the bath. 'Why d'you not put it in the toilet Mummy?'

'I got a fright.'

There was a set of plastic wheels and scoops suctioned to the tiles. Bright reds and blues, they were a favourite bathtime toy. Cath chose a red lattice shovel and screwed up her eyes.

'Mee doot. Mee doot.' Daniel was clapping his jobby hands.

'No, Mummy do it. Now move.' She chased the turd around the bath, pushing it into the side. A lacrosse flick and into the shovel it went. One hand made a basket beneath, to catch brown drips, as she swung her wet bundle across to the loo. The jobby dropped without dissent, slipping neatly down to its rightful home.

'Bye poo-poo.' Daniel waved his smeared fingers.

Eilidh tugged at Cath's jumper. 'Does it go to the sea now Mummy? Is it away to the seaside now? Will we see it when we go to the beach, Mummy?'

'Right, here you.' Cath grabbed Daniel's wrists. 'Do not touch anything. Eilidh, flush the loo please. Yes, it goes to the sea now.'

'No way. S'all jobby-poos. *You* do it.'

'Just do what you're told Eilidh.' Daniel was reaching for the plastic shovel still clutched in her hand. 'No. No touch, Daniel. Dirty.'

'Done a poo Mama.'

'Yes, clever boy. But we keep the poos in our potty, okay? Eilidh, will you flush the bloody toilet!'

The smell was overpowering.

'Snot fair. You did a swear at me, an it was him did a jobby in his hand. I hate you,' Eilidh screamed. And she was off again, slamming doors and kicking walls.

By the time Cath had scrubbed Daniel, scrubbed the bath and scrubbed herself, there was no point in going to Tumble Tots. Daniel's freefall backflips would have to wait. They could still make it to the primary school in time, if Eilidh would come out from under her covers. Cath sat on the bed, and pulled the duvet back. Dark damp fronds clung to a sobbing head. She singsonged her daughter's name. 'Eilidh-cakes. Eilidh-cakes.'

No response. Tried stroking her hair. 'Mummy's sorry.'

Eilidh jerked her head away.

'I was mean to shout at you when you hadn't done anything wrong. Daniel was the naughty boy, not you.'

One eye opened. 'Will he get a smack?'

'No pet. He's only little.'

Eilidh sat up. 'But you smacked me, an A'm only little too.'

So she was. Cath pulled her close, kissing sweat-curled hair. 'Oh baby, I know you are. I'm sorry. Mummy's sorry. I'm a bad mummy.'

'No you're not.' A little hand patted hers. 'You're a good mummy. You're *my* mummy.'

Cath hugged her. 'And you're my wee girl.'

'Will I always be your wee girl, Mummy?'

'Always.'

'Even when A'm a old lady?'

'Even when you're an old lady.'

Eilidh sighed, moulding herself until they were the same curve. 'Mummy.'

'Hmmm?'

'You smella pooh.'

By the embankment, a dog is crouching. It is mean and wiry, and slevers from a grey tongue. If it were human, it would have tattoos. Later, gangs will congregate in this lane, with their bottles of lurid mixtures, their thick, sweet tonic wines made by English monks. A thrilled nausea billows in her throat at the thought they might find her here, so she sits on a bollard to watch the dog snuffle and scrape at the earth. There are rows of bollards on the path, spaced at regular intervals, to stop joyriders enjoying the cycle track. Few cyclists venture here. They are too visible, too vulnerable in their fluorescent yellow and their spindly legs. Other cities can have secret spaces, and fountains and canals and greens – places that just quietly are. Not here, where a rampant fungus, a bindweed of spray paint and pishing and trolleys and filth encroach like shadows on breathing lungs.

The dog yelps, a wicked, triumphant howl, and she realises what he's seeking. A tiny rabbit jerks from between his paws, lurching in a blind scrabble across her toes. It is raining, but she prefers her sandals. They match her anorak, and never get scuffed. She scoops down her hand, like guddling for fish, and wins the rabbit from the scabby dog. The hound bares its teeth, and she kicks it, hard. Inside her fist, the rabbit trembles.

It was official: Eilidh loved school. Mums and siblings were left in the assembly hall while the Primary Sevens escorted the new intake to the gym and the dinner hall and the television room. Eilidh had come back wearing a white polo top with the school crest on, and a Polaroid the teacher had taken of her new group. 'We're called the Sunshine Group an A'm sittin beside a girl called Sarah and her there.' She pointed at the photo, 'Her's Gelly or somethin.'

'Gelly?'

Eilidh shrugged. 'Gella, Ah think.'

'Angela?'

'Don't know. And look Mummy, look.' She lowered her voice at the damning evidence, handing the photo to her mother. 'There's boys too.'

'Wow, so there is. Now mind you don't start kissing them, madam.'

'*Mu-um.*'

Cath could hear Eilidh now, in her room, arranging her dolls into groups. She, of course, was the teacher. Daniel was pegged out in his playpen, lulled by the tune from *Bob the Builder*. Cath turned off the telly and just stood. A low, still silence she could taste. Tiny snores of her son and a steady drone from the fridge. The soft beat of the house. She stretched to fill the space, sinews singing in her calves as Daniel stirred and mumbled in his sleep. Cath took Eilidh's photo and pinned it on the wall, next to another class picture. Adults this time, almost. Thirty neat figures in the black they called blue. Her husband at the rear, grinning beneath his hat. Tulliallan Castle in the background, and a woman with sharp blonde hair just *so* beneath her cap, one row in front of Jamie and pretending to smile. Anna Cameron. While the rest of these new police recruits looked eager and scared, Anna was calm, observing the photographer as you would a window.

Beside that picture, a framed newspaper clipping. Three glamorous black women linking arms with a wide-eyed cop, her shy smile folded in a youth-plump face. All strutting beneath the headline: *The Fourth Degree*. It was a photo of Cath, a few days in the job as a beat cop. For some reason, the Three Degrees (sans Diana Ross) had come to Glasgow to open a new cash-and-carry warehouse. A freshly minted Cath and her neighbour had been sent to deal with the crowd control. Either no one had told the locals, or no one cared, because the crowd, when they got there, consisted of the shop owner, two men and a stray dog. Struggling for a photo, the assembled snappers had coaxed Cath into the picture, and there she was, giving the singers *the fourth degree*. Nothing to the bollocking she got from her sergeant later.

The face in the picture was kind and naive. A relic of the old days. Nothing like the paramilitary, T-shirt toting, combat-ready cops of today. Look at her, white shirt, black tie, white vinyl top to her hat, which had to be taken off the hat to get washed and then would never fit right again. Radio harness dangling like a dog lead. And the handbag. God, the handbag. When Cath first joined, policewomen wore tunics without breast-pockets. Pockets spoiled the bust line. Instead, they were given smart black handbags in which to place the miscellanea of police work. Radio swinging from one hip, handbag from the other; Playtex straps lifting and separating breasts in a caricature of the clippie from hell, dissected and encumbered by leather and bulk, but with the most powerful catchphrase in the world. Simply this:

You wanting the jail?

'You wanting the jail, Daniel?' Cath asked. A sleepy Daniel looked up from his playpen and smiled, wet gums smacking like a little fish. Fish. Oh shit. Fish that she'd meant to buy for tea when they were out. Well, they'd just have to get a carry-out, because she wasn't getting them all togged up again to go outside. She moved slowly back from Daniel, still smiling, backing away till she was at the couch and he'd lost interest in her, turning instead to his toes. Up close, the couch was filthy, but she lay on it anyway, folding over a cushion to support her head. Yesterday's paper lay on the floor and she stretched to pull it over. The death-mask last look of a Middle East hostage stared, pleading with her. She turned to the TV section.

When Jamie got home, the kids were fed and the dishes done. Cath had an idea of family meals, all four around the table, chatting cheerfully about their day. But it never seemed to work, slipping instead to a grumbling, taut mess. Fractious bickering about the telly, Daniel painting mince into his hair. Jamie fighting with Eilidh over how to use a fork. Bathing was okay though; that was fun. Sometimes the three of them would squeeze in together, so 'Mummy could have a nice rest'. Aye, listening to water gush and slop on the floor. A daddy bath was the best bath, Eilidh said, because he never made them wash their hair.

'Good evening, starshine.' Jamie kissed the side of Cath's head.

She moved from the sink. 'Hiya. Why you in your overalls?'

'Had my first firearms turn today.'

'Did you? What was it?'

'Escaped bull. Done a runner from the abattoir and was rampaging through Tollcross. I was the nearest AFO, so off I went.'

'And?'

'And what?'

'Did you kill it?'

'Naw. Dunno why they sent me. It's got to be a marksman does it. But the vet got there first anyway, with a tranquilliser.'

'Good.' She wiped across the worktop.

'What d'you mean good? What d'you think's going to happen when it goes back to the abattoir?'

'I know, but . . . well, I'm glad you didn't hurt it.'

'Jeez.' He shook his head. 'What you going to be like if I shoot a person?'

'You know you're never going to shoot a person.'

'Where do you get that from?'

'Well, stats and stuff. I mean, that's you been qualified for three months, and your first turn's a runaway bull.'

'Cath, you don't know what you're talking about. Things have changed a lot since your day. There's weans at school can get hold of a gun nowadays.'

She hooked the dishtowel over a drawer handle. 'Oh, so you're going to start shooting wee boys, are you?'

'God, Cath, I'm just saying.'

Yes, there he goes. Into the fridge for a can of lager. Jesus, he'd not even taken off his jacket.

'Well, you don't need to patronise me. "Since my day." I do read the papers you know. And the chief constable's report—'

'Why?'

'Why what?'

A clash of tin on melamine. 'Why on earth would you read the chief constable's annual report?'

She shrugged, like a child caught with her hand in the biscuit box. 'Don't know. Keep up to speed, I suppose.'

'Yeah, but why?'

'Am I not allowed to take an interest in the outside world?'

He raised his hands. 'Och, just leave it Cath, okay. I've had a long day.'

'Yeah, playing Old MacDonald had a farm.'

Jamie shook his head, stomped upstairs.

She wanted to ask him what it had felt like. Getting the call, being told he was authorised. Was he scared? Elated? Disappointed he didn't get to shoot? That would be why he was such a crabbit bastard. She heard the sound of running water. Good, he must be bathing the children. Then an angry yell.

'Jesus Christ, Catherine. What the hell have you been doing?'

She ran up the stairs, worried one of the kids had got hold of some scissors, or unlocked their stair-gate, or something else that would, ultimately, be her fault. Jamie was standing in the bathroom, watching a circle of gritty brown bubble around the plughole. Bugger. There must be a bit of it stuck down there. She was sure she'd got it all out.

Eilidh held her daddy's hand. 'Mummy put a poo in the bath, Dad. And I got a new T-shirt. Look.'

'Just a minute Eilidh. Mummy did what?' He stared at Cath.

'You know Jamie, I was that bursting, I just didn't have time to make it to the loo. You've no idea what it's like here, stuck at home all day with these two, not even a minute to go for a crap . . .' She paused, waiting for a glimmer of something.

'It's a joke. Feel free to join in any time you like.'

A whistle of thin air through his teeth.

'It was an accident. Daniel had been using his potty, and—'

'No, I don't want to know. I'll go and get a plunger from the shed.'

'No, I can get it. If I stick a toothbrush down—'

'Cath, will you bloody leave it? Go and make the tea or something.'

'Well, I thought we could get a curry . . .'

'I thought we were having fish?'

'Can I not change my bloody mind?'

'But how are we paying for it?'

'Pardon?'

'You said this morning you were skint.'

She felt her jaw slacken, then clench. 'The money for *our* carry-out will come out of *our* joint account, which is full of the wages that *I* enable you to go out and earn while I stay at home feeding your children, cleaning your house and ironing your bloody clothes.'

'Ooh. Temper, temper.' His eyes rounded in a mirror of his mouth, and he was kidding, he was, but it was too late to stop the flaring, rising, her voice all high and ridiculous. 'Don't you dare speak to me like that!' Helium words, losing their impact. 'Don't you dare speak to me like that, you selfish, arrogant bastard.'

She saw Eilidh's nose, pressed into her father's side. Saw Daniel in his room, building Stickle bricks. Saw a door through which she could walk.

But she didn't. Could have done that three years ago, when it really mattered, and Daniel was becoming in her womb, and she *knew*. Knew he'd been with that woman, Anna. All at once, her husband had cleaved her heart and claimed her belly. And, like a crab without a shell when a predator circles, she had crawled back in.

Well, what was there left to be scared of now?

It isn't bleeding, not even bruised that she can see. Just frozen in its fear until she warms it with droppered milk. Her brother had all sorts of needles and measures and plungers. She'd taken one thin glass tube from a bottle of nose drops – his nostrils were cracked with whatever crap he inhaled. She squeezes the rubber bulb at the end, rinsing it under running water until the oily slicks wash from the glass and it no longer smells of hospitals. Every morning, there is a bottle of milk outside the flat across the landing. That morning, she spills it, first carefully siphoning off enough for a day's feeds. They'll think it is an accident – the milkman, or the paper boy careless in sleepy haste, but if she'd taken the whole bottle . . . oh yes, the bad bit was in her. Her gran was right to wash her hands of the lot of them.

The rabbit hunches in its box. She knows not to lift him, just eases the box gently from beneath her bed and drips the milk slowly at the side of his mouth. Some goes in, and maybe he will taste it. His fur is velvet, but she won't touch him yet.

3

'C'mon boys. Keep moving the ball up the left. Pace him, Jimmy, pace him!'

A muddy horde thundered by; a seething single mass of hair and snot, caterpillar legs trundling. Jamie watched the referee run to quell a scuffle, saw wee Benji stick out a foot to trip the St Patrick's boy who was marking him, saw the ball appear from nowhere – surely that was a different ball? – and smash into the back of the St Pat's goal.

'Fucking chaos, Mr Worth!' yelled Benji, whooping by to join in the celebrations.

Jamie rubbed his hand down his stubble. The rain was teeming down, splashing his neck and eyes, his tongue tasting drops each time he shouted at the kids. He caught Cath's eye. She and Jenny were in the stand; Eilidh waving in delight at her famous daddy.

'You're the boss of them, Daddy? All those big boys?' Eilidh had breathed, wide-eyed as she and Cath had arrived with Jenny at the ground, before the match. Jamie had the whole team doing star jumps and press-ups.

'Yup. They've got to do exactly what I say.'

'Jus like me?' she'd simpered, coy as you like. Wrapping her hair in twirls, as she wrapped him round her finger.

He turned towards the mêlée. The referee was berating one of the St Pat's kids; for getting mud on his nice clean top, by the looks of it.

'It's a stitch up, ref,' shouted Jenny.

After the Tamburrini murder, Jenny had applied to go job share. Said she wanted to spend more time with her wee girl, which was fair enough. Wouldn't everyone? The council had built a new travellers' site just off the M8, and they were keen for the police to form 'closer links', now the travellers had nice new toilet blocks and electricity plug-ins to replace the boggy field of before. Thus Jenny became 'Ethnic Liaison Officer' for the travellers. One of her more avant-garde ideas had been to set up a community youth club for the kids, so the travellers and locals could mingle. The council had backed the project, brought in youth workers, provided accommodation – the only problem was getting the kids to come. Even with Jenny playing big sister in civvies, and a cool youth worker with several piercings, the pool table lay unused, the crafts unworked. A few girls drifted in and out, but none of the boys – local or traveller.

'Well, it's shite, isn't it?' Alex had said, after Jenny had dragged them around the project. 'When I was a wean, I hated youth clubs. You want to be out drinking and shagging, not playing ping pong with the local pigs.'

'What about a competition? Maybe getting the kids to design a poster, or a sunflower growing . . . ?'

'Och Jenny, get real,' said Jamie, 'you've got to excite them. Not how Alex said, mind. He was obviously far more advanced than me.'

'Still am, pal.'

'I mean, when I was that age, all I wanted to do was play football.'

'Football!' Jenny had patted his back. 'That's it. Let's get a team going, get some trials organised, coaching and stuff. A Townhead team, for the whole area, not split into schools or religions or backgrounds. I know, the Townhead Tykes!'

Alex had started singing the old Coke tune:

'I'd like to teach the world to play, in perfect harmonee . . .'

'Aye, but who *would* they play Jenny? You need a bit of competition to make it exciting.'

'I don't know. There must be a junior league, or a schools' league. You know about football, Jamie; you used to coach, didn't you?'

'Aye, before Daniel was born.'

'Well, there you are then. You look at how we'd organise it, and I'll start—'

'We? We?'

'Ah, but Jumbo, you'd be the perfect role model. Tall, handsome, supremely skilled on the field—'

'Piss off.'

And so, Jamie had ended up coaching the Townhead football team. At first, it was just the kids who lived in the nearby streets that came. Bunch of wee toerags, most of them, more keen on vandalising the changing room walls and fighting than learning how to dribble. But there were a few good players amongst them. Jenny put up her posters on the site, talked to some of the families, but still, none of the travellers turned up. Well, not to play. A little gang of them sometimes sat on the wall, throwing stones and pithy phrases as the footballers neared. Jamie made a point of saying hello, then just ignored them. After a while, they stopped chucking things, but the trade in insults continued. Jamie was clearing up one evening when he heard shouting behind the pavilion. He'd run out to find three of the local kids punching lumps out of a traveller boy. Or it seemed that way at first. As he got closer, he'd realised the traveller boy – Benji, as it turned out – was lying on his back on top of one of the kids, whilst kicking out furiously at his other two assailants. Benji had landed a couple of kicks on Jamie too, before he'd managed to unpick the four of them from their tussle.

He'd ended up taking Benji home to the campsite, to be met with dogs and stares. The head man, a tall, broad seventy-year-old, with brown cured skin and a lustrous silver bouffant, had beckoned Jamie and Benji into his van. Like a Tardis inside, all chrome and leather and smelling of pipe smoke.

'It wisny me, Papo. That polis bastard fitted me up.'

'Benjamin, that's enough. Go to Berta's wagon.'

Benji had scowled, folded his arms.

'I said NOW!'

The head man's voice was like a cannon crack. Benji scurried off, pausing only to give Jamie the finger.

'Sit down.'

The cushions were green and gold velvet. Soft as anything against Jamie's back. 'Mr . . . ?'

'Thomas. Just Thomas.'

'Thomas, I came here to tell you that Benji's done nothing wrong. Just in case you heard anything, or had folk up here complaining. It was the local boys that were ganging up on him. Gave them a good run for their money mind. I think he felled about four of them.'

Thomas inclined his head. 'It's usually our lads get blamed for everything. Most folk find it – easier.'

'Well, that won't happen with me. By the way, your boy's got an excellent left foot on him. He should come along one night to the football practices. Tell him to bring his mates.'

Before he knew it, on his days off, Jamie was coaching fifteen grubby, spirited kids; a motley mix of Townheaders and travellers. Some of them even lied about their age, so they could play in the primary league. There was still the odd internecine bust-up, but, for the most part, the kids played as a team. Last week, they'd thrashed Ruchill Primary: five nil, a nasty gouge and a couple of black eyes. And it looked like they were on for another victory today. As long as the referee continued to be off the ball. Jamie followed the minute hand on his watch. Five . . . four . . . three . . . whistle. Yuss! They were home and dry.

If only. Jamie stood, chittering in his tracksuit, as the kids did their victory stampede. Rain driving in his eyes, seeping from the ground through shoes and socks. When he was little, he'd dream of having a transporter, like they did on *Star Trek*. Some devious device to hurl your atoms through space, instantly taking you far from danger or mundanity, to the bolthole of your choice.

'Well done, coach.'

'Bit wild out there the day, eh?'

Parents were moving forward to gather up their children. Jamie would have to take some of the Townhead lot home; he could cram four in the car if Jenny took Cath up the road.

'Good match, Jumbo.' Jenny lit up a fag beside him.

'Thought you'd given up?'

'No, it's just there's no bloody places left to smoke.'

Jenny didn't usually smoke when her daughter was around.

'Where's Catriona?'

'At her dad's. I know, don't ask. Court says he *has* to get access. Anyway, means I get a whole Saturday afternoon to go shopping.' Jenny picked a fragment of tobacco from her tongue. 'So, what are you guys up to for the rest of the day?'

'Well, I've some of the kids to drop off, then hot bath, a curry and an early bed for me.'

'Aye, very good,' said Cath. 'You remembering we've got Gem's do tonight?'

Cath's sister Gemma was off to work in Australia – the latest of her many, varied enterprises – and she was having a farewell do in Shawlands. There was a family meal tomorrow, but Cath wanted to go to this thing too. And he'd forgotten; something else to incur Cath's wrath. Jamie was knackered. He'd been up with Daniel half the night, then training and the warm-up with the team, then running up and down the touchline for ninety minutes, then after he'd taken the kids home, he'd have to get Eilidh to her dancing class. By the time he finally got to wash, the kids would have hogged the bath, and all the hot water. One cold, quick shower later and that would be him, halfway through his one weekend off a month. What had he actually done for himself?

'Shit Cath. Your mum's having us all for dinner tomorrow anyway.'

'God's sake. What's wrong with wanting to enjoy yourself?' said Cath. 'This is for Gem's *friends*, Jamie. The youngsters, not all the old aunties.'

He'd met some of Gemma's friends before. Had nothing in common with any of them. All his real pals were polis. Who else would go for a pint off the nightshift but another cop? Or play golf at 3 p.m. on a Thursday when the early shift was done? It was hard to join in with the real world when you worked odd shifts and weekends and had days off through the week. Police time was not real time; it was a fractured, grabbed-at cycle of feast and famine.

Plus, it was natural to gravitate to what you knew. Where you could relax and not have to justify yourself. Where the conversation didn't always work its way round to : *I've nothing against the police, but . . .*

But he went; he went to keep the peace and to show face and not show Cath up and they were five minutes in the pub before it happened again.

'This is great, isn't it?' said Cath, as they opened the plate-glass door. Music boomed through lurid lights and the sizzle of fajitas, and all Jamie could think about was how much he needed his bed.

'What?'

'You, me. Out.'

'Yes.' He kissed the top of her head. 'It is.'

'Look, that's some of them over there.' Cath waved at a table where nine or ten other people sat. Gemma, of course, drinking a vat of something green, a few folk he recognised from another party, a team that looked like they were from Gemma's most recent workplace – selling advertising space on bus shelters – and Gemma and Cath's cousin Mark, who waved back at Cath. So did . . . ach, no. It was Gemma's mad pal . . . Josie, Lucy, something like that. He kept wanting to call her Juicy. Only met her once before, but once was enough. Oozing from her dress, all glossy lips and too much perfume. She was squeezed beside a fleshy-lobed business type, and a fairish-haired lassie chewing at her hair. The girl was too meek to be in advertising, but the man just had to be. Check out the screaming shirt and self-important sideburns.

Mark pulled out a chair. 'Hi, Cath.' He kissed his cousin on the cheek. 'We got a round in for you two already. Alright Jamie? Good to see you.' He lowered his voice, 'Eh – Gem's a wee bit . . .'

'Wee bit what? I'm abso-bloody-lutely wunner . . . ful. Jamie!' Gemma flung her arms around him. 'My favourite big brother-in-law. Everyone! Meet Jamie!'

'Evening all. Been hearing all about you, officer. Don't worry,' the man with the fleshy ears raised his glass, 'the wife's driving tonight.'

'Aye, you've really got to watch yourself,' said an earnest little chap in a red tank top. 'Now, don't get me wrong, I've nothing against you lot, but a mate of mine, one beer he'd had. I'm telling you, one beer, and the traffic police stopped him . . .'

And so it begins.

'That's Pete. He's our illustrator, and this here,' Gemma hiccuped, blowing a kiss at rubber ears, 'is my boss, well, ex-boss Garry and his lovely wife . . . ?'

'Claire.'

'Thass right. Claire-bear!' Gemma giggled.

Jamie felt Cath nudge between him and the group.

'And I'm Cath, just in case anyone was wondering. Gemma's sister. Jamie's wife.'

'Pleased to meet you, Jamie's wife,' said Garry. 'Here, have a seat. Olive?'

'No – Cath.'

'Funny lady. I *like* you.'

Jamie took the dish from Cath. 'Here, you go easy on the snacks, missus. Remember you've to fit your bikini.'

Stupid, thoughtless, serrated banality, on which he would be hung, drawn and quartered. If he gulped hard, swallowed quick and hid his face in the chilly fluff of his Guinness, maybe Cath would think she'd imagined it. Would think not even Jamie would be stupid enough to use a public forum to imply his wife was watching her weight. A slow eye sideways. No, she was still staring. It would ferment for days now. There was no point in saying he hadn't meant it.

'That's right, you're on holiday, aren't you?' said Mark.

'Four days to go.'

'Where you off to again?'

'Majorca.' Jamie manoeuvred into the only free seat – the end of the couch where Josie sat. 'Can't wait. Get away from this pishy weather.'

'Ooh, I can just picture you in shorts. So, occifer –' Josie leaned close, one varnished nail tracing the air above Jamie's waist – 'that a gun in your pocket, or are you just pleased to see me?'

'Don't be daft. They don't carry their guns off duty,' said Claire. 'Do you?'

'We don't have guns full stop.'

He wasn't getting into this, a debate with half-cut strangers.

'Ach, it's only a matter of time though,' Garry nodded. 'In't it Jamie?'

'I hope not,' said Cath.

'Och, c'mon.' Garry was eager now. 'Don't kid yourself. The world's going to hell in a handcart. Everyone's got guns. It's only fair the polis can fight back, eh Jamie? Blast the bastards to fuck, eh?'

Cath, as Jamie knew she would, couldn't resist. 'You can't have the police tooling up en masse. The neds'll just get bigger and better guns. And before you know it, they'll be frisking weans as they go into school. Do you want to end up living somewhere like America?'

Garry laughed. 'Think that's a bit naive, Cath.'

Jamie saw his wife's mouth quiver. She was going to flay the guy with her acid tongue. Cath in full flow was an impressive torrent, particularly if directed at someone other than him. Her eyes were gleamy, the soft space above her breasts flushed. Suddenly, he wanted to taste her collarbone, slide his flesh upon hers.

'I agree with Cath, actually. Now, can I get anyone another drink? Claire, how about a cocktail? You're a Cosmopolitan kind of girl, aren't you? Garry – another pint, pal?'

'Eh? Oh, aye. Cheers.' Garry's mouth hung limp, like it was marking time. 'But how can you say—'

'And you'll take a wee hauf too?'

'Now Garry, you know what you're like,' breathed Claire.

'Aye, a whisky'll be great.' Garry readjusted his trousers. 'Single malt, if they've got it.'

'Gemma? Another bucket of meths for you?'

'Yes . . . but make sure they put a brolly in it.'

Cath and Jamie leaned together in the back seat of the taxi on the way home. The tartan rug draped behind was itchy, red floating fibres making Jamie want to sneeze.

'I'm sorry about the bikini thing, Cath. It was just a joke. You know you look gorgeous.'

'I'm sorry too,' said Cath.

'For what?'

'For noising them up. That Garry's a diddy.'

'Och, he was just trying to make conversation. He could've been talking about cars.'

Jamie assumed Garry's drawl, 'Say Jamsie-boy. What d'you think about the AK-47. Is that a better model than the 46?'

'Maybe it turns him on,' Cath laughed. '*Oh, Claire baby. Gonny pull ma trigger.*'

'Yeah, baby, yeah.' Jamie's voice was over-loud. He saw the taxi driver clocking him in the mirror. 'I wanna pump you full of shot, baby.'

'Thanks for sticking up for me.'

'It's a pleasure. I'll stick up for you any time, pardner.' His mouth brushed the tip of her nose. 'Know what I mean, doll?'

Cath laid her head on his chest. The heat of her head was on his shoulder, digging a little into the bone; a tiny pain he was reluctant to move from. Perfume playing beneath his nose, the same perfume she'd always worn, with a name that always escaped him. He stroked her hair, as the taxi rumbled on through the night, passing lighted windows and darkened doors. In an upstairs room, a woman drew the curtains, her silhouette stretching to pull them tight.

'And bloody Josie. I think she was trying to get into your pants.'

'Well, does that not make you feel good, that I'm still desirable to other women?'

The taxi shoogled over a bump. Cath pulled herself away. 'Not really, no.'

She hadn't spoken another word by the time they went to bed. Well, she had to the babysitter, and she had to Eilidh, who had woken and demanded an audience. But nothing to him, save clipped responses. Undressing in silence, slipping her satin nightshirt over her head. Him standing now, behind her, blowing warm breath at her ear. Not understanding, not wanting to. 'Come to bed, honey.'

'In a minute.'

'Come,' a hand across her breast. Rigid. 'To,' thumb circling her nipple. A tiny yield. 'Bed.' His groin nudging at the parting of her legs.

Cath reached to turn off the light. 'Why?'

'So we can, you know.' He pushed harder into her.

'Talk?'

'Body talk . . . hmmm . . . body talk.' Crooning his way to the pillow, her part-laughing, part not there. Until he moved his hands between her legs and made her fall onto the bed. Lying half on, her nightshirt round her waist, and him climbing on top. The breadth of his chest pressing down on her. He could crush her with his weight, do anything he wanted. His wife pinioned beneath him, unable to move unless he let her. He felt his penis jerk as she ran a damp finger around the glans and then it was he who was weak, snuffling at her breasts. 'I love you.' Meaning it with all his soul. 'Cath, I love you.'

'Don't speak with your mouth full,' she whispered.

'Do you love these?' came Anna's voice, clear above the two of them. Offering up her own breasts, round and perfect and with no scent of milk. Like the curve you can't see, but know is on the horizon, just outside the edge of your eye.

'I love my wife,' said Jamie.

Her father has come back, and there is another party in the living room. She'd watched from her window, as he came up the path. Struggled to trace their similar noses, and wondered why. Maybe today. Her belly begins to flutter like a web-bound fly.

As the front door opens, she hears him slur, Where the fuck's my welcome home banner? *Hears him lurch towards the kitchen, where all the bevvy is piled in crates. A voice shouting* Alright, Brizzers? *and a couple of whoops. She waits still, for him to come and see her, and passes the time reading the newsprint on the floor. It's good to practise her reading. A scuffle of feet in the lobby, and she sits upright, tugging her anorak so the sleeves reach her wrists.*

It is her brother, and he is holding a gun. If it works, it will be sudden. And loud. Her father will hear the noise and come in. But her brother, of

*course, can still make it torture. He traces the snout of the pistol across
her face, along the back of her neck, then around her shoulder and down
to where her heart must be. The gun is short and ugly, like him. Foul
breath close to hers.*

'*Right, fuckface. I'm saying this once. You've got to hide this, right?
Ah couldny gie a fuck where, but my da's no to see it, right?*'

She nods.

Packing. That's what most folk did the night before their holidays.
Shorts and towels and flip-flops, mind. Not themselves. The
cabinet was freezing. Well, it had to be, to keep the bodies fresh.
It had been a while since Jamie last packed himself into one of these
thin metal channels. A two-inch gap separated his nose from the
steel above. In Italy, before the kids were born, he'd seen a whole
cemetery like this, a multistorey concrete layering that he'd
thought at first was chicken coops. Then, as dusk fell, he watched
from their balcony as electric candles flared en masse at the front of
each coop, and a red, neon crucifix lit up the whole of the pyramid.
Small vases of carnations shone, ghost white in relief. You could
see the cross for miles around the valley, brighter than all the signs
for the pubs and clubs, and he'd thought what it must be like to
sleep for all eternity beneath hotels and a neon cross. He liked to
sleep in the dark. Total darkness, not even the hall lamp on for the
kids.

A sliver of light lit the top of his toes; they'd kept the drawer very
slightly open, to let in some air. Even Jamie had limits. He may be
Mr Game-for-a-Laugh, but even so. You had to breathe. It was
only a comfort blanket though, the paleness at his feet, a chink on
the horizon. Little illumination was afforded by the mortuary
nightlight. From the outside of the squat, sandstone building,
an eerie blue buzzed through opaque, pockmarked windows,
hinting at experiments and electricity. Inside, white-tiled astrin-
gent expectation was frequently punctured by the appearance of
the cat. A fat black monster, it stalked the mortuary with satisfaction, lending a homely air to proceedings. Or so the attendants
thought. Perhaps they brought it in for a petting session, to soothe

a grieving widow, and it never left. More likely, it was a fortunate feral, plucked from the rancid lanes behind the Saltmarket, where stray humans shared the gutter with the cats and rats, plying a sad and meagre fleamarket of single shoes and grubby underwear, swapping raincoats and string for a bottle of meths.

However the cat had arrived at the mortuary, it was clearly thriving. Cruel rumours abounded that it was fed scraps from a bucket. Sam, the head mortuary technician, did nothing to counter this belief. *'Aye, well,'* he'd say when challenged. *'It's a bit like fixing a car engine, see. There's aye some bits left over.'*

Jamie knew the cat was there now, watching him. Could sense it through the dark; its unblinking, questing eyes considering this anomaly. The humans it saw daily did not shift and wriggle, did not try to get comfy in their shells. Would the cat run, like Lassie, to fetch help; yowling its concern? A faint slurping gnaw from outside suggested it was engaged in cleaning its bits. Or maybe eating something . . .

'Psst. Alex,' he hissed. 'You there?'

Another slurp.

He closed his eyes and waited. Anna's wee cat used to chase his fingers. Launch herself and cling in a furry ball, kitten pinpricks anchored on his hand. Did Anna think of him when she looked at her cat? After all, he had found it; seen the soft, silent mewling, and thought of Anna.

Women remembered these things.

Women like Jenny. His mind was off now, wandering through the dark. Let it go. He knew Jenny knew, knew that she knew that he knew this. Always acute, now she was barbed, punishing him for *her* bad luck with men. It was none of her business what had happened between him and Anna, yet she made him feel it was. Little digs about 'Inspector Cameron', how *she'd brushed them all off without a backward glance. Eh, Jamie? Eh? Cath says she doesn't hear from her either.*

Ignoring Jenny didn't make it go away. And Jenny was friends with Cath. Close enough, yet far enough that he could never quite be sure where Jenny's loyalties sat. Jenny was his mate too, and that was where the real fault lay. It made her think she could say what she bloody liked to him. Mind, she'd always been like that.

Then there was the gun thing. She'd caught him this evening, just before their nightshift, when she was heading home. 'Oooh, look who it isn't,' said Alex. When the Flexi Unit had disbanded, Jamie and Alex ended up on the same shift. Alex hated being a run-of-the-mill cop again, his social life buggered by rigid shifts. 'It's Part-Time Patti.'

'Shut it, pretty boy. Here,' she said, thrusting a bottle of Grouse at Jamie. 'That's for you.'

'Eh, cheers. Why?'

'S'not from me, my love. It's from Thomas at the site. Here you,' she plonked herself on Alex's knee, 'I need a massage. I've had a hoor of a day.'

'And where would madam like massaged exactly?'

'Keep your hands above my shoulders and your mind above your dick.'

'But why?' asked Jamie again.

'To say thanks for what you've done. With the kids. Harder, there. Oooh, you're good.'

'I know.'

'Shit, they only won a football match.'

'Jamie, it wasn't so much the winning – although I believe the headmistress of St Pat's will be lodging a formal complaint about the "manner" it was won – it was the fact you got them playing at all.' She opened her eyes. 'Thomas says you're "a man of honour".'

He looked at his whisky. 'That was very nice of him.'

'Though I don't know what he'd say if he knew the latest string to your bow. Shot any good neds lately, Jumbo?'

'Och, don't start Jenny, okay?'

'How not?'

'Jenny,' Alex pushed her off his knee. 'Gie the guy a break. You haven't a clue. You're all cosy up there drinking tea and getting your palm read—'

'And getting information and making links and preventing future crimes.'

'Crap. You need to get back into the real world.'

'And you need a few more brain cells, then you'd be a retard, sweetcheeks.' Jenny folded her arms. 'I mean, c'mon Jamie. We've got CS spray, bigger batons. We don't need folk like you hoicking guns around.'

'So, what about wee China then?' said Alex. 'Much fucking use CS did him. If he'd had a bloody gun he'd still be alive today.'

'Alex, shut it,' said Jamie. 'What d'you mean, folk like me, Jenny?'

'Och, I don't know. You're just not – och, forget it.' She zipped up her jacket. 'I'm going home to talk some sense with my wean.'

Jamie was still angry with her. Here in the clinical darkness, wreathed in wall-to-wall inertia of gas-heavy bodies. *Someone like him?* Did she not think he knew what he was doing? Did she think he was a gun nut too? Someone like that Jinky Robertson? The whole point was: someone had to do it.

It started small. Challenging someone smoking on the bus. Asking a lassie if that guy's annoying her. Intervening in a shop when a parent thumps a child. Someone had to say: No. That's enough. Stop it. That's why he wanted to be a cop. Volunteering to carry a gun was the same thing. Not something he'd taken lightly. Well, it was at first. Gave him a big macho hard-on. But it also made him feel brave, and good, and worthwhile again, and he was sick of feeling guilty for that.

Alex had kept chuntering on, even after Jenny left. 'Well, if they told me I'd to do it, I would. I'd carry a gun—'

'Alex, you're a bunkernut. I wouldny trust you with the panda let alone an H and K. Here, give me the keys.' Jamie had grabbed the car keys from him as they went into the yard.

'Chill, man. You should be on the wind-down.' Alex seized Jamie's shoulders from behind, rubbing as sensuously as he'd done for Jenny.

'Piss off.'

Alex was facing him now, singing,'Oh, this year I'm off to sunny Spain . . .'

'Y Viva Majorca,' replied Jamie. 'Aye, ten hours and counting.'

He should have been off tonight. He and Cath were flying out tomorrow. But the gaffer had said he could get a flyer, so why waste a day's annual leave? If he was in bed by four say, that would give him a couple of hours' sleep before they'd to be up and at the airport. Could catch a few zeds here too, while he was waiting . . . What the hell was keeping them?

A new sprog had started on the shift this week. Cheery wee guy, with the unfortunate name of Trevor Whistle. And, in time-honoured fashion, his tutor cop was bringing him to the mortuary, to confront real-life death in the chilly, smelly raw. And, in time-honoured fashion, Jamie was lying in the fridge, waiting to jump out at the boy when the drawer was pulled. He'd a shroud thing to pull over his face whenever he heard them clatter in. But he'd been here ages, and his calves were beginning to cramp. The smell was starting to make him queasy, that chemical sourness of air fresh-ener masking shite. Blue-black, weighted air pushing on his chest, and not a soul around.

Five more minutes and he was out of here.

It lies in a glistening pile, quivering in the half-light. Its blood looks like pizza sauce, spilled across the box. No longer a he; a soft heaping of sticky fur and partial flesh. Matted. The velvet is all matted, a mat to stamp your feet on. Great boots of steel-capped leather, on her brother's cloven feet. Yet somehow the rabbit lives, one visible eye darting wildly blank. She'd left it too late to stroke him, and now she'd never know. Shouldn't move him, why she doesn't know, but it's what they always say on telly. Where would she take him anyway? Nowhere is safe. First her one shoulder, then the other, slides beneath her bed. She is bigger now than the first time she hid here, but still skinny, and the dark and dust seem to grow wider around her. She tugs the box in towards her stomach. Cradles his head in her palm, whispering her love that is melting, hot, down her face, running like milk into his panting mouth. The mouth she seals with her other hand, gripping his desperate throat and nose to take away the pain.

★   ★   ★

Jamie could hear footsteps. A gruff voice saying, 'In you come son.' More feet, several pairs; they must be selling tickets. Slowly, his hand slipped up towards his face, drawing the shroud across his cheeks and eyes. Thick cloth gloved his mouth with every breath in. He waited for the signal, but there was only silence. A great long pause of nothing. Had they gone already? Maybe the boy had fainted, but there would be some clamour surely, some noise? Bugger this, he'd had enough. How much oxygen was coming in that tiny gap anyway? Suffocation was not part of the deal. Being aware that voices had come and gone made him feel more alone than before. Heart leaping, straining for sound. Thought he heard a sniff, not sure, shit, he didn't like this.

Then a voice, deep and booming not an inch from his ear.

'Fucking freezing in here, in't it?'

Jamie screamed, his head jerking up to crash off the steel above him. Pain slashed his skull and he was tearing the cloth from his face, but it was wrapped around his neck and he was fumbling for something to tug on and slide out.

'Jesus Christ,' he yelled, battering on the walls that skimmed his sides. 'Get me out of here. Someone get me out.'

A rush of cool air and then he was looking up at Alex, Willy, even Trevor the bloody sprog. All creasing themselves with laughter as he scrambled and fell from the drawer.

'Ah, Jesus, Jumbo,' wheezed Alex. 'You should see your face.'

'Nice one, Kevin,' someone hooted. The drawer to the left of the one Jamie had been stuffed in slid open, and Kevin Clark arose like Dracula, arms crossed across his chest.

'Good evenink, Mr Worth,' he purred. 'Did you haff a plisant sleep?'

'You bastards.' Jamie cradled his aching head. 'You total fucking bastards.'

'Ach well,' Alex patted him on the back. 'S'about time the tables were turned pal.'

'See you, you shitebag—'

'Woah, don't blame me, pal. It was the sprog's idea!'

Young Trevor was beaming from ear to ear.

'Hey Jamie!' Andy Duff came running in from the street. 'Jamie, is your radio still off?'

'Christ, my bloody heart's switched off, let alone my stupid radio.'

'No, listen. Area Control have been shouting you.'

'Ah, very funny.' Jamie looked at his watch. 'I'm away on my holybags, as of five minutes ago.'

'No, seriously Jamie. They're looking for you. Some firearms thing, over in the South. The ARVs are tied up at an incident in Dunoon. You're the nearest AFO.'

4

The rendezvous point was at the back of a chip shop. Binfuls of fishy entrails spilled onto the cobbles, inside-out guts blowing sea tangs across murky night air. Acid and salt. A ventilation shaft hummed, and it seemed louder to Jamie than the buzzing in his own head. Like a bee trapped behind his eyes, and he tried to shut it out.

Huddled there already was the local shift inspector and a couple of beat cops. And, thank God, another AFO, muffled in protective gear. When Jamie had gone to get his carbine from the armoury, the duty officer couldn't say if they'd found any other AFOs yet. They were still ringing round divisions in a panic, and the Support Unit were down at Dunoon too. He couldn't do this on his own. The grand total of one attendance at a turn so far, and that was a bloody bull and even then, he hadn't drawn a gun, and this carbine felt so heavy with its magazine. Real bullets that would pop and burst. Then the other AFO took off his helmet. It was bloody Jinky Robertson. The blind leading the blind, though Jinky would never let on. In fact, he sounded born to it, lecturing the inspector on procedure. 'Well sir, oh, hiya Jamie – we'll bring you up to speed in a minute – as I was saying, it's highly unwise to deploy single AFOs. Ideally, we should work in pairs.'

'But there isn't anyone else.'

The inspector was young; an Accelerated Promotion man perhaps. He had that studenty eagerness about him, a naive idealism nurtured by careful, screened progress through the ranks, where two-monthly secondments equalled two years' hard graft to mere plods.

Jinky sighed. 'Right Jamie, the situation is—'

The inspector cut in. 'Constable Worth? I'm Inspector Coltrane. Now, listen up.'

Did the boy think they were on *Hill Street Blues*?

'The situation is as follows. We've had a report of a firearm being discharged from the close at number sixty-two. Believed to be from a first-floor window. It's just on the corner of Gryffe Street and Spean Street.'

'No sir, it *is* the first floor.' One of the beat cops was relaying information from his PR. 'That's a definite. Golf Mike Two confirms the window there is smashed.'

'Fucksake.' The other cop was scanning the frenetic radio traffic. 'Get them bloody back . . . sir there's two . . .'

A white nylon clad local was sauntering towards them. 'Haw big man, is that chippy no open? We're needing fags and ginger.'

'Get back,' yelled the inspector. 'This is supposed to be a sterile area.'

His companion raised besovereigned hands. 'Woah, cool your jets man. I'm fucking pristine, so I am.'

'Aye, he's sterile all right,' honked his mate. 'He's a total Jaffa. Firing blanks all the way!'

The two beat cops ran towards the neds.

'Get them hunted,' shouted the inspector. 'And you two stay back round there. Make sure this fucking containment holds. Bloody hell. Right.'

He puffed his cheeks, turned back to Jamie. 'Right, in a nutshell: Golf Mike Two saw a lassie in one up left, waving a gun towards the street. Bottom line is, the on-call Tactical Firearms advisor is down at frigging Dunoon, as are the Armed Response Vehicles, the nightshift super and every other bloody AFO in Strathclyde Police it would seem. So, you're it, guys.'

'And what's the story with the girl, sir?' asked Jamie.

'Well, like I said, she's been seen and heard firing a gun out the window onto the street.'

'What kind of gun?'

'Em . . . something bluntish. A sawn-off shotgun maybe?'

'Maybe?'

'Well, my guys didn't hang around to find out.'

'But they've seen her with it?'

'Are you questioning me, Worth? You heard it yourself: Golf Mike Two confirms they saw her.'

'But have *you* confirmed that sir?'

The inspector's face glowed yellow beneath the security light. He took two steps nearer the chip shop door, then swung back round. Neat as if he'd rehearsed it. 'Who exactly do you think you're talking to?'

Jinky nudged Jamie in the back. 'Okay sir. Sir, sir, do we know her name?'

'I didn't go up and fucking introduce myself, Robertson.'

'No sir. Neighbours, friends – does anyone know who she is?'

'I'm just about to get someone on that. I'll . . . we should check the voters' roll.'

'Might be a good idea, sir,' said Jinky. 'As a start. Maybe look at what firearms licences have been issued in this area too? Just in case, like.'

The inspector moved away slightly, spoke into his PR.

'Go easy on him, Jumbo,' hissed Jinky. 'His uncle's an ACC.'

'So?'

'Right.' The inspector was panting. 'They're going to check who knows her. But we can't speak to the neighbours obviously . . .'

'Neighbours? Sir, are there still folk in the tenement?' asked Jamie.

'Yes. I thought that would be safer. My guys have been shouting at them to stay inside. I mean – what if she takes a pot-shot . . . ?'

'No, that's fine sir,' said Jinky. 'That's fine. Have you closed off the roads?'

'Well, Gryffe Street's been sealed.'

'But what about the streets running top and bottom? If they're in her line of sight . . .'

'And what about negotiators?' said Jamie.

The inspector's moon eyes began to dart.

'It's okay,' said Jinky, 'we can negotiate if we have to, can't we Jamie?'

An almighty crack rang out across the night. All three radios shrieked in cacophony, frantic messages relayed, orders yelping.

'Fuck me – is *that* confirmation enough for you?' yelled the inspector. 'Now just get round there, the pair of you. One at the front and one at the back. Just bloody keep her in check till we get some more AFOs.'

'Okay.' Jamie was running now. 'Just find out her name, will you? Find out as much about her as you can.'

'I'll take the rear,' panted Jinky beside him. 'I'll secure the back close and stair windows, okay?'

These southside tenements were squatter than their city counterparts. Three storeys high, crenellated windows with geraniums spilling from generous balconies. Trees and shrubs rustled as Jamie jogged past them and tried to think. Think.

'D'you not think we should cover the front door of the actual flat?'

'Go inside the close, you mean?'

'Aye. What if she tries to come out?'

'But what if she keeps shooting out the windae?'

'Shit, I know.' Jamie slowed down. 'We can't do this with just the two of us.'

'That's what I bloody tried to tell Coltrane,' said Jinky. 'Shit, I don't know, pal. What d'you think?'

'It's a no-win situation. Either we both cover the inside door, keep her from getting out, or we cover front and back and just contain her till the cavalry get here.'

'And what if we *are* the bloody cavalry?'

Jamie liked Jinky better when he was a pain in the arse. 'Right. If it's a sawn-off, the pellets are going to scatter everywhere. So she's gonny do more damage firing in the street, yeah?'

'I suppose.'

'So: we'll go with Plan A. Cover front and rear, like you said.'

'Fine.' Jinky laid a hand on his arm. 'Now, nice and slow Jumbo. Make it look like we know what we're doing.'

Jamie went towards the front. The cordon melted back as he strode through, cops holding up tape and human traffic for him.

He spoke to a policewoman as he passed. 'Can anyone tell me anything about the girl?'

'Not much. She's a bit of a local misfit. Lives there with her dad, I think. And there's a brother too.'

'And where are they?'

'I don't know.'

'What's her name?' he called, as he was swept forward by a cop.

'Looby Loo!' came a shout from the crowd.

Gryffe Street ran down towards a river. Bushes screened it from the road, but Jamie could hear the sound of water rushing, muffled through his helmet. There were trees and a couple of cars providing some hard cover. Crouched behind the second car was another cop, his yellow jacket glowing like a beacon. Jamie knelt down and crawled over.

'Alright pal?'

'Jesus, am I glad to see you. This is about as close as we can get.' He pointed to a sandstone tenement across the street. 'It's that house there.'

Jamie shouldered his carbine, and trained it on the flat. One bare balcony, no flowers, no washing on a line. One single, curtained window: slightly ajar. One main oriel window: three sides shut, flat blackness behind.

'Have you spoke to her at all?'

The cop shook his head. 'I got the call about forty minutes ago. Anonymous report of a firearm being discharged inside the flat.'

'Just the one shot?'

'There's a bit of confusion about that. I went and spoke to the ground-floor occupant, who confirmed she'd heard a bang, then I went up and chapped the lassie's door.'

Jamie's earpiece crackled.

'Control to Alpha 409, Constable Worth.'

'Go ahead.'

'Inspector Coltrane asks is that you in position?'

'Affirmative. I have unrestricted views of the front windows and close mouth.' He glanced at the cop by his side. 'You did what?'

'Well, the woman wasny very clear about what she'd heard. And we weren't gonny call you guys out on a wild-goose chase.'

Jamie turned his eyes back to the first-floor window. 'But that's what we're here . . . anyway. So, you went up and chapped the door. Then what?'

'Total silence. Then a fucking loud bang, so I legged it back here. Been hunkered down ever since. My sciatica is bloody killing me.'

'And that bang – was it a shot too?'

'Could've been. But it could've been that chair hitting the ground, too.'

Jamie realised the front pane of the oriel was not closed, but empty; almost devoid of glass. Beneath it, on the roadway, a dining chair in pieces, legs splayed at awkward angles.

'So you didn't see it. Whether it was the chair or a gun? Are you not from Golf Mike Two then?'

'Naw, I'm just on foot patrol. And I shouldny really be, not with my back. How?'

Voices in Jamie's ear again. 'Message from Inspector Coltrane. Quote: "He wants his officers back within the outer cordon. Ensure they have adequate cover".'

'Can you tell the inspector I'm still trying to establish—'

'Constable Worth. He says that's an order.'

'Roger, Control. Can you put me on talk-through then, so I can liaise with Constable Robertson?'

'G Golf to Constable Worth. That's you now on talk-through.'

'Obliged.'

First a tickle, then a trickle of sweat, running down the inside of his helmet. Jamie tried blinking to push it back. Maybe the cop could swab him like a surgeon? 'But it's definitely a girl with the gun?' he said.

'That's what the inspector says.'

'What about that last shot, just there?'

'Oh, that came from inside.'

'Who fired it?'

'I don't know. I just heard the bang, same as yous.'

'I thought you had seen her.'

'Naw, I told you. We're no Golf Two. I just know that the wee woman downstairs says there's a lassie and a guy living there. Doesn't know their names.'

'Okay, right,' said Jamie. Stuff it, he'd ask him. 'Here, pal – what's your name, by the way?'

'Callum. Callum Grant.'

'Right Callum. There's a hanky in my overall pocket. Could you grab it for me?'

A rustle of paper being scrunched into his outstretched fingers.

'Cheers.' Jamie lowered the carbine to rest on the bonnet of the car, right hand still covering the trigger, and quickly scrubbed his forehead with the tissue.

'Okay. I want you to inch your way slowly back to where the first car is. From there, you can see the outer cordon.'

'Fine.'

His radio again. 'Robertson to Worth.'

'Go ahead Jinky.'

'All quiet at the rear. Suggest if there's any talking to be done you do it, big man, since you've got the front-row seat.'

'Cheers, Constable Robertson.'

The inspector's voice broke in. 'There'll be no negotiating with the suspect till we get reinforcements.'

'Sir,' said Jamie. 'We're not trained for that anyway. That's why we suggested you call up some negotiators. But, if she makes a move, we'll have to try and make contact. Sir?'

A pause, then a curt, 'Stand by.'

A longer pause. Jamie studied all the windows in the close. Most had lights on. One, the one directly above the flat the gun had been fired from, had an open window. Grey curls appeared above the sill. 'Officer. Officer. Can we come out yet?'

'Get back madam,' he shouted. 'Keep away from the window.'

'Oh. Alright dear,' she quavered. 'But I'll need to take my dog out soon.'

Frantic waving motions with his free hand. 'Stay back until you're told to move.'

Too late, the panic ripples spread. Another window opened,

then another. 'We need to get out.' 'Look what happened at September the eleventh. You need to let us out.'

He lifted his head slightly higher than the car. 'This is Strathclyde Police. Armed Police. Stay inside and shut your windows. Keep as far back from this side of your house as possible. You will be told when it's safe to move.'

His earpiece zizzed. 'Inspector Coltrane here. I've liaised with the duty officer at Force Overview, and he agrees you can communicate with the suspect. But only if required.'

'Too frigging late,' whispered the beat cop. 'As per usual.'

Jamie tapped the leg squashed beside his. 'Right, you get back first, pal. If at any point I tell you to stop, you get your arse down on the ground and don't fucking move. Okay?'

'Aye.' The cop licked his lips.

'And well done, by the way,' said Jamie. 'You didny need to stay so close.'

'Well, there's all those folk in the tenement see. I should've got them out first . . .'

'You did fine. Now, back away slowly. Worth to Robertson.'

'Go ahead.'

'I have an unarmed officer returning to the outer cordon. Please advise of any movement to the rear.'

'Roger Jumbo. Still quiet.'

Jamie waved his arm behind him. 'Right pal, scarper. Gie's a shout when you get there.'

Soft whispers of leaves and watching eyelids. A shuffling crunch and scrabble as the cop slithered away. Moon passing cloud, pale butter wrapped in silver.

Light-dark flickers. Silhouettes. Every window but the one he was fixed on had some sign of life. The moment seemed to droop, languorous, like it didn't matter and it was all on TV.

'Golf treble four,' said the plastic at his ear. 'That's me back in the outer cordon.'

'Roger treble four,' replied the Controller. 'Be advised you're on talk-through. Golf to Alpha 409 – was that last transmission noted?'

'Ah Roger,' said Jamie. ' Control, are you in a position to update me regarding any personal information on the suspect?'

'That's a negative.'

Jamie uncricked his neck, and a distorted apex reflected back from the car window; a wrought-iron finial over a row of swings. There was a play park behind him, silent and grave. Up above, a whirr of wings. To fly. To close his eyes and be somewhere else. That button which you could press when you were trapped or scared or; that would be too easy. Then you wouldn't stay around long enough to feel the buzz, the steady calm that knew all eyes were on you.

At once, fast and shrill and sharp through dark, a single, ripping scream that spoke of agony. Then . . .

Then . . .

Nothing. Only withered, flapping shadow-sky, hanging flaccid in the aftermath, and a volley of birds whumping up from the trees.

'Worth, Worth! What the fuck was that? You need to make contact with whoever's inside.'

'Sir, advise we should just hang fire till—'

'Worth, she could be dismembering someone in there. Initiate immediate contact with the occupants – that's an order.'

Jamie cleared his throat. Shouted, 'Hello!'

The word drifted, soft and stupid.

'Hello, in there. This is the police. Armed police. Can you hear me?'

The birds in the tree above him flapped and murmured, settling themselves back on their branches.

'What's your name, eh? Who is it I'm talking to?'

'Robertson to Worth.'

'Go ahead.'

'Jumbo, I've a visual on what looks like the kitchen window. Can make out a figure through the blinds.'

'Okay. You want to try talking to her from your side?'

'Roger.'

A pause, then Jamie could hear a raised voice around the back, but with his helmet on, his radio crackling, it was only modulated noise. Then a flurry at the curtains he was watching, a gash of light. One pale hand and a flash of something grey or silver that was gone when he looked.

'Robertson to Worth – shit – I think I freaked her, pal.'

'Hey, Hey. It's okay,' yelled Jamie at the single window. He could still see a shape, something human there. 'It's alright. I need you to calm down. There's people here could get hurt.'

'Fuck off!' screamed a girl's voice.

'Well, I can't do that,' shouted Jamie. 'Not when you're shooting at folk out your windaes.' At least she'd acknowledged he was there. And he knew it was a female. His breath was coming quicker now. He puffed once. Twice.

'What's the problem, eh? Will you come out and we can talk about it?' Straining to hear over the voices in his head, pouring from his earpiece, looking for updates, barking out ETAs. Trying to rise above the cacophony, like the pigeons. She didn't speak.

'Okay, well, my name's Jamie. Look, I need you to talk to me. I need you to tell me what we can do? What is it you want, can you tell me that?'

The curtain moved again.

One insistent voice prevailed at his ear. 'Control to Constable Worth.'

'Go ahead.'

'Believe we may have established the occupant of the flat. One Gerard Brisbane, just out the Bar-L. Serious assault, housebreaking, reset – the usual.'

'Partner? Brother?'

'Father, I reckon. DOB Nineteen fifty-six. No indication of firearms, however. Can you try using the name and see if you get any confirmation?'

'Roger. Listen,' Jamie yelled. 'I need to know your name if I'm gonny help you. Is it Brisbane? Is your name Brisbane?'

'Noooooo. No No Nononono.' An ululation of an animal in pain, the discord tore at the moon, tore through his helmet like shrapnel. 'Not Brisbane. Nooooooo.'

A hand struck glass, and the open pane shattered, raining shards. Two or maybe more arms flailing at the window, in a twist of curtain, then they disappeared. Jamie's heart leaping from his chest, battering to get out, falling back in. Still his finger never left the curving edge; insinuating his flesh with its metal grin. Grim. Set. Waiting.

'What's going on?' Like a wasp at his ear, Coltrane again. 'What can you see? Worth?'

'Nothing.'

'Robertson?'

'Kitchen light's gone out.'

'Right. I want you to go in. Get in close to the house.'

'Sir – strongly advise against that.' Bloody sweat again, dripping in his eyes.

'There's people in that building, Worth.'

'And there's people outside – *sir*.' Could taste it in his mouth, like tears.

'And what if she runs out with all guns blazing?'

'Control to Inspector Coltrane. Have details on another male sometimes residing at the same address—'

'Robertson to Worth. Robertson to Worth, Jamie can you see her?'

'Negative. No movement at the front. Have—'

'Inspector Coltrane to Worth—'

'Control to Worth—'

'Inspector Control to Coltrane—' Nipping at his eyes.

'To Nightshift Superintendent – ETA ten minutes two AFOs at the scene. Roger sir. Control to Constables Worth and Robertson—'

'Robertson to Worth – Jamie I can—'

'Worth to Robertson – what was that Jinky?'

'Negative Alpha Mike One – no further assistance required at present. Golf to 474 – can you attend a report of a noisy party at Nine Sefton Street – complainer's a Mrs—'

'Robertson to Control – can you put us on a separate channel? We canny—'

'Robertson to Worth. Robertson to Worth – Jamie I can see her. Running down the stairs, SHE'S JUST PASSED THE LANDING – JAMIE—'

'Coltrane to Worth – Get ready. She's coming out. Get bloody ready—'

Licking the moisture from his upper lip. Rocking on his heels stay still stay still. Cushion the butt against the recoil. Remember to shout. Remember to wait. Remember your children that you'll never see grow.

He felt his bowels slip, clenched his arse. Coltrane screaming in his ear, but he couldn't hear words, just moans as his vision narrowed, like the tunnelling on the range. Just you and the target and you and the target and the gun and the target and your finger and the target and it's moving it's a target and the whining's growing louder and there's nothing else but you and the door through which she runs and she raises her arms so you lift and you aim and they're screaming at you from another place, but they're not there and you are and you feel your finger squeezing as the air freezes. The air is stopping and you are watching this. Up in the tree with the flapping pigeons. Twenty minutes in a taxi would take you to your own house and you swoop back down with a silent gasp.

I don't want to die so close to home.

But it's too late. He hears a bang, a huge bang that comes from inside his trembling finger.

And as he's thinking, she's falling. Over backwards, slow, so slow. If he runs he could catch her and break her fall. All he can hear are her movements, though his helmet is deadening. Can hear the rustle of her anorak as it flaps outward to catch the smoke that is everywhere. White billows spilling like vomit are her pillow as she lands, then bounces once, like on a trampoline, or in a bad movie where they drag it out. Then the sweat is in his eyes again so he can't see his legs, which are trying to walk on their own. They spasm with his hands as he stumbles forward to where she sprawls. Dirty blonde hair spread in a puddle that is coming from her chest. There's a pack, he has a pack somewhere with bandages and lint, but he can only find the tissue stuffed up his sleeve and he tries to stem the flow that is belching and spreading and someone is screaming at him to get back, get back and how he wishes that he could.

5

Cath couldn't get the button through on her cuff. It was a stupid thing, shaped in a thin metal link, needing two hands to work it through the slit. Jamie always did it for her, but she'd given up waiting. So much for getting a flier. At this rate, Cath would be driving the kids to the airport herself, and he could follow in his car. Where the hell was he? They should be leaving the house in twenty minutes and he still wasn't home. *You're cutting it fine Worthless.* She glowered at his shorts. Still damp, she'd tried spinning them in the microwave for five minutes. Now they were warm and damp, with a hint of defrosting prawn.

Eilidh lolled on the couch, one arm around Liony's shoulders. She had on her new striped sundress and a straw hat with cherries, which were being crushed against the side of the cushion.

'Hoi miss,' Cath patted her gently on the arm. 'Don't you go back to sleep.'

'M'not.' Eilidh raised her Barbie sunglasses. 'Look Mummy. M'awake.'

'Good girl. Now, you sure you wouldn't rather wear this nice baseball cap? The one they sent in your travel pack?'

Eilidh looked at the blue logo on the front. 'It's for boys,' she said firmly. 'Give it to Dan-pants.'

'Daniel's got his own.'

Daniel was wearing his hat on his foot, leg poised mid-air towards his mouth, like a cat about to groom.

'Ha–gh,' he agreed.

The fruited hat Eilidh wore was hideous; a granny gift. 'Okay,'

Cath patted the plush toy her daughter was clasping. 'Well, Liony's a boy, and he'll need a hat, so will we take it for him?'

'He has a *mane*, Mummy,' Eilidh sighed.

'Raa-aarr,' screeched Daniel, dropping his hat and tugging at the lion.

'Leave him,' screamed Eilidh. 'You hurted his hair.' She thrust one palm against Daniel's chest, pushing him to fall onto his padded bum.

'Enough,' shouted Cath. 'If you two don't behave, we'll not be going anywhere.'

Both kids began to cry. 'Will I phone the aeroplane man now and say we're not coming?'

'Noo,' wailed Eilidh. Daniel licked the snot down from his nose. 'Wan Liney,' he sobbed.

'Well, you can't have him. He's Eilidh's.' Cath's open cuff wiped against the bogies as she reached to blow his nose. '*Shit.*'

'Oooh Mummy. You swored.'

And now, an interview with Alice Heys, the seventeen-year-old star who's turned the jazz world upside down . . .

Cath glanced at the clock on breakfast telly. Fifteen minutes or they'd miss their check-in. Where the hell was he?

'Right, I'm just going to put the suitcases in the car, and then I'll phone Daddy's work. Eilidh, will you please look after your brother, and make sure he doesn't touch anything, okay? I'll just be a wee minute. You're in charge, okay?'

''Kay Mummy.'

Cath heard a bump, then a squeal. 'Bad Dan. Don't sit there.'

Only one case had wheels, so she rolled it out first. A smirr of rain was coating the pavement. Good. She always liked going on holiday when it was raining. Jesus, this was heavy. *And* she'd left out half her shoes. As Cath lugged the case upwards, her loose cuff caught in the handle. The twist of the fabric nipped her skin. She slammed the case into the boot.

'Morning,' said her next-door neighbour. 'That you away then?'

'Eh, just about.'

'Off somewhere nice?'

'Majorca.'

'Oh, lovely. I mind when I was in Fuengirola—'

'Sorry, Mags, I think I can hear the kids fighting again . . .'

'Well, I was actually wanting a word about that. See when I'm out in my garden—'

'Look, better go. Speak to you later, okay?'

Cath hurried back inside, out of hex's way. Bloody cheek; and her with her slabbery big dog, which barked if you so much as sniffed the air outside. Bloody woman. Bloody blouse. You *will* fasten. She raised her wrist to her mouth. If she poked the stupid, skinny button half into the slit with one hand, she could pull the remainder through with her teeth. The metal tasted cold against her tongue, harsh like taint. She clenched the protruding edge between her front teeth and began to tug. Reversed the action in the mirror.

And now a round-up of all the news and stories where you are.

The hall was too dingy, she couldn't see what she was doing. Wee bit more . . . she began to wiggle the button from side to side. Could feel it slipping on saliva. Biting it tighter, just one more pull.

And, here in Scotland: Police shoot teenage girl.

One elbow nudged the door to the living room. The button was nearly through, and then they could go. Stuff him.

A thirty-seven-year-old Strathclyde police officer is being questioned following the shooting of a teenage girl in the Cathcart area of Glasgow earlier this morning. Neighbours in the quiet south side street report hearing several shots being fired by police marksmen . . .

One more pull.

'Fuck!'

A sliver of enamel fired off her front tooth and arced through the air.

'Jesus Christ.' Cath held her mouth, ran back to the mirror in the hall. Grinned at it. A ragged chunk of tooth was missing from her stricken smile. A ghoul-smile, with several tiny vampire fangs where the straight line should be. Nerve fronds unfurled in the new-found breeze; agony like ice cream.

'Jamie,' she sobbed. 'Where *are* you?'

*Police are refusing to comment on reports that the young girl was
unarmed.*

Eilidh galloped into the hall, cherries bouncing above her earnest
eyebrows. 'Mummy, what's wrong?'

'It's okay, honey.' Cath tried to stop crying. The ache was
intense. 'Mummy's hurted her tooth, that's all. C'mon, we'll get a
seat, eh?'

*The officer concerned is believed to be stationed in the city centre, and
was responding to a call for assistance.*

Cath caught the last few words as they trailed from the set, and
the stab travelled right through her spine.

No.

A flat dryness wound around her tongue.

No.

Someone would have phoned her.

Any minute now, he'd come bouncing in the door, full of
excuses. And he'd flash that smile that would rip your heart
and she'd give him a mouthful and they'd be off. Via the dentist's.
Cath tried drinking cold water, squishing it in her cheeks, across
her gums to rinse in numbness. Ten more minutes and she'd have
to go without him. God, please.

*Somewhere, a girl sprawls in darkness. Air blasts inside her chest,
surprising her with its ferocity, as there is none inside her lungs. Her
chest is raw and shrieking; the only part of her that's real. Pricked stars
above her head, tiny light paints fading shadows. Dimming, dimming
to varying shades of night.*

*Something is on her, part of her, sobbing as if its heart would break as
her own heart falls like heaviest basalt and is cold is hot is deafening.
Bumping, brighter lights, the rawness is an ache: it is only from the strain
of staying, and if she falls back into this burning snow, she will never know
how it ends but already it is spooling . . . spooling back and is it true that
you see everything, rushing backwards in reels like streamers, and she is
back, back at the beginning of the end and now she sees it, sees it all . . .*

And she sees it all in the pitch black.

*   *   *

Cath raised her head, half asleep. Felt his shadow at the front door. Moved to the hall and watched him stand there, head pressed on glass. Yet she didn't open it. The kids had fallen asleep on the couch, wee fat feet in brand new sandals. They were too late now. Too late for this flight. They looked so peaceful, the kids. Just stay out. If she ran and yelled *where the hell have you been?*, like clashing pots, would that exorcise what was coming in? Then she heard his key turn in the lock and a damp gust of morning followed.

'Jamie? At last! You do realise we've missed the bloody . . .'

His skin was wet, greyish-yellow. Eyes narrow in a stone-pallor mask. No movement, no sight. And she didn't want to see it. It was her husband and it was not. Some pathetic shade of him, stretching out with flailing fingers to find the light switch for their gloomy hall.

'Jamie?' She moved forward. 'You okay?' When clearly, patently, obviously he was not, but that was what you said to stop the silence and keep the kettle boiling.

She removed the jacket from his rigid shoulders. 'You're soaking.'

'Where's the kids?' His voice was low.

'They're in the living room, asleep.'

He nodded.

'Look at you, you're soaked right through.' Cath squelched his T-shirt with her fist. 'Jesus. You been swimming? Look, why don't you go for a bath and I'll phone the travel agent's, see if there's another flight today, your shorts are still wet by the way . . .' She was gabbling, gabbling into the void, and waiting for him to explain, giving him all these chances and he wasn't and she had to fill the space. 'Why are you so late?'

He put one hand on the banister. 'I need to go to bed.'

'Okay, fine. But will you tell me what's happened?'

'I just need to sleep.'

'Jamie – I saw the news.'

Please tell me you were in a car crash.

'Honey, please. You have to talk to me. What's happened?'

Trying to be calm, and her tooth was screaming at her. She kept tonguing, a constant flicking pressure at the ragged fissure, prodding it to further reaches and her brain was booming – what about Majorca? – and he kept walking up the stairs.

'Jamie – please!'

He stopped, looked down at her. 'What did it say on the news?'

'I don't know. Something about a girl being shot by police . . .'

Still he stood, swaying slightly against the banister. His torso was twisted, legs facing up the stair, eyes on Cath below.

Maggots in her belly. 'Tell me it wasn't you. Tell me it's got nothing to do with you.'

He frowned, puzzled like a child.

'Talk to me – God!' She tried so hard not to shout.

Slowly, his knees sagged into the stairs, hands squeaking down spindles until he was staring at her like a monkey in a cage. 'I'm sorry.'

Then she was beside him, squatting down low and cradling his precious body. Feeling him tremble; hard, spastic movements that juddered her breasts.

'Sssh. Sssh.' She kissed his hair. 'Jamie. What happened? Is she dead?'

'Yes she's dead. She's dead, alright? Can you not just fucking hug me?'

And he clambered away, limping on all fours up and into their room, leaving Cath sitting on the stairs nursing a broken tooth. There was a sickness in her stomach. Rocking helped, very gently like you would to quell a period pain, using the warmth of your own body to soothe the ache.

Please God don't let this be true. Please don't let my husband have killed someone.

They should be tucking into a plastic meal. Enjoying a beaker of too-warm wine and toasting their holiday while the kids bounced with glee. First time on a plane – she'd had it all planned. Travel packs and crayons and secret little toys; barley sugar for their ears; sick-bags and a change of clothes. By dinner, they'd be on a terrace, choosing pizza, linking hands. Passports and Euros were stashed in a little wallet, perched perky on the hall table, all set to go.

Images of beaches dripped with bodies sprawled in sand. Her tongue probing deeper in the cracked enamel, tooth on fire. How young was the girl? The girl that her husband has killed.

Go on, say it.

It was a joke. That's what you said. When you were told you'd got the sack or your granny had died, you'd say 'You're joking', because it bought you time, like saying 'Um', or 'That's a very good question, I'm glad you asked me that'; time for your brain to switch on and turn and chunter into gear. And time to rewrite history, so that your first thought, the very first, deep-in-your-soul thought was not '*I wonder how much she's left me*', or '*What about Majorca?*'

Someone is dead because of Jamie. Yesterday they were alive. When we woke up yesterday and argued about how many pairs of shoes I could take, that person was alive, making coffee maybe. Scratching her arm or yawning in the mirror.

She'd seen dead bodies before. At work, when Cath had a life, she'd always been struck by their warmth. Most bodies the police saw were pliant and moist. Still hinting at life, and underscoring the messiness of death. Not at all what you saw in reverent parlours. Stiff and painted, that's how her granny had been. No sense of the chafing from her bedsores and pads, which leaked and were rarely changed and must have rubbed her every day. In life, her mouth was slack, room only for a straw or spoon. In death it was firm and rouged, prim and primed for the great hereafter.

That girl, the girl Jamie has killed, will still be soft. Her heart will have stopped and the blood will be clotting, but her flesh will be supple yet. Today was . . . what day was this? Wednesday. Wednesday. The girl would have been at school and they'd be on their aeroplane. That girl would have a mother, who would want to view her now. Now, immediately, and not be told to wait because it was procedure, but to hold her baby's head on her breast and trace her dimples before they set for ever.

For ever. Her husband had.

Her husband had.

And what would happen to them all?

And what about Majorca?

Cath folded up her insides and waited. Outside, cars were revving for the morning's business. Doors slamming and the screek of their gate as the postman whistled up the path. Long red hair, shaved at the sides; this village postman really did whistle; cheery airs by AC/DC, and other stuff she didn't know. Two brown envelopes and a fat white one slid onto the carpet, on top of the newspaper that was already there. Would it be banner headlines? Would she read all about it, over two rounds of toast and a nice pot of tea? Cath picked up the paper from the floor and scanned the front page. There, in the late news column, a small trail of jumbled newsprint. She screwed up her eyes to stop the words from shifting so fast.

POLICE GUN DOWN GIRL IN CITY STREET

Police were last night examining firearm incident procedures after the fatal shooting of a teenage girl in the Cathcart area of Glasgow. The victim's details have not been released, but it is believed she was a pupil at King's Park Secondary. Neighbours report hearing loud bangs prior to the arrival of police, but no confirmation has yet been given that any firearms were recovered from the scene. Strathclyde Police are also refusing to comment on reports that a volley of shots was fired by firearms officers in an attempt to bring the situation under control. It is believed that an internal investigation into the incident is currently underway, and a report will be made to the Procurator Fiscal.

Cath could hear movement overhead. She'd fill up the kettle. Maybe he'd like a coffee. Secondary school. How old was that? Twelve, eighteen? It said '*officers*', not just him. They'd probably all been interviewed, and that's why he was late. They could still go tomorrow, once they'd got it all sorted out. Did insurance cover things like this? God, he'd need a holiday. Should she take the coffee up? Put a brandy in it? Brandy, whisky – that worked for teeth. Her dad used to dip some cotton wool in whisky and hold it to her gums whenever she had toothache. The pain was thumping harder than before. If they weren't going today after all, she could try for an emergency appointment. The address book was in the hall, on the wee table below the mirror. 'D' for dentist or 'M' for McFadden? She tried 'D' first; doctor, Donaldson, dentist. As she reached for the phone, it began to ring.

'Hello?'

'Hello. Can I speak to Mrs Worth please?'

'Speaking.'

'Hello. Cath isn't it? This is Barry Grey. I'm ringing from the *Daily Report*.'

'I'm sorry?'

'Scotland's favourite newspaper? Look. It's about this shooting – we know how hard it must—'

Cath dropped the phone, then picked it up again and slammed it down on the receiver. She remembered a horror film, where a tongue or a hand or something came reaching out of the phone. She kept looking at it like it would bite, or growl, or ring. Again. And it did. And again, it kept calling her, until she slipped the plug from the wall.

A slow creaking to her left. Jamie was lowering himself down the stairs, shuffling like he was ninety, with his wet black police T-shirt on over his pants.

'It's alright, honey. Just go back to bed.'

No, don't. Come down and talk to me.

'I need a drink.'

'I was just going to make you a coffee. D'you want a coffee?'

'Who was on the phone?'

'Och, just a wrong number. Look, should I phone the travel agent's?'

'*What?*'

'It's just, well, will I tell them to cancel Majorca?' The words sung through the gap in her teeth, tugging at the edges. 'It's just – the kids – I mean, are you free to go on leave or what? God, Jamie, you have to tell me what happened. *Please.*'

'Well, fuck me; have I upset your plans?'

'Keep your voice down—'

'Christ, and I'm shouting and all? I am *so* sorry.'

'Jamie, *stop* this. I can't help you if you don't talk to me.'

This was the pattern of their everything; she would push, he would pull away. With the impetus of one countering the retraction of the other; until Anna Cameron had sent the whole careful construction spinning out of sync.

Anna Cameron. That torn-faced spectre. Cath couldn't stop her swimming unbidden into view and wedging herself between them; all looming blank visage with covetous eyes. Why couldn't she be dead? Why couldn't he kill her? *Dear God forgive me take that back, I take that back.*

Jamie rubbed his hair back from his eyes. 'You think you can help me? Okay. Great. Hey, thanks, Cath, for coming to the rescue.' He walked past her, and on into the kitchen. 'Am I getting this coffee, or what?'

'Well, yes, if you . . .' Cath quickened her step to follow him, watching his buttocks contract and pucker below his pants. One side was hitched higher than the other. She wanted to pull his T-shirt down to cover him.

'Jamie. Let me help you. Please. Talk to me.'

He wheeled around. 'Talk to you? What do you want to hear, Cath? That I mowed down a wean? That I sent a volley of bullets ripping through her flesh and then, apparently, crawled over to where she was lying in a puddle of my very own making; that I was trying to stuff her guts straight back inside her – in fact, that's it: you're good at sewing. Maybe you could—'

'Stop it!' Cath shouted.

'But I thought you were going to help me,' he yelled right back. His breath was foul; night-breath and blood-breath, smearing her dripping cheeks. Face all contorted, like the mask had slipped; and she could see nothing underneath but red.

'Is that blood on your face?'

Again his puzzled frown, like Daniel when he woke up. Her lion-tamer fingertips traced his cheekbone, ready to whip back at the snarl. Stretched skin trembling – either his or hers; the several pinks and yellows merged as her eyes lost focus and she felt the stain.

'I don't know,' he whispered. 'Is it? Jesus! Is it? Get it off me!'

He fell against her, eyes closed. 'Catherine – help me.'

Words buzzing against her neck, his body threatening to drag her down. He was pleading, groaning, and she wanted to run away. Hide from this slobbering mass and wait until it had passed. Jamie never cried.

'I killed her. It was me: I killed a wee girl. Oh Jesus Cath, oh Jesus.' Violent shaking and then he was grabbing at his head, clawing at hair like it was flames and if it were then she would dive in too and let the burning scour her clean. No words, no sense, just a conflagration of the world that was folding hard above her. And she *wanted* to be buried and she wanted to be burned, far away from this fact that could not be. She wanted to scream and scream at his soft, wet face, his mouth wheezing in, sobbing out, her forcing his hands down, cupping at his face. His weight bruising her once more and the shudder and the heave, wet particles on her lips until she was breathing him in.

And she couldn't let him fall.

'Jamie! Jamie. Stand up straight. Come on now, I've got you.'

She raised his arm across her shoulder, led him towards the dining room, away from where the children might hear. 'Sit down.' Slapped him into a hard-backed chair. 'Sit down and look at me. LOOK at me.'

His shoulders felt so strong beneath her clenched fists. She held him fast, crouching down so his eyes were in hers. 'I'm here, Jamie, I'm here. Look at me.' His eyes stopped rolling and she moved her hands to hold his face instead.

'Can you tell me what happened?'

'I don't know.' His voice was monotone. 'We were covering the house.'

'What house?'

'The girl's house. We were waiting for her to do something and then I saw her running out and everyone was screaming and – I just lost it. Christ Almighty – I lost it. I saw her and I fired—'

'That's what you're there to do, honey. It's okay—'

'Don't patronise me!' Jamie jumped up, crashing the chair onto the floor. 'When I said I lost it, I fucking lost it. I was shooting into her and she didn't even have a gun. I didn't know – I didn't.' He kept pulling at his hair, berserk jigging.

'Stop it. You're scaring me! Just tell me what happened.'

'Stop asking me questions.'

The door swung open.

'I can't remember.'

'Mummy, it's after the o'clock.' Eilidh, tiny and self-possessed, dwarfed by her father. She touched him on the leg. 'Daddy, can we go now?'

'What?'

'We need to go the holidays. And Danil's hungry.'

Jamie grabbed at Cath's arm. 'Help me.'

'Eilidh sweetie, you go into the kitchen and get something for you and Dan.'

'Biscuits?'

'Yes, take the biscuits.'

'Can we have the choclit ones?'

'Yeah,' Jamie shouted, 'let's all have fucking biscuits!'

Cath tried to move towards her daughter, but Jamie was dragging on her arm, holding her back.

'On you go pet, quick now. Daddy's not feeling very well.'

'Mummy, we're going to miss the airyplane.' She spoke to Cath, but her eyes never left her father's face.

'It's okay. We'll get another one.' Cath was inching towards the doorway, Jamie slumped around her neck. 'On you go now Eilidh, please.'

Barely blinking, the child backed into the hall. Cath shoved the door shut with her foot. 'For God's sake get a grip of yourself. You're terrifying her.'

'I'm sorry. I'm so sorry.'

Jamie dropped his arms, lurched against the wall.

She led him back to the chair, righted it. 'Will I get the doctor? Jamie tell me, what do you want me to do?'

'I don't know,' he whined. Head on his knees.

'Did anyone – has a doctor seen you already? At work?'

'I don't know.'

'Did they let you drive home like this?'

'What?'

'How did you get home?'

'I don't know.'

'Right, I'm phoning the doctor.'

'No. Christ no, don't.' Red eyes up at her. 'Please don't.'

'Jamie, you need something to calm you down.'

'No, please, no. They'll think I'm a loony Cath please, please. Just sit with me, please.'

Neither of them heard the door brush open again. Or saw two frightened children slide inside, until an urgent little hand knocked Cath's thigh. 'Mummy. It's past the big o'clock. Mum-*mee!*'

Eilidh was tugging on Cath's skirt, 'You said we had to go at the big o'clock, and it's gone round two times. Look at the wee hand, Mummy.' She held her Barbie alarm clock out for inspection.

'I know darling, I know. Look, can you just, oh honey, Daddy's not feeling well – I think we'll ask the plane man to take us another day.'

Eilidh stared at her father as he hugged his legs.

'Is Daddy hurted, Mummy?'

'Yes darling, he is. But it's okay. He just needs a wee rest.'

Daniel shuffled out from behind his sister. He waddled to where Jamie sat. 'Da-h.'

Cath caught his hands before they landed on Jamie's thigh. 'Just leave Daddy, Daniel. Go and watch the telly. Eilidh, will you put on *Fimbles* please?'

Cath's jaw couldn't get any tighter, crushing down on the searing tooth, pushing it to the point where pain would no longer register.

'But we've got to go to My-orcy,' Eilidh gasped, the enormity of all that loss and breath-in flushing her cheeks. 'You *said*, Mummy. We've got new sannils on.'

'Baby, I know.'

Smooth cheeks crumpling. Still her little baby, mouth screwed up in disbelief. 'Mummy, we're sorry.'

'But you've not done anything—'

'We're sorry we were bad,' Eilidh heaved, swinging on Cath's skirt. 'Please Mummy, I'm sorry. Danil can have Liony—'

'Shh Da Da.' Cath saw Daniel reach for Jamie's hand, chocolate smeared on sticky fingers.

She felt Jamie's nails dig further into her skin.

'Get them out.'

'Please, Eilidh, please will you take your brother through to the living room.' Cath untangled Eilidh's hands from her skirt. 'Please Eilidh; will you just do this one thing for me. Please?'

Eilidh's face was scarlet, fevered. 'But, Ah'm sorry Mama. Ah'll wear the hat.'

'For God's sake . . .' Cath felt her hand lurch out and strike the child's leg. 'Take Daniel into the living room now, do you hear me? NOW!'

Eilidh's tears, shock-stopped. Her lips tinged like cornflowers, thinned. Too thin. She took her brother's hand. 'C'mon Danil,' she whispered, leading him from the room.

A smarting, tingling in Cath's right palm, like a brand flaring. Him on the left, clinging like a child. Eilidh in the next room, hating Cath beyond her years. Daniel stinking – she'd smelled him when he came over. Her insides out. Her insides fucking out. But she was stronger now. She kept telling herself that, every time the light of day threatened to take her back to before. To a time when she would sit and shake like her husband was doing now, but over a dropped lasagne or an unfound shoe. When a week would pass and she hadn't dressed, or washed or eaten or played with her baby. Poor Eilidh had suckled on venom and bile – no wonder she was like her mother.

Nothing would drag Cath back to that place. She stood up.

'Right, Jamie. You need to let me go.'

'Don't leave me.'

'I'm just going to make you coffee. And I need to check on the kids and make a few phone calls.'

'I'll come with you.'

'No, Jamie, just sit.'

'*Please.*'

'Right, fine. Come with me then.'

They went into the kitchen and she switched the kettle back on. 'Can you get the mugs out while I check the kids?'

He didn't answer.

The children were cuddled together on the couch, watching the weather man. Daniel hid his face when Cath came in, tucking himself under his sister's armpit.

'Did you not put on a video?'

Eilidh shrugged.

'Here, will I put on *The Railway Children*, eh? You love that Eilidh, don't you?'

'Don't care.'

'Darling . . .' Cath knelt down in front of her, and felt her daughter flinch. 'Eilidh, Mummy's really sorry I smacked you. I didn't mean it.'

Eilidh scrubbed her fist in her eye.

'And I'm really sorry about Majorca too, but Daddy's not well. I'm going to phone Gran, see if you two can go and see her, eh? Get away from horrible Mummy for a wee while, alright?'

Eilidh melted. 'You're not horrible Mummy, you're not.' She flung her arms around Cath's neck. Coconut wafts from such soft hair.

'I love you, Eilidh.'

'Love you too.'

'Love oo!' squealed Daniel, delighted to be happy again.

Cath stood up. 'Okay, I'm going to phone Gran. See if we can get a nice holiday with her.'

'To abroad still?'

'Oh, I don't know pet. Somewhere nice.'

'Ganny-goat!' clapped Daniel.

'Now, don't you let her hear you call her that, you two.'

'But Daddy—'

'But Daddy nothing, miss.'

Jamie was standing in the hall. 'I didn't know where you were.'

'I was just in the living room,' said Cath. 'Has the kettle boiled yet?'

'I don't know.'

'Well can you . . . ?' she sighed. 'Right, I need to phone my mum, then I'll make it.'

He sat at the foot of the stairs. 'Okay.'

As soon as she plugged the phone back in, she grabbed the handset before it could ring again. Dialled the number she'd learned to recite as a child.

'Hello, Mum?'

'Catherine. Why are you still here? Are you at the airport?'

'No, Mum, listen. I need your help. I need you to take the kids for a few days.'

'What? Why? Catherine, what's wrong?'

'Mum, please can you do it?'

'Well, we're supposed to be having lunch down at Troon today, but I suppose I—'

'Mum, listen to me. We've had to cancel the holiday. The kids are really upset.' Cath stole a glance at Jamie. His head was on his knees again, arms wrapped around his skull. 'Mum. Something's happened at Jamie's work. Someone's been killed.'

'Oh God,' quavered her mother. 'Is Jamie dead? Oh, my precious girl.'

'No Mum, no. But he's . . .' Tongue in her tooth again, spearing the nerve ends. Say it. Go on, say it. 'We think he's maybe – he's shot someone and I need you to help me. Please come round now, Mum.'

She could hear her mother panting on the other end of the phone. Oh for a maid with smelling salts, and how could she even think that as her life was imploding?

'Catherine, I'm leaving now. Alright?'

'Alright.'

As she replaced the receiver, the phone began to ring again. She switched on the answering machine and let it mop up the messages. 'Hi, Mrs Worth. Barry Grey again. Look, I know this may be a bad time, but I really need to speak to you. I'm on my way over, so give me a ring on my mobile.'

'Ho, Jumbo, it's Alex. Gie's a call pal, eh?'

'Hi there. This is Sally Burton from the *Evening Post*. I know you must be desperate to speak to someone about all this, Mr Worth – strictly off the record of course.'

'Mrs Worth. Barry again. That's us outside now. It would be really good if we could have a few words.'

Cath watched the numbers build. Six new messages, seven. Jamie hadn't moved from the stairs. She walked past him and into the kitchen. Poured lukewarm water from the kettle and stirred the grounds in the mug. Nudged his back. 'Here, drink this.'

He looked up. 'Thanks.'

'Jamie, you're shivering. You need to take that wet T-shirt off.'

'Will you come up with me?'

The doorbell rang. 'Mum, oh God.' Cath opened the door wide to a stranger in a leather jacket. He craned his head to look past her at Jamie. 'Hi, Constable Worth? Barry—'

'Fuck off.' She forced the door shut.

The letterbox rattled. 'Mrs Worth, I understand you're upset. We just need to get your side of the story. Is it true your husband's been suspended?'

Cath turned off the hall light.

'Jamie, what's the number for Pitt Street?' she whispered, scrabbling through their address book.

'What?'

'What's the number for Force Headquarters?'

'I—'

'It's okay, I've found it.' Cath turned her back on the silhouette at their front door. 'Hello. Can you put me through to Corporate Communications please? Jamie,' she hissed, 'it's okay. Drink your coffee. Hello, this is Cath Worth here. Who am I speaking to? Gillian? Hi, Gillian.' Cath scribbled the name on a pad. 'Listen, can you help us? My husband's a serving officer and he's been involved in an incident on duty. We're being bombarded with press enquiries, and we'd really appreciate it if someone could come down here. Yes, no, the press are actually on our doorstep. Sorry? Worth. James Worth. Uh-huh, the shooting, yes. Pardon?' Cath put down the pen. 'But we've got two young children in the house . . . I'm sorry – is that not what you're there for? No, that's not – let me speak to someone in charge please. Let me – well, can you get them to call me back then? Do you know when that – hello? Hello?'

Cath rested the receiver back on the cradle. 'Jamie,' she asked softly. 'What do you want me to do? I don't know what we should do.'

She watched her husband rock back and forth, still sucking on his bare knee like it was a lollipop.

6

Anna Cameron slipped on sunglasses and breathed it in. Newark Airport unfolded before her, hot and brash and bubbling with kerosene. She paused for a moment at the top of the stairs, tasting throbs of petrol and power, until a man behind clipped her with his carry-on.

'Excuse me . . .'

The voice was Scottish.

'Where's the fire, pal?'

Deliberately slow, she held both railings, took her time descending from the plane, although she knew if she was the one being stymied she'd have been equally impatient, tutting and frothing at this impediment to her great, important haste. But she wasn't, and they were going nowhere till the luggage came through, so he could damn well wait.

'Better watch they don't lock you up,' the man murmured, as he overtook her on the tarmac.

'Pardon?'

'Going on about fires and that. Don't you know we're in a heightened state of security?' Dark eyes blinked beneath sleep-tousled hair, then he was gone, long strides carrying him miles in front of all the other passengers.

Immigration was heaving, queues at every bulletproof booth. Anna waited in line, clutching the green form they'd all been given on the plane. Varying shades and styles of uniform milled at every entrance and exit, chewing, staring and toting guns. They couldn't all be cops. Some must be security guards, some would be – Jesus – that one was pushing a cleaning trolley. And, yes – he had a holster too. Mind, it looked like it was holding a can of polish.

'Next!'

Anna moved up to the booth. A large banner declaring *America Welcomes All* swung proud above the hall. 'Hi there.'

'Remove your shades, ma'am.'

'Oh, sorry. Yeah.' She put the glasses in her pocket, handed over her passport and paperwork. Immediately, the guy turned over the green form, and pointed to one specific box. 'Not complete,' he drawled.

'I'm sorry?'

'Not complete. Go to the end of the line, ma'am.'

She looked at the box. 'But it says here: *To be filled in by US Authorities.*'

'You fill it in. Next.'

'Oh, okay. Could I borrow your pen please?'

'Go to the end of the line, ma'am. Next.'

Anna noticed several other arrivals were being turned back. 'Excuse me – there seems to be a problem with these forms. Perhaps if you made them more clear . . .'

The officer stood up, looked her in the chin. 'Ma'am, you are now in breach of US Security Procedures. If you do not return to the end of the line, I will require you to be detained for interview.'

He too had a gun.

'You ever heard of small man syndrome?' Anna snatched up her forms and passport, and made her way to the back of the hall.

Another queue had built up at the rear counter, where dozens of people were writing furiously on their forms, cadging advice and pens off each other. Anna wedged herself into a space. She pulled a Biro from her bag, started to write in the offending box. No ink came out, only gouged, dry lines.

'You been sent to the dummy desk too?'

It was the man from the plane. Anna whipped the form over to scribble on the back. As she did so, the side of the card sliced against her flesh, opening up a paper cut. Little rubs of orange blood smeared her form. 'Shit.'

'Ah, see.' The man handed her his pen. 'More haste, less speed.'

His hands were slim and tanned. White cuffs and expensive suit. The pen, a beautiful Schaeffer, weighted smooth and heavy against her crooked finger. 'Ditto,' she said.

Anna filled in 'Reason for Visit'.

'Ditto, ditto.' The man was looking over her shoulder.

'What?'

'Me too. I'm visiting the UN as well: look.' He waved his form at Anna. 'David Millar: delegate to the UN. You want to put that instead of just 'business', don't you? Sounds much more important.'

Though boyish from a distance, up close he was about her age. Few greys, few lines. No wedding ring.

'Anna Cameron.'

She held out her hand. Wondering what he saw as he shook it. First, he would notice short, clean nails and blue-white skin. As he raised his head, he would see tasteful, light make-up, masking the beginnings of broken veins. And a frown line that was begging for Botox. Pale blonde hair, smooth as silk. As he drew back for that final sweep, he would take in good, high breasts and a firm bum. And would, about now, be making his final assessment: bit skinny, mid-thirties, no kids, no ring.

'It's a pleasure.' David Millar squeezed her hand just tight enough.

'Here's your pen back, fellow delegate.'

They both moved to rejoin the surge of pre-queuing queue.

'So, what you delegating about then?' he asked.

An efficient Hispanic woman in grey fatigues ushered David forward into the throng. She too, naturally, had a gun. 'Okay sir, move it along now. Join the line sir, that's it, join the line.'

Anna was nudged to the opposite booth. 'Nice knowing you,' she grinned, as he looked back and curved his hands around his mouth.

'Farewell, Anna Cameron! I'll see you in the lifeboats.'

It was the same booth she'd been at before. Of course it was. The officer picked up her form and turned it over. He pointed at the blood smear. 'What's this ma'am?'

David Millar had gone through his queue, and was standing by the exit. Was he waiting for someone? Anna pretended not to see him when he waved. 'It's blood. I cut myself on the paper.'

The official pushed the form towards her with his pen. 'That, ma'am, is a biochemical hazard. You shoulda warned me about that. We got procedures, you know.'

'Oh, for God's sake. I don't have any contagious diseases, I'm not a drugs user. Can we just get this over with?'

The official cleared his throat, picked up his radio. 'Eduardo, we have a situation here at Booth Six.'

Within seconds, 'Eduardo' appeared. His uniform was grey, and was embroidered *NJPD*.

'Right, I've had enough of this,' said Anna. 'You a cop?'

'Officer Gardello, this lady is being abusive,' said the official.

'Officer Gardello,' repeated Anna, 'are you a cop?'

She opened her bag to produce her warrant card, and found her wrist being spun roughly against the window of the booth. Anna tried to pull her hand down, but Gardello forced it back against the Perspex, while at the same time gripping her other wrist firmly by her side.

'For fucksake. What are you people on?'

Her palm, being forced inwards. Firmly, emphatically, Gardello was contorting her wrist in a perfect gooseneck, while a crisp metallic grinding from the booth told her that cuffs were being ratcheted. Jesus Johnny, that would be something to add to her application. *Furthermore, I have an innate understanding of the United States judicial system, having been arrested on arrival at New York.* She had to try and calm this down; much as she wanted to knee Officer Gardello in the bollocks.

'Look officer, I am not being abusive, I am simply pissed off.'

Gardello was an older man, with a hint of Sean Connery about him. Anna held his gaze, prised her eyes to a wide, placid welcome. 'I'm not a security risk, I'm a police officer from Scotland. Here on business. If you look inside my bag, my purse, you'll see my warrant card.'

The official in the booth snorted. She could see Gardello kneading his gum as he watched her. Then he turned her around slowly, so her brown leather bag hung close to him. His grip loosened slightly as he shifted to reach it. A hiatus, then she heard him speak. 'Okay Mori, I got this.'

The pressure on her right hand lessened, as Gardello's body weight eased off.

'Okay ma'am, let's move it out of here, yes? You stamped the lady's papers Mori?'

His touch became light, just guiding her elbow. 'This way, ma'am.'

Mori scowled as he handed Gardello her paperwork. Folk had gathered in clusters to watch, Anna's heart shouting at her in furious, sick-making spurts. She could afford to be angry now. 'Do you have CCTV here? Do you? I insist we look at the tape right now, then I want a copy of it, so I can use it when I sue you.'

'Hey,' Gardello checked her passport as he walked her through the crowds. '*Anna*. If you're as smart as you look, you won't wanna piss me off.' Still holding her elbow, he leaned right in till his lips were inches from her ear. 'You so much as sneeze in here, and I own you. Now, I know Mori is an ass – but you wanna spend all day here and then get sent back to bonnie Scotland? Would that look good at your station house?'

'No.'

'Well, you just be goddam grateful that I'm a nice guy. I guess it's in your interests as much as Mori's if we say there ain't no tape to speak of, huh?'

She nodded, glowering beneath her fringe. A thirty-six-year-old child who knew tantrums were bad. But sometimes you couldn't help it.

'Now, you shift your cute butt out of my airport, and don't go making no diplomatic incidents for me, okay?' His grey moustache tickled the side of her face.

They were nearing the exit where David had stood. He must have gone through already. Only empty white walls and a fire extinguisher to see her mortification. Anna snatched her papers from Gardello, cool air fanning as they brushed past her face.

'Hey, *Inspector.*' Gardello called her back.

'What?'

'You have a nice day.'

It was midnight when Anna arrived at her hotel. She ordered a beer and some fries, then crawled, knackered, to her room. Nice big bed, clean sheets, soft pillow . . . Tomorrow was a big day, and she had to be fit for it. Eyelids closed, jaw unclenched. Her face squished on crisply creasing linen smelling of outdoors. She should have flown out earlier, got herself acclimatised, but there'd been a big report to finish, and she'd a case to hand in yesterday. Which she could have done weeks before, if she'd been organised and methodical, with all the time-management skills and self discipline she'd described on her application form.

Her application form. Had she listed all her projects from Policy Support? She switched on the light, pulled the copy out, again, from her handbag. Scanned page two, page three; yes, all there. Light back off, brain nosing itself awake. What time was it in Scotland? If this was home, Alice would be keeping her company, throbbing purrs massaging the back of her legs. Would Alice be lying awake now, wondering why the house was so quiet? Her upstairs neighbour was going to feed her, let her have the run of both flats, so she didn't get too lonely, but still . . . Shut up Anna. She tried to compress the babble into a single thought. Sleep.

And it came, of a sort, in a teasing glimmer that she couldn't quite catch. As all her other senses dulled, her ears refused to go quietly into that dark night. Rather, they became aware of every noise. Once heard, each one was there to stay, no matter how many wads of tissue Anna stuffed inside her ears. All night, an extractor fan railed and grumbled beneath her, its muffled drone punctuated by sharp horn blasts and hollers from the streets below. That and her body clock still being on Glasgow time kept zinging her back awake, and then it was her nerves singing red hot, and her excitement, and her nerves, and then she was practising what she would say, and then the practising was getting stuck on a loop, so that each time she drifted towards slumber, her brain would screech: *It's imperative that a model of democratic and inclusive policing be developed throughout the world,* or: *As a woman police officer currently with an interest in human rights law . . .,* or: *Basically, I just want to travel and do good works for charity and be kind to animals. And I'm 36, 25, 36.*

By six a.m., she'd given up. Through the gap in her curtains, Anna watched the New York dawn. A steady, gelatinous pink smeared up across navy sky. One by one, the skyscrapers took shape, no longer dark lumps, but fine, thin sentinels. She had pinned so much on this – even missed Billy Wong's funeral to take her initial test in Edinburgh. Something she was not proud of, but Billy would have understood. He had ambition, dreams like hers. He'd spoken about going into Special Branch. *Talk about inscrutable,* he'd laughed. *Those guys would have nothing on me.* And part of her, since she'd not seen his coffin being swallowed up in fire, part of her could imagine him still alive. Just about to send her an email, or, in that beep which signalled she'd just missed a call; out there, somewhere, on the end of a line. So, really, it was best she hadn't been at the funeral. And no part of her at all could care less about seeing Jamie Worth. That hadn't been the problem. There was no problem there; there was nothing. Anna curled on her side in the big strange bed as sunlight polished a thousand hopeful windows. A tightness burned along her collarbone, below the place you would span your hand while coughing. Sweet and sour, like all her memories. But it was cleaner to have no contact, with any of them.

She'd been moved almost immediately after the hearing. A 'hearing' where nobody listened to Anna, just read the discipline papers and looked disapproving. Sad, even. The audacity of a police officer getting involved in a case she wasn't actually investigating. *And* catching a killer to boot. But (that steady pause; *you lucky little cow* drifting in silent parenthesis above the panel's heads), seeing as there *had* now been an arrest for the Wajerski case, they were prepared to overlook her other indiscretions. Of course, she couldn't stay working in A Division . . .

It was a sideways punt to the Training School at East Kilbride, not the inspector's job she'd been angling for. Did they think she'd stay there, buried and grateful? Of course she would never black-mail Martin – he knew that as well as her. Might still phone him a couple of times, then hang up after one slow breath. Or send to his home, perhaps, a photo of him in a mystery pairing, the tacky paper torn on the corner, just where the woman's neck would have met her shoulder. Enough cleavage left showing though, to prove it was, indeed, a female. A history of shagging a sordid super-intendent had to have some bleak advantage attached.

It was shortly after that she was given a Force Panel for Inspector, passed it, then got her own shift at Easterhouse. Which was fine, but once you'd met the local councillors and got to know the local druggies and seen the local deprivation and been invited to the local Open Day and eaten the buffet at the local church or the local school, you had experienced everything you were ever going to. Then the cycle would repeat itself, and off you'd go again.

This job, oh, this job, though, was heaven-sent. It offered an escape to something wonderful. UK representative on the Police and Justice Task Force – for the United -bloody-Nations! This was the start of a three-month secondment, based in New York, where she'd be involved in drawing up plans to maintain law and order in areas of . . . what was the exact wording? Her application file was lying on the bedside table.

'. . . *worldwide areas of unrest. Furthermore, the successful candi-date will be expected to bring their knowledge and experience to ensuring the protection of human rights in locations undergoing civil crises.*'

Wonderful in itself. But the glorious prize at the end of it was the possibility of a long-term attachment. Two entire years in New York – and being made up to acting chief inspector for the duration. Getting approval to apply from Strathclyde had been torturous, but her impassioned presentation to the Force Execu-tive had finally swung it. She'd worked for months on it; an investigation into human rights abuses against women, based on her time at the Flexi Unit in Glasgow. Even though Anna had left the Drag for Easterhouse, the Drag hadn't left her. She knew too much about these women for them ever to revert to just bodies to be jailed. Angela, the prostitute who'd lost her baby, had died last year, high on heroin too pure for her addled veins. Her sister, Francine, had disappeared, and all her secrets with her. But mumsy Lily and poor, scarred Linda and all the hundreds of other defiled, drugged-up women still plied their trade there, battling with 'they Balkan lassies' who stole their punters and didn't know the rules.

One final turn before she'd left A Division had been what set Anna on this crusade. They'd raided a new sauna up in Park Terrace, where the sandstone townhouses were all being cleaned, and the up-and-coming neighbours didn't like the open-all-hours 'health club' that was ever-closed, but always busy with single men. In a room at the back, they'd found fifteen girls – some just early teens. Yellow skin taut over Slavic cheekbones, all clutched in cowed huddles. They had stared from dull, pained eyes, painted black and green and all manner of garish hues, like children trying out adult make-up. One girl, barely a teenager, had begun to cry when Anna pulled her to her feet. And Anna had held her, and rocked her and told the cop who was trying to cuff the child to piss off and leave them alone.

None of the terrified women would testify to anything. They were handed over to immigration, and returned home; to be beaten, or raped, or resold. The wee girl too, sent back to the place from which she was bought, and to the family she had shamed. The UK had not signed up to the European Convention on Trafficking, and so, unlike other European nations, was not obliged to give any period of legal sanctuary. Anna's proposal was to set up a 'safe house' project, where trafficked women would be given time for rest and counselling and medical examinations, before making a statement, or giving intelligence to police. Getting this UN job would give her the contacts, the backing and the experience to make her paper plan a reality. And, each day of this secondment, she would be on trial; all leading up to that final assessment. Anna showered and got ready, drying her hair flat and straight.

United Nations Headquarters was in East Manhattan. She'd chosen this hotel for its proximity, but although the grid pattern of the roads was similar to Glasgow, 'a block' here was not like a block back home. Each strip of longer, brasher, wider street was a great straight line to infinity, numbered sequentially and latticed neatly in a right-angled Big Apple piecrust. Though the framework was rigid, the stuffing of the place bubbled out everywhere, people and car horns and bagel shops and skyscrapers, and she had to fight the urge to leap on a car roof and sing the theme tune from *Fame*. Do a quick boogie too perhaps, if only her heels weren't chafing. Eventually, she gave in and hailed a taxi.

The morning traffic was heavy. Anna clenched and un-clenched her fists in her lap. When she got stressed, her hands got sweaty. Cod-fish hands, her grandpa had called them, all clammy and damp. And there would be lots of other hands to shake today. She wiped her palms on her skirt, willing the driver to move it. Damp circles spreading, seeping into silk. The jacket should have been discarded as soon as she entered the cab. Now, she was stuck wearing it for the entire day. Had she brought any perfume? Her aching head told her she was grinding her teeth again. At last, she could see the entrance to the compound, heralded by the United Nations flag; a circular map of the world, framed in olive branches.

Set in acres of land, the UN building looked like a huge postmodern airport. Or a cubist drawing of a funky church. One long pale chunk of curving concrete stretched hundreds of feet lengthways, while a black skyscraper soared steeple-shaped off to the right. She couldn't see if the two were joined. Another domed building lay behind the pale one, or grew out of it in a giant cupola; it was hard to tell. Jolly colours broke up the minimal monotones of the buildings. Flowers and flags, so many it felt like Christmas. Flag upon flag fluttering like gaudy bunting, stretching right along First Avenue. It was ten past nine when she finally arrived, according to the clock in the foyer.

'You're late,' said an impossibly slim woman, all power slacks and clipboard. 'Breakfast was at oh-nine-hundred hours.'

Anna was told to wait in a room with the other secondees. She checked her timetable again, like she didn't know it off by heart.

The format was to be a morning of group exercises, then a formal briefing in the afternoon. Then there would be a weekend conference called: *Global Village, Global Problems*. After that, they would be flung in at the deep end, expected to commence duties in the newly formed Task Force, working on whatever projects were already under way. It sounded a bit like being an intern; the UN would get their pound of flesh, tapping into ideas and experience from law-enforcement agencies around the world, and those doing the donkey work would be lured to give their all for three months solid, with the juicy carrot of a real job at the end. As far as Anna knew, there were four long-term attachments on offer; but one of them was a dedicated UK appointment. Seemed little Britain still had enough muscle to demand special treatment. She assumed there must be one candidate each from Scotland, England, Wales and Northern Ireland. A one-in-four chance of getting it.

As Anna entered the room, she saw at least two dozen people jiggling cups, saucers and various sticky buns in an awkward tableau. Everyone was clustered in twos and threes, nodding and munching. Who looked friendly? A small woman with braided hair glanced up and smiled. Anna started to smile too, then turned away. Maybe that was wrong; she didn't want to come over all eager puppy. Okay, so who looked the least approachable? Scanning the group, she saw a tall, dark man wave at her from the buffet table. He was with another man, smaller, stockier. As they came towards her, she realised who one of them was. Felt a ripple through her belly.

'Well, hello, fellow delegate. I wondered if I'd see you here.' David Millar flicked some croissant pastry from his lapel. 'Coffee, Inspector?'

'How come you're here?'

'Same as you I expect. Look, d'you want this or not?' He was holding two cups, each with a Danish pastry on the saucer. She took one, sniffed the cup. Mega-strong black stuff. Anna only liked milky coffee.

'Don't look so happy. Here's me thinking you'd be pleased to see me.'

'Oh, I am . . . I mean, I'm just not clear. Are you involved in this selection thingy too? I thought I was the only Scottish candidate?'

'Ah, for the polis maybe. But Joe here's the case for the prosecution, I guess. And me, I'm just along for the ride. Well, for the conference, actually.' He set down his coffee cup. 'Allow me to introduce myself officially. David Millar, Procurator Fiscal Depute, Argyll and Clyde.'

'Oh. Right. Anna . . . well, you know that. Inspector at Easterhouse . . . em, Glasgow.' She wished she had a more exciting title to offer.

'No Mean City, eh? And, speaking of scary places, this is Joe Murray, PF Depute at Paisley.'

Joe shook Anna's hand. 'Pleased to meet you. Look Dave, I just want to catch up with Rutger before we start. Will you guys excuse me?'

'Nae probs. Catch you later.'

David gazed around the room. Today, he was wearing a grey suit, and a sky-blue shirt with little fabric twists at the cuff. 'Yeah, it's not just Brits either; these interviews are for the whole of Europe. Every country can put up two candidates, one each from police and prosecution agencies. It's a major, major bit of work.'

'How do you know all this?'

'Same old story: we're always better informed than the plods.'

'Your arse,' she laughed. 'You lot couldn't function without us keeping you right. That's where it all goes pear-shaped, soon as we pass our cases into the great black hole that is the Procurator Fiscal Service.' Anna stuffed a big chunk of Danish pastry in her mouth.

He sighed sadly. 'I hate to mention the lost productions, missing evidence, dodgy notebooks, non-attendance at court – and that's just the Dumbarton polis. God knows what you're like in Glasgow.'

'Bloody good.'

'I'm sure you are.'

A crumb of white icing hung from his lip. Should she tell him it was there? Should she brush it away, all casual, no big deal? Most people never had Anna down for a cop. Schoolteacher maybe, or accountant, but few could imagine her laying down the law in its most literal sense.

'How did you know I was in the police?'

He smiled, licked the icing from the corner of his mouth. 'At what point, exactly, do you think I left the arrivals hall?'

Shite. Shitey-shite-shite.

'Okay people, My name is Marla, and I'd like to welcome you on board. Can we move it into the seminar hall please?' It was the skinny clipboard woman, appearing in a doorway at the back of the room. People began to drift towards her, draining cups, finishing their food. The girl with braids swiped another quick pastry as she laid her cup on the buffet.

'After you,' said David.

'No, no, after you.'

He squared his shoulders, shirt stretching over his chest. Did he mean to wear his clothes that little bit tight?

'I insist.' He was at least a head taller than Anna, even with her heels. She stepped back a pace, waved her arm in invitation.

'Age before beauty. Anyway, you're always in such a hurry.'

'Bossy cow, aren't you?'

Here goes. No pressure, Anna – just the job of a lifetime. Anna took a deep breath, as they walked side by side into the adjacent room. Sometimes, just sometimes, she wished she could pray.

7

One day. Three days. A hundred days, no days.

Mornings happened with Cath bringing Jamie coffee and toast. This act distinguished night from day, but not sufficiently for him to do anything about it. He'd leave the toast to go cold, then she'd come back upstairs and tut. He'd pretend to chew, get up, follow her around the house like a collie dog. Stand in the kitchen while she was washing up, sit at the table while she ate her Alpen. Today was the day she would scream at him. He could feel the air swelling like a sandstorm, whirlwinds whipping as the pressure grew. But he couldn't stop it, couldn't be alone.

Sounds and images kept flashing, like a video out of control. Pictures of the dark and the girl and her bleeding and someone keening. He kept going over it, willing the end to be different, but every morning was like waking after the night before, each solid lump of reality splattered on the ground. It was as if Eilidh or Daniel had been killed. Every time he woke, there was a beautiful moment of normality as he came to, then the heaviness of lead in his chest as he remembered and wanted to die. He truly wanted to die.

'Jamie, you going to shave this morning?'

'What?'

'I think you should shave. Maybe have a bath?'

He raised his shoulders, wishing Cath could just sit by him. Silent and stoic, nursing his head in her lap.

'I'll run it for you, okay?'

There'd been no word from work. Nothing official anyway. Alex had called round, and Derek, and Jenny, but Jamie didn't want to see any of them. The only person he wanted to speak to was Jinky. Did he see the gun? He must have seen it when the girl was running down the stairs. They'd separated them, back at the police station. Taken Jinky into one room and him to another. Seized their weapons – no, that was before, at the locus. Jamie's memory kept twisting. They'd taken his gun there, and a woman had asked him questions – someone said she was from the Fiscal's office. As she was talking, they were taking photos, then the wee girl got lifted up. Put in an ambulance and driven off with blues and twos. And even though he'd seen the hole that split her anorak, split her skin, split her breastbone wide apart, even then, he thought there must be hope. Why all that rush if there wasn't hope?

Whatever he'd said to the Fiscal, she'd scribbled it down in a spiral pad. God knows what the woman looked like, but Jamie could picture the pad, white paper-rags whirling from black twisted wire, the woman's face so close that her breath made pages dance. Then the Fiscal had gone to see Inspector Coltrane, and Jamie was put in a car. By himself, in the back seat, staring out the window. Every part of that car alive and screaming colours at him. Seats oozing wet black vinyl, ochre stitching undulating in the grooves. Moulded plastic on the door, shaped like an elbow jutting out, an invisible pattern in the grey that raised up to stroke his fingers. Yellow jacket slung in the parcel shelf, one arm against his shoulder, its reflective bands flashing at the streetlights. Dot dot dash. Dot dot *dash*. In out, *sigh*. Blue folder tucked half beneath the seat, nudging him. He saw it by his feet, by scarlet-splashed black boots which he rubbed with his tissue. The pores on his hand seemed huge and scaly, then someone snatched the tissue off him.

'Fucksake, don't touch anything. Your gear'll need to be seized.'

They drove him back to Govan, where his mate Dean worked in the Fraud Squad, but he wouldn't be on duty at that time in the morning. Jamie looked for him anyway, as they brought him through the back door. Just in case.

His clothing was taken right enough, and they lent him a jumper and some too-small jeans. 'Have you got civvies at Stewart Street, son?' the OD asked.

Jamie nodded.

'Give us your locker keys and I'll get a boy to run over for them.'

They put him in a room and left him, leaning on a melting table gleaming orange brown and black. He rested his head on its coolness, surprised that his cheek didn't sink right in. All was calm, all was bright. So quiet, he could hear the sea. Ears whining, like he was on a plane. Jamie sat up, held his nose to make them pop, but the buzzing only intensified. Footsteps passed back and forwards, never coming in. Eventually a head popped around.

'Alright, pal? Sammy Aitken, Govan CID. Gonny just write up your statement the now and we'll let the boss have a look at it.' The man put a pen and a couple of sheets of headed paper on the desk in front of Jamie.

'How's the girl?' asked Jamie.

Aitken frowned. 'How d'you mean?'

'Is she dead?'

'Fuck, aye.' He half laughed. 'Both barrels pal – what do *you* think?'

There had only been one barrel. It hurt to swallow. 'Could I have some water?'

'There's a vending machine out front. You want a coffee or something?'

'Just water, please.'

Aitken sighed. 'I'll see what I can do.'

'Is there a phone I can use?'

'Why?'

'I need to phone my wife.'

'Hold on a minute.' Aitken left the room. Jamie stared at the two blank sheets. What was he supposed to write? Age and service, that always came first. He tried to pick up the pen, but his fingers were thick, trembling. Worse than his auntie who had Parkinson's. She often held one hand with the other when she was drinking a cup of tea. He tried that, clamping his right hand down on the page, but the pen still skittered and splattered ink.

Aitken reappeared, carrying a chipped mug. 'Here you go. Listen, the boss says best to wait. Just get this written up, then you can head. No need to ring your wife.'

Jamie sipped the lukewarm water. 'What – where d'you want me to start from?'

'Och, it's just a few notes we need the now. Usual blurb; on duty and in uniform when requested to attend, blah, blah, blah.'

'Have I – am I getting a debrief?'

'What?'

'We're supposed to get a debrief after every firearms incident.' He sounded like a kid, cheated of a prize. But he needed to talk this through with someone. With Jinky, Coltrane, anyone that was there. None of this made sense.

'Eh, I think you'll find they're all debriefing each other at the moment, pal.' Aitken yawned. 'Just write it up, and then you can get shot of this place.' He turned to go.

'Wait.'

'Aye?'

'Do you know what her name was? The girl . . .'

Aitken shook his head. 'Havny a scooby pal. Something Australian rings a bell.'

'Brisbane.'

'Aye, that's it.'

'No, I mean her first name.'

'How, does it matter?'

Jamie picked up the pen, forcing it into paper. 'No.'

No one was around when he'd finished writing. He went into the uniform bar. The shift had changed, and a new OD was fixing on his epaulettes, using his PC screen as a mirror.

'Can I leave this with you, sir?'

'What's that?'

'My statement—'

The OD scowled. 'For what? I'm no the bloody postman.'

'About the shooting last night.'

Immediately, the guy shot upright. 'Oh, fuck, aye. Yes, I'll take that.'

Jamie opened the back door out into the yard. It was morning, proper bright morning, and it was raining; a soft burr humming on his face. The yard was deserted. Damp grit soaked into his borrowed socks. He stood for a minute, turned his face up to the sky, then remembered: his car was at Stewart Street and he was at Govan. A tightening threatened in the glands beneath his ears. All he wanted was to go home.

'Ho, son.' The nightshift OD leaned out his car window. 'You wanting a lift?'

'No, it's okay.'

Why did people say that? Was there some acceptance etiquette, where you had to refuse twice before being cajoled into taking what you wanted, and what was offered freely in the first place? Of course he needed a lift.

'Sure?'

'I mean, yes, please. Just to Stewart Street, sir.'

'Hop in.' The OD leaned over to open the passenger door. 'Did you get your gear?'

'Oh . . . I forgot. Can you – d'you know where it is?'

'I left it at the bar. Wait the now, I know where it is.'

The OD nipped back inside, came out a minute later, carrying a black bin bag. 'There's your locker key too.'

'Thanks.' Jamie took the bag on his knee, and closed his eyes.

'You sure you don't just want me to drive you home?'

'No, I'll be fine, thanks. I'm just tired.'

He felt the OD swing his car through the gates.

'Jesus son, you've nae shoes on!'

Jamie opened his eyes and looked down. Neither he had. 'They took my boots.'

'Have you something in your car then?'

Jamie shook his head. 'Don't think so.'

They slipped on to the dual carriageway, passing over concrete turrets that raised them high above the motorway. Turrets that, legend had it, held Merlinesque underworld bodies, chipped in at the mixing stage by some canny Glasgow gangsters.

'I've some wellies in the boot,' said the OD. 'What size are you?'

'Ten.'

'Ach well, they'll do.'

The car smelled of pipe smoke. They wheeled round a round-about and down onto the M8. Rush hour hadn't yet begun and they got a clear run towards the Kingston Bridge. 'Another half-hour and this place'll be mobbed,' said the OD.

Jamie nodded. From his window, the sleek silver tower of the Science Centre stuck one impudent finger at distant university spires. A plane soared lazily overhead.

The little girl never missed her father when he went away, for then Robbie came, and he was nice, with his long fair curls and his gentle smile. He'd bring presents wrapped in paper, which her mother would seize and they'd cook strange dark smells sweeter than the oils on the bathroom shelf. Her brother would watch in fascination at the grinding and the rolling, and would gladly run for lemon juice, but she just watched, and listened as her mother whispered and worked, trying to find the right time to ask what was for tea, or if she could go swimming with the school. It was the last day to take the note back, and she didn't know what to do.

So her brother ticked the box and did a scribble and she went, all excited for she'd never been in this magical glass dome of echoes before, where watershadow rippled on tiles and a bright sharp smell nipped from the little scoop of pool you had to walk in. It was different than on the beach. Here, there was a changing room, and you never took everything off in a changing room.

Because down there was private.

Her classmates laughing at her, tinies all, with orange-puff arm-bands and pretty ducks on their costumes. And her, wearing her vest and pants beneath her swimsuit. Only the second time she'd worn it, and already too small.

Muffled voices, cloying, stucky sticky covers whipped off. Cold. Cold.

'Jamie!'

He made his eyelids part. Cath, face like a fishwife, scowling down.

'What?'

'Your water's freezing! I put it on ages ago.'

'Sorry. Must've gone back to sleep.'

'Well, get your backside out of bed and get washed.'

'Where's the kids?'

'I told you, they're with my mum. Away to Cornwall for the week. Remember?'

'Oh. Yeah. Cornwall.'

Cath sat on the bed, took his hand. Just that part of him, a band across the knuckles and his pinkie and a thumb's-width of palm, turned warm and safe.

'Look, you.' She spoke gently. 'Why don't you get washed and dressed? You'll feel . . . well, it'll help.'

'That and a nice cup of tea, eh?'

She let go of his hand. 'It's a start. Then I want you to phone the doctor. And your work, in that order.'

'I'm fine.'

'Jamie, you've rolled yourself up in a duvet for three days now. And when you're not sleeping you're just . . .'

'Getting under your feet? Moping around the house? Sorry Cath,' he rolled his legs out of bed, stretching toes to locate his slippers, 'I've not read "Post-incident procedures for murderers" yet – I'm not sure—'

'Would you see the priest?' she cut in. 'Father Graham's called round already.'

'Who?'

'From St Joseph's. He's new.'

His feet made contact with felted cord. Sheepskin inside, all cosy. 'How come you're so up on the parish news?'

'I went to see him.'

'When?'

'The day after . . .'

'Fed up with your Proddy meenesters were you?'

'No, I thought . . .'

'You thought what?'

'I thought you might talk to a priest.'

'Cath, I haven't talked to a fucking priest since I left school.'

'Well, you won't talk to me, you won't talk to your mother and you won't talk to the doctor, so . . .'

'So bloody what? Maybe I don't want to talk to anyone. Just cos you'd go crawling off to church for a wee greet doesn't mean I have to.'

Flecks of spittle stung against his chin. 'And, see my mother . . . what does that sanctimonious old cow know about anything? Kids on she's such a nice wee woman – well she was a bloody old witch when I was wee, she thinks I've forgotten and I haveny. I fucking havny, okay?'

'Jamie, you're talking shite again.' Cath picked up the breakfast tray. 'Just go and have your bath. *Please.*'

'What d'you mean I'm talking shite again?' he shouted after her.

She came back in. 'You've been burbling a lot of filth since it happened.'

'No I bloody haven't.'

'Yes you bloody have: in your sleep, in the kitchen. Watching telly. All of a sudden you burst into profanities – muttering *cunt* and *motherfucker* and words I've never heard of.'

'No I don't.'

'Yes you do!' she shouted. 'And you don't even know you're doing it, and it's scaring me. And I can't have the kids back in the house while you're like this, and I miss them. I miss my babies and I miss my husband.' She slammed the tray back on the bedside table. 'Don't you understand? You're frightening me!'

'Cath, please don't. It's still me . . .' He reached out his arms to her, but she dodged away.

'Just bloody wash, will you? You stink worse than one of Daniel's nappies.'

Swirls of blue and cream on the bedcover, spiralling like comets in a scrambled mess. How he'd love to push off down one of those twists, birling and twirling further into duvetland. Away from this, from Cath, who he didn't mean to hurt. He didn't mean to hurt anybody.

Jamie left the crumpled sheets and went through to the bathroom. The bath was only three-quarters full, enough room to top it up with hot. He climbed stiffly over the side, and sat in the lukewarm water, stripes of ice and heat slapping across his thighs as the tap gushed. His penis bobbed between his legs. A sad wee fucker, shrivelled like the rest of him. The whole of him spent and limp, rotting from the inside out. Again and again he dragged his mind back, counting down the stages, ordering the sequences that insisted on switching. Back and forth, in and out. First it was Jinky; he was saying she had a gun. Then Coltrane, screaming at him to fire, telling him to shoot. But it wasn't up to Coltrane. It was up to Jamie. He was trained, he was trained, he was bloody well trained to scan the scene, assess the risks, count down the options in that split second of choice afforded him. Trained not to get it wrong.

The decision is yours.

Cilla Black bobbed where Eilidh's duck was; all toothy smiles and a lorra lorra laughs. Pointing at him, at her, at that dead little soul, lying not-looking at the stars. Jamie sees her face, watching him, and she is trying to speak from a mouth already gaping. He starts to shake and water goes over the top, sending him over the edge and slipping through the enamel, through the lino, through his skin which he wants to strip. And the waves rise up and there are people in them, faces that bay for his blood and they will always be there and he will never be alone and he cannot be alone and this fear is overwhelming as it rises and it pauses and it breaks across his face, crashing liquid terror over short cropped hair, a drenching all-consuming panic that wets inside his flesh. He tries to stand and the water is melting him, tendon dissolving from bone, until only the truth remains.

He is a murderer.

'Cath. Catherine!'

She comes running from wherever she has been and wraps him in towels and arms. 'Don't leave me,' he pleads, and the towels are warm, but the shivering remains.

On the fourth day, Derek called round again. This time, Cath had made Jamie come downstairs.

'So. What do you think?'

'What?'

Derek leaned in towards him. 'About the strike?'

'What strike?'

'I'm just bloody after telling you. Apparently around half the AFOs in Strathclyde have downed tools. They're refusing to carry out firearms duties until this is all sorted out and you're back at work.' Derek beamed. 'That's something, eh?'

Jamie tasted his coffee. Cath had made it too bitter again. 'So? What's the point?'

'Jesus, man, the point is they're sticking up for you. Okay, so you might have been shafted by the gaffers, but *we* know it's pish. Plus, it's the thin end of the wedge. Fucksake, nobody's gonny volunteer to be an AFO if it means you end up in the frigging pokey . . . um . . . Jeez.' Derek put his Penguin back on the plate. 'Eh, sorry pal, I didny mean it like that.'

Jamie felt the stubble on his face. 'Like what?'

The rasp was satisfying, granular grits across his skin. 'Like you mean I killed her? Like murder? Ten out of ten, my friend: I shouldn't have shot her. That's the bottom line.'

'Jesus wept, Jumbo!' Derek's face was flushed. 'Gonny no talk like that. See you pal, you're gonny have to pull yourself together. You've a wife and two weans need to eat, so you'd better get your finger out and take a long hard look at yourself in the mirror.'

'Why?'

'Cause you're a bloody state, that's why. Look yourself in the eyes, Jamie, and get a fucking grip, man. Jesus,' he rubbed his hands across his eyes. 'Is there nothing I can do for you? Nothing at all?'

'Can you rewind time, Derek?'

'Naw . . . but . . . what about the weans' football? Can I help you with that, eh?'

'The weans' football.' Jamie shook his head. 'Aye, you do that, Derek. You take over the Townhead Toerags – cause that's way at the top of my priority list, you know.'

Cath popped her head round the door. 'Everything okay? Derek, can I get you a refill?'

'Eh, no, Cath, thanks.' Derek stood up. 'I was just heading actually. Jean's given me a list of messages to do. Women, eh? Bloody slave-drivers, eh Jamie?'

'I'll see you out, Derek. Jamie,' Cath spoke sharply, 'that's Derek away.'

'Cheers for now, pal.' Derek patted Jamie's knee.

'Aye, cheers.'

He raised his mug and pretended to sip from it. Could hear whispers in the hall. Cath saying, 'I'll try.'

On the fifth day, Jamie opened the door to a detective super-intendent. Cath was at the shops, said she had to, cause they had no food, and he'd tried ignoring the knocking, but then they shouted *Police!* through the letterbox, so he thought it would be okay. The media had stayed a day or two, then something had made it all go quiet, but he still wanted to be sure, so he made the man show him his warrant card. *Simon Mackay,* it said, *Strathclyde Police.* So he thought it would be okay.

Mr Mackay had a female colleague with him. Black-haired and thin, with an air of Anna Cameron about the eyes.

'Mr Worth?' she said. 'I'm Nikki Armstrong. DCI. May we come in?'

The hall was narrow, and Jamie had to shift Daniel's pram into the kitchen to let them stand two abreast. Armstrong smiled at him, at the pram, and he realised he'd been holding his breath for four days now. He tried to smile back, wanted to hug her. One of his own.

'Jamie, please, ma'am.'

'Jamie. Mind if we sit down?' She walked into his lounge, patted the arm of the couch. There was a Winnie the Pooh blanket on the seat, and Jamie whipped it away.

'Sure. Fine.'

'Thanks.' She smiled again.

'Jamie . . .' Simon Mackay leaned forward in his chair, resting praying fingers beneath his chin. 'You'll gather why we're here.'

'Yes, sir. The shooting.'

'First of all, can I apologise for the delay in coming to see you—'

'It must be very isolating at the moment,' Armstrong interjected. 'Not knowing what's happening. Have you spoken to anyone connected with the enquiry?'

'No ma'am. I've not – I've not been sleeping well. I can't really . . . No.'

She smoothed out a cushion cover, nodded encouragingly.

'Jamie,' continued Mackay, 'I'm the investigating officer in this case. I've spent the last few days speaking to all available witnesses, with a view to preparing for a Fatal Accident Inquiry.'

'Yes sir, I understand.' Jamie was watching Armstrong's legs. First one foot, then the other, shifting like she was treading air. As each heel rose, so her buttocks lifted slightly from the seat. She slipped one hand under her backside.

'You need me to give a further statement sir?'

'Well, yes, yes I do. However . . .'

Now Mackay was watching Armstrong, who was delving deep beneath herself, clawing like she had worms. 'Jamie, this is a little awkward for me to say. I'm afraid we need to make this statement more official . . .'

'Ach,' Armstrong cried, pulling out a plastic teapot. 'I wondered what I was sitting on.' She beamed at Mackay. 'Sorry, sir. You were saying?'

'You were saying you had to make this more official, sir?' said Jamie. 'How d'you mean?'

The panic was hovering again, but then Armstrong smiled. 'It's just a formality Jamie,' she said. 'But we're going to have to Section Fourteen you. Do you need me to go through the whole rigmarole, sir?' she asked Mackay.

'Yes, Chief Inspector, I think we do,' said Mackay. 'Mr Worth has the same rights as anyone else.'

Armstrong gave a tiny sigh, and stood up. 'James Worth, I am detaining you under Section Fourteen of the Criminal Procedure (Scotland) Act. I have reason to believe you may have been involved in a crime or offence punishable by imprisonment and wish to make further enquiries to establish the facts. As such, I am conveying you to Govan Police Office in order that I may question you further – blah-di-blah-di-blah. Okay, Jamie? You know the score. Six hours max, but it won't take that long, I promise. We just need to do this by the book, clear a few things up, all right?'

Mackay patted him on the shoulder. 'Grab your coat, Jamie. It's a bit dreich out there.'

So the constable followed the chief inspector and the superintendent out to the waiting, unmarked car. Stomach curdling, head fuzzy, but he thought it would be okay.

As they drove towards Govan, Jamie watched the sky whip by. First time he had been outside since it happened, and everything was the same. His life had flipped forever, yet the air was still placid, the street still damp. Bellahouston Park still rolled its green banks down to the busy road, and there was still an artificial ski slope perched on one side. The fat red box of Ibrox stadium still sheltered Glasgow Rangers, and Asda was still open 24 hours a day.

Jamie didn't want to go back to that night. He would have to relive it all in this interview, try to align thought to action, and to logic: *This happened, and I knew this, so I did that.* But he knew he couldn't and his chest constricted as the panic took hold again. It was a fear of the unknown; and the unknown was him. Deep inside, you never knew what you were capable of. Only Jamie *did*. He knew he was a failure, who let the dark and his adrenaline and his fear and his inexperience and his confidence misinterpret all the signs. So highly attuned to the threats and gestures and circumstances which chant their prelude to violence that he just couldn't see a scared wee girl.

Who didn't have a gun.

That's what the papers were saying and his mother was saying, because she'd heard it on the news. What Derek was omitting to say, but was thinking all the same. And even if she had died clutching a sawn-off shotgun, would it really make a difference? Would she be less dead? More deserving of death? His finger less heavy on the trigger?

They parked in the yard, went in through the back door. Jamie turned automatically to where he knew the interview rooms were, but Armstrong halted him, one manicured hand on his arm, pushing him forwards to the charge bar. 'Sorry, Jamie, but we've got to do this right.' Her smile was clipped at the edges now, as she held his wrist, while Mackay took the other side.

'Sir.' The duty officer behind the charge bar nodded at Mackay, then Armstrong, his eyes stumbling over the space framing the figure in between them. He was the same man who'd taken the statement from Jamie on Thursday morning. He *must* recognise him.

'Section Fourteen, Gordon,' said Mackay. 'James Francis Worth, the Brisbane shooting.'

The OD read from the form before him. 'I need to advise you of your right to have a solicitor informed regarding your detention.'

'Pardon?'

The OD glanced up. 'Do you have a brief?'

'Eh – no.'

'Do you want one told you're here?'

'Well, I don't . . .' Jamie turned to Mackay. 'Do I need one?'

'Have you not been in touch with the Federation yet?'

Jamie shook his head. 'No.'

'The Federation use Hargreaves Simpson. I can call them,' said the OD. 'Or I can get you the duty solicitor?'

'No. No, it's alright. I'll be fine.'

Getting a solicitor would just escalate this. All Jamie wanted was to answer their questions, get it all on paper and go back home.

'Okay, Mr Worth,' said the OD, 'can you empty your pockets for me, please?'

This had to be a joke. Jamie hesitated. 'Mr Mackay?'

Mackay was reading over some notes, but his eyes were fixed on one line. Never moving, no matter how hard Jamie stared. 'Just do as the man says Jamie.'

Dull realisation dawned. Slowly, his hands jittering worse than ever, Jamie placed a crumpled hanky, some coins, his door key and his wallet on the counter. 'You want my belt and all, sir?' he asked the OD.

'Eh, aye. Better do this right.'

Jamie slid his belt from the loops of his jeans, dropped it like a snake beneath the OD's nose.

'And what about my shoes? They've no got laces, but I suppose I could beat myself to death with the heels?'

'No, Jamie,' said Mackay. 'You can keep your shoes.'

Armstrong tugged his wrist away from his side, raising it to shoulder height.

'Je-sus. You're really enjoying this, aren't you, ma'am?' said Jamie.

Armstrong ignored him, sticking her beaky neb straight ahead, like the smell of him was too much. Could she feel the quivering in his arm? Was it giving her a wee thrill? The civilian turnkey lifted the edge of the counter, but the OD stopped him. 'Just leave it, Andy. I'll do this.'

Barely touching, the OD skimmed his hands across Jamie's arms and down his legs. He had a bald patch at the back of his head, surprising tonsure-pink amid lush curly surrounds. His fingernails were yellowed and serrated; Jamie had never met a duty officer who didn't chew their nails. His hands reached mid-thigh. Jamie tensed, and he stopped. 'That's you, pal,' he muttered, head still lowered. He only eyeballed Jamie when he was back around the other side of the bar. Embarrassed brown eyes, sad-dog droopy. Jamie stared at the poster on the far wall. The wall was a one-way mirror, screening the Control Room behind the bar – where everyone would be staring at him – and the poster was stuck with tape, silhouetted below and to one side in the rippling glass, light refracting across letters. He kept reading the first line, something about cracking crime, there it was again, the same words, running on a hamster wheel, crack crime, it was a cracking crime, crackling time, lunchtime . . .

'You sure about the solicitor?' asked Mackay.

'Note that down,' said DCI Armstrong. 'He's declined the services of a solicitor. Number one free, Gordon?'

'Eh, yes, but I thought you'd be taking him straight up . . . ?'

'Yes we are,' said Mackay, 'if that's alright with you, Detective Chief Inspector?'

'Sir.' Armstrong's fingers nipped tighter against Jamie's skin, and he pulled away, daring her to grab onto him. Instead, she folded her arms. He could see her reflected in the mirrored wall, forming a crescent slit with her mouth.

'One other thing, Jamie,' said Mackay, 'do you have your firearms authorisation card on you?'

Cracking time. Do the time. 'Pardon?'

'Your AFO authorisation?'

'In my wallet.'

'Can I have it please?'

Jamie took the white laminated card from behind the picture of Cath and the kids, and handed it to Mackay.

'Thank you. You do understand, I have to withdraw your authorisation, don't you?'

'Yes sir.'

Jesus, like he'd ever want to pick up a gun again. Take it, take it and burn it till the plastic puckered and the sneering little words of permission curled into oblivion.

'Right, Jamie.'

Armstrong's spindly, tanned hand on his back again, nudging him forwards like he was her pet. The bar officer went ahead. Jamie hadn't paid any attention to him before, but there was something familiar about his gait; a slight limp on the left that made his right hip jut. As he unlocked the gate to the cell passageway, Jamie realised the bar officer was a cop he used to play five-a-sides with – Allan something-or-other. Jamie nodded at him and the bar officer twitched his head in reply, a nervous little dart like a lizard.

Fingerprinting first. He remembered being taught how to do it. A whole squad of probationers, giggling like they were at playschool. Ink on faces, smearing white shirts, the sergeant bawling at them to *bloody well grow up*.

Now they used an infrared pad, but the technique was just the same. It was important to relax the hand. Go limp like a puppet and not try to fight the hand that rocked you. That lifted and laid each separate digit, rolling from right to left. It was important to make a good impression. To stand up straight and take it like a man. A camera was rigged in front of a plastic chair, and the bar officer motioned for him to sit. 'Turn your head a wee bit to the left. Ta, that's it.'

FLASH. White light across his face.

Like an out-of-body experience, Jamie was above all this, observing the calm recordings of his fingers, of his face. And now of his flesh. Up close and personal, the bar officer was breathing into Jamie's mouth, fingering a cotton swab. 'I'm really sorry about this, Jamie.' His breath was cheesy, with a hint of coffee bean. 'I've to take a DNA swab from inside your cheek and all. It's just a scrape, okay?'

Mouth already open, Jamie gurgled his response. Armstrong was leaning in the doorway, propped against the frame like none of this mattered. Perhaps that was the best way. Detached, dispassionate, no conciliatory pats and nods. Wasn't that how Jamie always did it? You could taunt a ned, wind him up or banter him into grudging submission, but once Jamie got them up to the cells, the fun was gone. Watching a person being slowly dehumanised, split into samples and siphoned into a cell made him uneasy. So it was simpler to remove yourself from the process, replace Jamie with a stone-faced cop, who *was only doing his job*.

The bar officer slid the swab into a plastic cylinder, and snapped on the lid. 'Right, ma'am. That's us.'

'Okay, Jamie. Let's get this over and done with, eh?'

Back down to the interview room, passing people who stared like he was in the zoo. *Polis Fuckupitis: a mangy breed provoking pity and disdain. Fear of cross-infection will lead to rejection from the main herd.* Jesus, his head was mince. None of this was real.

And all of it deserved.

Mackay was already seated in the windowless room. 'Right Jamie. Just to explain: there's two separate investigations going on here, okay? One is a procedural one, which will be carried out later by Complaints and Discipline, and this one, which is a criminal investigation. Do you understand the difference?'

'Aye, yes, but you said this was for a Fatal Accident Enquiry sir.'

'No, Jamie, that's not what I said. I said I began this investigation as I would any other. However, circumstances have led me to believe that this could in fact be a murder enquiry. Hence the taped interview.' Mackay nodded at the machine whirring quietly on the table between them.

Armstrong pulled out a seat. 'Sit there.'

She walked around behind Jamie, pausing briefly at the back of his head. He waited for her to do something, could feel her inches from his hair. A rustle, then she moved to the opposite side of the table.

'Okay, Jamie.' Armstrong hung her jacket on the back of her chair. 'So. Before we begin I have to caution you that you're not obliged to say anything, but that anything you do say will be noted down and may be used in evidence against you. Do you understand?'

'No, aye. Yes I do understand that.' His mouth was dry. 'But are you telling me you're doing me for *murder*? Jesus wept. It was an acc—'

'We're not "doing you" for anything,' said Mackay. 'We're trying to get to the bottom of what happened that night.' His head was down, scribbling again. Looked like a bank manager, with his pen and his pinched specs.

Armstrong's ochre face had that neutrality Wee China had specialised in. Implacable, immutable. She leaned forward. 'You'll understand our dilemma, Jamie. We have a fifteen-year-old girl – a little backwards by all accounts – gunned down in the street by an armed police officer. Now, despite some confused reports to the contrary, no gun was found on Sarah Brisbane, nor in her flat, nor in the immediate surrounds of the property. No witnesses report seeing her with a gun as she fled the house—'

'But what about Jinky—?'

'Please don't interrupt me. As I was saying, we have an unarmed, vulnerable teenager, potentially trying to flee from a dangerous situation, being shot at not once, but twice . . .'

'But she was running towards me—'

'. . . by a gung ho, trigger-happy cop. As you can imagine, the Chief Constable, indeed the *Force*, is under tremendous scrutiny, both from the public and the media, to try to explain what went wrong. Now, we've spoken to everyone else involved in the incident, we have your somewhat vague operational statement here, and what we want now is a fuller account from you of what actually went on that night.'

Jamie's brain was struggling to process what was being said to him. But what did he think, what did he think was going to happen? The room began to bevel in and out. Trotting here like a lamb; he'd thought they were going to help him.

'Did she have a family?'

'Who?'

'Sarah.'

A sibilance he'd never spoken before, a name he'd never met. But that *was* her name, and it was real; she was real.

'Yes, a father and a brother,' replied Armstrong. 'Why?'

'No reason.'

'Well, stop fannying about and—'

Mackay raised his hand. 'So, Jamie. Tell us what happened. You got the call to attend Gryffe Street . . .'

'Yeah, I – we were told she had a gun.'

'Who told you that?'

'Em, Inspector Coltrane, I think. Yes, it was him, definitely – I think he'd seen it out the window – or no, maybe that was the car crew . . .'

Armstrong had moved around the table again. 'Which was it, Jamie?'

'Inspector Coltrane ma'am, definitely. So, we took up positions: me at the front; Jinky, I mean Constable Robertson, at the rear.'

'And at any time did you see Sarah Brisbane brandishing a gun?'

'I thought I did. Something flashed at the window.'

'Something "flashed"?' said Armstrong.

'Yeah. I mean it was dark . . .'

'You had your Kevlar helmet on?'

'Yeah – then she disappeared – well no, she shouted first, said her name wasn't Brisbane, then Constable Robertson said he could see her coming down the stairs and—'

'C'mon, Mr Worth. You're a bloody cop.' Armstrong pursed her lips. 'This sounds like you're making it up as you go along.'

Jamie's heart was racing, his conscious self struggling to find Gryffe Street once more, while his unconscious pulled and yanked and dragged the other way. His breath was speeding, his blood was spiking and he could see the girl running out of the door, little hands spread wide and open.

Empty.

His voice charged on as his schizo brain strove to keep up. 'I thought she was going to shoot me, ma'am.'

The words dropped out in sobs. 'I was all keyed up, you know, Christ I was wound up to fuck, and there were people shouting and, Christ, you've no idea – I just panicked and I squeezed and kept squeezing to keep her back – God, sir, you have to believe me. I didn't mean it.'

Mackay took off his glasses. 'I do believe you, Jamie. Now, tell me this. As she was running towards you: did you see her with a gun?'

His head fell on his chest. 'No.'

'I see. So, you knowingly fired on an unarmed civilian. A juvenile. Is that correct?

'Yes.'

Armstrong stood up, clicked the tape machine. 'Thank you Jamie, I think that's all we need. Mr Mackay?' She jerked her head towards the door.

Back bowed, Jamie listened to his heart thump. Toes curled inside his shoes, body waiting to be hit. With release, forgiveness; anything but this never-ending liver-eating.

Voices rose outside: a vulture and a boar. Jamie knew vultures; they would peck and peck until they got their way. As Armstrong's voice became more resonant, so Mackay's diminished, until, at last, it faded right away.

Armstrong came back into the room. Mouth entirely horizontal, like her gaze, which rested somewhere just above him. There was someone else with her, but Jamie's eyes were too blurry to see.

'James Francis Worth, I have to remind you that you're still under caution. I am now about to charge you with the murder of Sarah Joyce Brisbane. Do you understand?'

He was going under. 'Yes ma'am.'

8

Rising everywhere beneath her, above her, bold beacons of orange light, squared up and up like giant, luminous building blocks. Each one the window to an office, or gym, or home. If Anna knew which way to look, she was sure she would see it: one jarred, dark patch of negative space on the so-familiar skyline. The wind shivered through her coat, but she didn't care. Anna loved this place. New York was like a new friend you couldn't stop talking to, evoking a giddy excitement of recognition as you slid, compact and perfect, into your slot. This city was made for her. This job too. The more workshops and assessments they did, the more she heard from women like Dlia Bejko, the more she knew it.

There had been hundreds of people in the hall this afternoon, not just Anna's lot. Ambassadors and officials, politicians and powerbrokers, all here for 'Global Village'. The surplus of people meant the conference had no interaction or workshops with which to wake you, just speaker after speaker after hour. Inputs from the Coalition Against the Trafficking of Women had taken up most of the afternoon, painting a grim canvas of the growth in human trafficking. You could sense an air of restlessness from most of the delegates, that slight shifting of posture, a casual glance ceiling-wards. Anna could see one guy mouthing numbers; he was counting all the little dotted spotlights.

And then, at last, it was the turn of the final, keynote speaker. A slight young woman, maybe twenty, twenty-one, introduced simply as Dlia Bejko. She took centre stage in the UN auditorium, dwarfed by the pomp and panelling and all the pennanted colours

of nation speaking unto nation, and, in slow, precise English, told
them her tale.

'My name is Dlia. I am a lecturer in women's studies and ethics
at the University of Tirana, in Albania. I am also a representative of
CATW, and have much experience of dealing with the causes and
the effects of women being bought and trafficked into sexual
slavery.'

A few coughs. Some watch-checkings and paper-shufflings. It
was getting late, Anna's bum was tingling from hours in her chair.

'As the world becomes smaller,' continued Dlia, 'as border
controls weaken, as countries endorse sexual exploitation by
decriminalisation, as travel gets cheaper, we see an exponential
growth in sex tourism, and also in the sale of young women to be
pimped and abused abroad.

'Young girls – children – are particularly prized: small, tight
virgins who will cry and bleed.'

Dlia elongated the 'e's in 'bleed', so there could be no doubt as to
what she had said. The woman next to Anna wiped her mouth.
Good. They needed to be shocked, this audience. How many of
the folk sitting here had held a kiddie's hand as the casualty
surgeon tried to stitch her whole again, stroking and murmuring
platitudes like *you're going to be fine*?

'I believe the perpetrator is made to feel powerful by doing this;
somehow, more of a man. Most of you will have seen the
devastation that sexual abuse wreaks in a domestic setting. But
imagine, if you will, being kept like an animal, locked up, beaten,
usually malnourished, sometimes chained to a bed, where you
might lie in your own excrement. And then, being sexually
assaulted, day after day after day, until your insides are torn
and your heart is dead and all hope has been blasted from your
existence. Seeing your friends raped beside you, *dying* beside you,
from haemorrhaging, starvation, despair. Listening, in the filthy
blackness, to girls weeping.'

Dlia stopped to take a drink of water. Thick, still air in the
auditorium, curdled like nausea. Not a whisper nor a throat-
clearing to fill the void.

'You see, I know at first hand what these places are like. I searched many of them, looking for my sister.'

Another, slower sip. Some murmurs around the hall.

'Justina was only fifteen when she left our village to find work. We were all so excited; a man in the next town had a brother in England, who needed women for his factory. The pay was more than Justina could ever hope to earn in our country. My mother and I, we waved her off. Then we waited, for a letter or a phone call. But nothing came. And then the rumours started, about how other girls had been duped by this man, about what they had been forced into doing.'

Dlia lifted a little bundle up towards the audience. A video camera flashed it up on the screens behind her, enlarged so everyone could see. It was a tiny piece of wood, like an old clothes peg, wrapped in bright cloth, and with black wool stuck on the top for hair. 'In my culture, we have a tradition that, if a loved one goes away, we make a little doll like this. A totem, if you like, of the person who is no longer with us. I carry this doll with me always, to tell me never to give up fighting.'

She laid the doll back on the lectern. 'I want to appeal to you, sitting here in this nice bright room. Don't talk about "sex workers", and the "sex industry". Don't try to normalise cruelty and domination by pretending it's just a job. Did you know, during the World Cup in Germany, they built drive-through brothels, where men could drive their cars into big cubicles, have sex and drive back out in a matter of minutes? That woman lying in the cubicle could be my sister. She could be *your* sister. I beg you, all you lawmakers and law enforcers, don't continue to legislate for tolerance zones and licensed brothels. Legislation does not protect the women; it simply protects the men. Legalising prostitution says that society thinks this subjugation and humiliation is okay. It allows the sordid market in human trafficking to flourish, and it encourages more depravity – because men don't want the legal stuff, they want it younger, and more savage, and more sick. Legalisation simply says society has given up.

'Remember that, when you sit in your conference rooms, discussing how to tackle the international sex trade. I have seen girls in brothels in Bangladesh as young as eight years old. Please, let the world make a stand and say: this must stop. And you, here today at the United Nations, are the representatives of that world. The onus lies with you.'

Anna had never heard such strange applause. Loud, fevered clapping, yet not a single call or comment. Most conferences she'd attended ended on some happy clarion call. Not this one. Anna had left the auditorium without speaking to anyone else, walked quickly towards the river, and room to breathe.

This wasn't the end, anyway. Tomorrow was the day the real work began, when the candidates stopped jockeying for position, and asking oh-so-intelligent questions, always observed by folk with clipboards, scribbling and ticking as the group dynamics played out. All this collective assessment did Anna's head in. Tomorrow, though, she could get her teeth into some real work, be allocated a project in the Task Force and earn her keep. But tomorrow also meant that, with the conference over, David Millar would be going home.

She could see him up ahead, walking with some of the others. Right next to Pilar, that Spanish lawyer with the put-on lisp. All through dinner, Anna had sensed a thin gloss spun around David and herself, so fine that no one could see it for sure, but seemed, by an avoidance of their shared space, to acknowledge it all the same. Yet, in the slip from restaurant to the neon madness outside, they had reverted to separate entities. Anna had purposely held back, to see if he would too. But David kept going, caught up in the swirl of bodies and lights. She saw him stop, take a photo of Pilar with her arms around Rutger, the beardy *kriminalinspektor* from Berlin. Anna didn't care. Walking alone simply meant she could bite off more of the opulent, creamy flesh of this Apple. New York was everything Glasgow wanted to be. She could gorge on it forever, cramming it far down her throat until the juice was washing her face, her belly stretched sore and full. They were in Times Square, which was not a square at all, but a hard, vast street of glitter and grime. Everywhere were crowds of people, all milling and gawping and pointing at light-polluted sky. Huge electric billboards screamed adverts and flashed promises of fun, swells of snapping sightseers capturing it all for posterity. All the atoms of the city danced in a live kaleidoscope, shimmering and shifting in arrangements of stark, bright movement.

'So,' said Marla, linking her arm through Anna's. 'What d'you think of our little town?'

'It's fantastic. I don't want to go home.'

'Hey, well, maybe you won't, kid. I heard you were doing real well. But, you know how these things go. They pick a guy from one country, they pick a girl from another. And if one of them's a cop, the other's bound to be a lawyer.'

'But why have they got so many candidates?'

'It's all political. This is a brand-new task force, and there was quite a bit of resistance from some of the, uh . . . less powerful member states. Who says what model of policing *is* best practice, that kind of thing. So, this way, they choose from as wide a pool of candidates as possible, and they also get to build up a shortlist for the future too.'

'How d'you mean?'

'Well, the attachments only last two years, then they'll want replacements. Without the hassle of going through all this selection crap again.' Marla waved at someone. 'I mean, all this careful analysis and consideration.'

It was David, walking back towards them.

'Anyways . . . I'll leave you guys to it.' Marla smiled, and went to join the others.

'Thought you'd got lost,' said David.

'Thought you'd got fed up.'

Anna knew she'd had one glass too many; a nonchalant, hurried sipping that knew exactly what it was doing, but the Martini had tasted so sweet and it made her so sparkly. Now it was time to sober up and get a good night's sleep. Recently, in the mornings, she'd observed a stranger's face in the mirror, one that was baggy instead of taut, with a clear deepening of the lines that ran from nose to mouth. And Anna, being Anna, couldn't even call them laughter lines. Only furry Alice truly made her smile. Hence the lure of fizzy happy juice and handsome, spice-scented men. She could taste cloves, or ginger, burning close. He was going home tomorrow. And that would be that for evermore. Should she let him go gracefully, maintain her enigma?

'Och, cheer up you.' David had taken out his camera again. 'Let's get you in front of Toys Я Us. Beside the Big Wheel.' He moved backwards to frame the shot. 'Say cheese.'

'Apples!' she laughed. 'Big juicy apples.'

'Hey you, move it.'

A warden or guard or one of those multipurpose cop types she'd seen at the airport was jabbing an old dosser with his nightstick. The tramp had settled in the doorway of the toy shop, filthy greatcoat swaddling filthier skin. After a few half-hearted battings at the stick, he rose, grumbling, and lurched forwards. As he pulled his coat around him, something slipped from the pocket; a brown paper bag that clattered onto the step. The clinking made the tramp turn around, stagger back to retrieve it. But the security guard barred his way. 'I . . . said . . . move . . . it.' He punctuated each word by pushing the old man's chest, driving him backwards until he fell off the kerb and into the road.

'Ho, wait a minute you.' Anna started to walk towards the guard.

'Anna, just leave it,' said David. 'How would you like it if some tourist started telling you how to do your job?'

His hand was on her shoulder, the camera still swinging from a strap around his wrist. The old man was struggling to his feet, ignored by all the passing legs and shopping bags and sweatpant-clad backsides. At last, he stood upright, got back on to the pavement.

'Don't let me see you back here, buddy,' said the uniform. He swung his stick back into his belt. Should they throw money into his cap, clap out some staccato applause? Did Anna look as feral as that when she was working? David ran his hand from her shoulder down her arm. She wanted to tell him to piss off, but she also liked the heat his touch generated, the little bursts of effervescence pricking at her skin.

Swaying on the spot, the old man fought to keep his balance.

'I'm warning you.' The guard pulled back his jacket to reveal the dull grey pistol in its holster, and the tramp finally tottered off.

'Arsehole,' said David.

'Bet he's got a tiny prick.'

'Bet they all do.'

'All who?'

'Och, you know; all those inadequates who need to tool up to get some respect.'

'Yeah,' she laughed, 'like that National Rifle Association guy who did the input yesterday. Did you check out his sideburns—?'

'No, I mean the whole lot of them: gun-nuts, soldiers. Your mob too.'

'My mob?'

'Police.'

Anna paused midstride. David's gaze met hers: perfectly serious, perfectly calm.

'So, what would you suggest we do then? Hand out sweeties to convince an armed robber to put down his gun? Maybe stuff a few flowers into the barrel while we're at it?'

'Oh, come on, Anna, you're a smart girl.' He put the camera back in his pocket. 'You must see it more than anyone. It's bad enough getting your rocks off by ordering folk about, humiliating them like that wee arsehole over there, but then you get the worst of them going: *aye, gie's a gun and all. Then I can just shoot folk into submission.* Stuff trying to *engage* with people.'

'And how do you engage with someone who's out their head on crack cocaine and waving a shotgun around a crowded bar?'

'Bullshit. How often does that happen?'

An ugly sneer. How could she have thought that mouth was soft?

'Anna, you forget. I see these people all the time in court. In fact, I take the time to talk to them, try to understand them a bit – which is more than the police ever do.'

'I can't believe I'm hearing this . . .'

The rest of the group had melted away. The toy shop was closing for the night. One by one, the window displays darkened, bonbon bulbs snapping into shadows. The Big Wheel in the window had creaked to a halt, just a shimmer of swing around the vacated gondolas. She should have seen it before now. David was a typical lawyer; throwing nuance and suggestion into the spinning of his words, snapping arguments from his sleeve and 'facts' from fragile air — yet without a clue about life in the real world.

'Most of them are alright,' he went on. 'They're just ordinary, decent human beings who've had a rough deal, and deserve a break.'

'Aye, of their necks. I've never heard such unadulterated pish in my life. Your trouble is, you're just a—'

'A what? God, you're so easy to wind up, Inspector Cameron.'

David seized the ends of her scarf, swinging her around until they were face to face. 'Just you watch they don't get you going like that during the selection interviews. When I'm not here to protect you.'

She pulled away from him, he tugged her back.

'Hey, huffy cow,' he grinned, 'I was *joking*.' Traced his finger down one side of her face, warm as a kiss.

Oh, Anna. you're not even trying to walk away.

How long since she'd felt this steady, growing disquiet; since her nerve ends sung louder than her senses? His lips carved from day-old stubble, that was all she could see, then he, or maybe she, stepped one pace further and her neck was lifted back and his tongue was on her tongue, his hand inside her bra. His mouth *was* soft, and beautiful, pushing life into her veins. For a long, blissful moment, she was savouring the kiss, the abandon of his hands on her. Then freezing night flicked her nipple awake, and she pushed him away.

'Hey.' Her hands smoothed the skin on his face. 'You want that guy to come over and jail us?'

'How?' He bit at her bottom lip. 'What are you going to do to me?'

'Nothing. Not here.'

Her hotel room wasn't far, but it could have been on a different planet, one where air was laden with musk and a night breeze carried peals of cars and shouts from far away.

'You know I'm going home tomorrow.'

'Uh huh.'

You stupid card-thing, get in the lock. Just click on the green light. Click, damn you.

Butterfly breath at the nape of her neck. Arms sliding around her waist, hands on her haunches. His thumbs gentle wheels, hypnotizing her hipbones.

'So how are you at long-distance relationships?'

'And how are you at no strings sex?'

Why did you say that, Anna? What's wrong with you . . . bloody click.

At last, the green light. *Go, go, go.*

As she shut the door, he was on her, mouth to mouth, bodies tight. Touching naked flesh, pulling at his shirt until she felt wisps like fur, and she thought of Alice's belly, then she thought of flying as she was dropping, dropping back, him taking her feet from beneath, forcing wide her thighs, but it didn't hurt as they found the floor. Carpet burning her back, sawing her skin with nylon teeth, and him, measuring handfuls of shoulder and buttock, panting into her neck, hot-wet in her ear, her eyelids blurring shapes. Only the red dot of standby on the telly staring back at her, crimson against blocks of grey and the blacker bulk of him above her, in her. Pressed beneath his clammy-solid chest, her breasts splayed sideways, nipples flat. His smell no longer clean, but brackish on her tongue, so rough against his teeth and it still wasn't enough. Opening more, as it all slipped by, these slick, slick washes, so oiled and damp against the hardness, flesh sticking like damp rubber. Up into another place which was not here, was not Anna. Just ebb and flow and the bruising of hidden rock.

Can't breathe. *Make it finish.* Don't stop.

But she was losing it, the desperate, fleeting, fronded grasp becoming a hopeless yawn and . . . it was gone, as he lurched and heaved and crushed her. She felt her body ache, the weals she knew would appear tomorrow glowing hot on her shoulders and back. Still lying on static-fizzing carpet, he wrapped his arm beneath her, tracing sweat pools on folds of flesh.

They lay for ages, each waiting for the other to speak as the air between them grew cooler. Her legs were cramping; she needed to move.

'I need to get dressed. I'm freezing.' She shifted David's arm.

'No, really, the pleasure was all mine.'

'Mine too.'

'You sure?'

Darling, you were wonderful. You didn't make me come, but that's my fault, obviously. I wasn't concentrating enough . . . I've got a lot on my mind . . . you were squashing me . . .

She kissed him hard. 'I'm sure.'

'Let's get under the covers then, and I'll warm you up.' He pulled her upwards, onto the bed.

'Um . . . let me just – I need to . . .' Anna nodded towards the bathroom.

'Okay. Don't be long.'

They should have gone to his hotel, then she could have slipped discreetly away, digested what they'd done. Considered the after-taste as she brushed her teeth. Would tomorrow bring warm glows and smug purrs, or a chill douse of *what were you thinking?* Black Widow spiders; now there was a species that had it sussed. No *will he ring me?* or *did my bum look fat?* for them.

'Anna? Anna. You okay?'

'Just a minute.' She ran the tap.

'Take your time, why don't you? I'll just watch some telly while I'm waiting. Don't mind me.'

His glib, chiding humour was wearing thin. Ach, she was just tired and cranky, on the comedown from nearly-there sex and green Martinis. She could hear David scanning channels until he found the plummy tones of BBC World. Anna had been trying to ignore the outside world since she got to New York. No TV, no papers, no charge in her mobile. She hated her mobile, with its blank will-it, won't-it silence, then its sudden, strident wail. No escape from being available and accountable, twenty-four hours a day.

She opened the bathroom door. Saw David jump back from her laptop, flip it shut.

'What you doing?'

'It was making a funny bleeping noise. I think the battery's running down. How? D'you think I was stealing all your secrets?'

'I keep my secrets in my head, not a computer.'

'Very wise. I keep mine in a nice oak chest my auntie left me.'

'Aye, right.'

'No, I do.'

'What secrets are those, then?'

'Och, you know. Files, documents. Cases I've worked on . . .'

'You boring bastard.'

'Come on, Anna. You've got to keep track of where the bodies are buried. Never know when you might need a bit of leverage.' He smiled at her. 'But I put other stuff in too. Photos, keepsakes . . .'

'Don't tell me you save old cinema tickets. And pretty pebbles from the beach.'

'So what if I do? Anyway. Will I put this on charge for the morning?'

'I thought I had . . . yeah. The cable's just there.'

As he rolled to reach the plug, David leaned on the remote control. The volume shot up, as a familiar sandstone tenement backdrop appeared on screen:

'Here in Glasgow, locals are still reeling from the recent tragedy.'

Surprised, Anna listened more intently. Not often you heard a Scottish accent on American TV. What had happened in Glasgow that merited worldwide coverage? Had Rangers and Celtic merged teams? Or had the last fish and chip shop closed its doors forever, forced out by the relentless rise of organic cafés? Nah, just your usual bloodshed and mayhem, by the looks of it.

'We speak live now to her brother, Craig Brisbane, who's just returned from Manchester to comfort his father.'

The camera swung to a narrow, white face with black strings of hair gelled onto a prominent brow. Beside him stood a middle-aged man with a similar puckered brow, but his hair was dirty blond. The boy licked his gums, sniffed hard before he spoke. 'I canny believe what's happened, man. My sister was a pure doll;

she wouldny harm a fly. In fact, she was a wee bit . . . slow, know? We were aye looking out for her. She wisny street smart, put it that way.'

The reporter nodded. 'And how do you feel about the fact police are alleging she had a gun?'

'That's a total load of crap, man. She wouldny know what a gun was.'

'But it is true your father's been jailed for firearms offences in the past? Mr Brisbane, perhaps you'd like to comment . . . ?'

The older man looked blankly at the mic.

'So?' interrupted the boy. 'Does that mean the polis can start shooting weans? Just cause someone's dad's been in a bit of bother? *She* never done nothing wrong, did she? Listen, I love my . . .' His face contorted. 'I loved my wee sister. My dad's had some problems in the past, aye, but he's alright. I'd never have left them if I didny think they'd . . .'

The boy shook his head, wiped his eyes on his sleeve.

Another man in a dark suit interjected. He'd been standing at the back, like a smartly dressed minder. Or a reporter with a nice fat cheque. 'What I think Mr Brisbane would like to say is that he's mounting a campaign to have the officer responsible brought to immediate justice.'

Craig Brisbane leaned into the mic again. 'Bloody right we are. The man who murdered my sister is still a polis. Even though they've charged him. Any other murderer would be on remand, but he's still getting paid to sit in his house watching telly . . . while my sister's . . . my wee sister's lying on a slab in the frigging mortuary . . .'

His sobbing grew louder, till the reporter cut in.

'And there we must leave it; one family fractured by a moment's mindless violence. Only this time, it appears, the violence was caused by the very forces of law and order we expect to protect us. Police are refusing to comment further, other than to repeat that a thirty-seven-year-old man, stationed at Glasgow's Stewart Street Police Office, has been charged in connection with the death of Sarah Brisbane.'

Anna sat on the edge of the bed. David's chatter, the voices on the telly, the hundreds of questions screaming through her head; all noise and nonsense. Only one dark certainty, swirling at the centre. Of course she knew where Jamie still worked. Of course she knew his age. Of course she had watched his trigger-happy progress.

Of course it would be him.

Because Anna was a contagion.

9

Cath drove out of her street and turned left, travelling through the village. At the end of this road was the church; old and squat, but picturesque, shrouded by ancient trees and gravestones. There was a little bothy inside the gate, left as a reminder of the days when relatives would stand watch over freshly dug graves, guarding against the body snatchers. The village was only a few miles from Glasgow. Or it had been. Now, it fought off intruders on every side, as urban sprawl made a mockery of the green belt. But here, passing the church, where you couldn't see the tower blocks, it was still quiet and beautiful. A good place to raise a family – if you had a car and could get to the shops, since the baker's had closed and the butcher's shop was now flats. And if friends came to visit and keep you company. And if you didn't mind drunk neds from the estate, pissing on your gatepost as they staggered home from a day in the country. Or didn't mind being painfully visible, even when you fought to keep your head down. A great, corpulent, gossip-worthy carp in a tiny, churning pond.

'Mummy, my tummy's sore again.'

'No it's not.'

'Is, is, is.'

'Bzzzbzzzz,' echoed Daniel.

'Shu-up, Dan-pants. Me's talking.'

Cath checked the rear-view mirror.

'Stop fighting you two. Eilidh, you're going to nursery. You were at Cornwall with Gran, then you went to Auntie Jenny's, then you missed all of last week, cause of your "sore tummy". You've had the whole weekend to get better. And you managed to eat a big bowl of ice cream last night, so I think you'll be fine.'

Silent scowls from the back seat. Cath switched the radio on, then promptly switched it off again. It was nearly time for the news bulletin.

'Mummy?'

'Yes?'

'What does Daddy do when I'm at nursery?'

'I think he's going to have a wee rest today.'

Cath turned into the main road. They could have walked to the nursery, along with lots of other mums and buggies. But that meant facing people.

'Mummy, is Daddy hurted?'

'No darling, he's fine. He's just tired. Will we put some music on? Let's see what's on the CD.'

'Bo Buldah!' cheered Daniel.

Cath switched on the CD player, and Snow Patrol drifted through the car. Instantly, sound twined with memory. The last time she'd listened to that CD was three weeks ago, when she went to pick Jamie up from Govan Police Office. The day after they had charged him. The day that should have found them halfway through their sunny Majorcan holiday. That horror of coming home from the shops and finding him gone. Thinking him wrist-slashed or hanging. Not wanting to look, and praying as she ran, searching every room. Then a man phoning to explain that Jamie had been charged, that he would be appearing in court from custody – oh, he was very sympathetic. Lord Advocate's guide-lines, he said, when it was murder; nothing he could do about it. All these phrases came oozing from the phone that Cath had come to regard as her enemy, and she just wanted to say *wrong number* and hang up. But she'd thanked the nice man, who told her where Jamie would be taken to the next day – a judicial hearing at Glasgow Sheriff Court. And no, Cath couldn't come, it would be held in private, but that he'd phone Cath himself when they got back. Cath had wanted to laugh, just there, at the pleasantness of it all, like they were arranging a trip, and she'd written down all the details on a smudged piece of scrap that she took up with her to bed, and then knelt like Christopher Robin and thanked God it was only the Sheriff Court and not the mortuary they were taking him to.

That night, Cath had lain on the floor. Imagined it was concrete and kept herself awake with images of keepers throwing meat through the bars of a cage. Three calls in the morning: one from her mum to say she'd bring the kids home from Cornwall on the Saturday, one from Philippa, offering to take the kids when they came back – her poor babies, passed like lost luggage on a carousel, and one from Jenny, who was taking her for lunch. *No excuses*, she'd insisted, until Cath told her. Until she'd whispered that Jamie was lying in a cell.

'Ah,' was all she said. Tart-tongued Jenny, never lost for words. Then a silence, then a: 'Listen.'

'What?'

'Has he got a lawyer?'

'I don't know.'

'You tell him to go for Len Mackenzie. He's on the Federation's list. And Cath . . .'

'Yeah?'

'Please don't read the *Daily Report* today. It's a lot of shite and it'll only upset you.'

Too late. Cath had already clipped out the page, added it to the scrapbook she was keeping.

CONTROL OF GUN COPS URGED

Calls are growing for a check on the number of police officers licensed to kill, in the wake of the Sarah Brisbane shooting. Leading human rights campaigner Mairi Kinsale said: 'Police are refusing to reveal the actual numbers of gunmen in their ranks, for reasons of "operational security" – but this is nonsense. You cannot hide behind such trite statements when officers are killing young children in the street. We need to know how many there are, how closely they are supervised, and what kind

of psychological screening they undergo. Quite clearly, something needs to be done to stem this backdoor militarisation of
our police service.'

Ms Kinsale's comments were echoed by the father of the dead
girl, Gerard Brisbane, who spoke yesterday of his grief. 'My
daughter was everything to me. When I think of what the police
did to her, I just want to explode. I'd never wish this pain on
anyone, not even the man who pulled the trigger. But he has to
be dealt with. He can't just kill someone in cold blood and get
away with it.'

Cath had filled several pages of the scrapbook those first few days.
All the initial reports, then the leaders and editorials, opening out
the global from the local, growing more strident in their calls for
action. Lists appeared of all that had gone before, spreading the
debate yet wider and louder:

In the last 15 years, thundered a broadsheet, *police officers in
England and Wales have shot nearly 40 people, many of whom, it
transpired, were not even carrying a firearm. And not one of these police
officers has been convicted of any criminal offence. Is this a clear
example of one law for the public, and another for the police?*

But this was Scotland. This was Jamie. This was their life. Did
nobody care about him? Cath had got so angry, when she'd picked
him up after the judicial hearing. Waiting in Govan's front office,
people peering at her through partitions, seeing him stumble out
and refuse her touch.

'Just get me away from here, Cath.'

For once, he had wanted to talk. It had all poured out of him, like
a valve had been unscrewed. How they'd kept him in a cell, fed him
breakfast from a plastic tray. What had happened at the hearing;
how he'd been sneaked out the back door and driven to the court.
Put in front of the sheriff in a private room, and the charges read
over to him.

She and Jamie had parked up by the Clydeside, on rubble that
was once Garden Festival green. Not just green – flashes of azure,
gold and mauve and roller-coaster red too, all the buzzy colours of

creation. It had been so beautiful in bloom, this stretch of waste-
land; Cath had even bought a season ticket to the festival. Long
before she met Jamie. It had been a gorgeous, long summer in
1987, and she and her mum had taken picnics, ridden the working
trams, enjoyed the artificial beaches. Giant spirals and loops of
flowers everywhere and feelings of hope and healthiness. Glasgow
was shaking off the soot, lumbering to her feet again. It was a
wonderful time to be growing up. They'd bought a stone urn for
the garden; her mum still had it now. The trouble they'd had,
lugging it over the bridge to the car, rolling and dragging, taking
turns. Laughing as they begged a passing man to help. So much
life had been planted here, springing up from dragon's teeth.

And disappearing just as fast. When the festival finished, the
people left. Turf was rolled up, rides dismantled. Metal arbours
went back to scrap, the sand returned to the builder's yard. All that
remained were some jagged new apartment blocks, fashioned on
an angle to catch reflected sun. Snapped up in the artificiality of
the moment, then stranded by the rutted water's edge when the
party was over. The poor people that bought them had purchased
a dream of cosmopolitan living, chic little riverfront bistros, gentle
evening strolls, that even now, twenty years later, were still just
plans and promises.

'The sheriff kept asking me questions. Just to "clarify the case".'
Jamie was slumped against the steering wheel; he'd insisted on
driving. 'God, Cath, yesterday I was sitting in the living room, you
know? Today I'm being talked through my murder trial. Fucking
murder. I don't . . .'

He stopped, pushed back his hair, black strands through fever-
ish fingers. 'It just got surreal then. I switched off. They were
asking me questions that I couldn't answer. I tried to stay calm, you
know, analyse what was going on, but . . .' He shook his head. 'I
couldn't distance myself from it. That it was me, there.'

'What happens now?' she'd asked.

'The sheriff said they would fix a date for the trial and that I was
free to go. With "normal bail conditions attached".'

'What does that mean?'

'Oh, I've not to talk to any witnesses, or anyone involved with the case. Sign on at my local pol . . .' He'd started crying then, and she'd cried with him.

Just like she was crying now.

'What's wrong, Mummy?' asked Eilidh from the back seat. 'You sad about Daddy still?'

'What about Daddy, darling?'

''Cause Daddy's all sad. Has he hurted someone?'

'What?'

Eilidh's mirror-face stared woefully back at her, downcast where dimples should be.

'Hurtit,' squealed Daniel, thumping his rattle off his sister's skull.

'Bad boy, Dan-pants. You horrible bad boy. I'm gonna kill you dead.'

'That's enough, you two. We're nearly there. Now just you behave, or there'll be no sweeties at home time.'

A week after the judicial hearing, Jamie had been called into Headquarters for a discipline hearing. That was when Cath got in touch with the lawyer. She phoned the number Jenny had given her, was told Mr Worth would need to come in himself. So Cath made an appointment, offered to drive him there.

Stop treating me like a bloody child, Catherine. I'll go myself.

She made him phone the Police Federation too, to ask for support, welfare, any help they could give him in preparing his case. He'd paid his dues for long enough. But no Federation rep ever turned up at Headquarters. At the discipline hearing, the Deputy Chief Constable charged Jamie some more, just in case murder wasn't enough. Told him he was 'suspected of having committed a criminal offence' and that the hearing would be continued until after his court appearance. Something to look forward to. Jamie wouldn't let her drive him to Headquarters either. She had to stay, waiting for a reassuring call that never came.

It was only after he brought his shattered self home, that Cath realised Jamie still hadn't spoken to the solicitor. Turned out he never went to the appointment. That was when she most wanted to leave him. Just scoop up the kids and walk away from the whole tragic mess. So angry, when she saw he was prepared, willing even, to let their life slide down the pan. He'd gone in to the whole thing unadvised, unprotected, and come out in pieces. Jamie probably would have crawled into jail right then, if they'd offered it, gladly taking the medicine – and the refuge. Thank God for Leonard Mackenzie LlB. Cath finally dragged Jamie to see him just yesterday. A small, blunt man with a Pancho Villa moustache and a vintage, lime-green Capri. So brusque that his lucid, forthright words actually seemed to penetrate Jamie's skull.

'But you won't get it,' Len had poised ironic index fingers in the air, '*"reduced to culpable homicide"*. Don't you understand?'

They'd been sitting in Len's office, overlooking the Broomielaw, where the Clyde once hummed with passenger ships and roaring trade.

'Look. Let me make this simple for you, Mr Worth. The law is quite plain. You, as an authorised firearms officer, either have a complete defence, in that you were acting within the law, using proportionate and necessary means to defend yourself and others, or, if the court decides that you used excessive force, you have *no* defence. No defence whatsoever.'

Len was wearing a yellow and brown sports coat, and the checks throbbed like pus as he swept around the room, occasionally striking a table or a pile of books for effect and punctuation.

'Can I make this any more plain to you here? We can't go plea-bargaining saying, "Ooh, I know my client killed the little girl, but he didn't really mean it." You bloody did mean it: that's the point. If you made a mistake in law, if you used too much force, then there is *no middle ground at all*. At all!'

His nose was inches from Jamie's face, and Cath wanted to cheer as her husband flinched. He was actually paying attention.

'So, what you're saying is that it's murder or nothing?' Cath said.

'Exactamondo, Mrs Worth.'

Len's heels clicked as he resumed his pacing. 'Either your husband pleads guilty and goes to jail for life, or we move heaven and earth to prove that you, Mr Worth, acted with good intent, that you genuinely believed your life to be at risk and that there was NO OTHER OPTION AVAILABLE TO YOU!'

He took a little glug from a crystal tumbler. 'Are you with me, Mr Worth?'

'But I did shoot her . . .'

'Good God man. Do you want to see your children growing up?'

Jamie was silent.

'Well, work with me here, Mr W. Work with me, eh? There's a dear.'

Cath had faith in the flamboyant Mr Mackenzie.

She pulled up at the nursery. She'd left it until the last minute, so most of the kids would already be inside. But the mums, the bloody mums, still stood and blethered and locked their radar eyes onto her as she parked the car. One or two raised hands or smiled as she bundled the kids out. Most snapped their heads back into the default position, talking, talking as if Cath wasn't there, hands flapping in time with their mouths. About 'something else' of course. Cath felt like climbing on the bonnet of the car, ripping her blouse open and doing a Tarzan yodel.

Yes, my husband's been charged with murder. And it's shite and I'm dying here. Just say what you've got to say, and get it over with.

She hunched herself up as small as she could and hefted Daniel on her hip, her other hand reaching out for Eilidh's tight fist.

'Hey, Cath!'

Philippa left the huddle she was in and came straight over, her daughter Skylar skipping beside her.

'Hiya, Eilidh. Good to see you back. Miss Patterson says you're making banana bread today.'

'To eat?'

'Oh, I'm sure you'll get to try a bit. Why don't you go in with Skylar?'

'M'on Eilidh.' Skylar seized Eilidh's hand. 'Alan Hodges wetted his pants at story time.'

Philippa shook her head. 'That boy's never been properly potty trained. Too many au pairs traipsing through. Anyway, how you doing, missus?'

'Okay. Did you wait for us coming?'

'Well, I didn't know if you'd want to face the playground mafia. I know how hard it is. And I'll bring Eilidh back too, if you like. Save you the bother.'

Cath had forgotten about Philippa's own appearance in the *Infamous Women of Westerton Mains'* roll of honour. When Philippa's famous husband left her, the media had spared no mercy in spreading her shame. Within a few days though, Philippa had been back at Mums and Toddlers, taking her turn with the tea rota. Cath hadn't known quite what to say to her; didn't remember if she'd actually said anything useful at all. But she did remember inviting her around for coffee, loudly, after two bitches in the kitchen had been trilling about: *well, she has let herself go. I mean, all those kids. Think what it must do to your tits.* And then, after that time . . . after Cath had been injured in the fire, Philippa had come to visit her in hospital. Had provided nutritious bean stews which made Jamie fart and beg Cath to tell her to stop. And they'd been friends ever since.

'Thank you. I was dreading coming here, to be honest. Especially after what they said yesterday in the *Herald.* They're trying to whip up a frenzy. It's as if they want a scapegoat.'

'You need to stop keeping all those press cuttings, Cath. It's not healthy.'

'I can't.'

Philippa reached out and pulled Cath close. Such a simple gesture. Two arms around a torso, in full view of the world. The pressure of skin, a sharing of sin. It felt powerful, like her body was filling up. Touching Jamie sucked all the life from her now. Beyond Philippa's shoulder, she could see one of the other girls she was friendly with, who'd been there the whole time, now moving purposefully towards her. And there was Carole, getting back out her car to come across.

'Philippa, I need to go. I can't do group hugs right now.'

One final squeeze.

'Don't worry, I'll cover you. Now: run!'

When Cath returned to the house, Jamie was still in bed. She took him tea and toast, drawing the curtains so prying daylight flooded in.

'It's the final today,' he said, by way of greeting.

'Of what?'

'The kids' football tournament.'

'Is it? Good. You getting up?'

'In a while.'

'Well, I could do with some help around the house. The grass is getting really long.'

'That my therapy for today is it?'

'No Jamie. That's life. Houses get dirty, grass grows.'

'People die. I know, I know.'

'Just drink your tea.'

Passing through the hall, she noticed the phone was off the hook. One of the kids. Eilidh liked to play at 'offices', sporting her mother's heels and handbag, and, usually, one of her father's ties. Cath replaced the receiver and went into the kitchen. In his highchair, Daniel munched on toast and honey, wiping most of it in his hair. But he was happy. All chubby and beaming, and she loved him for it. Last night's dishes congealed in the sink; smug and greasy and crowing *we told you so*. Jamie had said he'd do them after dinner. Which dinner? Easter, Christmas? She scooshed in some Fairy Liquid, turned on the tap. White-hot bubbles, each polished with a promise of purple and blue. She scooped their softness, pressing palms against bouncy foam. Above the splash of suds, the phone was ringing.

'Mrs Worth. Len Mackenzie here. Did we get cut off earlier?'

'No, don't think so.'

'It's just, I tried to phone about fifteen minutes ago. I'm sure someone answered, but then the line went dead, and you've been engaged ever since.'

They were all at nursery fifteen minutes ago.

'Sorry. Must have been one of the kids.'

'Anyway, I need to speak to Jamie. Is he around?'

'Not at the moment. Can I help?'

'Well, I really need him to come in and see me. Today, if possible.'

'Is there a problem?'

'Potentially. We really need to meet face to face.'

'I'll make sure he comes in, Mr Mackenzie. What time suits?'

'I'm in court most of the day. Shall we say five-thirty p.m.?'

'That's fine. We'll see you then.'

Whatever it was, Cath was going too. Philippa would take the kids – she'd ask her when she brought Eilidh home. And she wasn't even going to tell Jamie they were off to see Len, until she had him in the car.

Cath and Jamie spent their day, as they spent most days, in separate, bumping orbits. Meeting in the hall, him moving his feet as she hoovered, her finishing off the grass when he went in for lunch and forgot to come back out. He stayed in the bedroom all that afternoon until, just as she was getting ready to take the kids over to Philippa's, Cath heard a strident knocking at the front door. Jamie appeared before she'd got halfway up the hall. Lots of laughing and clapping, as Jenny entered with a grubby little boy.

'Jamie, Jamie! We won it.' The boy was brandishing a silver cup. 'We fucking gubbed them!'

'Benji,' said Jenny. 'There's a wee girl in this house.'

'Sorry, miss. We fucking slaughtered them! It was brilliant.'

He flailed the trophy around his head, one finger looped loose through the handle.

'Careful, you,' said Jamie.

'Mr Waugh said we wurny to bother you, but I telt Jenny and she said to—'

'I said you'd be very proud of them.' Jenny smiled. 'Hi, Cath.'

'Jenny.'

'This is Benji. He's one of Jamie's star strikers.' Jenny ruffled Benji's hair.

'Haw, you, watch the gel,' said Benji.

'Gel? Feels more like glue to me.'

'Are you no going to the party then, Jamie? There's loadsa your lot going. Mr Waugh said—'

All the smiles switched off. Cath saw her husband freefall. No parachute, no net. And Cath smarting with the same indignant impotence she felt when Eilidh didn't get invited to scabby little Shona Black's *Princesses and Ponies* party.

'What party's that, Jenny?'

'Och, just a few of the boys.'

'What, like Derek?'

'Aye. But I mean the kids . . .'

'And Alex?'

'I guess.'

'And were you invited?'

'There wasn't exactly invites.'

'We're going out anyway, Jamie,' said Cath.

'Are we?'

'Yeah, into town. In fact, we need to leave right now, to miss the rush hour.'

'Oh well, there you go then, Jenny,' said Jamie. 'No need to get embarrassed on my account. You'd best go and enjoy your party, Benji. Tell the boys well done from me.'

'Can you no come too, Jamie?'

'Evidently not.'

A skew-eyed stand-off, until Cath opened the door.

'Well, thanks for coming, Jenny.'

'Cath, I'm really sorry. I didn't mean to upset anyone.'

'I know. Look, we really need to go. I'll speak to you later. Bye Benji, nice to meet you.'

The boy stuffed his hands in his pockets. 'Fucking shite, this. You're the coach Jamie, no that fat old—'

'Bye, folks,' said Jenny, closing the front door.

On the way into town, Jamie fiddled with the radio, seeking a static-free station that didn't exist. Cath hadn't asked who would drive, just assumed the position, and he made no protest. Whether it even registered was unclear. Driving her mad, that frizzle and crack, but she said nothing; a whole journey of saying nothing. Oh, she had many potential detours. A few false starts, which phuttered to nothing even as they formed. Cath, being a good driver, was always thinking ahead.

That was great about your team, eh? **It's no my team any more.** *Nice of Jenny to come over.* **Aye. And rub my face in it.** *I'm sure they thought you'd feel uncomfortable.* **You mean they'd feel uncomfortable.**

I wonder what Mackenzie wants? **To tell me I'm totally fucked?**

So Cath swallowed each sentence and let silence prevail. She tuned in to the fiddle music Jamie had settled on, grateful for its sawing relentless upbeats, and thought about driving hard-speed to slam the car into that wall. That one there. All she had to do was not turn the wheel. Let it run straight and true, trust the camber to tilt the chassis, put her foot down. One fast-blasting shudder, a crumple and a snap. Then it would be over. Only for an instant, mind.

So. No.

They got to Len's office slightly late, but at least the city streets had emptied a little, so they got a parking meter right outside.

'Why are we here again?'

'Not sure. He maybe wanted you to sign some stuff?'

'Did you not ask?'

'He just said you'd to come in.'

All Len's office staff had departed. Just him and his whisky waiting.

'Take a seat, people. How are you, Jamie?'

'I'm alright.' Like an old, old man, lowering himself stiffly into his seat.

'Good, good. Well, I'll get straight down to it. Bad news I'm afraid. We've got the statements in from most of the police witnesses, and, as I suspected, Inspector Coltrane's one is virtually diametrically opposed to yours. Take a look. I've highlighted the particular areas for concern.'

Jamie held out his hand to receive the piece of paper.

'*Gave clear instructions not to engage with the (now deceased) suspect . . .*'

Even his reading was slow, finger-moving. His face flickering between confusion and animation.

'Well, that's bullshit. He told us to speak to her . . .'

'*. . . At no time did I indicate there was any confirmation that a gun had been discharged.*'

Jamie dropped the document, spun anxious eyes from Len to Cath and back to Len. 'But that's just not true. That's not what he said at all.'

'Are you absolutely positive?'

'Yes. Look, just get the tapes of when we were all on talk-through. You'll hear it then, he was screaming at me to get ready to shoot.'

'And that's another little problem. No tapes.'

'But it's standard procedure. It's bloody automatic.'

'Oh yes, I know it is. And the controller insists all his equipment was working correctly. Unfortunately, there's absolutely no trace of any of your radio traffic from that night. We've checked with – Airwave is it you call it? Where all your radio stuff's controlled from?'

'What about getting statements from the other cops that were there?'

Jamie's head turning, a frantic gulping motion. Looking at her – at *her*? What could she do? Cath panned over this faraway scene; her husband pecking, panicking, Len sighing, her retreating backwards.

'Already done. Here.' Len fanned out a sheaf of papers. 'Take your pick. They're all the same.'

On day, date and time specified I was on . . .

On duty and in uniform when . . .

Anonymous reports alleging gunfire. Attended locus

'Golf Mike Two – ah, now they're the ones that definitely heard something.'

Jamie's face relaxed a little, tongue peeking timid from the corner of his lips. Cath knew what was coming, prayed it was not.

'. . . *Anonymous report . . . noises . . . No trace. Unable to confirm with any witnesses. As cautionary measure, AFOs were called to scene. While they were in attendance, I heard one loud bang. I have no firearms experience, and would be unable to state if this was in connection to any weapon being discharged* . . . blah, blah – *possibly car backfiring or chair being dropped from window.* But they bloody reported the other bang themselves.'

'What, the first one?'

'No, another one. We were told there was one noise like a firearm being discharged prior to the police attending. That was the anonymous report. But then Golf Mike Two called in to confirm they'd heard another bang – *when* they arrived. Not the one I heard. It's all there in my statement.'

'Unfortunately, it's not in anyone else's.'

'What about forensics?' asked Jamie. 'What's that showing about a gun being in the house? Fucksake, if it was fired from there then there must be some residue somewhere? Or casings in the street, even?'

Cath had already seized the outline forensics report from the strew of papers. She scanned through it as the men were talking. It was saying that Sarah had evidence of gunshot residue particles on her upper body, face and hands. In particular, there was a trace of lead inside her mouth, but the report said that could have come from a variety of sources, even household keys.

'Not a jot of evidence, I'm afraid. Burn marks around the cooker – hold the front pages! Animal blood in the back bedroom – well, we knew she was a bit of an oddbod. But nothing conclusive found to indicate a gun was discharged in the flat. And the only two casings found in the street match your gun. Basically, we've no corroboration of your account of events in the statements, no radio recordings to back up your version and no forensic evidence to suggest Sarah had possession of a gun. In short, someone has either been very slapdash, or extremely tidy, with this investigation.' Len took a sip of single malt.

'What do you mean "tidy"?' said Jamie. Len didn't answer.

'But, Mr Mackenzie,' said Cath. 'It says here that she had "*lead, barium and antimony*" particles all over her.'

'Well, she would do, dear, seeing as she'd just been shot. Unfortunately, gunshot residue gets everywhere. It's like talcum powder. Jamie, you say in your statement that you went over to the girl, after you shot her?'

'Yes.'

'Did you touch her at all?'

'Well, yes. I was trying to—'

'There you go, then. Prosecution will simply argue the residue is as a result of one: the initial entry wound and two: cross contamination.'

Len drained his glass.

'You'll also notice that the report says the furniture in the flat was broken, and all the mirrors smashed. The prosecution are likely to suggest that this wrecking spree was what created all the noise the neighbours heard.'

Len's glass looked huge, all jaggy-diamond cuts, too big for him to lift. Cath felt like she was shrinking, looking up at them both from inside a little black box. Pointed corners shutting, closing off her lines of sight, until just one 'oh' of light channelled all the noise and movement in the room. Len still droning on, his voice like raining pebbles.

'Still, if we can prove you acted in good faith, that all the signs suggested she was armed, that you were advised as such by the officer in charge – and, that, crucially, this can be corroborated – then we still have a fighting chance.'

A fighting chance? All that did was conjure visions of a battered man in a bare-knuckle fight, flailing blindly through the blood, knocking down one, maybe two, as ten more men spat on their fists.

'Albeit, there's the not insignificant matter of the fact we haven't yet received Constable Robertson's statement yet.'

A few more dropping stones.

'Why not?' said Jamie.

'Prosecution state he's suffering from post-traumatic stress, and can't be contacted at the moment. But we've still got plenty time to have a wee chat with Mr Robertson.'

Len shuffled his papers, peered directly at Cath. As if she were his ally.

'Don't look so worried, Mrs Worth. It'll all come out in the wash.'

Being locked in a box wouldn't be so bad. Sinking down, all those corners in which to curl up and die. She'd quite like that, really.

Blue Peter *again. Tuesday afternoon, the last before Christmas, and the lady on the telly was twisting tinsel over coat hangers The girl tried to make notes, while eating crisps and fighting with her brother over whose feet had more claim to the couch. Then the noises started. A steady distant drum pulse, getting closer. She was six.*

'You fucking dirty hoor!' her father was yelling. A hollow, vicious, drawn-out clatter, like a xylophone of bones. 'Did you think I wouldny be back?' Her mummy's skull, being rattled off the banister. The door open, the mirror above the fire reflecting the Mad Hatter and the Queen of Hearts and the off with her head.

'I don't want to hurt you.'

Louder rattle roaring. Voices soaring. She heard them, hundreds of voices, all chanting for blood.

'I don't want to fucking hurt anyone.'

Crunching crisps till her jaws ached, covering her ears, her brother hunched over her, his arm pushing her head down, face muffled into his side, counting with his panicked heart. One eye still on the telly. They were singing 'Hark the Herald Angels', and a crowd of kids marched into the studio, holding lanterns as her mother fell bleeding into the living room, hugging her belly.

Then her father kicked her, and spat in her face.

10

Suspended on full pay. Relieved of his warrant card. Locked in a cell, next to junkies and scum. Taken before a sheriff, taken back to Govan, to the stares and headshakes. Handed back his property, his jacket and his shoes. Told to leave the office and not speak to anyone connected with the police, or go to any police office unless it was to report a crime. Turned on by his own, no truth, no substance. No trust.

Excommunicated from his family of sixteen years.

Jamie had been a cop longer than he'd been married. It was who he was, like being good at sports, a dad of two, the joker in the pack. A cop. Cased in a uniform, part of a club, might be a bit officious, but you'd always tell your wean to go to one if they were lost.

But not a cop who kills.

A cop who kills, who has shed his skin and slithered sideways into desert, knowing they will come after him with sticks, and wanting them to. Days become pointless, food becomes dry. Shame beats down, and he finds he has nowhere to hide.

Cath seems to go on as before, taking the kids out, dealing with the lawyer, talking to her mum, to *his* mum. Going to the shops, wiping bums, answering the phone. He is aware of all this going on in the background of his life, and he huddles indoors, knowing he is using her as a buffer, trusting that she will absorb everything outside, knowing that he cannot cope with what is inside. It's possible she may hate him. Probable, in fact, for he hates himself.

There are no solutions to this state of suspension, no action plans he can draft, no shortcuts he can make. He is hanging out to

dry, to be cured in hot blasting air. Only a leather-sprawl remains
of who he was, and he is conscious of all this, which makes it worse.
But still, there is hope. There must be hope, and faith in friends.
Those cops in Govan, they weren't his friends.

Jamie lifted the phone. There was that faint grating sound on the
line again. He'd need to phone BT and get it sorted, but he hadn't,
wouldn't, because then he'd find out that they'd bugged his phone
and that he was not just paranoid but under surveillance. Under-
hand, underbreath, six feet under. Under. So he'd just let it be the
wind and the trees tugging on the wire. Of course it was, he was
insane. It was only a phone. He dialled Derek's number, but the
machine clicked in almost immediately.

'Hi Derek, it's Jamie. Jenny told me my lads trounced Blair-
dardie Boys. Sounds like it was some final. So, tell them well done,
brilliant. And eh, keep me in the loop eh ? All the best for now.
Hope you're all well.'

He went to hang up, then changed his mind.

'Listen, I'm sorry I was a grumpy arse with you before, Derek. My
head's fucked at the moment. I . . . you were right. I need to get a
grip. So, I was wondering if you and Alex fancied going for a pint
maybe? Or, yous could come round here – right, who am I kidding –
it'll *need* to be here, unless you want to be on the front page of the
Sunday Saddo. Anyway, I could really do with seeing a friendly face,
know? And, really, all the best with the team. Tell the boys I'm dead
proud of them; they've done fantastic. Okay? Bye now.'

He became aware of an angry shape, waiting at the corner of his
vision. All accusatory angles and tapping feet, Cath stood, her
dishtowel quivering.

'What do you think you're playing at, Jamie? Derek never
bothered his arse telling you about the final, so why congratulate
him now?'

'Because he did really well.'

'I certainly wouldn't have bothered if I was you.'

'Well, you're not me, Cath.'

She clattered back to the kitchen, toward sounds of running
water.

Jamie had taken to reading the dictionary. Every morning, at random, opening a page and learning it all. There might be signs in amongst all the tight black lines, telling him what to do. There, see: 'Try'. And 'try' came right after 'truth', which was profound. But after 'try' came 'trygon', which was a type of stingray, and meant nothing at all. He waited for Cath to come back in, give him another doing, but then he heard her car start up. Must be time to pick up one of the kids. Or maybe she was going to get some lunch.

Jamie chucked the dictionary across the room, and picked up the remote control. Maybe there would be signs in daytime TV. A phone-in for first-time felons. Or a life coach offering six-point plans for successful rehabilitation after committing murder. Behind the couch, Jamie had hidden a bottle of whisky. Stuffed it there last night, when Cath came back early from her mum's; and it was calling to him now. A couple of gulps would calm him down. It wasn't his fault: Cath had got him all uptight. A couple of glasses would just deaden it.

It was late when Jamie woke, the room lit only by the blue chattering of the telly. He stumbled to his feet, switched it off.

'Cath! Cath!'

The house was dull and empty. He went to the window, craned his neck. Cath's car still wasn't there. Where were they? His breath started to come in spurts, leapfrogging over his diaphragm. *Blow away the badness. Blow.* Forcing himself to slow down. It was okay. Cath had left him on his own before. Just not for this long. He went into the hall, switched on the lamp. It glowed pinkish beneath the mirror, almost a red light, warm and welcoming. Winking at him, making him look.

An old man leered back, septic-skinned. Yellow gaunt face, shadowed at the jowl. Pink eyes rimmed with red; greasy hair; mean lips. He stretched the pads beneath his eyes. For a minute, they were his eyes again, then he looked right into them.

And jumped away from the mirror.

Breathing rough, panting; he needed air. Opened the door, went outside. He'd not been out on his own, not since they charged him. Not been out at all since Cath drove him to the lawyers. God, it was big; all that sky. Stuff towering, trees and houses, lamps all glowing. Angry colours, oranges and reds. Deep greys and plums in the sky. Everything was angry at him.

He walked briskly through the village, through streets too narrow for the cars that straddled them. Walls reeling with nightmare shapes; a jogging shadow following him, rocking and mocking his flailing gait. He bumped into a dog, or something that yelped, trying to get past the shapes that were stretching, becoming trees and gravestones. Real ones, toppled and mossy in a messy frail pile. Silent walls squared up to him, silver-green panes in an arch. His lungs were hurting, his body flagging. It was the grey stone church where Eilidh was baptised. He must have gone from one end of the village to the other. Beyond this, no pavements and black country roads.

No one was about. The door stood ajar, and he pushed it further, tasting musty damp tangs. Nobody there.

Jamie went inside. It shouldn't be left unlocked like this. Closed the heavy wooden door behind him and walked down the wooden aisle. Dusk light played through leaded windows, making shadow diamonds on bare stone walls. He sat at the end of a pew and bowed his head. Slowed his breathing and tried to focus. It wasn't enough. He wanted to kneel, but you didn't do that here. Wanted to belly crawl across the splintering floor and prostrate himself before the silent altar.

Would you talk to me then?

He sat scrunched and leaden. A stillness descended, but it wasn't serenity.

Tell me what to do. Someone tell me what to do.

In the Church of Scotland, there are no candles to light. No statues on which to pin your thoughts, no beads with which to clack and pray. No intermediaries, invocations or favours. Just you and your maker – gaunt and stark, stripped to the bone.

How that aches, air sharp on your bones. Hanging vulnerable, waiting to be saved. Yet they never showed the body. No rack, no nailed muscle, no contortions or bloody thorns. Only glass above the altar, reflecting dark sky and two thousand years of imagining the worst. Was the wee girl somewhere warm?

Sitting, waiting, waiting in the quiet. A drowsiness descended, that same stretched sense of time yawning and poised that he'd had before. Jamie went with it, glad of the balm, but knowing he'd have to wake. A single lantern hung over the pulpit, with an Iona cross picked out of the brass. It wasn't switched on, nothing to illuminate the closing gloom. He breathed long draughts of Pledge and lilies, and watched the light fade, slower and slower till everything was like ghosts.

When Jamie finally got up to leave, it was completely dark outside. He stumbled back to the house. Saw only his car in the drive, not Cath's. Where were they? Jamie opened the front door. It wasn't locked. His car keys hung on the hook by the door, untouched since that morning he'd driven home.

The house was so quiet. He needed noise, distraction. Someone there.

Driving was easy, after all. Like a bike, you never forgot. He had a vague idea of where Jinky lived. Out Paisley way, in the new houses up by the mental hospital. As long as Jamie kept his hands gripped tight and his eyes wide open, he'd be fine and as long as he kept to the speed limit and, God, oh God not again please . . . no, he'd missed it . . . it was a fox, not a kid . . . and stopped at red traffic lights, he'd be fine. He remembered the house had a black door and white walls – Jinky supported St Mirren – that was it, there, the one with the BMW in the driveway. Jinky's wife had a beauty salon – he'd been handing out flyers for it at the range.

It was her who answered the door when Jamie knocked it. He just chapped it, hard with his knuckles, as soon as he got out, because if he stopped to think about what he was doing he'd get straight back in the car; and then he knew he'd never come back.

'Yes?'

Must be nails she specialised in; hers were sugar-pink with white tips, so long they curled slightly at the ends.

'Is Jinky – John – in please?'

Her hair didn't move when her head did, shimmering sleek and solid and whitest blonde. 'Who's calling?'

'Can you just tell him it's Jamie?'

She shut the door over. There was a heavy lace curtain behind the glass and Jamie could see two shapes there, then an arm waving, or pointing. One shape moving off, heels clackclacking in angry Morse code. A door slammed somewhere inside.

'Jamie!' Jinky flung the front door wide. 'Good to see you, pal. In you come.'

Jamie hesitated on the step. His trainers were grubby on the shiny red tiles. 'Are you sure? Look, I know we're not supposed to talk to each other . . .'

Jinky gripped his shoulder. 'Ach, away and don't talk shite. I was just about to give you a ring, pal. Get yourself in here and don't be so daft.'

As Jamie entered, a huge husky-type dog galloped into the hallway, shaking her fur like a mane. 'Down, Sheba. It's the wife's.'

They went into the front lounge, a light, pale room that reminded him, fleetingly, of Anna Cameron's flat. Only less stylish somehow.

'Here pal, take a seat.' Jinky offered him a choice of cream leather couches, set at right angles to one another. 'Can I get you anything? Tea? Coffee? A beer?'

Jamie shook his head. Unzipped his jacket, folded it over his arm. Now he was here, he didn't know what to say. *Please help me* sounded too desperate; *what have you told them?* too childish.

Each of them took the end of a separate couch, close, but far enough apart that their knees didn't touch. They looked at each other across the corner of a slim glass coffee table.

'So,' said Jinky, 'how you doing then?'

'Alright I suppose. You?'

'Me?'

The way he said it, like it was a surprise, like why should anyone be asking about him, because he hadn't done anything wrong, had he?

'Forget about *me*, pal; it's you we need to worry about. What have they said to you then?'

'Well, you know a trial date's been set? They're talking about September.'

'Aye. Tough call, man. I was just saying to the wife; there but for the grace of God. See if I'd gone round the front instead of you, pal . . .'

But you didn't. YOU didn't. God was graceful to you; He steered you round the back.

'Look, I know, but anyway . . . nothing we can do about that. What I want . . . fuck . . .' he heaved a sigh deeper than he meant, all wet and quavery, and filled with phlegm, 'Jinky. I need to know. What are you speaking to? Who's interviewed you? What have they asked you?'

'Och, Jamie, man. How can you ask me that?'

'Jesus, I'm sorry. I know I'm putting you on the spot. But—'

'Naw, I mean, why should you have to ask me? I'll speak to whatever you want me to, pal. We were a team that night, and that's what we are now. Fucksake Jamie, what kind of a neighbour d'you think I am?'

'Did you tell them she had a gun?

Jinky brushed some fluff off the arm of his seat. 'I telt them exactly what happened: that Coltrane *telt* us the lassie had a gun.'

'But did you see a gun? Did you see anything?'

'Did you?'

Jamie rubbed his eyes. There was an ever-present patina, smeared across everything he could see, like sap had oozed from his tearducts.

'I saw a flash of something grey at the window.'

'Me too. When she was over at the back.'

Jamie reached over, seized his hand. 'You did? You saw something metal? Oh, Jesus.' He began to weep. 'Oh Jesus, thank you. I was starting to think I'd gone mad. You definitely saw it?'

'Aye.'

Jinky eased his hand from Jamie's grasp, cheeks pinker than his wife's nails. Jamie had probably mortified him, snottering all over his shagpile rug.

'Oh, Jinky, you've no idea what that means to hear that.' Jamie stood, searching his pockets for a hanky. His jacket slid to the floor. 'Don't panic. I'm no going to hug you!'

Jinky stood up too, slapped him on the shoulders. 'Nae worries. I'm only glad I can do something to help. It's bloody shite this. We get shafted just for doing our job.'

Jamie blew his nose, vaguely registering the tentative, supportive *we* instead of *you*. Ach, Jinky was brand new right enough, not the fly-by-night chancer Jamie had him down for. *That* was what he loved most about the polis: when the chips were down; whether you hated each other's guts or not, your neighbour would back you up. United we stand: it was a given, a code. And a lifebelt.

'But listen,' said Jinky, handing Jamie his jacket, 'I don't think it's a good idea if we meet up again, know? Just in case it jeopardises anything . . .'

'Absolutely. Look, I'll put my hood up on the way out, in case anyone sees me!'

Jamie the joker was back. For an instant, the weight had lifted and his lungs could take a breath. Just an instant, mind, then it slammed back down, dousing him black as the sky outside.

Someone had sent Cath flowers. Widow flowers, Jamie supposed. Well, as good as. They were waiting in a vase in the hall when he got back from Jinky's. So was Cath, hunched and wrathful as Tam O'Shanter's wife. He'd grunted at her questions, gone straight up to bed, pausing only to take one of the flowers with him. He didn't know why; it just looked pretty. He still had the flower nearly a week on, long after Cath had binned them. An iris, blue with a stab of yellow. He'd kept it out of water, in his bedside cabinet. Each day the petals drew in on themselves, the yellow bleeding into blue. Now it was just papershades of ochre, crumbling into the bedroom carpet if he touched it.

Daniel was smiling up at Jamie when he came back from the bathroom. He was holding the remains of the fanned-out leaves. 'Da!'

'Hey there, wee man.' Jamie crouched beside his son. 'What you doing in my sock drawer?'

'Wee flowa.'

'You got a wee flower? So you have.'

Daniel beamed, crammed the leaves into his mouth.

'Uh, uh. No, dirty boy Daniel. Dirty!'

'Dir-ee! Dir-ee Da-ee!'

'Daddy's *not* dirty, Dan-pants.' Eilidh stood in the bedroom doorway, skirt slung around her neck. 'Daddy's *not* bad.'

'Hiya honey. Dan, no. Give that . . . Eilidh where's your mum?'

'Downstairs.'

'Well, here – you take Daniel down to see her, eh?'

'I need to get ready for nursery, Daddy.' Her lilt became a whine.

'Oh, for goodness sake, don't be so selfish Eilidh. Just take him downstairs.'

'But Daddy . . .' she started to cry.

'Christ, will you just get out of here? I canny take any more of your moans.'

'Mummee.'

Jamie could hear her wailing all the way down the hall. He scooped up Daniel and the remains of the flower and followed his daughter downstairs.

Cath was waiting at the bottom. 'What's going on?'

'Och Cath, she was doing my head in.'

'She only wanted you to put on her skirt. She can't do the zip up.'

'Well, I had Daniel to deal with. God, I can't do everything, Cath.'

'Apparently I can. C'mere Daniel. Let's get your breakfast sorted.'

She carried her son towards the kitchen.

Jamie hesitated. He desperately wanted coffee, but that would mean going to sit with them all. Refereeing over Sugar Puff squabbles. Listening to the radio or seeing the news.

Cath leaned back out the half-closed kitchen door. 'Oh, by the way Jamie, I wasn't going to mention this. But, seeing as you're *such* a concerned parent: your daughter got into a fight yesterday. I've to go up to the nursery after lunch.'

'Is she okay?'

'Not really, no. Lost a clump of hair and she's got scratches all the way up her arm.'

'But when? I never saw.'

'No, you wouldn't have, would you?' Cath shut the door.

There was some vodka in the bathroom cupboard; a wee miniature that came in an aftershave gift set. Jamie took it back to bed, and waited till the front door slammed and the house went quiet. Cocooned under the covers, he could've been off school sick with the measles. Or skiving. He'd only ever done that the once. Once was enough, mind. Crept in the back door and saw his mum getting humped red raw by a man in a tweed sports jacket. Balls a-slapping on her fat pink arse. *That* was who had called her Dee-Dee. His dad's mate Bert.

This vodka *tasted* of aftershave. Maybe it was one of those flavoured ones, like they had down the Polish Club. He'd gone there once, with Anna. She'd know of course, what he'd done. Everyone would know. What would have happened, if he'd left Cath for Anna's familiar-strange embrace? They'd have passed their honeymoon stage by now, maybe shagged themselves out of lust already, and he'd be paying child support and . . . the thought bit him. And she wouldn't be here. Anna Cameron wouldn't hang around a loser.

So, what did that make Cath?

Jamie heard the front door close, stuffed the vodka down the side of the bed.

'That you, Cath?'

Footsteps coming up the stairs. He pretended he was just getting up, but she didn't come in. Two sets of feet walked by the door, then he heard another door opening across the landing.

'Now, in you get to bed, teeny-bash,' said Cath, 'and I'll get you a hot-water bottle.'

Eilidh's voice came back. 'Okay Mummy, can I watch the—'

'No you cannot, young lady. If you're really not well, you're going to sleep. Right?'

Eilidh sighed, 'Yes.'

Jamie went through to see them. 'What's up?'

'I'm off sick too Daddy,' his daughter smiled. 'Same as you!'

'She wouldn't go into nursery today,' muttered Cath. 'Said her tummy hurt again.'

'Something she's eaten?'

Cath turned away from him.

'I'll away and get your hot-water bottle, sweetie. Now you snuggle down, and maybe Daddy'll read you a story?'

There were pills lying downstairs. Pills the doctor had said 'would help', but they didn't taste as good as alcohol. He was sure there was Martini downstairs too, bought for Cath's mum last Hogmanay.

'Will you Daddy? Can I get the one about the teddy that got lost? This one, Daddy, ple-eease?'

The book was called *Nothing*. It was one of her favourites, and he always read it in a squeaky, small voice.

'Right.' Jamie shuffled up on the bed beside her. 'But it's not a teddy, remember? It's a cat. Okay, it's moving day, and the family have taken all their stuff away – all except this wee box lying in the attic . . .'

His daughter snuggled against him. 'Pooh. You smell yuck. Have you brushed your teeth?'

'Eh no, not yet. Anyway, he gets up onto the roof—'

'Do the sad voice Daddy, when *Nothing* sees the stars again!'

'*Can you imagine how it felt, to see the stars again after all that time?*'

That would have been the last thing she saw, that wee girl. Looking up at the sky.

'Daddy, what about the fox voice? Dad-*dee!*'

Eilidh read at the same time he did, stopping him from missing out any words or pages. And they were doing fine, until it came to the bit when the cat started sobbing: *I don't know who I am. I don't know who I am!* His throat began to tighten as he mimicked the tears of the toy. The cat who'd lost his markings and his ears and was unrecognisable as anything at all. But they made it to the end, then he tucked Eilidh in and slunk back to his room. It did stink in here, that stale, dank smell you get under rocks.

The doorbell went as he was dragging on some joggers. The lawyer had said he would call round as soon as he had any more news. Jamie couldn't bear the silence. The Federation were supposed to keep him informed, but all they'd done was punt every phone call Cath made back to Len Mackenzie. Lawyer, trial, defence, all nonsense. What was the point? What could a lawyer do to undo the undoable? Last time he'd checked it was still only Jesus Christ could raise the dead.

'Jamie!' Cath shouted up. 'Jamie, can you come down here please?'

It wasn't Alex. It was an inspector and that DCI who'd charged him. Déjà bloody vu.

'Mr Worth? DCI Armstrong again. We have a warrant here to search your premises in relation to the murder of Sarah Brisbane. Step aside please.'

'Whoa, wait a minute here . . .'

They brushed past him. 'Euan, you take the ground floor, I'll do upstairs.'

'Excuse me, what's going on?'

'Your wife has viewed the warrant, sir,' said Armstrong. 'Excuse me.'

'But what is it you're looking for? I gave all my gear in to Govan. Ho! Ho – you!'

The inspector was heading up the stairs.

'My daughter's up there you. Get your arse back down here. NOW!'

Armstrong shoved him into the dining room. 'Unless you want done for a breach – which means straight back to jail, do not pass go – I suggest you sit on *your* arse and keep your mouth shut.'

Cath's hand pressed down on his shoulder. 'DCI Armstrong,' she said, 'I want to accompany your inspector up the stairs. My five-year-old daughter is in bed, ill.'

'You just plonk your butt beside your man's, Mrs Worth. It *is* Mrs isn't it? Or are you just his bidie-in?'

'Yes, it is *Mrs* Worth, Chief Inspector, and your inspector is not setting foot upstairs unless I'm there. I am *not* having my daughter terrified by some strange man.'

'You mean, apart from her father?'

Cath moved away from Jamie, walked towards the door. He saw Armstrong's eyes dart as she moved. If that woman put one hand on her, he'd rip her stringy throat out. But Armstrong let her go, then Jamie could hear Cath running up the stairs.

He sat like a dunce, watching as this polyester-clad, sweating woman pulled his home apart. Armstrong began with the sideboard, upending drawers, then the cupboard where their good glasses were. Next, she got down on her knees, so close Jamie could have jumped her, could have kicked her bony long head to kingdom come. Armstrong tugged at the corner of the carpet, yanking until it came free from its nails.

'Got a hammer?'

'What?'

'You got a hammer? I need to take these boards up.'

Jamie's hands twisted into the side of the chair. 'Can you not just tell me what it is you're looking for?'

'If you've no got a hammer, I'll just use one of these.' Armstrong reached for the old fire irons that had been Cath's gran's.

'In the kitchen. Drawer next to the fridge.'

When Armstrong opened the door, Jamie could hear Eilidh, crying overhead. Instinctively, he jumped up, and got two steps before he was thrown to the ground. Armstrong was above him, one foot crushing on his balls. 'Police assault, breach, resist arrest. Not to mention obstructing an officer in the course of her duty. It's just as well I'm a nice girl, eh?'

Armstrong flexed her heel one more time, then stretched out her hand.

'Right. Get up, and don't do anything stupid.'

She hauled Jamie to his feet. 'I have no desire to cuff you, pal. Now sit like a good boy, eh?' Smiled as she held skinny hands down on Jamie's chest. 'None of us like doing this, do we?'

Jamie watched Armstrong shove the drawers back in the wrong order. Cath would freak. Armstrong scratched her backside, then paused. Bent down to retrieve something from under the sideboard. A small black rectangular book, embossed with gold. Eagerly, she flicked through its pages.

'Aha. Thought we wouldn't find it, eh?'

'My notebook? It was in that top drawer all the time. I'd have just given it to you if you'd asked.'

'Bollocks. How did you not hand it in on the night of the shooting then?'

'I thought I had. Then I found it later, in my bag of clothes.'

'Aye, and I came up the Clyde on a bike.'

Armstrong put the notebook in her shoulder bag. 'Remember, we're only doing our job. A shitey one, mind, but someone's got to do it.'

She left Jamie sitting on a hard-backed chair. Upstairs, Eilidh was still crying, and fury beat on impotent fury, each sob and slamming door and clunking drawer like stinging slaps. He could hear Cath shouting, and a deeper voice barking back. In their bedroom; another man telling his wife what to do.

11

It wasn't like dressing for a wedding. Or a funeral for that matter. The outfit had to convey dignity, quiet assurance, vulnerability and hope. Only Cath couldn't afford the sustenance that designer jackets, tailored to fit in all the right places, would give. She had picked out a dark suit, a kind of sage green, which she'd bought last year in Dorothy Perkins. Chosen on a good day, when she thought it might work for interviews. As soon as Eilidh was at school and Daniel was in nursery, she was going to look for a job. Save some money in a secret stash, then, when the time was right and the kids were old enough, she could make a move for freedom; leave visions of Jamie and Anna far behind.

That was the plan that had kept her seething her way through the last three years.

Still some way off, this future, but there was nothing wrong with being prepared. So she'd bought the suit with birthday money from her mum, and it had lain in her wardrobe for ages. Until now.

This now, this here and now, where Anna Cameron seemed somewhat inconsequential. The moment when the world had caught up and overtaken Cath, mocking the biggest huff in history. Sweet, sweaty irony of failing to kick your husband from the marital bed, then learning he'd be taken anyway. Against your will, because of your will? Decide or procrastinate. Stay or go? Keep/ dump? Lovehate? Like heads and tails holding all the answers: when the obverse flicks and spins its downward spiral and it lands the wrong way up, well, that's when you really know. The crystallisation of what you didn't want, flat and grinning up at you from the floor.

How can you be prepared for this? For months they'd been waiting, suspended in confusion and dread and resignation and maybes. They had lived their summer in a curtain-drawn daze. Eilidh's first day at school; a shuffled depositing, a tight, small wave. No daddy, no camcorder, just heads down, in and out.

May to September, a slow dying of days. Trying to explain to your daughter why dog shit was smeared on the letterbox. Or why Mags next door wasn't talking to them any more. Minimising your trips to the shops, asking friends to come to you. Not many did, but they phoned. Sometimes. Wanted to be kept up to date, and to tell her they were thinking of her. But then, even the phone calls got less. Alex forgot to meet Jamie for a pint. Derek's wife discovered they'd been double booked for Sunday lunch, and emailed them to cancel. Emailed them. How quick Cath's certainty they'd be seen alright dissolved. *In the polis we trust* – Cath always had. Her standard response to *Frontline Scotland* or any of these exposés on miscarriages of justice had always been 'no smoke without fire'. Even when they trundled out the 'wrongly imprisoned victim', she'd always think they looked guilty. They must have done it. You only had to look at them, sniffing and weak.

Defeated, just like Jamie.

The police would never stitch up one of their own.

Cath's confident, unshakeable belief had shattered, as the juggernaut of impending justice bore down on them, as cold shoulders turned to ice from which to slip and slither. The one defining moment had been that meeting with Len Mackenzie. After that, a gentle snipping of lifelines, a tiny turning away as they drifted further and further from the mothership. Calls to work unanswered. Minutes of meetings lost. Len telling her 'this was to be expected'. Cath, curled alone on the couch with the plangent night-chimes of the downstairs clock, wondering if her husband was a liar. *Knowing* her husband was a liar, who even now carried the secret of Anna Cameron coiled inside like a pale, segmented maggot. If he could carry that deceit so close to home, then what other truths could he contort to save himself from prison? How easily could he fashion some great pretence that this was all a conspiracy?

But if it was all an act, wouldn't he be fighting? Yet all Jamie showed was ambivalence about saving anything. It was she who was pushing and pulling. He was simply fragmenting. All summer, Cath had been trying to glue the bits back together. Him, living inside a whisky bottle, self-pity sousing reason. Sleeping the day and pacing the night. Refusing to eat chops and roast lamb. *No meat* he'd say. *No meat. I don't want to eat dead things.* It was Cath who had dealt with all the legal stuff. Cath who had insisted a psychologist, a psychiatrist and however many doctors it took examined him. Who fed him the pills that gave him visions and her peace. She could have walked away, said it was nothing to do with her.

So. This was it; the day Jamie's trial began. A procedure that would decide his fate and hers, because they were bound grimly up, for better and for worse. They'd tried to prepare themselves last night, clinging to each other in a last-chance cocoon. Whispering words they should have said a lifetime ago. God, he'd even tried to tell her about Anna Cameron then, but she didn't want to hear it. '*Cath,*' he had started. 'There's something I need to tell you.'

'Don't,' she breathed. 'Please don't.'

If Cath had to confront that now, she would collapse. Her innards would curdle and she wouldn't be able to cope. He would be defining her choices: leave and be brave, or stay and be a martyr. If they didn't talk about it, she didn't have to deal with it. *One day at a time, sweet Jesus.* Just don't make me do honesty right now.

The green of the suit made her skin look dirty. She was ready far too early. Jamie wasn't even up yet. Cath watched him now, still sleeping. He'd been awake till the early hours, sipping in the dark. She'd heard him, sensed his need and pretended to be asleep. Now she'd have to put him in the shower and feed him coffee. Oh, he wouldn't be drunk; he was too well practised for that. Just small and shabby and softly gone.

His jaw was tight, smooth cheekbones hollowed, little grating noises from his teeth. Cath's tongue strayed to her own rough front tooth. It still hurt: some days shrieking, some days a constant throb. Other times only if she poked it with her tongue. *Nothing I can do,* said the dentist. It was only a tiny chip, too small to fill. *But it hurts,* she'd whimpered and he'd shrugged. Said he was sure the nerve would 'calm down', and suggested she use Sensodyne toothpaste. Some nights, when the pain was driving her mad, Cath smeared the blue paste over her tooth and gums, then packed her tooth in cotton wool. It would still be sore, and feel slightly porous in the morning, when she'd wake with rabies dribbles on her pillow, and a face like a foaming gerbil. So she'd learned not to prod it, and to bite fruit with the other side of her mouth.

Her hand rested above Jamie's head. If she touched him, he would wake, and then it would be their last, proper day. *There's honesty for you, m'lud. I think my husband will go to jail. I am fighting and praying, while he has given up. I think he wishes they would hang him.*

A wooden headboard was propped against one wall; he never did fit it onto their bed. They'd have to sell the house. They'd put so much work into it, especially the kids' rooms. Even if Jamie was found not guilty, there would still be Police Discipline. Two bites at the cherry. And even if, suppose if, just suppose in the most amazing of twists *if* he still got to keep his job, what then? What was left for him in Strathclyde Police? No future, no faith. No friends.

Derek had come round, one more time. Last night in fact, with a bottle of malt. His face, painful; his timing, impeccable.

'Look, pal,' he'd begun.

Cath wouldn't let him over the door. 'Piss off, Derek.'

'No, let the man speak,' said Jamie. It hurt Cath to look at his eyes, bright like a puppy's.

'Jamie, I . . . . Christ, I just want to wish you all the best tomorrow, alright?'

Derek kept playing with the zip on his leather jacket. Up and down, up and down, till Cath wanted to slap his hand away, like she did when Eilidh picked her nose.

'Look, pal, this is really difficult. Can I come in?'

'Aye, away—'

'No.' Cath stood in between them. 'You can say what you have to say here Derek.'

'Fair enough.' Derek stepped back down on to the path. 'I know I've not been around much . . .'

'*Much*! God—'

'Cath. Please be quiet. Derek, come away inside.'

It wasn't worth the fight. But he could stand in the bloody hall.

'Aye, well,' Derek mumbled, 'look, basically we've been warned off. Telt that if we come into contact with you, speak, phone, anything, then we're fucked too, you know? I mean, as far as the job's concerned. You know what they're like, Jamie.' He sounded whiny now. 'I mean, they telt us it would be worse for you too, because of bail and that. They said you shouldn't be seen talking to any of us either.'

'Och, that was very noble of you, Derek—'

'Cath, please.' Jamie touched her elbow. She wished he would put his arm around her instead. 'I know, Derek. They said that to me too.'

'So, anyway.' Derek offered the whisky again. 'This is from me and Alex. Hopefully, it'll all be over by next week, and we can all get back to normal, eh?'

Cath took the bottle from Jamie's hands and gave it back. 'But we didn't need you next week,' she said. 'We needed you *now* Derek. We needed you last month, today, tomorrow.'

'Look, what can I say? I'm a shitebag, okay? But I've got a family to feed too, Cath. I – I'm sorry, right?'

'That's okay Derek,' said Jamie. 'I appreciate you coming round.'

Derek clapped Jamie's shoulder. 'Take care, pal, alright? We're all rooting for you.'

'Cheers.'

They all stood and looked at each other for a minute. She was buggered if she was making this easy for Derek.

'Well, I'll away the now. Eh . . . keep me posted, okay?'

'How? By bloody telepathy?'

'Christ, Cath . . . I . . . cheerio, alright?'

Derek headed back down the path, still clutching the whisky. Jamie had pushed past her, out the door and after his mate.

'Derek!' he called.

What the hell was he doing, making a scene in the street? She could see Mags next door peeking through her curtains.

'Derek. I'd really like it if you could be there tomorrow. If – if you're not working, I mean.'

'Well . . . I'm supposed to be . . .'

Zip, zip, zip with his jacket. Cath thought she would scream.

'I'll try right. I'll do my best.'

'Tell the guys eh? It would mean a lot to me,' Jamie repeated.

'I'll do my best, okay? I promise.'

'Thanks pal.'

She'd wanted to slap them both: Jamie for being so pathetic, Derek for being a two-faced bastard. Then she'd wanted to hug Jamie, kiss him where it hurt and make it all better. Until he shoved past her, straight for the decanter on the sideboard.

There were some dregs still, there on his bedside table. Cath took off her jacket, lay back down on the bed. It was still too early. There was a brown stain on the ceiling, where the rain had seeped in last winter. So many plans had gone unrealised in this house: a conservatory one day; possibly an *en suite* under the eaves; all the aspirational accoutrements they said 'added value' to your life. They had it all planned. Soon as they'd seen the old cottage, Jamie's imagination had galloped wild. He'd darted from room to room, tugging Cath behind him. 'Look here, this could be the dining room . . . And if we knock through this wall . . .'

She'd laughed and kissed him. 'If you say so, honey. Just remember, there'll be three of us soon.'

Had that really been them? Cath newly pregnant, Jamie strutting with his tail in the air. Full of love and dreams, new life burgeoning like spring in her belly. She'd felt young and special, Jamie treating her like she was the eggshell, not the box. God, how she'd loved him. The man who swept her up with schemes and dreams and kept her safe with kindness.

She knew she would marry him after Corfu. Their first holiday, and they'd been in a bar. One of those beach ones, set up outdoors, with strings of lanterns and earthen jugs of wine. Raucous noise, some karaoke, and, in amidst it all, a tiny kitten, perched on the rock-face wall that sheltered the bar. It was mewling and tottering above the heads of the crowd, quite high, maybe fifteen feet or so off the ground.

'Look, Jamie, look.' She'd grabbed his arm. 'Oh, the poor wee thing. It's stuck.'

'It's a stray,' said Jamie. 'It's fine.'

Then other people noticed, and some kids started throwing stones. The thing was terrified, circling and backing and looking upwards. A moonlit tail swept along the top of the outcrop. It was the mother, pacing back and forth, too far up to reach her kitten on the ledge below.

'Oh, shit, Jamie, it's going to fall.' A table of pissheads were jeering at it, one dragging his chair over towards the wall. ''Ere kitty, kitty.' He shimmied his Union Jacked chest. 'Come ter daddy.'

'Only pussy you'll be getting tonight!' shouted his mate.

'Jamie, do something.'

Jamie put down his pint, kissed her forehead. 'Alright, alright. I'm going.'

A few deep strides, a friendly pat on the back for the Cockney rebel, and Jamie was on the wall. Hewn from cliff stones, the rocks were rough and staggered, but he scrambled up easily. Probably most folk could have climbed it, but it was *him* that did. Within seconds, he'd reached the kitten, scooped it in his fist, and clambered a little higher, to where the rock was smooth. One hand clinging to stone, he'd raised the other up like a trophy, depositing the kitten beside its mum. A cheer went up from the bar as he dreeped back down to earth and Jamie, her Jamie, had solemnly taken a bow – winking at Cath as he flourished his hand.

Cath turned the pages of her scrapbook. She still kept it under the bed, inside a shoebox. The pages were thickest in the days after Jamie had been charged.

SACK DEATH COP NOW

Cathcart councillor Christine Harold today appealed to the Chief Constable to sack the killer of local schoolgirl Sarah Brisbane. The family of Sarah Brisbane were outraged to learn that the thirty-seven-year-old Strathclyde police officer, who was last month charged with the murder of fifteen-year-old Sarah, has been suspended on full pay.

Ms Harold, who is a member of the Joint Police Board, has been supporting the Brisbane family in their struggle for justice. She said, 'I think it's outrageous. Not only is that officer at liberty to go about his business, but he is still being paid from the public purse. What kind of a man can go home at night to his family, and continue to pocket taxpayers' money, knowing he's deprived another family of their own child? The police are meant to uphold the law, not create it on the hoof.'

Sarah Brisbane's grandmother, Elizabeth Brisbane, joined with Councillor Harold in urging for a swift resolution. 'If this was an ordinary punter, he'd be in the jail by now. My wee granddaughter will never see daylight again – I don't see why he should.'

A spokesperson for Strathclyde Police commented, 'We can confirm that an officer has been suspended on full pay. As with any criminal case, a suspect is deemed innocent until proven guilty. With regard to being remanded in custody, that is a matter for the Court to decide.'

Cath couldn't face reading the papers today. She hadn't even read the notes Len had couriered over to them yesterday evening. Each finite, hamstrung particle of her energy was focused on simple survival. Get one day over with, then focus on the next.

It wouldn't be Len defending them this morning. You needed a Queen's Counsel for the High Court and, at last, they had one.

Crispian Traquair. Not their first choice, nor their second. They'd tried for all the big names, advocates with fame, influence – at the very least, big football club connections. No takers. Jamie was an embarrassment, it seemed. Was he also primed to be an example? There'd been so much build-up in the news; some media suggesting the future of society was predicated on the result. In the blue corner, you had the nodding heads, stuffed full of their own dinner-party sagacity:

'*A civilised state functions when law and order are upheld. What then, if the very functionaries of law and order are called into question?*'

What a taxing philosophical dilemma. Aren't you so lucky you're not living it, Cynthia . . . Cynthia . . . Cath scanned down the column: Cynthia Douglas-Clarke? While, in the red corner, liberal wolves bayed for blood: '*We have to guard against paramilitary RoboCops, administering summary justice.*' Subtle, measured stuff like that.

Cath closed the scrapbook, pushed it back under the bed. Philippa had taken the kids overnight, and the house seemed very quiet. Like it was waiting for something to return. Yet, everywhere, if you strained hard, were soft whirring particles, muffled but there, in the whisper where nothing was ever really silent. Cath lay down beside her sleeping husband and cupped her hand against his skull. Didn't stroke, just held the plates beneath her fingers. Resting her hand like it was a hug, feeling him flow through her skin, gentle pulses, sliding her hand slowly, firmly, past the cranium to rest on the soft gristle where his spine began to bud. One finger of her other hand reached to trace his face. Hesitated, then swept across his forehead, moving to a delicate, feathery sketch, first one eyebrow, then the other. Tickly hints on flickering lashes. More pressure down each side of his long, straight nose; his perfect nose that she wanted to place her lips around, and feel its hardness in her mouth. Then he snickered and she laughed at her desperation. Smoothed the rough, high cheekbones that he'd need to shave, but it was their stubble that made her want him. That and the spring of dark hair reaching from his naked chest. Hair on which she would rest her cheek, which could rub and tease her breasts to orgasm . . . she climbed on all fours and stretched her tongue to the corner of his mouth.

Jesus.

Drew back at the stench of necrophilia.

'Jamie,' she snapped. 'Jamie. Time to get up.'

He mumbled and stirred. Smiled vaguely, not remembering, then sat stiff against the pillows.

'Time to get up,' Cath repeated.

'Jeez – what's the time?'

'It's okay, we've plenty time yet. You go have your shower and I'll sort breakfast.'

'Mgh.' He shook his head. 'I don't want any.'

'Bacon sandwich?'

He jettisoned the covers and stood up. 'I told you. I'm *not* eating meat.'

'Eggs?'

'God, I don't want anything. Stop fussing, will you?'

She made him food anyway. Scrambled eggs and mushrooms and toast, and he picked at it like Eilidh would. Breakfast telly droned in the background. Another bomb, a lottery winner and some woman extolling the South Beach Diet. Local news.

At the High Court in Glasgow, the trial begins today of—

Cath leapt to switch the telly off.

'What?' Jamie stopped pushing his fork around the plate. 'So they're saying the trial starts today. We know that.'

'I know. I just – we're eating breakfast.'

'So?'

'So I don't want to listen to it, alright?'

The room was sullen without the telly's glow, and Cath pulled the curtains wide. Two cars were parked on the wasteground opposite, a favourite place for neds to dump their stolen wheels after a night of joyriding. Unusually, both vehicles were intact. No charred bodywork or missing wheels.

'Looks like there was another road race last night,' she said. 'Will I call—'

'No,' Jamie cut across her words. 'Let the police do their own dirty work.'

She said nothing. As she straightened the curtain, she saw a head dip up from the back seat of one of the cars. 'Jamie, there's folk still in them, look.'

He came over and stood behind her. Immediately, a flash went off across the road, illuminating Jamie's face in the morning murk.

'Shit.' He ducked behind the curtain. 'It's bloody reporters, that's what it is.'

'You're joking. Why?'

'Cath, don't be naïve. First cop to be convicted of murder. They're going to put my head on a spike, as a warning to others, didn't you know?'

'Stop bloody talking like that, Jamie. Len Mackenzie thinks you have a good case. You and Jinky can both vouch for the fact Coltrane told you she had a gun. He bloody ordered you to shoot her. Neighbours say they heard shots, there's loads to—'

'Not this again! To what? To prove I was right to shoot her Cath? But I wasn't.'

'You . . . you acted in good faith,' she said, weakly. 'To protect the public.'

'Faith,' said Jamie. 'And what if that wee girl had faith I'd protect her too?'

'Well, it's too late for her.'

He flinched like she'd punched him.

'Think of your own wee girl Jamie. *Please*. She needs her daddy.'

He pushed his hair from his eyes. 'Right, c'mon. Action stations. What have we got in the way of disguises?'

'Pardon?'

'Well, I'll need to do a Betty Burke, won't I? Dress up in women's clothing and sneak out the back door in glorious retreat. You can be Flora MacDonald.'

'Now you're just being manic.'

He slapped his hands against his thighs. 'I can't win with you, Cath, can I?'

'Just shut up.' She took Jamie's hands, placed them on her waist. Wrapped her own arms around his neck and held him close until he gave in and hugged her in return, like Daniel having a tantrum. Body soft, then hard, then soft. They stood together in the vortex, and, just for an instant, Cath could feel the air rub against her.

12

Everything was cold. From the thin beige marble walls to the splatter-pattern stone floors. Even the towering, circling pillars that dizzied the entrance were the colour of pale, dirty ice. Twin metal detectors stood side by side, a police No Waiting cone acting as flunky. Cath put her bag on the table as instructed and passed between the plates. Nothing buzzed, no one stopped her. She looked around for a sign or a noticeboard. The foyer was huge; ubiquitous fig trees weeping all over the shop. Cool yellow shone from rounded lights, hung like giant footballs in the sky.

They had entered the High Court separately, Jamie in Len Mackenzie's car, spirited somewhere to the rear of the building. Cath had found a space near Glasgow Green, where the car would no doubt get screwed by passing trade, but she'd driven in circles for ages, so it would have to do. And she was beyond caring; nothing seemed real this morning, not the changing of gears or the colour of lights or the tremor at her husband's mouth. Her own mouth was filled with a damp silveriness.

Reversing into the gap, Cath could see a tunnel of grass and trees behind her. Glasgow Green: the stoic and grubby half-lung of a cheerful smoker, who'd lived to be eight hundred and thirty, and eaten pies all his life.

Carefully, Cath had peeled the Tulliallan sticker from the windscreen and placed it in the glove box. Two wading birds flanking a crest, with little black and white chequered bands to discreetly flag up you were 'in the job'. No point in advertising the fact here, so close to the Saltmarket, where an aggrieved friend of the accused might vent his spleen with a brick through a cop's car window. Held back only by the crying female, shouting, *Naw Malkie leave it: it's no worth it.*

A female just like Cath. For now she was one of these defiant, skulking women. Clipping briskly into court, eyes right and left as she swallowed and glanced, carefully casual, for a noticeboard, a sign. Over to one side was a curved reception desk, all low-lit like in some trendy hotel. She made her way across, past cops she might have known, but didn't look at.

'Excuse me,' she asked the security guard seated at the desk. 'Could you tell me what court the case against Mr Worth is?'

The guard turned around the list he had typed on a paper in front of him. Scanning down, Cath read:

HM *versus James Francis Worth. Court 3.*

'Thanks.'

The arrow on the sign above the desk pointed right for Three and Four. Cath made her way along an open passageway to the door marked Court 3.

'Haw, 'scuse me hen.' A wee barrel in a security guard's uniform appeared from behind a plinth. 'Where is it you're off to?'

'Court Three.'

'Canny go in yet, pet. Public gallery doesny open for another hour.' She smiled. 'You're keen, eh?'

'Sorry.'

Cath's seen-it all-got-the-T-shirt façade must be so transparent to this woman, who really had seen it all. Marching in and staring straight ahead had been Cath's only defence. Now what was she going to do? She'd begged her mother not to come, or her father, nor anyone that could see her for what she was.

'Can I wait down here then?'

'Aye. Course you can, hen.' The woman gave Cath another smile, one of those frowning, pained ones that showed solidarity, and seated herself back behind the plinth. From the side, Cath could see the woman continue to nod and grimace, desperate to catch Cath's gaze.

'Terrible, wantit, hen?'

'Sorry?'

'Court Three: that lassie getting shot. Terrible, eh?'

'Yeah,' whispered Cath. 'Terrible.'

'Someone close?'

'Pardon?'

'Sorry, pet. None of my beeswax. It's just, well, you seem that agitated, know?'

Agitated? Sitting quiet as a tiny rodent with her handbag on her knee, shoogling only slightly to keep out the cold? The woman kept frowning at her, with her black bun eyes.

'I think . . . I think I'll come back at ten.'

Cath lifted her handbag and went outside, half running across the Saltmarket, skirting the chain of buses and vans until she was under the graceful, lonely McLellan Arch that led to Glasgow Green. She leaned one arm against the cool stone, trying to slow her breathing. It had never crossed her mind that the Brisbane family would be there. But of course they would be there, full of grief and righteous anger – as Cath would. So focused on her own family that she'd rarely thought of the Brisbanes, except once, when she read in the paper that the girl's mother was dead. It mediated her pain that there was no mother left to grieve. For that was too sore to contemplate; the overwhelming desolation of a mother losing a child, seeing the literal flesh of your own flesh, lifeless and decayed.

I made you, a mother whispered. *I kept you warm inside me and fed you good things and went without. I stroked you through the stretched skin of my stomach, seeing your breath rise and fall within my own as you swam, shapeshifting and leaping in the jelly I grew to cushion you from life.*

Nothing could compare to that.

Cath's jacket sleeve had fallen back from her raised wrist, flesh sticking to the icy stone. She pressed her arm deeper into the carvings of the arch, feeling the rub of chiselled edges break against her numbing skin. In court, Jamie would have to face the girl's father. Across a crowded room, he would have to look him in the eye. Or look away. Cath's arm was aching, tingling as she compressed all her body weight against it. Skinny wrists and ankles: the sign of a thin person, bursting to get out. Probably her weakest point, these bony hiccups. Crushing on the numbness, her breath coming in gasps now, tasting pain in puddled reservoirs at the back of her tongue. Pressing, then pushing until her hand was thinnest, weakest veal. Were she to slash her wrists now, little blood would flow.

Cath eased her arm back down, pulsing her fingers back to life. Glasgow Green stretched before her, along the northeast bank of the Clyde. Socialist heart of the city, the Green was more a big back garden than a park. A melting pot for marches and rallies, it was once a popular place for hangings too, and laundry, sheep-grazing and prostitution at various times. Tucked to one side, Cath could just make out the fine pink sandstone of the People's Palace; a museum of Glasgow's people, the real ones, not the famous ones. In the distance, adjoining the Palace, the Winter Gardens glittered in low morning sun. A lean-to of grandiose proportions, the huge conservatory arched high with wrought iron and exotic plants, offering tropical escape from the city's urgency. There'd be people there now, unfurling newspapers in the glass-magnified warmth, perhaps sipping a latte and wondering what they'd do today. It was somewhere to walk to, somewhere wide and light.

Cath always wished she was other people. Studying for her prelims, she'd trudge home from school, glowering through stacked windows at the shop-girls the same age as her. Girls arranging jewellery or flowers, gift-wrapping gorgeous bits and bobs for Christmas, girls who were planning their office parties and not looking forward to an evening of cosines and hydrocarbons and bloody World War One. When Cath was a cop, she'd tut at sergeants, knowing she could do their job so much better, and didn't they understand how tough it was out on the street? Even now, she'd envy the yummy mummies in the supermarket, who wore matching clothes and had clean, Stepford children that did piano instead of nose-picking. And, not that long ago, Cath had wanted to be Anna Cameron. A woman in control of her life; sharp, authoritative, with a career, beige clothes and smooth blonde hair. And Jamie begging to be inside her.

How many times had Cath pictured the scene, then shoved it away like turning a page? But these pictures kept morphing. Her husband, rutting at Anna Cameron. His mouth open, telling her how much he wanted her. Was it tender or rough? Did he kiss her? Did they shove up against a wall? Were his eyes closed? And, if they were – who did he see when he fucked her?

This time, Cath let the feelings come in a bloodletting. She had no energy left, no make-up to smudge, so the tears didn't matter, and it hurt too much to hold them back. Her belly twisted as the air hit her lungs, rage rolling like an avalanche that could sweep foundations clean. With it came debris of pain and shame and yearning which Jamie would never understand. Only now, when he was slipping so fast, so far, did she realise how much she wanted him. Not through desperation, or fear, but through love.

Palms pressed on eyes, black circles like targets inside her eyelids. Anna Cameron better not show her scrawny face here, playing belated champion as the buzzards circled. After all, it happened at funerals: the mistress and the wife, all stoic dignity and huge black sunglasses. But Cameron was no mistress, just a sad wee cow. All that was left, all that was important, when your world and your ambitions and your dreams and your life was sucked into a big black hole, were the people you loved the most. Your children, your husband. Your bulwarks against the world. But what if they could never talk properly again, her and Jamie? What if all the words that were left unsaid remained that way?

Cath wished she was anyone else in the world: that man over there with the brush and the cart, who was sweeping up the leaves. Nothing to worry about but the wind whooshing through his piles. And his daughter playing up at school, and his wife's operation and the fact his boss was a bully . . .

Enough.

She was Cath, she was here and she had to go back.

Ancient, bulbous trees waved spindly fingers at her, shooing her back down the path. This was the route they used to run as probationer cops, when Strathclyde's training school had been an old, ramshackle building in the Gorbals, not the shiny new-build that it was now. There were twenty guys in Cath's intake; guys who'd streak on ahead in their smart blue shorts, leaving ten thundering young women to bring up the rear, breasts heaving and buttocks jiggling inside the navy-blue gym knickers they were forced to wear. A rare treat for the jakies nursing their meths. Cath looked behind, then moved one hand beneath her jacket to tug at her own knickers. Blew her nose, and walked back through the park.

The Saltmarket was much quieter now that rush hour had passed. But, as Cath approached the High Court for the second time that morning, a small posse of lights on legs moved as one, sweeping across the pavement to block her path. Blinding whiteness, rapid fire from every side. Some lights flashing, others shining continual piercing darts in her eyes as she twisted back, trying to find a way past. A clutch of furry knobs wiggled under her nose, their owners shoving and jostling and calling her name.

Mrs Worth: how does it feel to see—?

Mrs Worth: do you feel that the police have let you down?

Mrs Worth: is there anything you'd like to say to the family of—?

Hands in her face, grabbing at her jacket. They were going to rip the sleeve . . .

'*Cath.*'

She pushed on forward, making it to the front entrance.

'*Cath.*' It was Jenny, elbowing her way through the crowd. 'Ho, you. Shift your arse,' she spat at a photographer who refused to move. She kept pushing Cath, tripping over feet, banging her into the revolving door.

'Here, you a cop or a frigging tailor's dummy?' Jenny yelled at a court officer who was standing just inside the foyer.

'Ah, it's yourself Jenny,' he smiled. 'My job's just to keep them out. And can you see any snappers in here?'

'That's no the bloody point, you big tosser . . .'

'Jenny, please.' Cath could see the security woman glaring over at her. *That's right missus. I'm tainted me. Wife of the accused, not a tearful auntie.*

The guard stomped over. 'The lassie's right John. That's a pure sin, so it is, and you just staunin there watching. C'mon hen, straight through now.' She put one arm around Cath and ushered her and Jenny through the metal detector. 'Turn right, then first on the left. There's a wee seat up at the back for you. Okay?'

'Yes. Thank you.'

The woman squeezed Cath's arm. 'You'll be fine, hen.'

The girl never remembered her mother crying before that night. Such a fresh-sour memory, the woman slipping into the girl's half dreams, dark hair dripping over sleepy skin. Winding arms beneath her waist, the girl's back melting into her mother's belly as she sang soft words. That mother tongue, sobbing sorry, sorry – but for what? For whom?

She didn't ask. Didn't want to know because it was never said; the girl had only heard it in her sleep, in a nightmare that slithered under her brain, kept hissing its lies for happy never after, whispering that what it spoke was truth. That her mother was alive, but hadn't come back for them. Instead, the girl could dream that he'd thrown her under a train.

Though she knew she saw her mother leave with her rucksack in the dawn.

'Court!'

Third day of the trial. The start had been delayed by nearly two hours, lawyers arguing in private over legalities and submissions, then stopped abruptly for lunch. They ate in a nearby pub: Cath and Jamie, Len and Jenny, and Jamie's mum Doris. His dad was doing a shift with the kids. Doris kept asking Len what would happen next, and Jamie kept asking if anyone had tried the puddings here, and could they turn the sound up on the telly? Cath had eaten quietly and missed her children and wondered what she'd done so wrong. Every pea and chip a tiny prayer. *He was only doing his job, God. He's a good person. Why are you doing this to us?* Deliberately jabbing pie crust in her ragged tooth. There was still a piece of meat lodged there now, squeezed in the narrow space between her front teeth. She pushed her tongue into the gap.

Yesterday had stopped and started too, and day one had . . . Cath could barely remember day one, which might have been a year ago. Each evening, she would try to analyse the day's proceedings with Jamie, though he didn't seem to care. Initially, she found it hard to look, let alone listen. To see her husband white and humble in the dock, his tie too tight and a little off to one side. To see her mum take turns with her dad, and her cousin, who'd all ignored her pleas not to come, and see Jenny, and Jamie's folks sitting alert and afraid, squeezing hands, patting shoulders. To watch Sarah's dad, a stocky, coiled man with no neck and tragic eyes, sit apart from the troupe of wizened old ladies whose tongues clacked loud as knitting needles at the guillotine, and the bevvies of wide boys in shell suits. She'd seen Mr Brisbane's picture in the paper, and knew not to sit beside him. There was another man sitting alone today, a boy really, early twenties, neatly dressed, with well-gelled hair. She'd vaguely smiled at him a couple of times, in case he was someone Jamie knew. Because that was another thing which was hard to see: the absence of Derek, or Alex, or any of those bastards. Only Jenny hadn't turned her face away. She came when she could, between work and looking after her own family.

The courtroom was very modern; sickly beech wood in broad horizontal bands, which jarred with the archaic wigs and gowns. The three men in the prosecution team – the ones Cath used to call the goodies – sat around a small conference table to her left. Traquair, Len and a woman Cath didn't know adopted similar positions on the right. The Advocate Depute, the prosecution's main man, was toying with his ponytail as he chatted to the younger, dark-haired man beside him. Just another day at the office.

Pale, thick turquoise glass muffled the public gallery from the court. The court officer kept a seat at the back for Cath. Standard practice, he told her, so people would have to turn around to see her.

'Means you're a bit safer,' he said, 'it'll be fairly obvious if someone's trying to intimidate you.'

Good of him to point that out.

They all rose as the judge swept in, his robes a stream of red crosses on white silk. Cath could see all the faces in the public gallery, reflected in the glass. Her own face too, observing the players on the stage through her wan reflection. The macer, decked for dinner in a white bow tie and black robe, hung the mace in a sconce, at the same time as the jury entered through a door in the back wall. Fifteen men and women who would decide her family's fate. How should Cath sit? Head bowed, shoulders back? Should she look straight at them with clear, honest eyes? As if it mattered.

Then came Jamie, rising up from below. No shackles, just the slow shuffle of stairs up into the dock, flanked by two Reliance security men. The dock sat directly in front of the public gallery, so all Cath could see most days was his head. Occasionally, a hurried profile. She was never sure what he was looking for when his head flicked briefly round, but she always smiled.

'Advocate Depute,' intoned the judge.

'My Lord.'

And so the prosecution resumed. The droning lawyers' voices, with their Anglicised inflections, soporific, lulling, confusing even to those who listened as if their lives depended on it. What chance did the jury have of keeping up?

It was the turn of the tactical firearms advisor to be grilled by the prosecution.

'And so, to clarify what we touched on yesterday: what you're saying is that lethal force should always be the last option, yes?' asked the Advocate Depute. 'For the ladies and gentlemen of the jury, let's recap: you, as an authorised firearms officer, can only resort to firearms if – sorry, what was it again?'

The sergeant took a deep breath. 'An armed officer can only fire when he has reason to believe there is an immediate threat to life, to him or a member of the public, and where there is no other option available to him to remove that threat.'

'I see.' The AD chewed the end of his glasses. 'And am I right in thinking, Sergeant, that since the inception of the Human Rights Act, even having considered all these issues, even having arrived at the conclusion that you really have no other possible option than to raise your firearm – you still have to ensure you use,' his head bobbed to his notes, '"*no more force than is absolutely necessary*" to incapacitate the person posing this "immediate threat to life".'

'That's correct sir. All our training is directed towards protecting life, and using firearms as a last resort.'

'*Protecting* life, hm? In your professional opinion then, Sergeant, do you believe that firing not one, but two bullets at a juvenile – who, I might add, was posing no immediate threat to life – was *absolutely necessary*?'

'As I said, the firearms officer's role is to protect life. He has to make a judgement after each shot fired, to decide if the threat to life still exists. Any shot fired after that threat has been removed would not be justified.'

'Objection!' interjected Jamie's QC, Traquair. 'We have already established that there is no way of knowing if it was Constable Worth's first or second bullet that struck Ms Brisbane, therefore this line of questioning is irrelevant.'

'Sustained.'

Billings inclined his head. 'Forbye all that, Sergeant, surely when not one police witness present had even *seen* the girl present a firearm, let alone fire one, some kind of less lethal options should have been deployed in the first place, giving poor, young,' he glanced at the jury, '*terrified* Sarah a fighting chance?'

The sergeant cleared his throat. 'As a lone authorised firearms officer, Constable Worth would not have had access to baton guns or Tasers. These alternatives are carried within our Armed Response Vehicles. As you are aware, sir, both the ARVs and the Tactical Firearms Unit were unavailable to assist that evening, owing to another incident taking place some distance away. I was tied up with that myself, and was therefore not in a position to offer any advice.'

The QC smiled; a little, quick smile that said *of course, of course, I understand. Busy men like us.*

'But you would have done, Sergeant, had you been there?'

The sergeant hesitated. 'Well, situations like these are extremely fluid. Often, there is little time to establish—'

'Just answer the question, Sergeant: yes or no? *Had* you been present, even as a lone firearms officer, would you have advised the senior officers present to wait, until a less lethal option could be obtained? Bearing in mind the ambiguity of the situation, would you have advised that some other method be used in the first instance, to restrain this distressed young girl? Some other form of containment?'

A gentle slump of his shoulders. 'Yes sir, I would.'

'Thank you, Sergeant Green. No further questions.'

The judge nodded at Crispian Traquair. 'Your witness, Mr Traquair.'

Traquair shuffled to his feet. 'Thank you, My Lord. Um, Mr Green. Yes. A man in your position will, I'm sure, be "up to speed" – as they say – on current opinion and case law relating to "less lethal options" open to authorised firearms officers?'

'Em, yes sir. To an extent.'

'Of course, of course.'

Traquair looked like a horse, thought Cath. A knobbly old shire horse with a draped chin, who should be eating apples in a gentle field; not defending the rest of her life.

'So, would you concur with the oft-held view that using less lethal options is actually dereliction of duty on the part of the police? Ladies and gentlemen of the jury, if I might explain this viewpoint in its simplest terms: it could, and indeed, *has*, been challenged, frequently, I may say, that resorting to the use of say, plastic baton rounds, may be interpreted as a *failure* of the police to carry out their duty to protect life.'

'I'm aware of that view, sir, yes.'

'How so Mr Traquair?' asked the judge.

'Well, My Lord, if, as we are all agreed, the onus is on the authorised firearms officer to do his or her *utmost* to prevent the possibility of a death – where an immediate risk to life is foreseeable – surely merely slowing down an assailant leaves the potential for further violence to ensue? Particularly as these alternatives are often ineffective, and can merely aggravate the situation. As such, by deploying a less lethal alternative, the police are actually *neglecting* their duty to protect the wider public.'

Traquair swivelled back to face the witness box. 'Would you agree, Sergeant?'

'Objection!' sniffed the AD. 'The witness is not here to offer conjecture . . .'

'Sustained. Mr Traquair,' intoned the judge, 'please do try to keep to examining the facts of the case.'

'Indeed, My Lord, indeed. Very well . . . Sergeant Green,' Traquair ran a finger down the edge of his notes, 'tell me, in any case, these legal foundations my learned friend was speaking of; they're only a framework, aren't they? Guidelines, if you like. It is the *individual* firearms officer, the brave policeman who has volunteered to put his life on the line, who has to interpret these frameworks and flow charts and options in the *split second* of time he has available, yes?'

'Correct.'

'So, it is very possible that Constable Worth felt he did not have the luxury of "time to wait". Picture the scenes, ladies and gentlemen. It is dark, confusion reigns, neighbours are terrified, an allegedly armed suspect is running towards you . . . How can we . . .' Traquair twirled to face the jury. Wobbled slightly, then regained his composure, '. . . safe, relaxed, within the confines of this majestic courtroom, possibly substitute our own assessment of the situation for that of the officers required to act in the "heat of the moment"?'

'Objection,' called Billings. 'This is a matter of opinion, not fact.'

'I will allow.'

'Yes, sir,' replied the sergeant. 'It's extremely difficult; AFOs have to make instant decisions based on all the knowledge that's available at the time – but there's little room for error.'

'Quite an onerous task for the lowly constable, eh, Sergeant Green?'

'All our officers are rigorously trained—'

'No, no, I don't doubt that. We've already heard all about the laudable training programmes you have in place. But even so, Mr Green, even in the immediacy of the fraught, electric, and quite probably terrifying atmosphere that comprises a firearms incident, do individual firearms officers not require some level of guidance in arriving at that decision to shoot?'

'Sir?'

'Supervisors, Mr Green.'

Cath sat upright. Something in the smug 'ta-da' of his tone made her pay attention; made cautious bubbles rise inside.

'Ultimately,' Traquair asked the jury, 'who controls a firearms operation? Who deploys the resources and makes the decision to issue firearms? Who briefs the AFOs that attend at the scene, who monitors and controls events as they occur? Who processes intelligence and feeds it back to the officers on the ground?'

'The most senior officer present,' said Green.

'Precisely. Is it not the case, Inspector, that the Council of Europe Declaration on Police insists that, and I quote: "*Police officers shall receive clear and precise instructions as to the manner and circumstances in which they should make use of arms*"?'

'Yes sir, I believe so.'

'I thank you.' Traquair clicked his heels. 'No further questions, My Lord.'

'Mr Billings?'

The AD lifted his bum just slightly off his seat. 'No further questions My Lord.'

'Very well,' said the judge, 'owing to the lateness of the hour, we shall adjourn. Court will reconvene at ten tomorrow morning. Mr Green, thank you for your attendance. You are now free to leave.'

He turned his gaze on the jury. 'Once again, ladies and gentlemen, I charge you not to discuss this case with anyone in the duration.' One final drink of water, then the judge rose stiffly, fluffing out his red robes like a racy bride.

'Court!' shouted the macer, and everyone jumped to attention. The man with the slicked-back hair was quick to exit the gallery, but he caught Cath's eye and smiled as he left. She smiled back, waiting for Jamie's mum to make her ponderous way out of her seat.

'Who was that, love?'

'I'm not sure,' said Cath. 'Someone Jamie knows, I guess.'

'Och, that's nice. A policeman?'

'I suppose so.'

'Someone he works with?'

'I don't know Doris.'

Doris hirpled towards the stairs, leaning heavily on Cath's arm. 'What about yon lad Derek. Is he here? He's a lovely lad, so he is. D'you know he came and helped James paper over the kitchen for me, that time I left the gas on and—'

'No, Doris, Derek couldn't make it.'

'Och, that's a shame.'

Cath was watching Doris's feet, willing them to move a little quicker. Half the gallery had now cleared. At the door, they had to step aside as a man nudged his way back through. As he said, *I forgot my jacket* to the court officer, Cath lifted her head to see who it was. Sarah Brisbane's father looked back at her, his hand reaching for a crumpled coat on the back of a seat. Shame fired Cath's cheeks, and she pretended to rummage in her bag.

'Here, what's the rush?' piped Doris as the man tried to pass them once again. Hands on hips, she faced him down. 'I canny just jump out your road as quick as all that.'

Cath waited for the onslaught.

'Sorry, hen,' came the reply. 'I'm sorry.'

'Och, you're alright. This place gets to you, doesn't it?'

Cath tugged at her arm. 'C'mon, Doris, my mum'll have the car waiting outside.'

'Aye, it does that.'

'Are you here for James? That's awfy nice of you.'

'C'mon Doris,' urged Cath. '*Please.*'

'For who?' he asked.

'My son – James. That poor boy who's having to climb up in that glass box day after day . . .'

'Naw, missus,' Brisbane frowned. 'I'm here for my daughter. Sarah.'

'Oh.'

Brisbane had tattoos up and down both arms; Cath could see them dance above his twitching muscles. She looked for the court officer, but he must have gone through to the foyer. Then she saw Doris reach out her hand and touch Brisbane's cheek.

'I pray for you every night, you know. You, and her, and my boy.'

The man stood rigid, fists flexed. 'Is that right?'

Jesus, he was going to punch her.

'God bless you, well,' soothed Doris. 'I'm so sorry for your loss.'

Mr Brisbane put on his jacket and walked away. As Cath turned to make sure he'd gone, a hiss of blonde hair passed out of the doorway, one cream-clad shoulder swinging past Brisbane.

Doris tugged at Cath's arm. 'Oh Catherine love, that was awful. That poor man—'

'Would you just stop talking and get a bloody move on, Doris?'

Cath hurried into the corridor, but the woman had disappeared.

13

'Your mum nearly got a doing yesterday.'

'What?'

Jamie dropped the plastic spoon he was feeding Daniel with. He'd asked for the kids back, though it meant getting up at the crack of dawn each morning to take them over to Philippa's or his mum's or whoever they were being farmed out to that day. But he needed to smell them in their beds at night, taste their downy clean hair and peachy cheeks. It was something he always did, if he'd had a shite day, or been at a sudden death, or come back in from a filthy house; the kind where your feet would stick to the carpet, and the weans would be licking at bowls with the dogs. Blow away the badness, breathe in the goodness. Each perfect pore of his children's skin cleansing him quicker than all the showering and scrubbing in the world.

Cath continued tearing pieces from *The Herald*, angry twists of paper pointing up at him from the table.

'Well, not really, but she started talking to the Brisbane girl's father—'

'Sarah. Her name was Sarah.'

'Fine, Sarah. Anyway, she started telling him she was praying for him – I thought he was going to gub her.'

'What did he do?'

'Nothing. Just walked away.'

'So.' He scooped more spaghetti into Daniel's mouth, 'so she didn't nearly get a doing then.'

'What's a doin?' asked Eilidh.

'Eilidh, don't speak with your mouth full,' said Cath. 'No, not a doing, but she needs to—'

'So why say it?'

'Pardon?'

'Why tell lies just to wind me up? Sorry, Cath, am I not wound up enough for you already?'

'What's wound—'

'Eilidh!' they both shouted.

'Just eat your dinner,' said Cath, 'and stop interrupting. Lies? Lies. Yeah, let's talk about lies Jamie. After all, we're living one.'

Jamie wiped Daniel's bib across his mouth. 'Where the hell is that coming from?'

'Hell? God, aye, that's about right.'

'Cath. I don't understand. I've told you everything about that night.'

'What night?'

'The shooting.'

Cath threw her plate across the table. 'Well, I'm not talking about that bloody night!'

'Mum-mee!' squealed Eilidh. 'You're a very naughty girl. You splodged all over the table.'

'I don't care,' yelled Cath.

'But it's dirty!' breathed Eilidh. 'You gived Dan-pants a row for making messes.'

'Nuff Da! Nuff!' Daniel was shaking his head, pushing the spoon away.

'Okay son, ssh now.' Jamie undid the bib. 'Cath, you on drugs or something?'

'Jesus, that's rich,' she sneered, 'coming from the junkie.'

Jamie pushed his chair back. '*You* are a total cow. You know I can't sleep . . .'

'Well, let's be honest about something, eh? Junkie and an alkie, while we're at it. You go to sleep with a pill, wake up with a pill, and stay just this side of pished all the rest of the time to—'

'Catherine.' Jamie spoke quietly. 'Don't talk to me like that in front of my children.'

'Oh, but you can call me a cow though . . .'

'I did *not* call you a cow.'

'You bloody did.'

'You did Daddy, you did,' said Eilidh eagerly. 'You *bloody* did.'

'That's enough . . .'

'See Jamie. See. You've even got the kids swearing now. That's what it's like, living in this shitehole with you. I can't—'

'Moo – oo!' bellowed Daniel, clapping his tomato-smeared hands. 'Moo moo moo!'

'Clever boy!' squealed Eilidh. 'Clever boy. That's what the moo-cows say: Moo-oo. Moo-oo.' Louder and louder she shouted, encouraging her baby brother to do the same. His children screaming with desperate laughter, Eilidh's eyes pleading with him to say it was okay.

'That's right. Moo-oo!' Jamie yelled, waggling his fingers like horns above his head. 'Clever boy, Daniel.'

Cath ran from the table. 'Just shut up,' she sobbed. 'Shut up the bloody lot of you!'

The door slammed shut behind her.

'Oh, son.' Jamie bent to lift Daniel from the high chair. He kissed his fuzzy skull. 'Oh baby boy.'

'Daddy,' whispered Eilidh. He could hear her, but what could he say?

'Daddy.' It came again, softer even than before. Then a tiny sigh. Hiding behind his drooping fringe, he watched his daughter lift a napkin from the table, try to clear up the mess.

Day Four. The morning had gone badly. The controller who'd been on duty that night vowed he'd no clear memory of when exactly guns were mentioned, or by whom.

'You have to remember, My Lord, it's a very pressurised job, very reactive. That's why I don't take notes as such. Just update the incident on screen as it develops.'

Traquair had scanned the printout before him. 'Yes, very sketchily too. Let's see. *Constable Welsh attends. Report of gunfire . . . Confirmed by GM Two.* Ah yes, now this word "confirmed". Surely *that* is clear corroboration that gunfire was heard?'

The controller shrugged. 'I think they said they'd heard bangs or something when they arrived, but I don't recall them actually saying they'd seen anything.'

'Very well. Then, according to your update: *Nightshift superintendent advised. AFOs despatched and issue of f/a authorised.* So, plainly you deemed that there was sufficient evidence. Sufficient for your most senior officer on duty to authorise the deployment of firearms.'

'You'd need to ask him, sir.'

'Indeed I will, Constable. Thereafter, your update gets even more vague, doesn't it?'

'It was a very fast-moving situation sir – and I was relying on the recording . . .'

'Ah yes, the mysterious disappearance of the recordings—'

'Objection!' called the AD.

'My Lord, I am simply pointing out that this is a most unusual coincidence. The standard procedure, as we have been advised, is that recordings of all radio traffic would be logged immediately as productions. Now, we have evidence in the production log that this was done, but, alas, no sight of the elusive tapes.'

'Mr Traquair. Are you suggesting these recordings have been deliberately erased?'

A slight ripple through the jury.

'Well, My Lord . . .' Traquair arched one aristocratic eyebrow.

'Do you have any evidence whatsoever to substantiate a claim that this was done with malice aforethought? Or to indicate who might have done such a thing?'

'I do not, My Lord.'

'Then kindly avoid emotive language, and concern yourself with the facts at hand. It is for the jury to decide the significance, or otherwise, of the lack of consistent records here.'

The crew of Golf Mike Two were even worse when they came to give their evidence. The first cop claimed he thought his junior colleague had seen 'something' flash at the window. 'I just heard a bang, coming from round the front, and I radioed my neighbour to take cover. To be honest, I wasn't getting too close. We don't get paid enough to be heroes.'

The younger of the two looked nervous when he took the stand, all shambling gait and downcast eyes. Probably his first time in court, judging by the age of him. Jamie had felt very old, watching this pale young boy sway back and forth on his shiny shoes.

'No sir, it certainly wasn't me that said they saw a gun,' he said. 'We'd split up, you see, to check all round the tenement. Initially, I thought Constable Welsh had been shot at: he came running out the close as I arrived. Maybe someone said that to the controller? It was all really confusing, you know?'

'So we've heard. Tell me, then, just what you did see.'

'Well, like I say, when we got there, we parked the next street down, so my neighbour could go round the back lane. He told me to go to the front. I was just at the corner of Gryffe Street when I heard a really loud crack. Then my neighbour radioed to me to take cover.'

'Clearly, then, you both thought you were under some kind of attack?'

'Well, we didn't know what it was. It kind of echoed across the street. Like a sort of splintering roar is the best way I can describe it. You couldn't tell if it was coming from the house or the street.'

'So, in fear of your life, you then took cover?'

'No. I knew Constable Welsh had gone inside the flats. So, I started running towards the tenement – which was on my right as I approached. I then saw Constable Welsh running out the close. He waved at me to get back. Before I did though, I looked up, and saw the window of one of the first-floor flats had been smashed. Virtually the whole pane was out. Then I saw a girl's face – her head actually – half in, half out the first-floor window. Then her head went back in and it was just her hand. At first, I thought she was waving for help.'

'What made you think that?'

'It was a kind of frantic wave, like she was trying to attract attention.'

'Could it have been a brandishing type of action – ' Traquair shook his fist in the air – 'thus?'

'Objection! How can the witness state if a hand gesture is "brandishing"?'

'The witness is a professional law enforcer. I'm sure he has experience in discerning body language, My Lord.'

'Please rephrase the question, Mr Traquair,' said the judge.

'Constable, did it look like the girl was holding anything?'

'I couldn't really see; the curtains were flapping about in the wind.'

'So, what exactly did *you* report back to your controller?

'That I'd seen a girl at the window of the first-floor flat.'

'And did you say that she was armed?'

'No sir. All I could see was that the window had been smashed.'

'And did you notice the window was smashed before or after you heard the "loud bang"?'

'Oh, after.'

Jamie held his face between his freezing fingers. *Jesus wept, Traquair. You're supposed to be dismissing the 'it was just a chair' theory, not advertising it.*

Why was no one talking about the panic and the fear and how everyone was convinced she had a gun? Where was the defence's evidence to show that a firearm had been discharged inside the flat: the burn marks, the powder, the residue on Sarah's hands? Could they not have found anything, after all these months? And where was the bloody gun? He *had* seen a gun at the window; he had, he had, he had.

'Keep your chin up,' Len had whispered, when they adjourned for lunch. 'We've still plenty more witnesses to come.'

'What about Callum Welsh? You know, the cop that was hiding behind the car when I arrived? He's the one that was first on the scene.'

Len sighed. 'No show. He's filed a soul and conscience, I'm afraid. In hospital having his herniated disc shaved. Lovely.'

'Has my notebook turned up yet?'

'Not been lodged. No trace, no production label, and no mention of it on the productions list.'

Jamie couldn't face any more of his food. He pushed uneaten peas around his plate. The only veggie option they had on the menu was omelette, and eggs were just dead things too. The pub jukebox was competing with his mother's prattling: to him, to Jenny, anyone that would meet her eye. He pushed the plate away, feeling it stick on rings of spilt juice. A man at the bar asked for a half and a half. Rainbow prisms danced across Jamie's peas as the barmaid held a glass to the light, then reached up to the gantry. Jamie imagined lying on his back on the polished wood, pushing off hard with his feet and sucking from each optic as he slid across the length of the bar. How rich and brown the whisky would taste, smoky treacle burning down his throat, cut clear across with a shot of cool, clean vodka. Sweet perfumed gin was next, then more whisky, then . . . ach, stuff it, why not? A luxuriant dollop of Malibu to finish it off. What kind of Glasgow pub had Malibu on its gantry? Jamie sipped his pint of diluted orange juice. Cath had purged the house of every last drop of drink, and wouldn't let him out of her sight for a minute. He was already having a taster of the jail.

He wished he could die.

No one ate much. After lunch, they all walked around the back of the court, trying to ignore the cameras that preceded their every step. The reporters knew they couldn't question Jamie, or they'd get done for contempt of court. But, by God, they could film him. Record the anguished licking of his lips; film every time he tripped up on the kerb or pushed the wrong door open. Jenny had wedged herself in between the cameras and Cath, trying to shield them as Jamie and Len turned to go in the side door.

'Okay.' He kissed the top of Cath's head. 'We know what Coltrane's going to say, so try and not get too mad, right? I know what you're like.'

Cath smiled. 'Should I leave my dagger at reception?'

'Aye, probably for the best.'

Jenny whispered in Jamie's ear: 'Don't worry. I'll take the bawbag's legs from under him, one dark night when he thinks this is all over.'

'What's she saying about me?' asked Cath.

'Just that I'll sit on you, if you make a lunge for Coltrane,' said Jenny. 'Now, Jamesie-boy. You get in there and sit up straight. No picking your nose.'

One last time, Jamie pressed his lips hard into Cath's hair. 'Love you,' he mumbled. Then the big, heavy door swung shut and they were all gone. A security guard led him back to the cell passageway. He hated this charade. Allowed to eat lunch in public, then locked away in the dungeon until 2 p.m. Sitting in his suit, trying not to crease it or touch the grubby walls, listening to distant clangs and catcalls. Then being ordered to 'move it upstairs' by some jumped-up ned swinging a bunch of keys.

Back to the dock, gliding up the stairs like a pantomime baddie sprung from his trap. Right in front of the public gallery, leaving Jamie's back exposed and his face to the wall, towards the judge, and side on to the jury. Confronting damnation, or salvation; either way, it would be soon. He was flanked by two security guards, each of them puffed up and gallus, with not a neck between them. Quickly, he glanced behind him. Press were back again, loads of them, squeezed into the Perspex box that housed Sarah Brisbane's father and some other folk. They also knew it would be soon. Never once had Mr Brisbane looked at Jamie, never once had he done anything other than stare straight ahead. Jamie could see Cath, in her usual seat on the far right.

Every day the same, smiling faintly whenever he caught her gaze. Which he tried to avoid. He kept his hands down, clenched in his lap until the judge entered.

'Court!'

Everyone stood, waited till his lordship had eased himself onto his throne, and then the merry-go-round began again.

Coltrane looked young standing in the witness box. Big rabbit eyes and rubbery lips, which quivered as he gave his age and service. *Six years*, and an inspector already. Of course the guy had panicked. Had worried he would get the blame, lose his chance for promotion. But surely now, when he had sworn an oath, and he was standing there, looking at the man he might send to jail . . .

Look at me. Have the balls to look at me.

Surely then, before it had all gone too far, Coltrane would say he was mistaken and agree that perhaps he *had* said Sarah had a gun, and maybe he *had* been a bit too hasty to jump to conclusions and . . . *please, man. Dear Jesus, please do the right thing. I don't want to go to prison* . . .

A subtle, below-the-counter fist dunted him in the stomach. 'Haw, you, sit back,' muttered the guard. Jamie hadn't realised he was leaning so far forwards out of the dock, knuckles over the edge like he was contemplating a dive. He slumped back, the bench hard and unyielding as a chapel pew.

'Now, Inspector Coltrane. There seems to be some confusion over what actually happened that night; or, at least, that's what the defence would have us believe.'

Even though it was the Advocate Depute who had spoken, Coltrane gave a courtesy nod towards the judge, just like they taught you at Tulliallan. 'No confusion at all, My Lord.'

And there, in that cocky, careful phrase, Jamie knew he was lost.

'My recollection is perfectly clear. Following an anonymous report of loud bangs from the vicinity of Gryffe Street, I had our controller dispatch two officers in our Golf Mike Two vehicle to investigate. One of my uniformed beat officers, Constable Welsh, who was on foot patrol nearby, also picked up the call. Constable Welsh spoke briefly to an elderly resident – the witness Mitchell – who advised that the noises had come from the flat above. I believe that, without consulting me, Constable Welsh then decided to approach the flat in question. Around this time, Golf Mike Two arrived at the scene. As they arrived, they, along with Constable Welsh, heard another loud bang, but I understand they were unable to ascertain where it had come from.'

'And, at this time, from the three officers present, did you form the opinion that a firearm had been discharged?'

'Well sir, in these situations, it's always advisable to request professional back-up from AFOs – that's authorised firearms officers – which I did. They are, after all, the personnel trained to make these kinds of judgements.'

'Of course, of course. So, what else did you do, Inspector?'

'Obviously, I immediately attended at the scene, in order that I could control and plan the operation. I had my officers make the area secure, as a precautionary measure, until I received further updates from the AFOs.'

'And other than these mysterious "bangs", was there anything to indicate to you that this may or may not be a firearms incident?'

'I believe when the anonymous report was phoned in, the caller said it sounded like a gun going off. Of course, when the police receive a call like that, we have to be prepared. My controller, as well as alerting me, made contact with the nightshift superintendent, who, as the most senior officer on duty within the force at that time, can make the decision to authorise the *issue* of firearms.'

'So that doesn't mean authorising their use?'

'No sir, simply agreeing that firearms officers can attend the incident, and that the firearms can be taken from their locked box, either within a police office or within the firearms vehicle. Most certainly *not* authorising that they can be fired at will.'

'Objection.' Traquair raised his pen, as though he was taking bids at an auction.

'"At will" suggests a degree of wanton randomness.'

The AD smirked, 'And your point is, my learned friend?'

'Mr Billings,' intoned the judge. 'This is not a matter for levity.'

'Apologies, My Lord. Inspector Coltrane, tell me. Beyond the "loud noises" – any sign of a firearm? Any bullets on the ground? Any indication *whatsoever* that a gun had been discharged?'

Coltrane shook his head, more firmly and emphatically than was required. 'None at all, sir. However, I observed that a chair had been thrown from the window of a first-floor flat at the locus – a fact which I pointed out to the AFOs when they attended.'

Now wait a bloody minute . . . Jamie coughed, tried to get Len or Traquair to look at him, but they both were too busy, Len stroking his moustache, Traquair making notes. Or maybe doodling his initials on the blotter.

'I see. So you were in fact downplaying the threat of firearms?'

'I was simply pointing out to the men that there may have been another reason for the noises. However . . . I . . .'

'Go on, Inspector.'

'I felt the AFOs in question were both a little – um – gung-ho. Particularly the accused, Mr Worth.'

Is anybody awake down there? Say something, for God's sake. Was this why they made the accused sit through a trial? Not in the interests of fairness and transparency, but as an additional punishment, confirming your powerlessness in the face of confections and lies?

'Gung-ho, My Lord, means overly confident, in a reckless—'

'I know perfectly well what it means, Mr Billings.'

Billings nodded his contrition. 'Indeed, My Lord. In what way "gung-ho", Mr Coltrane?'

'Extremely keen to get involved in "some action", were I think the words that Constable Worth used.' A subtle head-shake. 'I've subsequently discovered that neither of these men had any real experience of dealing with a live firearms incident, which would probably explain their . . . excitement and eagerness—'

'Objection!' called Traquair.

At bloody last. The old tosser was awake.

'Sustained.'

'Hmm.' On slid the AD, smooth as his very own silk, '. . . and, is it difficult, in situations like these, to ascertain who is responsible for pointing, aiming and actually firing said weapons? Do you, as the most senior officer present, give that order, or is it a decision for the trained firearms officers?'

'I can really only provide the AFOs with the facts as I have them,' said Coltrane. 'It's then up to the trained AFO to make a professional judgement based on this information. Thereafter, my role is to assume overall control of the wider elements of the operation, deploying my officers in such a way as to support the AFO and minimise risk to public safety. Which I did: I had officers securing a cordon around the perimeter of the locus.'

He was like a kid who wanted a pat on the head.

'Tell me, at any time did you see a gun being waved or pointed from the window of the flat?'

'No, sir.'

'Did any of your men see such a weapon?'

'No, sir.'

'Just to be absolutely clear; beyond the anonymous call, there was no proof that a firearm had been discharged, or indeed was even present at the scene?'

'No sir, none at all – which is exactly why I urged caution and restraint, sir.'

Did you fuck, you lying little shite. You told me to blow her away to Kingdom Come. And you know *you did.*

'Thank you, Mr Coltrane.'

At last, Len deigned to look his way. Jamie shook his head, pointed at Traquair. Made his eyebrows rise up into his forehead, showing only the whites of his eyes. As many silent gestures as he could conjure to show frustration and despair. Eventually, Len whispered something to the QC, who nodded, rose.

'My Lord, the defence requests a brief adjournment to consult with our client.'

They moved through to a panelled anteroom, Len Mackenzie pushing Jamie inside. 'But would you listen to us, Jamie? Coltrane—'

'The bastard stitched me up,' shouted Jamie. 'He stood up and lied. Told them all *I* was a liar and that he'd never even said about the gun—'

'Precisely,' said Traquair. 'And we let him say all that. Just like he did in his statement.'

'Too right you did, *Crispian*. You gave him the chance to repeat it several times. How come you didn't jump about screaming "objection", "liar"—'

'Because, dear boy . . .' sniffed Traquair.

'Don't you patronise me, you old arsehole—'

'Right, you.' Len shoved a surprisingly firm hand into Jamie's chest. 'Now shut it and listen up. Don't you realise you're in the hallowed chambers of Her Majesty's High Court of Justiciary? Show a bit of damn respect!'

He fingered his ridiculous bow tie. Chartreuse green and burgundy, it toned with the green leather chairs and soft rose walls of the office they were in.

'As I was saying; we deliberately let Coltrane lead himself down the garden path, tie himself up in knots, so it's all on record. Then Crispian here will play with him a bit, teasing out his self-importance, bumming up the fact that he, Coltrane, and only Coltrane was in charge. That way, when Jinky Robertson testifies that Coltrane told you both, *specifically* that Sarah Brisbane had a gun, and encouraged the two of you, against your own professional advice, I might add, to take the offensive to her—'

Traquair interrupted. 'Then the blame, dear boy, slips from you to Coltrane, and shows him up for the liar that he is. You get the benefit of the doubt, and I – we – make legal history.'

'That's right, Crispian,' beamed Len. 'A nice little stated case. Corporate homicide: the time is ripe.' Len's moustache shivered. 'I can smell it in the air. Mmm. No longer will the poor solitary polisman have blood on his hands for a firearms incident that was clearly an operational balls-up from the beginning. There were more fingers on this trigger than yours, young James. Once your man Jinky Robertson takes the stand, we can prove Coltrane lost the plot. The wee shite couldny organise a ménage. Not only that, but he gave you duff information, has therefore lied on oath – and quite possibly destroyed evidence to protect himself. Once Coltrane's evidence crumbles, we'll get the controller back in the stand. I'm sure, with a little gentle coaxing, he'll remember a bit more about what exactly was said by whom to whom. So,' hands smacked firmly on Jamie's shoulders, 'what d'ya say, Jamsie my man? Do you trust your old Uncle Len? Not to mention Granpaw Traquair, eh?'

The court officer came in. 'We'll need to take you back through, Mr Worth. That's his Lordship finishing off his coffee the now.'

'Jamie?' said Len. 'Do you trust me?'

'I've no option,' he replied. Dry sand in his stomach, a dust-bowl breeze.

'Good man, good man.'

Jamie was led back into the dock. *Assume the position.* Front-row seat as well. Traquair took a drink, swished the water around his mouth. Placed the glass on the table. Picked up his pen. 'Tell me, Inspector. You say there was nothing – nothing that is, other than the significant concerns of an anonymous caller; other than the ear-splitting cracks that terrified your officers, other than the scenes of chaos and disarray that littered the streets outside – to indicate that a firearm had been used. Was it not the case that a check carried out on the occupants of the flat, namely one Gerard Brisbane, indicated that a dangerous criminal resided there?'

'Yes sir, but there was no mention made of firearms.'

'I see. So is armed robbery not . . . ?'

'I believe a knife was used.'

'Ah.' Traquair tapped his big horseteeth with his pen. 'Well, in any case, I put it to you that you did indeed advise my client that the female whom we now know to be the deceased, Sarah Brisbane, was brandishing a gun.'

'No sir, I did not.'

'Did you not state the following?' Traquair paused to look down at his notes: '*She's been seen and heard firing a gun out the window onto the street.*'

'No, sir, I did not.'

'Is that so? Are you absolutely sure about that?'

'Absolutely.'

Traquair addressed the jury. 'Ladies and gentlemen, I ask you to remember that statement. Note it carefully. So, Inspector, tell me this: did you at any time, during the ensuing confusion, urge Mr Worth to shoot?'

'No sir.'

'Did you utter these words: "get bloody ready"?'

'I don't recollect using any language like that. I may have told the officers to be prepared for any eventuality.'

'Objection!' Billings raised a languid hand. 'It's not Inspector Coltrane who's on trial here. *He* did not pull the trigger.'

Traquair spread his arms wide. 'My Lord, I'm trying to ascertain a very important principle here. As I mentioned previously, the Council of Europe Declaration on Police states that,' he pushed his specs high up on his nose: ' "*Police officers shall receive clear and precise instructions as to the manner and circumstances in which they should make use of arms."'*

Specs off, with a magician's flourish.

'It is therefore critical that we understand exactly what was said, what was instructed, and by whom. Regrettably, young Sarah Brisbane died in tragic circumstances on the night in question. And that is the desperate reality my traumatised client will have to live with for the rest of his days. But, whose fault *exactly* was it? Was it *solely* Constable Worth's decision to fire: this brave officer, operating in conditions of darkness, interpreting a movement as a threat to his life, given dangerous, erroneous, unconfirmed information and direction by his superiors—'

'Objection!' Finally, Billings seemed to be losing his poise. Mottled colour rose in his cheeks as he conferred with the young fiscal at his side. 'This line of questioning cannot be sustained. It's uncorroborated nonsense.'

'Indeed, My Lord, it can be corroborated. And it will be.'

The judge waved his hand. 'Very well, Mr Traquair, continue.'

'Or was it the fault of the commanding officer, Inspector Coltrane, who, by his own admission "controlled and planned" the operation? If my client's decision to shoot was based on an honest belief that he, his fellow officers, innocent members of the public, were at imminent risk from this volatile, allegedly armed, incoherent young lady – if he had been *categorically* told, by a superior officer, whom he's been trained to respect and obey – that she was armed—'

Billings rose to his feet. 'Really My Lord, this is unacceptable. Mr Coltrane has been most emphatic in his rebuttals of this spurious allegation.'

The judge nodded. 'Mr Traquair, you have presented no evidence to give credence to this claim, which is, in any case, a rather weak assertion of "reasonable belief".'

'My Lord, I agree. A reasonable belief on its own may not be sufficient for acquittal. This belief must be grounded in an objective background. And it is precisely this objectivity which I will endeavour to display, when I go on to question our defence witnesses.'

'Well, I look forward to that eventuality, Mr Traquair. Then, perhaps, all will become clear.'

Jamie rubbed his hands together, then folded them, tucking each hand beneath its opposite armpit. His fingers, toes, even his nose, all bitter cold. The only thing clear was that it was him and Jinky against the world. And that they should turn up the heating in this bloody courtroom.

14

Glasgow Grey. It was a specific blend of mackerel smells and persistent drizzle; decayed, sooty stonework and poverty-pallored flesh. It was the utter weight of despair that slumped Anna's shoulders as she switched on her office light and began another day. Back at her grubby wee sub-office in the least salubrious segment of Glasgow's east end. One of many grubby wee sub-offices that ringed the city, serving forlorn, still-fighting communities whose branding switched from *special priority* to *socially excluded* to *socially inclusive*, depending on who was in power. Yet they gave these places such pretty names: Easter House, the Bishop's Loch, *Chateaulait*. Nits' Hill was something of an aberration, mind.

She pushed her stupid pen-pot to the edge of her desk. *A present from Rothesay*, so it told her, left by the previous incumbent, who'd been so keen to escape that he must have fled the building, squealing '*hang the pen-pot, I'm out of here!!*' Anna flopped her cheek onto the vinyl blotter, let the poison pulse. She hadn't made the grade. All her preparation, all her commitment, all her desperate conviction that she could make her mark on the world; thrown away by her own stupid temper, her lack of self-control. Every word still felt raised and livid as a scar. It had all been going so well. But it wasn't Anna who was beginning a two-year stint with the Police and Justice Task Force at the UN.

They had taken it right to the wire: no one knew who had been selected until the absolute conclusion of the three months. And then it was a flurry of booking plane tickets and licking wounds, before trailing off in disconsolate dribs and drabs to the airport, leaving to the victors the spoils. Interpol, the Hague, Darfur Command Control . . . In half an hour, Anna had to visit a junkie, who wanted to complain the polis stole his stash when they jailed him. She checked her notebook. 14 Craigievar Street, name of Kerr. David Kerr.

David. As Anna registered the name, her insides turned. Just a little twist, like a fishtail through water. He had kissed her one last time before he left America. Staking his claim in the foyer, in full view of the rest of the delegates.

'Good luck, Inspector Cameron. I hope you don't get it, though.'

'That's not very nice.'

'Yes, but then I'll get to see you sooner.'

'So you will. Bye, then.'

Had David sensed she was distracted? Did he think it was the heavy-lidded torpor of a woman spent with lust? Some brave resistance against departure angst? Or could he simply tell she was thinking of another man; that impatient ushering out of the old to bring in the new? The night before, after the TV report, after she'd convinced David she was fine, and that it must have been something that she'd eaten, and when he'd finally, finally, gone, she had immediately picked up her mobile. Her memory card still held all her Flexi Unit's mobile numbers, but it was Jenny that she dialled. They had come to an uneasy truce, and Jenny knew her history. Plus, she'd adopted Alice's mum.

'Jenny?'

'Yeah?'

'It's Anna Cameron.'

'Anna? I thought you were in America, putting the world to rights?'

'Have you seen the news? The shooting?'

A transatlantic hesitation. 'Yeah.'

'Is it him?'

'Anna, you've got to keep out of this. There's nothing you can do—'

'I know. Just tell me if it's him.'

'It's Jamie.'

She had lain awake for hours. Same sad, frantic phrasing playing; Jamie, her Jamie, had killed a wee girl. All in a rush, it had come at her. Picturing him at home, his trembling hands through thick, black hair.

It was her fault.

She knew what Jamie was like. The rage, the machismo. The bold change of direction, becoming an AFO. The brash bravado he pretended was heroic. It had been his way of building up his self-respect. Aye, that wee, sleekit, cow'rin tim'rous beastie that Anna had kicked in the balls, then spat on for good measure.

She'd scanned through all the TV channels, trying to find out more about the shooting, and, as she scanned, she found her hands retracing David's touches. The bulletin was always the same, only with the brother's hysterics cropped off the end. She should have asked Jenny every detail, all the whys and whos and what-was-happenings. Maybe she could phone Easterhouse, see if there were any updates.

Then she'd got out of bed, dragged her suitcase down from the top of the wardrobe. She could get a standby flight, anywhere in the UK, then hire a car . . . or go to . . . Why was there wet on her face? Why was she weeping for him all over again? Eventually, she'd fallen asleep, and, in the sober morning, was grateful that sleep had intervened. What kind of an idiot would she have sounded, pissed and snivelling to one of her sergeants? Best thing all round that she was in America. Jenny had been right – what was it, truly, to do with her?

Keep everything locked away in different boxes; that's what Jamie had told her years ago. So Anna did. He'd have been proud of her. She just shut off all the clamourings, and shifted up a gear. It was easy, being so far away from home, focused on something else. She simply watched no more news, took on additional projects, worked from sky-waking dawn to sky-scraping dusk and jettisoned herself towards the top of the world. So close, so close, she almost touched the stars.

Most evenings after David left, she had one drink after dinner, then went to her hotel to study what they'd learned, maybe rewrite some presentation notes – even practise out loud in front of the mirror, once she'd drawn the curtains tight and told herself no one need ever know. The next two years were predicated on the very last presentation and interview, when it would be just Anna versus the selection panel. No competitors to drag her down or cut her off mid-sentence. She knew she'd been performing well. Then, so had most of them. Her proudest involvement had been working with the CATW team. They'd chosen her because of her submission proposal. Dlia was very enthusiastic; she'd already heard of Glasgow's efforts to bring together agencies like the council, the police, the health board and refugee organisations. 'Make sure you mention that at your selection board,' she'd urged.

And Anna had, regaling the panel with details of all the work going on in Glasgow: how they provided counselling, found interpreters, even steered women into jobs and further education.

'We call it TARA: Trafficking Awareness Raising Alliance. I believe it's the only organisation of its kind in the United Kingdom.'

Her interviewers seemed impressed, had asked her intelligent questions. Then, out of nowhere, one plumpish man had casually flicked a line so thin as to be invisible. As all the best lines are.

'You're clearly committed to women's rights, Inspector Cameron. Obviously, an important element of any job with the United Nations would be an understanding of cultural issues across the world – which may not always comply with your own, um, views.'

She knew exactly where this was going. Confident, she thought she would toy a little with the bait, then spit it out in a flurry of convincing rhetoric.

Jamie killed a wee girl, Anna.

Go away

'I understand that, sir. I believe it's vital to remain consistent in my approach to every person I encounter, irrespective of gender, sexuality, race, religion or belief. In my current role as a police supervisor in Glasgow, I liaise with many different community groups. And previously, when I worked in Gorbals, the largest mosque in Glasgow was virtually adjacent to my police office. I frequently attended meetings and events there.'

'I see.' The man nodded. 'You obviously have an insight into observing cultural mores. So, tell me this, Inspector, would you wear a veil if serving in a Muslim country?'

Her response was instant and instinctive.

'Absolutely not.'

'But surely – you've just told us that you respect diversity. If the veil is the cultural norm . . .'

Too late, too late, she began to feel the reel, splashing out of her depth as indignant anger buoyed her on. She realised she was furious. At whom? This chubby man?

'What if the cultural norm is female genital mutilation? Should I condone that too?'

What was he doing with a gun anyway? Stupid, stupid. How could he?

'Inspector Cameron, that is totally different. Female circumcision involves actual physical harm.'

'But it's still about the subjugation of women, no matter how it's dressed up. You can say it's about "respect" for women, or for their "protection", but, in reality, it's all about saying . . .'

Jesus Christ, she was sinking like bricks. But she couldn't, wouldn't stop. *And you never even phoned him, you cow.*

'. . . no, about physically *showing,* that women are unequal. Either they're wanton temptresses who need to be covered up, or they're so vulnerable that they have to be locked away from view, unable to participate fully in the world in which they live. Either way, a veil says a women is not considered to have the same rights as a man. And I would presume the United Nations would deplore such a view.'

She stopped, took a slow draught of water. All eyes were on her, waiting for her to say something that would remove the barbs, tell them it was all just a little misunderstanding, and *of course* she would respect local values.

The man looked as if he would choke. 'We deplore *any* views that disparage firm religious beliefs, not to mention those that dismiss a woman's right to choose how she defines herself. Miss Cameron, we're talking about centuries of culture here – surely you have to be sensitive to these things?'

'That's what they said about abolishing slavery. Look, the bottom line is, if I'm serving in a country as an officer of the law, I'll wear my uniform, and only my uniform, while on duty.'

'But you have to understand that, in some of the countries we work in, you will be viewed as a woman first and foremost.'

'So, by apologising for the fact I'm a woman, and colluding with this . . . this visual stigma, are you saying I'd then make the job of enforcing the law, in fact, of demonstrating and upholding nothing but respect and equality for *everyone*, all the more easy?'

Oh, Anna. All these eloquent phrases flying from your mouth, and there's your brain – missing in action.

'Visual stigma? Inspector, many women are proud to wear the veil.'

'Sir, this issue is absolutely not about my lack of respect or understanding for cultural diversity. This is about me. I don't define myself by my gender. It's my uniform, and how I conduct myself, that earns respect. And it's the office my uniform stands for, which I would be representing in any country I served in. *That's* what articulates who I am, not the fact that I have breasts.'

The interview ended shortly after that. Hands shaking, face puce, she'd avoided speaking to any of her colleagues, and slipped away instead to an anonymous bar. Where she'd behaved with all the dignity and decorum her uniform merited, and got pished as a fart.

So much meticulous, balanced preparation. And there was Anna, blasting out loose opinions that only turned to firm conviction in the very process of uttering them. She didn't know yet why she'd said all that stuff, or even if she really meant it. It happened far too often; her seizing on a good going debate, strand upon strand of billowing argument pleating fragments of dormant thought, and suddenly she would be on fire, advocating absolutes she never knew she believed. Why had she not just said 'yes'? *I'll wear a veil, dark glasses or a big straw hat if you want. Just gie's the job.*

But she'd not. And so, here she was, back in dear old Glesga toon. At least Alice had been pleased to see her, after the pre-scribed period of nonchalant bum-washing and flagrant refusal to come and be stroked. Anna wondered if anyone else would be. Now she was home, she could no longer ignore what was happen-ing to Jamie. Couldn't avoid it; it was the talk of the steamie at work. Probably canteen fodder in every police office in the country, but worse here, in Glasgow, where it all happened. She could not stand listening to the pontificating and mannered outrage. The speculation, the saddened shaking of heads. The sick jokes and cruel comments.

What d'you call a man getting shagged three ways?

Answer: Jamie Worth – one, by the job, two, by the fiscal, and three, by a hairy big bitchmaster in the jail.

They meant nothing by it, it was just their way of digesting the reality, shifting the spotlight, covering their ears and going la-la-la, what a stupid arsehole; that would never happen to me; there but for the grace of God go I. Anna had tried blocking her ears too, averting her eyes and never once remembering his beautiful mouth on hers.

She pushed her hair behind her ears. That was a lie. She'd crushed Jamie away out of sight for the last three years, and now he was back with a vengeance. Did he think about her at all? When his life was disintegrating, did he ever wish Anna was there beside him? Poor, poor baby. She didn't want to see Jamie's face, not for real. But then, just last week, she had found herself standing in the High Court, drawn to the room that held his trial. Pulled, as if wire hooks had pierced her skin and were dragging her down the passageway. Gaining closer, closer on him, tasting sour despair. Lurking in the doorway, in a netherworld, neither in nor out, just watching his wife in her rightful place, and the dancing and prancing of wigs and gowns. Wanting, so badly, to breathe the same air that he breathed. To smile at him, each crinkle of her eye, each small, tender comma around her mouth whispering: *it's going to be okay.*

It was much easier not to face Jamie. Or even the thought of Jamie, and the hell he must be living through. She kept slamming the door shut, but gaunt fingers would prise it open, buzzy voices would whisper through, surrounding her with Jamie white noise. It was probably why she'd pressed 'self-destruct' at her interview, if she was of a mind to probe the deepest recesses of her subconscious. And hey, if she was going there anyway . . .

Probably why she'd lost touch with David.

A few days after David had left the UN, he'd called her on her mobile.

'Where have you been hiding, stranger?'

'Nowhere.'

'I've been emailing you.'

'I know.'

'So why have you not replied?'

'Been really busy.'

The reception was bad.

'What?'

'I said, I'm really busy. Scunnered, in fact. I need a break.'

'I never had you down as a quitter, Anna Cameron.'

His voice was friendly. She was far away.

'I'm not. It's just . . . I'm always focusing, focusing: this job, the next step, who's getting promoted – and why isn't it me? I'm feeling a bit focused out, to be honest.'

'Well, just focus on answering your emails, that's all I ask.'

He waited for a response, then carried on. 'I wanted to tell you this in person anyway. You're now talking to,' he coughed, 'the new PF Depute for Glasgow and Strathkelvin; Sheriff and High Court of Justiciary, of course.'

'Good for you.'

Was it good for her? Possibly. In time. Her heart had puckered, a tight little rosebud.

'Means we might be seeing a bit more of each other – if you don't get the job, I mean.'

'Uh huh.'

'Where are you just now?' David's voice echoed down the line.

'In the bath.'

'Oh, baby. Don't do this to me.'

'Sorry, you're cracking up. I need—'

To press that little red button. Bye.

David phoned several times, sent more emails. She'd saved the last few:

Subject: Continual & Prolonged Rejection
If you don't reply to this one, I'll assume:

1. You hate me
2. My willy was too small
3. I have extreme halitosis
4. You've met a hobo and have set up shopping trolley together
5. You're finding yourself in NY, but promise to get in touch when you return.

(please tell me it's option 5)
D xxxx

Subject: Re: Continual & Prolonged Rejection
Option 5 – but I won't hold you to it, I promise. Have got a bit lost.
A x

Subject: Re: Re: Continual & Prolonged Rejection
Option 5 is available under an extended warranty, with interest-free credit over the next – ooh – 12 months anyway. Just heard you didn't get the job. Am I allowed to be happy? Please look me up when you get home. Don't leave it too long, or I'll have explored the Dear Green Place all on my lonesome – and I'd much prefer an experienced local to show me the ropes!
Take it easy,
D xx

So why couldn't Anna just go to the High Court to see him instead?

She opened a bag of pickled onion crisps, crunching spiky bursts of acid deep into her molars. She'd bought two bags this morning on her way to work, eschewing her usual latte. When she was little, she'd have a piece and crisps when she came in from school: soft pan bread topped with salt and vinegar. Her mother always gave her a row if she caught her though, so it was a habit to scoff them quick. Anna tipped up the packet and licked the fragments off her hands. Sometimes, you had to give yourself a wee treat. From her desk drawer, she took out a compact mirror, checked her chin for crumbs. Grinned at herself; no potato on her teeth. Hair still neat, still blonde. Just.

You know, you still look good when you smile, girl. You just don't do it enough.

Then she took a deep breath, opened her diary, and dialled David's number. One ring, two rings—

A sharp knock at her door. Phone smashing onto the hook.

'What?'

'That's the paper in, boss.' One of her cops dropped a tabloid on her desk. 'Front page again. I think—'

'Colin, I'm not interested in what you think. I'm interested in what you *do*, all right?'

A tiny shake of his head. 'Yes, Inspector. *Ma'am.*' As the cop pulled the door shut, she could hear him muttering to someone outside. The words '*time of the month*' seemed to feature.

Oh, no, pal. This lasts all year long.

'Killer Cop Was Desperate for Action!' bawled the newspaper headline. Anna licked more vinegar from her fingertips, then threw the red-top straight in the bin. She was sick of telling them she didn't read this junk.

In her room was a silvered mirror. It was old, the backing coming off, and she kept it under her bed with her other treasures, packed ready and waiting for when her mother came to fetch her. The girl held the mirror up, trying to see the top of her head, see if it was getting any darker. Her hair was yellow, like her father's, an ugly cow-shat straw. She took one hank in her hand, and wrenched and wrenched until it tore free, savouring the stings on her scalp and in her eyes. It was the most she'd felt in days. A deserved hurt for doing nothing. Some of the thicker hairs still had their roots, others wisp-weak.

'What you doing, ya daftie?'

Her brother came in, sat beside her on the bed. His fingers touched her head, came away red. 'Gonny stop doing that? You'll end up all baldie.'

He held open his other hand, to show her coins. 'Look. I knocked some dosh to get us chips. You hungry?'

She shrugged.

A hard-heeled banging coming up the stairs. That thick, sickening slur. 'Come here, you wee fuckers. Who the fuck knocked my dole?'

Her brother leapt up as the door swung open, dropping the coins onto her bedspread.

'Wisny me, Da. It wisny me.'

'You cunt, ya,' said her father, smashing his fist into her brother's nose.

15

The smooth walnut-cased clock ticked on and on, each coughing clunk another second gone. Jamie sat in the dark, listening like he did when he was a wee boy at his gran's, waiting for the low chimes of the quarter-hour. He shivered in his dressing gown. The lounge was cold, the heating long switched off. One hand rested on the telephone, as it had done this last hour. Jinky was up tomorrow, that squat wee git whom he never thought he liked but was now his only hope. Jinky's statement had finally come in, two pages that basically told the same tale as Jamie. It agreed that Coltrane had told them the girl was armed, that they had been reluctant to deploy. Two pages that were basic, perfunctory and lacked any of the sense of chaos and confusion of that night. Would it be enough? It would all depend how convincing Jinky was in the box.

Domb. A quarter-chime chunk from his life.

Jamie picked up the phone. No contact with any witnesses; it was a prerequisite of his bail. But what had he to lose? And how would they ever know? Quickly, before he changed his mind once more, Jamie dialled Jinky's number. That noise again. It would be the big tree in next door's garden, pressing on the wire. But it was getting worse. There was like an echo now when you spoke. He'd phone them tomorr—

He'd not be here tomorrow.

That's right, James. You think positive.

The phone rang three or four times before a sleepy voice answered.

'Aye?'

'Jinky. Sorry. Did I wake you?'

'Jamie? S'at you?'

There was a shuffling noise, something clicking. A light switch?

'Aye, look, I just needed to check you were okay for tomorrow.'

'What? I've got a frigging citation fae the High Court, pal. I'm hardly likely to do a runner.'

'No, I don't mean that. I know you'll be there. I just need to know. You know.'

'Know what?'

'Are you still going to say, well, what we spoke about.'

'John?' A woman's voice rose shrill in the background. 'Who the hell is that?'

'Look Jamie,' hissed Jinky, 'the wife's cracking up. You canny keep phoning me like this. I'll see you in the morning, okay?'

But he'd only phoned him this once. Slowly, Jamie put the receiver back in its cradle, and went upstairs. Without switching on any lights, he felt his way around Daniel's tricycle, around the pile of dirty washing on the bedroom floor, and slipped into bed. With dawn would come today, tomorrow and that would be it. Once Jinky took the stand, the trial would be over for better or for worse. He turned on his side, careful not to bump Cath.

For days now, all Cath had shown Jamie was simmering fury, and he didn't understand. She recoiled from his touch, then half relented, then looked at him like Medusa – worse even than when Eilidh was a baby, and he'd thought Cath was truly going mad. He'd learned then just to leave her alone. Jamie could hear the hiss of her inbreaths now, regular as the clock tick echoing from downstairs. It was probably the stress of the trial. Each of them wrapped in separate anxieties, ready to explode, or implode, or both. And so they danced around one another, snapping and grunting, when they should have been bound together.

He eased the quilt a little further over his shoulder. Traquair had talked a good game today, mind, speaking a hybrid language that both the judge and jury could understand. Maybe they still had some kind of case. Jinky's testimony would back it up, prove that Coltrane had told them about the gun, that Jamie thought he had reason to shoot, and maybe – please God, maybe – he'd have a chance. But Jamie couldn't allow himself hope, not yet. For, if he imagined freedom, if he imagined that tomorrow the judge would tell the jury there was no case against him, would apologise to him and tell him he'd upheld his duty and was free to go, if he imagined that he'd taken a flier that night and they'd had a lovely holiday, if he imagined that he'd never volunteered to carry a gun, never thought he could do some good by it, never thought he should stand up and be counted and say *Aye*. If he imagined that he'd become a bank clerk or a hotel manager or a window cleaner or a dentist. If he imagined that Sarah Brisbane was lying on her bed doing homework, planning how she'd wear her hair for the weekend.

If.

'Jamie.'

'What?'

'You awake?'

He reached for Cath in the dark. 'Well, duh.'

Shit, he shouldn't have said that. He tensed his arm, ready to swipe it away.

'Duh, yourself.'

Through the blackness, he could feel sudden dampness on his cheek. He stretched out his jaw. Blinked and blinked again. 'Can you not sleep?'

'Jamie, I need to talk to you. I need you to tell me something.'

'What?' He sat up.

'No. Please don't put on the light.'

It didn't sound like Cath, this disembodied voice beside him. She sounded younger, much younger, and very scared.

'Alright, honey. What is it?'

Such a silence, low and snarling. Like all his life was waiting to pounce.

'I . . . I can't . . .'

'Cath – what is it?'

'Jamie, you've got to help me.'

That wasn't Cath's voice. It was a little lost girl, a little girl he'd broken. Jamie licked at the side of his mouth. He could hear her blowing. Did she know about the badness game too?

'When all this began, well . . . there was something. There was something you tried to tell me. One night, when we were lying here, and I asked you not to.'

A cold sickness slid from his heart to his guts. 'Mm?'

'I need you to tell me what it was.'

Yes, she did. And, in that moment, he recognised his life was over. The life he knew and was trying, pathetically, to cling to had gone, and with it, his youth and his aspirations and all the beautiful promises that had beckoned to him from the top of the world. They'd disappeared long before he killed Sarah Brisbane.

Now he was skidding on the scree he'd piled so high, scrabbling to get back up, slipping further and further as the desperation grew, and even now, he'd do anything to halt it.

'I was going to tell you something,' he began, 'something that would make you change the way you feel about me.' Then, a tentative anchor: 'Do you still want to know?'

'Do you still want to tell me?'

'No, because it doesn't matter any more.'

'What if it matters to me?'

Coiled now, every sinew taut and quivered to the point it could not retract. Could only spring forward in the darkness.

'I slept with Anna Cameron.'

As he said it, he found himself reciting the Lord's Prayer in his head, like he did as a sleepless child when he knew the bogey man was lurking right behind his bed, like he did standing on a wall, being told to jump. Like he did in the moments after his son was born, pale blue and silent. Like he did when the eggy smoke died away and blood began to spew through low clouds.

Waiting, waiting for the end of days.

'I knew that.' Cath's words hung, devoid of any feeling. Just a bland acceptance of the facts. She didn't understand.

'No Cath, I don't mean at Tulliallan. I mean later . . . I mean after, you know. When we were together.'

'Uhuh.' Then, like a yelp: 'When?'

'Years ago.'

'When exactly?'

'When I was working with her. You know, the Flexi Unit.'

Each word another rip in their flesh.

'Just before I was pregnant with Daniel then.'

'Yes.'

One flesh. That made other flesh.

'I see. And that was it? This big thing you wanted to tell me?'

'Yes.'

'I see.' The words oozed out of her like a puncture. Silent hisses, growing louder as her body hunched into a shadow darker than all the rest.

'Well, like I said, I knew that. I fucking knew it, Jamie, all the time I had your son growing like a leech in my gut, wanting to tear him out because he had your genes, wanting to kill myself and her and you.' She was shouting now. 'Keeping it inside, letting it burn because I was too fucking frightened to be on my own, a postnatal nutter with two weans and no money.'

'Cath, please – the kids.'

'The kids? Oh, you're worried about your kids are you?' But her voice dropped low again. 'Christ, it's burned and burned till I had nothing left. Or, at least, I thought—'

'When? How did you know?'

'A letter. I got a *letter* from a concerned "friend", who thought I should know . . . how did it go again, oh yeah, that you were a "gaffer's tout".'

Jamie switched on the lamp. 'Who was – was it Jenny? That wee . . .' He stopped when he saw Cath's face. Green eyes dripping despair, like an animal about to die.

'Why?' she whimpered. 'Did *she* know too?'

'I . . . well—'

'Jamie, did everyone know?'

'No, I don't, I never – I think she suspected, that's all. I mean, no one . . . baby, don't cry. Please, Cathy – please . . .'

'Leave me alone.'

Cath turned on her side, away from him.

'I'll go and sleep in with the kids.'

'Don't. Stay with me.' Her voice was muffled in the pillow. 'She came to see you at court, you know. I saw her.'

'Oh, Cath. I am so sorry.' Once more, he bent his arms towards her. 'I love—'

'Don't touch me. Don't you fucking touch me.'

'Look, I'll go next door.'

'No,' she cried, 'I need to know. Did you ask her to come to court? I need you to speak and say nothing and tell me everything and shut it out. Please shut it out.' Her hands winding around her head, her elbows daggers at his face.

'I don't want to hear it and I don't want to see, but I do. Dear God, I do; every day, I see her. Her and you, her taking what's mine – I see it every day and it makes me hate you, but I hate me more for never asking . . .'

'Cath. I'm so sorry. No, I didn't ask her – I haven't seen her . . . since. God, I'm so sorry, I don't know what . . . it was once, only once, I swear.'

'But I see it every day.'

She took her hands away from her head, twisted her spine to gaze at him. Eyes swollen, her lips shrunk to bitter strings. 'Every day it happens. Don't you understand?'

He thought of Sarah, blood and body arcing to form a dying 'Y' as the pressure lessened on his index finger and the butt kicked hard against his shoulder.

'Yes, I understand.'

Cath curled up, her back once more to Jamie. Sick surges of guilt and misery washed him as his wife dissolved in their wake. What had he done what had he done what had he done? Then, without a word, she turned, laying her head hard across him. Fingers clutched through the hairs on his chest.

He lay awake for hours, scared to move. Listening to her ragged breath.

'Constable Robertson, do you swear to tell the truth, the whole truth and nothing but the truth, so help you God?'

'I do.'

'I'm so glad.' Traquair allowed himself a little smile as he smoothed down the edges of his gown. Each mannered gesture, each careful pause telling his audience: *This will be worth waiting for.* 'For it is on your testimony, Constable Robertson, that I believe the jury will decide the facts of this matter.'

Don't milk it, man, thought Jamie. For a second, Jinky's steady stare wavered, glancing wildly around the courtroom, bumping into Jamie's own gaze, then pulling rapidly away. Jamie gave him a nod of acknowledgement. Or perhaps it was pleading.

Traquair leaned on the edge of the witness stand. 'Now, Constable Robertson, I understand that you, along with Constable Worth here, were the only other authorised firearms officers to attend at Gryffe Street on the night in question. Relive for us, if you will, the events of that night.'

Jamie strained forward in his seat as Jinky began to talk. He could picture them both, by the bins at that chip shop, arguing with Coltrane. The stink of fish, the sweat of his hands, still sweating now, as he clenched them tight together. He found he was rocking slightly, building momentum with his body on that bench, squeezing silent energy outwards. As if, by the power of willing the words he could hear in his own head, they would slip from Jinky's mouth.

'Well, when I got there, Inspector Coltrane had already set up a cordon.'

'Was this before Constable Worth arrived at the scene?'

'Yes, My Lord. So, anyway, the inspector began to fill me in on what had happened. He said there'd been a report of gunfire, and his guys had heard another bang since they got there – but no one was sure what it was yet. I think he basically just wanted us to check it out.'

'When you say "check it out", what do you mean?'

Jinky shrugged. 'I kind of got the feeling he was covering his back, you know? He didn't seem to believe there was any gun. In fact, he actually said it's probably just kids larking about with fireworks.'

He said frigging what?

Jamie's heart, going fast as his breathing. His head turning to find Cath. And then he remembered. Her sore eyes this morning, the way she held herself like a broken dove. Listening to this was less painful.

'Indeed? You make no mention of this in your statement. Was Constable Worth present at this juncture?'

Jinky rubbed his ear. 'No sir, he arrived just after.'

'I see. Please continue.'

'Well, the officers on the ground had been told by a neighbour that the noises had been heard coming from the flat one up right at Gryffe Street. Inspector Coltrane told us one of his guys had actually heard one of the bangs himself. Then, while we,' Jinky turned towards the judge, 'eh, Constable Worth had arrived at the rendezvous by this point, My Lord. So, while we were talking to Inspector Coltrane, an almighty crack rang out.'

Traquair smiled. 'And, in your *professional* opinion, Constable Robertson – was this a gunshot?'

Jinky's neck seemed shorter than before, his head more down upon his shoulders.

'Your mind can play tricks on you, sir. It all sounds different in the night air rather than on the firing range – plus your helmet muffles everything. When Constable Worth and I got to the locus, we saw the window of the flat had been smashed, and a chair was lying shattered on the ground below. So, the crack could have been that. Or it could've even been a car backfiring.'

Traquair swallowed. Stretched his upper lip over his incisors. His teeth looked grey. Jamie's hands were grey.

'Just answer the question, Constable. In your opinion: could this have been a gunshot?'

'No, in my opinion it did not sound like a gunshot.'

Gun.

Shot.

The words began to unravel, tumbling syllables that made no sense. Cold, cold waves, lapping up Jamie's spine. He heard Traquair say: 'How so?'

'Well, the report of a gun, in those still conditions, sounds more like . . . a sharp clear boom. This was more . . . crackling, I suppose.'

'And did you say this at the time?'

'Yes sir, I said exactly that to Constable Worth and Inspector Coltrane. He – the inspector – agreed with me, but suggested we take up a defensive position just in case.'

Icy reality, crashing over Jamie's head. Pulling him under and down. Down. Jinky was going to perjure himself.

'A defensive position? Really?'

'Absolutely sir. Inspector Coltrane advised absolute caution. He said to remember that we had no definite confirmation as yet. About a firearm, I mean. And he stressed that we were dealing with a vulnerable young girl. On no account were we to make any moves without his express knowledge.'

'He said what?'

Traquair was rummaging through his papers as he spoke.

He was panicking. His brief was losing it. Again, Jamie tried to turn round, see Cath's face, but the security guard tugged his arm. 'Sit still.'

'We were dealing with a vulnerable young girl,' repeated Jinky. 'He made that very clear.'

'And did anyone else hear him say this?'

'Only Constable Worth, sir.'

Jinky looked down.

'But, but – it was my understanding that no identification had been made at that stage?'

'No, well, see, I used to work that beat. I knew the beatmen had seen a young female up at the window, so I told them it might well be the – excuse me, My Lord – the Barmy Brisbane lassie. I'd had dealings with the girl once before, see. Found her lying on the railway line up at Cathcart. Just lying there, like she was sunbathing. When I challenged her, she said she was waiting for someone.'

'Constable Robertson,' stammered Traquair, 'absolutely none of this information is in your statement.' Traquair seemed to be swaying slightly, or maybe it was Jamie's head smudging outlines: white face, black gown, white wig.

'I know sir.'

'So why, now, have you changed your testimony?'

Jinky gripped the edge of the box. Knuckles knotted, mirroring Jamie's own, which were clenched in a silent prayer.

Don't do this to me. Please.

The guard beside him pulled on Jamie's elbow.

'Keep your hands down.' His hand remained on Jamie's wrist this time, a silent, pressing threat.

'My Lord, I was coerced into making my initial statement. Threatened by Constable Worth. He's been phoning me – came to my house, too.'

Murmurs began to build, noises like animals chewing, like the seashore in Jamie's ear. They began to rise, unchecked, until a high, desperate voice shrilled clear through all the chaos.

'You lying bastard!'

It was Cath. Jamie pulled his wrist from the security guard's grasp. Twisted round, and all he could see was a court officer poking his finger in Cath's beautiful face. Then another hand, wrenching him back to face the front.

'I've bloody telt you,' said the guard.

A bang, two bangs, sharp firings of wood on wood.

'Kindly refrain from such outbursts,' barked the Alpha male, and the pack quietened. 'Mr Traquair. Do you know anything about this harassment?'

Traquair's cheeks were florid against grey-white.

'Indeed I do not, My Lord. May I request a brief adjournment whilst I consult with my client?'

'I rather think you'd better, Mr Traquair.'

'My Lord, I'm so sorry about this.' Jinky sounded like he might cry. 'I just didn't know what to do. He even called last night, when my wife and I were asleep. She's been terrified. That was the final straw. I knew I had to come in here today and tell the truth. No matter what.'

Jamie was no longer in the courtroom. He was in this strange, echoing chamber, watching his last chance dissolve. And he couldn't stop shaking.

AFTER

16

Cath closed the book, then opened it again. Like she'd picked up his socks from yesterday morning, then dropped them carefully back on the floor. The book was heavy, hardbacked. It was a dictionary, not a novel, that Jamie had been reading. She smoothed the paper, touching where he had touched, the simplest thing, sitting here in his chair, reading. One rosy smudge smeared across the page. Her hangnails were bleeding again, where she'd been gnawing at them. She wound a tissue around her index finger.

When she was a teenager, their dog had died, put to sleep after a road accident. As soon as they'd got back from the vet, Cath had run through the house, gathering up every toy, blanket, feeding bowl she could find, and flinging them in the bin. Yet, when Philippa's husband dumped her, Philippa had left everything – his clothes, the letters by his computer, even his shaving foam – untouched. A shrine to a total shitebag. Cath turned down the page of the dictionary, then shut it over. 'Mumm-ee.'

She felt Eilidh, tugging at her arm. 'When's Daddy coming home?'

'Soon, pet, soon.'

Eilidh clambered onto Cath's knee, handed her a comb. 'But *when* soon? In a wee while soon? He's not had his tea or his breakfastses yet. Did you make him pieces?'

'Pee!!' Daniel, naked but for a grubby vest, clutched proudly at his willy.

'No.'

That tightening, jagging again, like ammonia beneath her nostrils. Gently, persistently nipping at her. *Blink, blink, blink.* If she wept now, surely stalactites would form, milky limestone dripping from her hardened heart. Would they feed him meat? Would he eat it? Could she bring him food? Every day, every day she could make up a lunch and a dinner, take it in. Breakfasts would be fine, he could have porridge or cereal or something, just ignore the bacon. Pig. Oh, sweet Jesus, what would they do to him in there, what would they hurt?

'No, I forgot.' And then the tears came. Not a gushing rush; low, simple sobs that asked for nothing.

'Ssh.' Her daughter's chubby arms reached up around her neck, cradling her. 'Ssh. It's okay, Mummy. We can make him pieces tonight. Is he on a big-big shift?'

That was what they called it when Jamie did overtime.

'Yes.' Cath kept her head pressed into Eilidh's hair. That beautiful hint of baby smell still lingered in the roots.

'Will he be back tonight?'

'We'll see.' Cath kissed Eilidh's head, then rubbed her scrunched-up tissue across her own eyes. Began to brush, like every other morning. Eilidh's hair was soft, the comb slithering like it had no teeth. Cath ran her tongue across her chipped front tooth. It was on fire this morning, aching, then shrieking from constant grinding. She slid a little flower clasp into that long front bit, which was growing back from when Eilidh gave herself a trim.

Next door's Alsatian was barking again. Maybe she could get a dog, a watchdog that would keep them all safe. Sitting up in bed last night, fully dressed, fully alert, chewing and rocking, Cath had listened for every not-noise and half creak and creep that wasn't there. All the times Jamie had been away on nightshift, all the times she'd worked nightshift herself, for God's sake, the dark had never fazed her. It had never felt so final. As the dog paused for breath, Cath heard a clatter outside their door. It sounded like milk bottles being overturned. That paperboy never looked where he was going. She squeezed Eilidh's shoulders.

'Peep peep missus, till mummy sees what that noise is.'

Eilidh slid off Cath's lap. Cath went into the hall, opened the front door, then froze. What if it was reporters? But the path, the street were empty. Was her family yesterday's chip papers already? She looked down. Sure enough, the milk had been knocked over, but there was nothing broken. As she bent to pick up the bottle, she noticed something else, lying on the bottom step.

A little flower sprig, knobbled white like knuckles stripped of skin. *Lucky white heather.* Somebody's idea of a sick joke. Cath scooped it from the step and took it to the dustbin at the gate. The little bell flowers jangled in her shaking hand. She lifted the lid and threw it inside.

'Mummy,' called Eilidh from the doorway, 'don't throw out the pretty flower.'

'It's not a flower, it's a weed.' Cath wiped her slippers on the hall mat, and shut the door, then put the snib on. Her pulse, her tooth, her fingers all throb-throb-throb. Who would leave heather on her doorstep? She blew her nose, smiled, bright as a button, at Eilidh. 'Now, you go and get your shoes on like a good girl. Gran's taking you to school today.'

'Ga-an!!' yelled Daniel.

'Not you, stinky bum.' Eilidh poked her brother in the tummy. 'Gran's coming for *me*.'

'No, she's coming for you both. She's taking Daniel this morning too.'

'Why? Where are you going Mummy?'

'Out.'

'Out to where?'

'Pee pee!' chortled Daniel, yellow trickles puddling at his toes.

'Oh, Daniel. Why don't you use the potty?' Cath went to get a cloth from the kitchen.

'Out to where?'

'Just out.'

Suddenly, Eilidh gripped her knees. 'Are you doing a big-big shift too? Please don't, Mummy. Don't go away.'

Again, the tears welled. 'It's okay, baby. I won't go away.'

It was a face made for slapping. Her gran was an evil old piss-head, croned before her time. Harsh-carved creases scored from nose to mouth,

*accentuating her muzzle. Black smudged eyes like cupmarks on knotted
wood. She stank of whisky and beer and her yellowed fingers stung like
nettles on your thighs. Even with the door shut, the girl could hear them,
two bawling, drunken grotesques.*

Like mother, like son. Night after night after night.

'How d'you no tell the weans the fucking truth?'

'Fuck off, Maw.'

'Naw. You fuck off, ya junkie arsehole.'

'Naw, you fuck off, ya raddled old cow.'

*Her covers were thin, she was cold. Needed muffling. The girl had
gone to her brother's room, tapping on the door. Then a gentle shove
open, reaching out for a little light.*

His twisted face above the covers. His furious growl.

'Fuck off.'

'Right. Arms up.'

Cath stood meekly as the female prison officer ran her hands along
her shoulders, down her sides, into her armpits. Like all the other
women there, Cath knew the drill, only she'd never been on the
receiving end before. She shut her eyes, listening to the clatter and
clamour resound from clinical walls. There was a smell of stale sweat
in the air, which she recognised from her days as a cop. It was a
butcher's shop smell of raw, gritty mince. A smell of poverty, poor
hygiene, of shellsuits, cheap bleach and well-we-dinny-gie-a-fuck.

The smell of the great unwashed.

'Okay. Bag.'

She opened her eyes. The officer was nodding to the counter at
her side.

'Here?' Cath placed it, open, before her.

'And?'

The girl next to Cath nudged her. 'You need to take the stuff out
yourself, hen.'

'Oh, sorry.'

Cath laid out the crisps and orange juice she'd bought, Jamie's
portable radio, some books. His slippers. She had no idea what to
pack, could only think: if he were in hospital, what would he need?

The prison officer held up the radio. 'This'll need stripped down before he can get it.' She put it to one side, shook the carton of juice. 'Sealed?'

'Yes, I just bought it.'

Cath nodded vehemently, feeling she was seeking this woman's approval. Then the officer pushed Jamie's slippers with her pen. They were navy, with a Homer Simpson cartoon on each foot, embroidered with *World's Best Dad*.

'I thought, you know . . . can he wear them here?'

'Aye. If he wants the absolute pish ripped out him.' She pushed them back across the table. 'Are they on his Proform?'

'Pardon?'

The girl behind her tutted. 'Gie her your chitty, will you?'

'I don't have a chitty.'

The warder sighed. 'Did your man no fill in a Proform?'

'What's a Proform?'

'Every prisoner has to complete a Proform if they want you to bring in property for them. And what you bring has to match up exactly with what's on the list.'

'I'm sorry. I didn't know.'

'First time, is it?' said the girl behind.

'Oh, hello again, Mrs Hill,' said the prison officer. 'Didny recognise you there. Well, it's certainly no your first time, is it?'

'Hello yourself, Magret. Still here then?'

'Aye. You and me both, eh?'

Cath clutched one of Jamie's slippers. 'Yes . . . I . . . nobody told me.'

'Well, you canny take any of that stuff in then. Have you any one-pound or two-pound coins?'

'I don't know.'

Surely she didn't have to pay some kind of bribe to take in a carton of Tropicana? 'Can I look in my purse please?'

'If you have, you can buy your man something from the canteen.'

'Look,' interrupted the girl, 'can she no just hand in some money, then he can buy his own juice and that at the canteen?'

The warder nodded. 'Aye, you could do that too. The Cashier's Office is in the atrium. You canny miss it, it's the one with a wee glass window. You can leave him up to twenty quid—'

'Aye – but he can only spend a fiver a week, tell him.'

'Thank you, Mrs Hill. Yes, you'll need to give his name and full prison number. Then they'll give you a receipt, and he can use it to buy his bits and bobs.'

'Right. Do I do that now?'

'Naw, wait till after your visit or you'll lose your place, hen. They don't let you in if you're late. No even five frigging minutes, and it's no been your fault that the bloody bus broke doon.'

The prison officer gave a rueful smile. 'Rules is rules, Mrs Hill. Talking of which, gonny empty your pockets, stop talking and open wide?'

'Oh, for fucksake. I'm no carrying – I'm pregnant.'

'Again?'

'Aye, randy wee bastard, so he is. Every time he gets out, I get banged up instead.' The girl laughed.

'My congratulations to you both.' The prison officer twanged a surgical glove, lifted from a pile in a Tupperware box. 'I'm sure the wean'll turn out to be a credit to his father. Now open wide.'

'This is harassment. I could sue yous.'

'Say ah, or you're no going in.'

'Aaaaggghhhh.' The girl grimaced at Cath as the prison officer inserted one rubber-gloved finger beneath her tongue. She looked no more than twenty – how many kids could she have?

Could Cath go through now? Nobody had said. Over in the corner of the room, a sniffer dog was panting at a baby in a pram. The mother was yelling at a male warder, who had attempted to lift the child up.

'Get your fucking dug off my wean!'

'Well, get that nappy off!' shouted the warder. 'I need to check everything.'

'M'on then,' said the girl who'd been behind Cath. 'That's us, just go through the scanner now. The name's Stella, by the way.'

A soaring, astral name for someone so pinched and earthbound.

'I'm Cath. And, thanks for helping out back there. I don't have a scooby what I'm doing.'

'No kidding? I've lost count of the number of times I've went through this rigmarole. So, what's your man in for?'

Cath thought of all the things she could say. That it was a terrible accident – he's not a criminal at all. He was just doing his duty. He's a good man, a kind man. It was dark, they thought she had a gun. He was only trying to help. If you knew him, you'd know how this had killed him too. IT WASN'T HIS FAULT.

'He shot someone.'

Stella snapped her hand, three sharp shakes like a gangsta rapper. 'Fucksake man, that's heavy. I've telt Brian; he ever picks up a shooter, and I'm leaving him. Nah, he's not that type. Just knocking stuff, folks' bags and that. For the readies, know? It's hard when you've got three weans and nay cunt'll gie you a job.'

Yes, of course. A man who mugged old ladies of their handbags, to feed his habit. In this inside-out world, that was morally superior to making a mistake. She decided she didn't want to walk beside this Stella any more.

'Eh, I'm just . . . on you go.' Cath plonked into one of the chairs that lined the walls. 'I need to get my head together a minute.'

Stella smiled down at her. 'Shite, isn't it? I mind how I used to greet and greet after I'd been here. Don't you worry. Just mind, when they screws sneer at you and make you do performing tricks – they've to live with themselves at night. Stripping weans and stealing orange juice – what kind of a job is that? You hold your head up high and sniff like you're smelling shite when they walk past. Remember: *you've* done nothing wrong, no matter what your man's done. Alright, pal?'

'Alright.'

'There you go, well. I'll no doubt be seeing you in the OK Corral.' Stella hitched up her shoulder bag and elbowed her way back into the snaking queue.

Cath looked at her knees. She'd put on a skirt, thinking that, somehow, ridiculously, it would look better. More respectable. Her thighs felt soft, squashy, where her fingers were squeezing in. Eilidh had wee dimples above her knees too. Cath had always had these dimples; used to push her mouth against them when she was little, all hunched up on the back stair, where her mother made her sit when she was bad.

She didn't want to be here.

Metal bars, walls, glossy floors, all shining like a migraine, wowing in and out louder than a Rolf Harris wobbleboard. If she pressed the walls, they'd be as pliant as her knees. The floor, rising to meet her, would be marshmallow, not tiles. All the world felt spongy, as it had since yesterday. She could remember her mum, helping her out of the courtroom, and Jenny . . . Jenny yelling at someone to fuck off as they pushed her into a waiting cab. Her mum holding Cath's head on her lap, all the way home, stroking her hair. The buildings of Glasgow tumbling past above her, high flats and terraced houses, all wonky and upside down. Cath could feel Doris, squeezed against her other side. Could hear the constant clicking as she worried at her rosary, muttering *but he's a good boy, Lord. He's a good boy.*

They made her tea and put her to bed and called her sister. Cath had heard her mum sniffling into the phone in the hall. 'No. It's not good. Not good at all, darling. They found him guilty. Yes, they've taken him already. *Prison* darling.' She lowered her voice, as if forced to impart a forbidden swearword. 'Barlinnie.'

A pause while her sister digested and responded. Hearing it out loud made it instantly real. Cath stuffed one pillow into her mouth, clamped another over her head, but still her mother wittered on.

'God, it's awful, darling. I just don't know what to do. They'll have to come and live with us of course.'

Oh no we won't.

Her knees were beginning to bruise. Cath clasped her hands and breathed deeply. The last of the queue was going through the scanner. If she wasn't quick, she would miss her flight.

So she came here today, alone, just to show them that she could. And because she had to. All thoughts of Anna Cameron, and revenge, were pushed away by the need to walk through fire to prove to Jamie that she loved him. But prove it here? This piteous, stinking, shiny sad place that was crueller than a zoo. Part of her would rather not see him at all.

An older warder called over to her. 'Are you coming or going lassie?' He had a nice, smiley, pitted face, like a potato.

One last big sigh. 'I'm coming.'

Barlinnie was the last of Glasgow's 18th-century prisons, looming on what was once farmland. Dumped away in the east end, like many things Glasgow didn't like to talk about, it squatted incongruous at the skirts of a modern housing estate, its brick perimeter walls tantalisingly low enough for the men within to catch glimpses of normal life. Designed to hold 1,000 prisoners, it held far more, receiving every male prisoner from the West of Scotland's courts. The leaflets Cath had gathered up in the waiting room advised that 'suitable' prisoners from its convicted population were sent on to other prisons. She prayed Jamie would be deemed 'suitable'. She'd need to speak to Len again. Or could she now? Was he still their lawyer? He was a Police Federation lawyer, after all.

Cath had been at Barlinnie a couple of times before, on escort duty, but had never been inside. Never thought she would be. Yesterday, she waited and waited in a little room at the court for Len to come, only for him to tell her that she couldn't speak to Jamie, or phone him, or go down to the court cells to say goodbye. She'd pleaded with him to do something. He'd managed to arrange this visit for her today, even though he said convicted prisoners were supposed to book their own visits.

'In you go, lass. Find a seat, pick a face. Any yin will do, they're all lovely boys in here.'

The visiting room resembled a teeming works canteen. Casual chairs and tables, not glass walls and phones like you see in the pictures. She searched the room for her husband. There he was, over at the far side. Head bowed, lips bitten, clad in prison sweatshirt. Bile surged unannounced, and she swallowed it back, somehow glad of the burning as she walked towards him.

'Hey, you.'

Cath laid her hand on the top of his soft black hair. Jamie looked up, like a dog begging to be put down. 'Hey. I wasn't expecting you.'

She leaned down to kiss him, felt him pull back.

'I . . . I don't know if we can,' he said.

Cath glanced around the room. Other families were kissing, hugging.

'I think it's okay. I – would you rather not?'

He shrugged, this familiar stranger staring from a fast-receding shore. Cath pressed her lips hard into his head, just as she'd done with Eilidh.

They sat facing each other. Cath doubted if he'd slept; his brow and jowls were so sagged and heavy, folds of pink upon yellowish beige. The only real colour came from the scarlet on his lower eyelids. She reached out her hand, spanned it over his.

'So? You okay?'

He stared at her, blinking, hardly registering. 'Am I . . . what? Okay? Aye, aye.'

'Has anyone been in touch? Len, the Federation?'

He shook his head.

'Well, I'll get on to the Federation today, find out what we do about an appeal. I thought if we got—'

'Cath.' He pulled his hand from beneath hers, like she was hurting it. Raised it, slow, to cup the side of his face. 'Don't you understand? There's no point appealing. I did it; I shot that wee girl.' He caught one trembling finger against the bridge of his nose, his wheeze almost lost in the chattering and clanging. 'I need to pay.' He tried to speak again, shook his head. Two steady streams passing down his cheeks, dropping from his chin, making pools on the table.

'Oh baby, don't.' She tried to cuddle him across the table, awkward, exposed, with her arse in the air and her breasts squashed on the Formica.

A warder came over to them. 'Ho! You alright there? You wanting back in your cell?'

They unlocked themselves, Cath sitting down, Jamie sitting up. 'No, no, I'm fine,' he said quietly.

'You sure?'

'Aye.'

Other prisoners were watching them. Some grinning, some shaking of heads. Cath wanted to pick up the table and brandish it around the room, wailing as she battered it into their ugly, thick faces.

The warder referred to his clipboard. 'Worth, is it?'

She was grateful to this man for his gruff concern. Surely he'd see Jamie was a decent human being, maybe look out for him.

'Oh, aye. Worth. I've got my eye on you.' The man scowled. 'Now why don't you grow a pair, and act like a fucking man, eh?'

'You cheeky bast—'

'Cath. CATH!' Jamie gripped her hands. 'Just leave it, eh?'

She saw his face, and shut up.

'It's okay.' Jamie nodded to the warder. 'We're fine, sir. We're fine.'

The warder winked at Cath. 'Aye. Can see who wears the troosers in your house. *Fanny*.' This last was directed at Jamie, as the man wandered away.

Jamie took her hand again. 'Cath, I'm okay, honestly. I'm sorry about that. I just, I wasn't expecting to see you today.' He sighed. 'We don't have much time left. Are the kids alright?'

'Yes, they're fine. They said to tell you they loved you and—'

'Where do they think I am?'

'I told them you were working.'

He nodded, more slow sad nails in his coffin.

'Eilidh will be twenty when I get out of here, Cath. I was thinking about it last night.'

'You're not going to be here fifteen years. We're going to get you out . . .'

'We? Who's "we" Cath? Haven't you noticed? We're it; there is no "we". I'm the head on the spike they needed, the cop that was finally made to pay.'

'Well, we'll find out why Jinky lied, and—'

'I was stitched up, Cath. Jinky lied because he was told to.'

'But *who*? Who told him?'

'I don't know, and it doesn't really matter. Call it what you like Cath. It's the system, baying for blood. And you can't fight the system.'

Each word punched Cath back further in her unyielding chair. 'Jamie, you sound like you've just given up.'

'Exactamondo, as our old friend Len would say.'

A buzzer rang, a warder shouted. 'That's time now, folks. Two minutes to time.'

That spongy feeling had spread from her lips, her limbs. It was in her brain now, thickening, muffling, and she longed for the sweet release of hysteria. But she wouldn't give in.

'I guess I'd better go. I'll see you tomorrow, then.'

'You can't. I'm only allowed three visits.'

'What a week?'

'No, a month.'

'Jamie. I can't wait . . .' Then she stopped. He didn't need this. 'Okay. Fine. When then? Do I need to book it?'

He shook his head. 'Apparently a timetable goes up each month. I've got to book the dates I want, then let you know. I can phone you, you know. But I'll need a phone card . . .'

'It's okay, I'm going to leave twenty pounds for you at the Cashier's Office.'

'An old hand already, eh?' His laugh was harsh.

'No, someone told me what to do.'

Jamie pushed his fringe out of his eyes. Cath longed to stroke his hair away herself, but was afraid to touch him again. He might not be real. Or he might just crumble and then she'd disintegrate too.

'I don't know what'll happen for the rest of this month,' he said. 'I think it's one afternoon, one evening and one weekend . . .'

'Well, make it a weekend then, and I can bring the kids.'

'Don't you bloody bring them anywhere near this place, Cath.' The heel of his hand, slapped hard down on the table-top. 'I'm warning you. I don't want them to see me here. Ever.'

A few heads turned again at the sound of Jamie's raised voice. That warder jangled his keys like a warning bell, as a dark-haired woman came towards them. She leaned over Cath's shoulder.

'Hello. Mrs Worth, Mr Worth? I won't take up a second. Just wanted to let you know I'm Isobel Rennie, the Family Contact Development Officer. We're here to offer you any support and advice we can. We liaise between visitors and inmates if required, and we can put you in touch with any outside agencies you might need. Now, I don't want to get in the road of your farewells, so can I just give you this?' She put a bright leaflet emblazoned with *Here to Help* on the table. 'It's got my number on if there's anything you need, alright?'

She smiled at Cath. 'Even if you just need a chat.'

Mrs Rennie had a lovely smile, warm and generous. Cath wished she could believe it.

17

Clunk. CLANG. The hatch slammed open, the eyes appeared. Twenty-minute checks, day and night. He must still be on suicide watch. No wonder, particularly after he'd started greeting in the visiting room. But he hadn't expected to see Cath there, was overpoweringly glad and ashamed all at once. He'd wanted her to cradle his head upon her breast, and sing to him like she sang to the children, nonsense rhymes and lullabies. The kind of songs he would never sing to his babies again, because soon they wouldn't be babies, and soon they would forget him.

No way were they ever coming here, to see the funny man behind the barbed wire and bars. It was his job to protect Cath, protect his family, and yet he was dragging her into a place where half the inmates would rape and murder her without missing a beat. Cath, appearing like a dream, luminous skin shimmering above all the swearing and sludge, like a flower breaking through a patch of dirt. And his great muddy boots, grinding her deep into the ground. Jamie stared at the eyes staring at him through the hatch. They blinked, vanished.

CLANG. Clunk. Signed-for, sealed. But not delivered.

Everything was clangs and keys; you could hear the rattling two corridors away, the constant grate of metal on metal. How did anyone ever sleep? But he was getting tired now, all the same. He'd never really slept since he arrived here. Not after the reception committee that had screamed their welcome across the quadrangle.

Your arse is mine, ya fuckpig hoor.

And not after his rude awakening this morning. It had been 6 a.m. when a prison officer told him to get up. Barlinnie prisoners no longer slopped out. Each cell was '*en suite*'; a thin partition between open, brown-stained toilet bowl and bunk. No sink, though. The stink of urine soaked each cell, which bled into each landing, which oozed down through each Hall. Jamie felt filthy, his body tarred and feathered, teeth furred.

'Is there somewhere I can get washed?' he'd asked. 'I mean properly. I need a shower.'

'Aye, but you'll need to get dressed first. And this'll need to be the last one, mind?'

'What do you mean?'

'You're only allowed two showers a week. We'll no count yesterday's, seen as you werny officially on my landing, but I have to record this one. So that leaves you one more from your allowance. I'd leave it to the end of the week if I were you.'

Since when did water become rationed in this pishy wet city? Even dogs could wash their own balls when they felt like it. But it was that or nothing.

'Okay. Fine.'

'Right. Haud on till I check it's clear for you.'

The warder had left the cell door open. Jamie pulled on his trousers, sat on the edge of the bed. He was just putting on his shoes, when the cell door swung open, and this apparition appeared. A bloke about five feet nine inches, with wild hair and a straggly beard. He looked like Catweazle, but with one grotesque exception: a blank socket where his left eye should be. The man was waving his arms, ranting: 'This is the score, pal. This is the score.'

Immediately, Jamie flew up from his bunk, all the adrenalin that fed his insomnia and frayed his head bursting out and up. This was it, his time had come – but not without a fight. Before the guy had a chance to lay hands on him, Jamie skelped him on the face and decked him, hard. Crushing his knee in the guy's chest, holding him steady, thumping his head.

'If you come in here again, I'll fucking kill you,' he yelled, each punch a pause between the words.

Then other arms clamped down on him from above, two prison officers pulling him off, flinging him face down on the bed. One restrained Jamie, hands wrenched high up his back, while the other picked Catweazle from the floor and part helped, part dragged him out.

'What the fuck was that all about?' The warder loosened his grip, let Jamie sit up.

'You tell me.' Jamie was breathless, his chest rasping with the panic and the panting. 'He just breenged in here and started screeching at me.'

'Och, that's just Murray. He rules up here; thinks he's in charge. Guy used to be in the Scottish National Liberation Army or something. Thinks he's a real terrorist. Mind,' the warder sniffed, 'he has murdered a couple of folk. He'll look after you, but. No one will step out of line while he's up here.'

'Look after me? I don't need anyone to look after me.'

'Well, it's up to you. There's a hard way and an easy way to do everything. It's worth having guys like Murray on your side, but it's your funeral if you don't.'

'I don't want a one-eyed nutter anywhere near me. Fucking loony.' He could hear his voice running riot, higher and faster than normal, shrill and girly in its indignation.

'Look pal, you don't have to *like* these guys. I'm no saying be their best pal, just tolerate them. Tolerate the system.'

Jamie shook his head.

The warder sat down on the bed beside him. He was about Jamie's age, a bit older perhaps. 'Fucksake. I know this is tough for you. I know they're all nutters, junkies and bad bastards, that you'd never choose to spend a minute with if you could.' He lowered his voice. 'I know you were a polis, pal. My brother-in-law's a cop too. You guys have it easy. You just lock them up. Wipe your hands and go back out on the street. We're the ones that have to babysit them. And it's shite sometimes.'

'How can you take it? Seeing them here day in day out, having to look after them, listen to them. Talk to them like they fucking matter?'

It wasn't the myopic madman Jamie was thinking about now, it was those bastards from yesterday. The ones that pissed in his food and clad him in shite and said what they'd do to his wife.

'Because they do matter, pal. Who's to say how any of us end up in here, eh?'

Jamie didn't respond. He leaned over to his locker, took out the prison-issue towel they gave him yesterday. It was still a little damp.

'Eh, I think we'll gie the showers a miss till later, yeah?' The warder stood up. 'Let things calm doon a bit, yeah?'

Jamie sighed. All the fight had gone out of him. 'Okay.'

'I'll see you later. The name's Cunningham, by the way.'

As the warder started closing the door, the walls began to shut in too. It felt so final, like they were pouring sand into a pyramid, and he'd never get out of this stinking hole again. Never get the chance to be anything more than a total mistake, who lived his life via a series of fuck-ups. Jamie shouted after him. 'No, wait. Look, what cell is it that Murray's in?'

'Number Twelve. How?'

'Can we make a wee housecall then, before you lock me up again? Let me get it sorted?'

Cunningham stared at him, considering. Scratching his belly.

Then he smiled. 'Aye. So long as you keep your hands to yourself.'

Murray was sitting on his bed, polishing a pair of boots when the warder rapped on the open door.

'Knock, knock, Murray. I've brung you a visitor.'

Murray looked different with two eyes. Still manic, only slightly more muted. And with the beginnings of a fine big bruise across his temple.

'Oh, aye?'

Jamie tried not to laugh. He walked over, held out his hand. 'I'm sorry about that. You know, back there in my cell. I thought you were having a go at me.'

Murray rose to his feet, took the hand that was offered. 'Nae bother, pal. I should've knocked. I was just wanting you to know what the score was here.' He tapped his left temple. 'Glass eye. I hadny put it in yet, see.'

Jamie didn't, but he nodded anyway.

'I'll see you right, pal. Any problems, any worries, just you come and tell Murray the Man. Alright?'

'Sure. Thanks. And, em, sorry. Again.'

'Nae sweat. We all go a bit loco in here at first. All water off a duck's back, know?'

They'd smiled a bit more, nodded a bit more, all the while Jamie wanting to punch him a bit more. Hands by his side, in, out, in, out. Nails in his palms, grit in his grin. But he'd have to do it; have to learn who to use, when to fight and what phlegm he could swallow down, because this jail was full of bile. He could drink it or drown in it. Better still, by far, to float on top, and if soothing the ruffled pride of a one-eyed nutjob was what it took, then so be it.

Didn't mean he meant a word of it. A final *nae bother, pal,* then the warder took Jamie back to his cell, left him with a *Daily Record.* He read the sports pages first, everything, even crap about the cricket. Then, when he couldn't pretend any longer, he turned it over. It still shocked him though, even though he knew it was coming. There, on the front, loomed his own grainy face, roughened and blurry like he was missing or dead. And he realised it was the photo from his warrant card, underscored with one black word:

GUILTY!

That exclamation mark. Like they'd been waiting for it. It was hard to rip a newspaper into pieces so small that no single sentence remained. But he managed; twisting and tugging till all was inky pulp, balled into several piles.

So, that had been Jamie's first full morning inside. Those grey lumps of papier mâché and the feel of unbrushed teeth were all he had to show for it. He closed his eyes, tried to doze awhile. Pretended he was lying on their double bed at home, and Cath was downstairs making breakfast, and all the bumps and the grunts and the shouting outside were just kids playing in the street. Lots of kids, playing at chases in the creeping warmth of early summer, running and running until it grew faded-dark and only one was left outside. A small girl, thin. Mid-teens, though you couldn't tell from the back. But she kept running, running on her own and he couldn't tell if she was running away or towards him and she was turning and he was running and she was turning or maybe spinning; spinning on the roundabout in the playpark, but even so she was still running and turning and as he raised his hands to reach out to her, he saw his fingers turn to a snub, black snout. Its muzzle began to roar and, as the girl turned towards it, she buckled, flew backwards through the air. And she was wearing Eilidh's face.

'No!'

A scraping, like something clawing to get out. Jamie jumped up from the bed, saw mucky primrose walls where he'd imagined sky. Realised where he was, what the noises were, as his door began to creak open.

'Popular the day, eh? That's you got another visit.' Cunningham was back, motioning to Jamie to follow him. Another warder, further down the landing, shouting 'Clear! Clear!' as he ushered men into their cells.

Jamie rubbed his eyes, quickly put on his sweatshirt, which he'd been using as a pillow. Foolishly, his first thought was that it would be Len, all geared up to plan out their next strategy. Regardless of what Jamie had said to Cath, he vacillated between wanting, needing, to serve his sentence and planning his desperate escape. And then he thought it would be Derek, his mate, come to console and bring him a breath of outside.

'Who is it?' he asked, as they walked through gate after locking gate. He could hear clanks of metal, catcalls and jeers, shouts of *dead pig walking* from behind cell doors. They'd locked everybody up, just so he could walk past. Would this happen every time he set foot outside his cell? It wasn't like America, all flailing hands through open bars. They couldn't actually see him, but still he kept his eyes on the end of the passageway. Fixed on the next locked door.

'Is it my brief?'

'Two guys. Look more like polis than lawyers: short hair and crap suits. With lawyers, it's more the opposite: sharp dressing and floppy fringes. Right into facial hair too, for some reason – and that's just the female ones.' He nudged Jamie. 'Boom, boom.'

They stopped outside an interview room. 'In here, pal.' Cunningham opened the door. Inside, two men sat on one side of a plastic table. An opened briefcase and two polystyrene cups of coffee lay in front of them. Jamie noticed there was no coffee for him.

The older man nodded at Jamie. 'Alright? I'm Duncan Forsythe, this is Mark Rodgers, from Complaints and Discipline.'

Were they not done with him yet? He was in jail for bloody murder. What possible discipline charges could they fling at him now?

'No point in beating about the bush here, Jamie. Now that you've been convicted, we're here to tie up a few loose ends.'

'Loose ends? Fucksake. I don't need this.' He turned to the warder. 'Gonny take me back to my cell, please?'

'Now, wait just a minute, Worth. This isn't an optional extra. I'm here to serve notice on you that a Strathclyde Police Discipline Hearing was convened in your absence this morning.'

'Oh aye?' He shuddered at his own intonation. Already, he'd adopted the institutionalised insouciance of Mad-eye Murray.

'And,' continued Forsythe, 'having been convicted of a serious criminal offence, the Chief Constable has found you guilty of conduct unbecoming of a police officer, and of bringing the service into extreme disrepute.' He nodded at Rodgers, who got to his feet. Haltingly, the younger man began to read from a sheet of paper. 'As a result, you are herewith summarily dismissed from the service of Strathclyde Police. You are required to immediately return all appointments, including uniform, batons, handcuffs and all other police property to any police office . . .' He faltered at this bit, looked at Forsythe.

'Aye, well, you can get your wife to drop them off at Castlemilk. That's your nearest office isn't it?' said Forsythe.

Jamie didn't trust himself to speak.

'On you go, Mark.'

Rogers looked at his piece of paper again. 'Your salary will cease with immediate effect, and you will no longer be eligible to receive any pension benefits—'

'Woah, wait a minute. My pension? What do you mean, "benefits"?'

'We mean you'll no get a pension, pal, that's what we mean.' Forsythe was looking at his watch as he spoke.

'But . . . I paid into that. I've worked for it; it's my money. What about my wife? What's she supposed to live on?'

'You'll get your contributions back.' Forsythe shrugged. 'You should've read the small print. Right, you nearly done, Mark? Just give him the paperwork and he can read it himself.' He drummed his fingers on the table. 'I want to get out of here. Place gies me the heebie-jeebies.'

Rodgers rummaged in the briefcase, took out copies of the paperwork he'd brought. He handed the papers to the warder, then dipped his head back behind the lid of the case.

'And what do I do with these?' said Jamie.

'I'll keep them for now,' said the warder, stuffing them into a plastic sleeve.

'You can give them to your brief.'

Rodgers was still shuffling papers, sorting them with his head inside the briefcase, like a kid under the desk at school. Forsythe tutted at him, leaned over to snap the briefcase shut. 'Oh, and obviously, you're no longer represented by the Scottish Police Federation. Therefore, you'd best have a think about how you're going to fund any legal advice from now on. Right Mark, is that you? C'mon, let's go, eh?'

Jamie and the warder stood back to let the Discipline guys leave first.

Cunningham held the door open for them. 'Alright boys, that you? Charlie down the passageway'll show yous out.'

Both men grunted as they passed, but it was hardly a goodbye.

'Couple of wanks, eh?' said Cunningham.

'Aye.'

'Tell you what, how about I get you some dinner sent up, eh? You didny eat any of your lunch, did you?'

'Nope.'

'And, as a special treat, I'll get them to gie you your own spoon. You can keep it, like. And your own plate and mug.'

Clammy sick taste, the same shame of yesterday, when the doctor had given him an internal. More stings of shock and violation. How much more could he take? And what would Cath do with no money? If he ever did get out of here, he'd . . . he didn't know. Sue the bastards for all they were worth? Kill some more folk, then come back for an encore?

'Here, you, don't look like you're gonny kick the shit out of me now, pal. It's a privilege, so it is. You're no supposed to get your own utensils if you're on suicide watch.'

'What, in case I spoon myself to death?'

'You'd be surprised, pal.'

His bug eyes made Jamie smile. 'What's your name again?'

'Cunningham. Alan Cunningham.'

Find grace in tiny things. It was on one of his mother's posters. She had them plastered all around the house: *The Sacred Heart* in her bedroom, *Desiderata* in the lounge, *Footsteps in the Sand* in the bog, above the bath. And that one, with lots of pastel flowers, and a tiny, wan angel. It was pinned over the front door, beneath a wood-effect crucifix from Lourdes.

'Cheers, Alan. For my spoon. Or should I call you Mr Cunningham?'

'Better stick with the mister, pal. Else I'll be seen as a soft touch, and you as an evil collaborator.'

'Fair enough.'

They walked through another mesh and metal door, back onto the hospital landing.

' Look, *Mr* Cunningham. Can you get me off of suicide watch? It's more likely to drive me crazy than anything else. I feel like I'm in the zoo.'

They were just outside his cell now. Cunningham took out another bunch of keys. 'How d'you think you'll hold out in solitary?'

'I think I'll prefer it that way. Keep my head down, stay out the road.'

'Hmm,' was all he said. 'In you go. I'll away and get some grub sent up.'

'Mind I'm a vegetarian,' Jamie said to the closing door.

'I'll see what I can do. There's nae meat in our mince anyway.'

Alone in his squat four walls, Jamie tried to swallow. Tried to stop the chill pitter-patter all through his veins. His stomach groaned. He was desperate for decent food, something homemade that wasn't grey. But, if he ate, then eventually, he'd have to crap, and he couldn't bring himself to do that. Not in the same room he slept in. Maybe he could time it, twice-weekly, for when he went to the shower block. Surely there were toilet stalls in there? His hands were sticky with sweat and grime, and still he hadn't washed. Already turning savage. A creature that lived on its nerves, baring its teeth for show, then shutting itself away. Only coming out for craps and to wash.

If he raised up on his tiptoes, Jamie could reach the sill of his window. The cell looked onto the motorway. Everything seemed so close; he could see cars driving, folk walking over the footbridge – everyone taking their freedom for granted. But it's a luxury, he thought. Don't you people realise that? Wasting your time in front of the telly, chomping on crisps, deciding you can't be arsed to wash the dishes. You lucky, lucky bastards. Just to be allowed to drive to your work. Life going on as normal outside, while his life was contained in a ten-by-ten cage.

Clunk. CLANG. Feeding time at the zoo.

A man in a suit stepped inside. 'Mr Worth?'

'Yes?'

'I'm Peter Hart, Assistant Governor. Just wanted to see how you were settling in.'

'I'm coping.'

'Mr Cunningham tells me you feel you're ready to come off suicide watch.'

'Aye. Don't know why I was put on it.'

'Unfortunately, we're not the ones to decide that. We've a prison psychiatrist you'll need to see. I've made you an appointment for tomorrow.'

'But they never even examined me to say I *was* a risk in the first place.'

'Standard procedure, with our vulnerable prisoners.'

'So I'm a vulnerable prisoner, am I?'

Hart leaned against the wall. Folded his arms like he owned the place. Which he kind of did. 'Mr Worth, you understand that you'll need to stay in solitary until we can get you placed elsewhere?'

'Am I likely to be moved then?'

'I think that would be advisable, don't you? I was in A Hall last night when you arrived.'

Jamie laughed, a kind of whicker. 'Aye. Good of them to help me settle in, eh? But d'you think anywhere else will be any different?'

'You're a Glasgow police officer, in a Glasgow jail. Plus, some of the guys here . . . well, they've got nothing to lose.'

'That's a sad indictment of the judicial system, Mr Hart.'

'It is indeed, Mr Worth. But you and I both know it's a fact of life. So,' he sighed, 'as I say, for the duration of your time with us, you'll be in solitary.'

'Suits me.'

'However, I strongly recommend that it's in your interests to get out.'

'You said it, Mr Hart.'

'I mean out of your cell, Mr Worth. I reckon you should start working in the prison; cleaning the doctor's and the dentist's offices, that kind of thing.'

'Don't think I'll break into the drugs cabinet then?'

Hart didn't respond. 'You'll still be totally away from everybody, but at least you'll be doing something.' He slapped his hand against the painted stone wall. 'Get you out of here.'

'Knock, knock. Who left you open?' Cunningham stood at the door, clutching a tray of food. 'Oh, hullo, sir. How you doing?'

'Right you are Alan, I can see it's tea time.' Hart nodded at Jamie. 'I'll leave you to it. Have a think about what I've said, Mr Worth – and remember: 10.00 a.m. tomorrow, Dr Foster's office.'

'I'll make sure he's there, sir.'

'Goodnight, both.'

'Cheers, sir.' Cunningham put the tray down. 'There you go: cheese salad and chips. Chips urny very warm mind . . .'

'Doesn't matter. Look, can I get a shower now? Please? Before I eat.'

'Swear I saw something move in there.' Cunningham shook his head at a limp cucumber slice. 'What? Aye. I suppose. Not as if it's gonny get any colder, is it? Wait and I'll make sure they're empty.'

He came back a few minutes later. 'Aye, we're all clear, but you'll need to be quick. There's a few due up from the gym, and they'll be way more minging than you.'

The closer they got to the showers, the worse that stink of piss grew. Jamie thought he'd got used to it already, but he realised it had been diluted with body odour, smells of paint and gravy. These fumes he could almost ingest were pure, concentrated, bitter-yellow urine, undercut with several shades of shite. It was hard to brush his teeth without gagging. There were four or five urinals, half a dozen toilet cubicles (good: plenty of crapping options there) and three primitive shower stalls. Jamie washed quickly with carbolic soap. Even the water was frustrating. He needed sharp stings and powerful jets. Instead, his skin puckered into gooseflesh beneath leisurely, tepid dribbles.

In the distance, he could hear a siren cranking up.

'Shite. Something's happening through-by,' shouted Cunningham, who was guarding the entrance to the bogs. 'Don't move Worth. Stay where you are. I'll be back for you in a minute.'

'I'm nearly done anyway,' he shouted back. But there was no reply.

The water had drizzled to almost nothing, and the soap was too dry and cracked to lather up. But at least he'd rinsed himself down. It was something. Water still dripping from his hair into his eyes, he reached around the side of the cubicle, to where he'd hung his scrap of towel. From nowhere, from silence, someone grabbed his wrist, yanking him out of the cubicle.

'You'll never wash that pig stink off,' whispered a voice, as more unseen limbs grabbed his torso.

He tried to shake off the man who was holding him, but his feet were skidding on the wet floor, his arm being wrenched backwards by the other one. Was it one or two? How many of them were there? The one trying to break his arm had a red sleeve, that was all he could see. Frantically, he tried to free himself, bending his knees and bucking back and forth, but he could get no purchase on the soaking wet floor.

A punch in the gut, a spit of: 'That's for you, Cunt-stable.'

At the impact of the blow, Jamie slipped on the tiles, cracking his head as he hit the floor. Could feel liquid running. Water? Blood? Another blow, deep into the kidneys. 'And that's fae Murray, ya stinking big cunt. He says to say he's got his eye on you.'

Jamie tried to shout for help, but a hand was in his mouth, tearing wide, hooking him like a fish as they dragged him to his feet, one in front, one behind. He screamed as Red Sleeve twisted his arm again, pain shooting up his shoulder. Once more, he lost his footing, bare feet scrabbling wildly on slimy tiles, held steady only by the brute behind him.

Red Sleeve started laughing. 'Like ice dancing too, do you? We seen you, ya fucking nancy boy. Greeting like a wean in the visit room. Some hard man, eh? Fucking polis poof.'

'Well,' said the voice behind him, 'you'll like this then.'

Jamie froze as he heard a zip being pulled down. Red Sleeve dropped Jamie's arm, grabbed both sides of his head. Pushing him down and down towards his groin, as the other man was fumbling with his trousers against Jamie's naked arse.

'Welcome to the jungle,' said Red Sleeve. 'Leo here loves fresh meat.'

Jamie knew he would rather die. Fury beat fear, and he flung his shoulder back, hitting the one behind him on the jaw. Jamie slithering, losing balance. Blood pumping, blinding, grasping wildly at the air. He seized the other's hair, swung his head down, low onto one of the basins. Felt the judders resonate up his arms as skull struck ceramic.

'Don't fuck with me, ya shower of fucking shite!' he screamed.

Opening his legs now, feet square, ready for the next onslaught, but the one who'd tried to assault him had already picked himself up, was making for the door. Red Sleeve lay where he'd fallen, groaning.

'Come on then,' yelled Jamie. 'Come ahead.' His hands pumping in and out, clenching. The one at the door had his mouth open, was speaking, shouting, but it was hard to make out anything at all. Thundering in his head, blood all churning, nowhere to go. Then thin, tapping beats, footsteps running down the metal-studded corridor. A panicked shout – Cunningham, possibly. 'What the fuck's going on in here?'

The crackle of a walkie talkie: 'Charlie, Michael. Urgent assistance in Shower Room Two.'

A hand on his arm, the roughness of a towel.

'Don't you fuck with me!'

Jamie bawled the words out, at the damp, peeling ceiling. Standing bollock naked in a puddle of blood and piss.

18

It was a beautiful morning; a sneaky Indian summer day of polished egg-blue sky, of beaming flowers and faces. Anna took her coffee out to the patio, shuffling barefoot, carrying her pile of newspapers. She'd got them on the way back from her run through the park. Most of them repeating yesterday's spiels, more photos, same bleak facts.

She'd wept when she heard the news. Literally heard the news, played through the speakers in the changing rooms, just as she was drying her hair. A jolly Radio Clyde DJ, segueing from Franz Ferdinand to Jamie to the Champions' League.

And that was 'Take Me Out', a top tune from one of Glasgow's finest. Talking of Glasgow's finest . . . we've news just in – South Side cop, PC James Worth, has been found guilty of murder at Glasgow High Court.

'Oh,' she had gasped, face hidden in a towel.

The jury, who had convened overnight in the Radisson Hotel, agreed on the verdict by a majority of—

Hot, angry blasts from the hairdryer, turned up as high and loud as she could. She didn't want to hear this. It was the first of her two days off. A nice day. She'd been swimming, was meeting a friend later.

This would kill Jamie. Truly, it would; they'd have been as well hanging him, got it over with quicker. She raised her finger from the press-down switch, wondered if it was over yet.

Celtic fans are delighted—

There. Anna slid the hairdryer back in its holder. Her bob was uniformly neat, but she'd need to get her roots done again. More grey was creeping in, plus the chlorine gave it a greenish tinge. Her eyes were pink. *Don't start snivelling. It's got nothing to do with you.* She scrubbed her face with the towel, then dabbed some face cream on, patting it gently like they tell you to do with 'slightly older' skin.

But it's Jamie. She'd seen the back of his head in court that day. Just the line of his shoulder, and his hair, still soft and black. It always smelled of trees and air. He would never survive. Locked up in a box, surrounded by shite. Her dam of self-denial burst, Anna felt the same urge to buy up every paper, watch every channel, like she had that night in New York. *Face your fears,* a wise counsellor once told her. That's all you can do, just face them, or they'll devour you.

She was meant to be meeting a friend after the gym. Lunch in a chi-chi little noodle bar. Her pal's mobile went straight to voicemail. 'Hi, Elaine? It's me. I'm really sorry about this, but something's come up. I'm going to have to give lunch a miss. But I'll definitely see you soon – I'll call you at the weekend.'

On the way home, Anna had stopped at the newsagent's. The *Evening Times* was out already; it ran three editions every day. Jamie's face, piles of them, all wrapped in string bundles. He was wearing a suit, grey like his face, pictured hurrying into court.

'No Licence to Kill', ran the headline.

'Can I take one?' she asked the shopkeeper.

'Sure doll. They're just in. Haud on till I get my penknife.'

With a deft slash he ripped one bundle open, handed her the top copy.

'There can be no exceptions, and no hiding place for police officers that break the law,' the piece began. She read on: *These were the words of Glasgow's Area Procurator Fiscal Arnold Crane today, following scenes of uproar at the High Court, as the first serving police officer ever to be jailed for murder was led away to begin his life sentence.*

The font and the photograph were both so big that she had to turn to the inside page to read the next paragraph. It was one of those 'specials' that ran to several pages, the kind they'd write in advance and have poised, all waiting, like when someone dies.

'Here, I'm no a library, hen,' said the newsagent. 'Are you wanting to buy it or no?'

'What? Sorry, yes.' She handed him some coins, and walked out, still reading.

A column on Jamie's career: *Never reached his potential.* Who gave them this rubbish? *Failed to achieve promotion . . . spent time in the seedy world of the Vice Squad.* What was that supposed to imply? There was an insipid paragraph from the Federation, reserving any comment until they had 'studied the judge's findings'. A résumé of all police shootings to date, laid out like a league table. Lots of information, broken into bitesized chunks, so you could digest it easily with a biscuit and a cup of tea. Even a bit about 'what motivates a cop to kill', from some psychologist, who probably didn't know his arse from his elbow. And this, a sincere, careful exculpation from the Deputy Chief Constable:

'We would like to extend our utmost sympathies to the Brisbane family, and express our sincerest regret on the loss of Sarah. I personally feel deep regret that one of our officers has been found guilty of the crime of murder. However, I take some comfort from the fact that justice has been done. I would also like to reassure the public that we will be examining every element of our already robust screening and training for firearms officers, to make sure that we do everything we can to avoid such a terrible tragedy in the future. We further acknowledge that, when individual officers do disregard their training and descend into criminality, then the full weight of the law must be brought upon them. We are therefore satisfied that this life sentence is an appropriate one in the circumstances.'

Wiping their hands of him. *Life.* Well, she'd known that. Life was automatic for murder. Fifteen minimum, so he could be out in seven. Seven years wasn't so bad. In seven years, she'd be . . . forty-three. Not that far from retirement. And Jamie's daughter would be a teenager . . . not much younger than the girl he'd killed. There was a section on her too:

Sarah Brisbane: the girl who hardly had a life.

Behind tightly drawn curtains, a family grieve today – as they have done since May – sobbing before a photograph of a teenage girl; shy smile, blue eyes, and long, straight brown hair. Fifteen-year-old Sarah Brisbane had wanted to be a veterinary nurse. She was studying hard at King's Park Secondary School in the south side of Glasgow, where staff described her as a quiet girl. 'She was always taking in stray animals,' said her father. 'Wild ones, too – we even had a baby rabbit once. She was that gentle with them.'

But Sarah's life was never easy. Her mother left home when she was six, and thereafter, her father struggled to raise both her and her older brother. This sometimes chaotic family moved from one address to another, as Gerard Brisbane fought to deal with his drug addictions, and keep his family together.

It is to this sad, tired-looking man's credit that neither Sarah nor her brother ever got involved with the law, despite their father's frequent brushes with it. A troubled family, perhaps, but a loving one. Sarah's brother Craig left the dark streets of Glasgow, to try and make a better life for himself in Manchester – returning frequently to care for his sister and father when he could. And it was Sarah's grandmother who stepped in when Sarah's mum left, providing a degree of care and stability that young Sarah hadn't known for some time.

'She was a wee angel,' said Betty Brisbane. 'A right quiet, shy wee thing. Good as gold, mind – which is why we can't understand what the police are saying about her, that she was ranting and screaming at them that night. It's been nothing but one lie after another from that lot.'

Indeed, finally, a life of crime did touch on poor Sarah, though not in the way anyone might have expected. She was snatched from her family in a hail of police gunfire, amidst claims that she was brandishing a gun and threatening to kill passersby. These claims were finally rubbished in court today, when a jury found Constable James Worth, the man accused of shooting Sarah, guilty of her murder. At worst, it seems that Sarah herself was guilty only of shouting out of an opened window. A moment of out-of-character confusion, a teenage tantrum, a cry for help? We will never know. But we do know that Sarah Brisbane died alone. And with no trace of a gun anywhere near her.

Today's papers would be more of the same. Anna pulled a wrought-iron chair out from the little table, sat down. A chirrup from the rosemary bush, as a sleek-limbed mini-tiger stalked towards her.

'Hello, gorgeous.'

Alice wound once, twice around Anna's legs, then stretched, gloriously long, and flipped onto her stripy back, baring a fluff-mottled belly for inspection. Anna rubbed her big toe deep into the fur, feeling purring throbs burr through her foot. Sunshine always brought out the best in folk, awakening glimmers of some deep-buried thirst. The parkie had raised his hand in greeting, the newsagent – that same newsagent – had smiled and said 'Good morning'. By now, Jamie would have spent his first night behind bars. Anna pictured him in his cell, looking out at the world he couldn't have. Only a bastard could have designed Barlinnie to be so close to civilisation. Although, to be fair, it had been there first. His window would be sealed, so he couldn't feel the sun. But he would see it.

She wondered if she should make contact with Cath. A note, a phone call. Should she send a card? *Congratulations on your Husband's Incarceration.* Cath didn't know what Anna had done to her. All she knew of Anna was distant, past connections: Jamie's boss a few years ago, Jamie's girlfriend a decade ago. Anna was Cath's almost-friend, who saved her life, then slipped quietly from the scene.

Would it look strange if she didn't get in touch now? She could text Cath, she supposed, offer some smiley emoticonned support. She still had her mobile number. Or did she delete it?

Anna, Anna. Live your own life, not theirs.

She checked her mobile, huffed a long, deep puff that stopped the cat in mid-lick. She'd not heard from David yet, and he must have known she'd tried to phone.

Ah.

From her work phone. The number of which he wouldn't recognise.

Bloody phones, emails – they were all too immediate. Scroll through your messages, stop typing at every 'ping'. And all too silent when there was nobody talking to you. Which just made her want to see him more. Whether it was for distraction, reassurance or just a need to be held, Anna didn't know. David had been an exciting possibility that she was saving for when she felt ready. But what was 'ready'? And how did you know, if you never even contemplated that first, brave leap? Again she thought of Jamie, and the girl he'd killed, and the days that neither would have.

Anna wanted no confusion, a clean slate.

An uncomplicated life.

The sun curled around her shoulders, on the back of her neck, cooling jog-induced sweat, stirring *I can do anything* resolve. She would go and see David. Start again.

But first, she'd have a shower. 'Well, Alice. I think Mummy's going to take a trip into town.' The deep purrs increased with the pressure of Anna's foot. 'And there's that nice fish shop beside the court, where they do the lemon sole, remember? Yes, we like sole, don't we?'

Alice quivered like she would burst. Anna knelt down, blew a raspberry in tender belly fur. At once, Alice sprang to her feet, and marched off, tail swishing at the indignation of it all.

'Ach, you'll be back, girlie, once you smell your dinner poaching.'

It always smelled of fish. Fish on a Friday, that must have been a school rule. She stood beside the bins at the back of the kitchen, watching the lines go in. She had nobody to stand with, so would wait until she could just walk straight to the counter. Pick up what was left, go to the nearest seat, bow her head and eat. Free school meals, and they always checked your ticket, pulled you up if you didn't go, so it was easier just to sidle in, shovel it down, then go back out and wait. Nobody wanted to know a girl with unwashed hair and a skirt too long, and that suited her fine. She didn't care. Secondary school was next year and it was bigger and wilder, so she could slink through the fray. Unseen, unknown. And then she'd go home.

Her brother's room smelled of fish, too. Of boy sweat and clotted tissues and that funny sweet perfume her mother made. Always, now, he was angry and sad, and she wished she could make him better.

The closer Anna got to the Sheriff Court, the stronger her desire to turn around. Guts grumbling – she should have eaten something. Could have just waited till he got home, then called him. Did this seem desperate, or wildly courageous? Like 'An Officer and Gentleman', she'd sweep him off his feet, and all those months apart would melt away. She'd timed her arrival for the lunch recess. Oh, she'd phoned the admin office and checked, she wasn't stupid. David was at the Sheriff today, case against Waddle and Brown. And the sheriff was Wutherspoon, who always liked a lengthy three-courser.

The steps outside the court were empty. Another few minutes, and it would discharge its effluent into the Clyde. Well, onto its banks.

'Oh, hi Anna.'

It was Rachel, a lawyer Anna had worked with before. 'You going in or out?'

'Neither, really. I'm hoping to catch one of the fiscals: David Millar? Is he still inside, do you know?'

'Oh *David*. Mmm.'

'What d'you mean, mmm?'

'You know. Business or pleasure?'

Anna laughed. 'What do you think?'

Rachel narrowed her gaze, tapped her chin. 'I never know with you, Inspector Cameron. But yes, I reckon he's still in court. It's been manic actually; he's been tied up with another big case across the river. We've only just got him back.'

Anna shrugged, dead casual. 'Och well, I'll just hang fire here till he finishes. Only one way out of this place, isn't there?'

Then she clocked the prison carrier, pulling up at the electronic barrier.

'Well, two I guess, if you count the big blue bus.' As she said it, she felt nerve prickles crackle her back. Yesterday, Jamie would have been put in that big blue bus.

'Why not just wait in our restroom?' said Rachel. 'C'mon and I'll show you; he'll need to come in to dump his robes and stuff.'

'It's fine. You're just heading out.'

'Och, it won't take a moment. And I wouldn't want you to miss him or anything.'

'It's not *that* important,' mumbled Anna, letting herself be led inside.

The room was like a teachers' staff room, all pinboards and posters, leaflets and dirty mugs. The only difference was the small cloakroom they passed through first, festooned with wigs and long black cloaks, hanging beside everyday overcoats and sports bags. One cloak had fallen from its peg, sprawled on the floor like a big dead crow. Rachel pushed it away with her foot. 'Behold the robing room. Dead glam, eh? Look, I'll have to love you and leave you. Grab a chair. Nice copy of the *Law Society Journal* there too, if you fancy.'

'Nah, you're alright. I'll just veg.'

'Well,' smirked Rachel. 'Enjoy your lunch. With the Divine Big D.'

'You enjoy yours.'

'Unlikely. A smear test at the Family Planning Clinic?'

'*Nice.*'

Anna stood by the window, looking out onto the River Clyde. It looked pretty in the sunlight, choppy little wavelets sprinkling glitter onto seagulls. The suspension bridge curved an elegant dip up to Anna's left, blazing white above brown water. She remembered standing there once, looking down at the ripples as they bled further out. Movement beneath, people appearing on the pavements below. Court was spilling, stretching. Getting hungry. She smoothed her hair, paced the floor. Footsteps. A couple of people entered. A woman, an older man. Not him. They nodded, one went to the fridge, took out sandwiches. Both left. More footsteps. A shout.

'Hey, Big Cheese. Hold up!'

'Hi there, mate, how are you?'

Anna stiffened. Anna soared. That second voice was David's. She could hear them approach the robing room, getting louder. Her heartbeat getting louder, throat drier. Would he kiss her?

'Tried to catch you yesterday. So, how does it feel to help make legal history then?'

'Feels good.'

She heard David's colleague laugh. 'What you doing for an encore?'

Anna could see a darkening pass over the crack between jamb and door. David was less than four feet away from her and she was staring at the shadow and then it swung out wide and he was . . .

. . . Even better than she remembered.

Taller, darker, smarter, sexier. His face blooming genuine delight, cheeks crinkling beneath his wide, wide eyes. Slowly shaking his head in joyful disbelief.

'Simon. Meet my encore.'

Anna feigned feistiness, when all she wanted was to hurl herself forward and thud into his chest.

'I've never been called *that* before.'

'What? You've never been asked for a repeat performance? I don't believe that.'

'Em . . . I'll just away and . . .' Simon's voice grew fainter and ceased to be.

David came close, fingered a strand of Anna's hair.

'Shorter. Nice.'

Electrical impulses shooting through fine filaments, her skin on end. Warm smell of his neck, the welcome of his mouth.

Enough. For now.

He stepped back, gripped her by the elbows.

'It's good to see you, Anna Cameron.'

An appetiser.

'Lunch?' he asked.

'You got time?'

'You got the money?'

'How much do you charge?'

As they left the court, David's hand was on the small of her back. With someone else, Anna would have found this presumptuous. With David, she was frightened to walk too quickly in case she lost his easy touch. Their conversation was easy too, gentle flirting masking beats of urgency. Anna let herself enjoy the rhythm. There was plenty of time.

Sarti's was an Italian deli-cum-bistro, rustic and simple. Great hams and salami dangled from the ceiling and wooden shelves buckled under the weight of cheeses and Chianti. Its doorman was not a pretension. The bustling little establishment was so perpetually busy, he acted as maitre d', taxi-finder, and, this being Glasgow, bouncer. He took Anna's jacket, and led them to a table. David ordered a platter of mixed cold meats and some foccacia from the open deli counter.

'You don't mind something quick, do you? I've got to be back in court in half an hour.'

He was squeezing her into his busy schedule. Anna tried to read signs. Was that good or bad? Was he so chuffed to see her that he was grabbing any time available, or was this a subtle slide away, to culminate in *I'll give you a call*?

'You've got to taste this ham.'

Instead of offering her the plate, David picked up a sliver in his fingers, held it out to Anna. She took the petal of meat in her hand, poked it in her mouth.

'Good?'

'Mmhm.'

He poured some water. 'So. You're back.'

'Yup. And you said to look you up.'

'I know. I missed you.'

'Did you?' Anna tore off a lump of bread.

'I did.' David put a hand over hers. 'No. Try it with the oil first.'
He took the piece of focaccia from Anna's fingers. 'Extra virgin.'
'Ha.'

He drizzled a little oil, just enough to make the bread glisten.
This time, she let him place the food in her mouth.

'Have you been back long?'

'Not really,' she said.

'Still in Govan?'

'It's Easterhouse.'

'Sorry, so it is. My brain's like a pound of mince at the moment.'

'How come?'

'Lack of sleep, too much hassle; I've been working on this nightmare case since I came to Glasgow.' He yawned. 'It only finished the
other day. Talk about micro-managing: I had the AD – smug git
called Billings – on my case morning noon and night, the press
wanting daily exclusives, and a bloody ACC who insisted I "look" at
every statement again and again and again. He was adamant we'd to
reinterview the witnesses as many times as it took.'

'As it took for what?'

'You tell me. To get the desired responses, I guess.'

The focaccia was sprinkled with little chunks of rock salt. She
crunched one hard, palate-popping sea breezes scouring her
throat.

'Meaning?'

'Well, this was one little fish that wasn't getting away, put it like
that. God, talk about closing ranks. When you lot turn on your
own, it's scary.'

'Our own?'

'Aye. It was that killer cop trial. James Worth?'

A sucking wheeze. Anna's breath, swallowed the wrong way.

'Ach, I didn't mind working it up him anyway. Guilty as sin, so
he was. You can just tell, can't you? It's in their eyes.'

Anna's first instinct was to hit him. She squealed her chair back
over terracotta tiles. It might have jarred against the table behind,
someone tutting *Hey, watch it* but all she really heard was her own
voice, viscous as spittle.

'You bastard.'

'Pardon?'

'That's a real person you're talking about. A guy who was trying to put himself between a rock and a hard place, trying to do his job, do his fucking best.'

'His best was pretty appalling, if you ask me.'

'Well, I'm not asking you. What would you know about risk, anyway? Scariest thing you have to confront every day is if your secretary forgets to put sugar in your tea. Had a good laugh when you sent a cop to jail did you? Big feather in your cap, was it? *Prick.*'

'What?'

What a sick, sick threesome: David screwing Jamie from behind, Anna in the middle, all righteous indignation.

'You heard me. Prick.'

Her intellect seared by anger, resorting to the comfort blanket of crude oaths and insults. She had to get out. Without waiting for a response, Anna fled the restaurant, fled David's baffled face.

I didn't mind working it up him. Ugly phrasing, ugly man. She was surprised at how quick her loyalties had leapt. No contest really. *You can see it in their eyes.* Aye, right. But this was wrong, all wrong, like some sick-joke jack-in-the-box, springing out when she'd stuffed it all down. David shafting Jamie. Everyone, deliberately, purposefully shafting Jamie. That was what David had said; implied at least. She made her way down Renfield Street, pushing through people, trying to wind back to when she hadn't really been paying attention, just gazing at David and thinking *yes, yes, yes.* Something about an ACC wanting the desired responses?

Her car was parked across the river, back on the south side. The suspension bridge rumbled as she hurried across, twanging sways that belied its sturdy metal frame. Anna could feel her cheeks burning, hands shaking as she forced her key in the lock. She threw herself into the driver's seat and started the engine.

Wanting the desired responses.

An implication that Jamie's trial had been worked from behind. And that David had been involved. Like water on salt, just there, he was dissolved. Was nothing. As was Jamie, she kept reminding herself. He was just a man she once knew. Someone else could worry for him. Someone like Cath. Pressing her foot to the floor, turning the wheel, not thinking, not planning. Knowing it was wrong, it was wrong and she couldn't do it. She couldn't walk away. Anna had to tell. Driving, driving and she had to tell. Yet what, exactly, was she telling? Only a snatch of some suspicion. A smug assertion from David that justice was not blind. Aye, well it wasn't deaf either.

Only one person she *could* tell.

Catherine Worth.

Cath's house hadn't changed. Still full of toys in the garden, still needing new paint on gutters and door. Anna had never been inside it, but had driven by, more than once. Not stalking, you understand. Just looking. A few cans and sandwich wrappers dumped by the front gate suggested someone else had been camping out here, biding their time. Little curls of Kodak film wrappers puttering in the breeze. Looked like the media circus had upped and left. The curtains in the front room were pulled part over, but there was a car in the drive. Anna banged on the door, too loud to miss.

'I've told you, I've nothing to say. Please go away.'

'Cath. I'm not a reporter, I promise you. It's Anna Cameron.'

'What?'

'Anna. I was in the Flexi—'

The door swung open. 'I know who you *are*.'

Cath looked awful. Puffed-up and blotchy, her hair wild and unbrushed. Greasy stains down the front of her baggy sweat-shirt, hand hoicking at towelling joggers which hung above her ankles.

'Hi!' Anna raised her hand, embarrassed. 'I know, bolt from the blue, this. And I know you probably don't want to see anyone now, but—'

'He's not dead, you know.'

'Who's not dead?'

'My husband. That's usually when these confrontations happen, isn't it?'

Anna shook her head. Must be water in her ears still. A little girl sidled up behind Cath, one arm snaking around the front of her thigh. Mini Jamie-eyes scowled from under a lopsided fringe. 'Whoozit Mummy?' The child spoke to Cath, but stared all the while at Anna.

'Nobody.'

Anna crouched down. 'Hey there. You must be Eilidh. Last time I saw you, you were just a little baby.'

And I was grabbing clumps of your hair, your leg, dragging you out a burning building. I bet your mummy never told you that.

'Who are *you*?' retorted Eilidh. 'My mummy's not well, and you need to go away.'

'Eilidh!'

'Well, Eilidh, I'm Anna, and I'm a friend of your mummy's.' She heard Cath snort.

'Cath, I know this isn't a good time,' she said, straightening up, 'and I know I haven't been in touch for ages. I'm sorry. I'm so sorry about Jamie, about everything that's happened.'

'Everything?'

'Yes. Of course.'

Why was Cath crying? Soft orbs of tears, pooling in the corners of her eyes.

'Look, I wouldn't be here if it wasn't important. I think somebody set Jamie up. Well, not set him up exactly; but I don't think the trial was fair. Witnesses have been coerced into lying, I'm sure. I don't know why yet, but—'

'Eilidh, will you go inside, please.'

'No.' Two wee arms winding around now. They dug in tighter to Cath's legs, puckering her joggers, Eilidh's face all pudged up on one side where she was squashing into Cath. 'I'm lookin after you.'

'Eilidh, I promise you, Mummy's fine. Away you go and see if Daniel's finished watching Postman Pat yet.'

Eilidh hesitated. One arm slid away, the other still holding Cath's leg. She looked doubtfully up at her mother.

'If he has, you can put on *Barbie Princess Tales*.'

The remaining hand immediately dropped down. 'Oh. Okay, Mummy. DANIL,' she yelled, running into the house. 'I've to get *Barbie Princess Tales* on. NOW! MUMMY SAYS!'

'Would it be easier if I came in?' asked Anna.

'No.'

A small, tight pulse flicked in Anna's neck. 'Oh. Right. Fair enough. But, I need to know what you think. You know, did any weird things happen in the run-up to the trial; midnight phone calls to Jamie, folk suddenly changing their tune about supporting him?'

'Fuck off, Anna.'

'Pardon?'

'I don't need this, and I don't need you. We're not toy figures in a dolls' house, that you can play with when you're bored.'

'Now, wait a minute here.' Anna moved up a step, so she was standing almost level with Cath. 'I'm just trying to help you—'

She wasn't prepared for the rapid, jabbing punch that caught her on the jaw, swinging her backwards so she wavered, stumbled sideways off the step. Landing awkwardly on her ankle, she grabbed at a climbing rose to steady her. Of course, it had thorns, big ones that bit her palm, her fingers. 'Shit-shit-shit,' she yelped, pulling her hand free, sucking on her thumb. 'For fucksake Cath. What was that for?'

'I don't do cat fights.'

'You could've broken my nose.'

'Guess I could have, if I'd tried. Then you'd be twisted on the outside too.'

'Cath, it wasn't me that sent Jamie to jail. I'm trying to help you here—'

'But it was you that fucked him, wasn't it, Anna?'

Anna stared down at her thumb. Two globules of blood, like a viper bite, stinging sorer than they looked. Her face smarting, crimson all across, brain whirling wild possibilities of excuse and indignation. Keeping her head down.

'How did you know?'

'He told me.'

'Did you know in hospital? When I visited you after the fire?'

'Kind of. Let's just say I had a strong suspicion.'

'But how?' She made herself look up.

Cath's eyes were wild things, scuttling shadows and firing sparks. 'I got a note. Several of them, in fact, from a concerned "well-wisher". Genuine green ink and everything.'

'Jenny.'

'Nah, the writing was far too neat for her.'

Green ink? Immediately, Anna thought of smarmy Gus and his vibrant pens. Gus, the sergeant who'd replaced her in the Flexi Unit, who was currently under investigation for touching up two female probationers at a night out. Who'd been jealous of Anna, wanted her out of the way. Who'd leered knowingly at her and Jamie, when they'd been standing too close or talking too quietly.

'Plus, that's not Jenny's style,' continued Cath. 'If she wanted you to know something, she'd just tell you to your face.' Then, quick and pointed as a dart, 'But I *knew* she knew anyway, so you can piss off there too. There's *nothing* you know that I don't, Anna. Jamie told me it all.'

'Oh, Cath. Please believe me,' said Anna, 'I wish it had never happened.'

'Me too.' Cath's fingers were clenched at her side, tugging at her sweatshirt.

'Can I do anything?'

'You can go away.'

Anna nodded. 'Okay. But, please, will you think about what I said? If there's anything that could give me a lead . . .'

'Because you're a dog? Anna: you don't go near my husband, you don't have anything to do with my family. You leave us alone – understand?'

It was an order, and a plea. Still, after all this time, after all the hurt he had wreaked on her, Cath loved Jamie absolutely. Anna could see Eilidh, watching them both from the sitting-room window. The little girl was chewing on her nails, hand curled tight against her lips. She remembered doing the exact same thing when her daddy died. Standing for hours, looking out and waiting, while you hurt yourself for comfort.

'Yes. I understand.'

The door clicked shut as she was walking back to the car. She looked round, saw Cath join her daughter at the window. Pale ghost girls behind the glass.

19

Jamie wiped bread around the edge of the plastic plate, chasing the last of the cheese sauce. Macaroni, again. A twinge of pain down his left side, at the back, where his kidneys were. Hanging on still, doing all their necessary filterings, but swollen enough to have him pissing pins and needles these last three weeks. Nothing much to think about in here but the pain. Still – he probed his fingers into his side – it was a small pain, in comparison to torn-apart flesh and bullets breaking bone. No books, no papers, no visitors, no privileges to make compartments of his day. They dealt with him the way he'd deal with Eilidh and Daniel. Not listening, not caring who said what to whom. Swift smack for both, then bed.

Not always. Mostly, he was a good dad. But on one of those days where he'd just got in from work, and Cath had locked herself in the bathroom, and the two of them were playing up, and he was trying to read the paper, insistent tugging on either arm, a scuffle, a squeal . . . Oh God. For one of those days now. Only this time, he would scoop them both into his arms and laugh, kissing their beautiful, clean, soft faces.

Jamie went to put the bread in his mouth, then thought of how the turnkeys at Stewart Street would just rinse the plastic plates under a running tap, after every prisoner's meal. No disinfectant, no industrial dishwashers. Not even soapy liquid, no scrubbing, nothing. And here was he, mopping up sauce that had soaked into the saliva of God knew how many prisoners, with God knew how many diseases and infections. He threw the bread back onto the plate. They probably did have dishwashers here, but even so. He'd never got his own plate and spoon, like Cunningham promised. Apparently that was one of his withdrawn privileges.

Scrape-clang at the door. Automatically, he handed up his plate to the figure coming in. Easier not to make eye contact, because then something would be said. It usually was, and he was too tired too argue. But it was a warder, not a trusty.

'Right, Worth. Get your gear together. You're moving.'

'Where?'

'I don't know. You've got three minutes.'

Cold, clammy terror. No, this was it, now. The real punishment. They were going to move him to another hall, out of the safety of the hospital wing and into hell proper. Quickly, though he wanted to go so slow, he gathered up his toothpaste and toothbrush, his spare socks and his little scrap of soap. A bookmark made by Eilidh, glossy with carefully crayoned-in flowers and birds.

'That you?' barked the warder. 'M'on.'

The familiar leprosy routine. Another warder, shouting 'Clear!' Him in his sackcloth, shuffling through. Passing Murray's cell, hearing a slithery whisper. 'Be seeing you, pal.'

Not funny any more, not at all.

They took him downstairs, back to the receiving area where they'd first brought him in.

'Wait there.'

Stood him by the desk, dark heads bowing over paperwork, ticking forms that were all about him. At the edge of his eye, Jamie could see a purple tie, black shoes, folds of grey, thick cloth, piled neatly on the counter.

His civvie clothes, the suit he came in with!

A wonderful thrill; sure that this was it. Cath had found some great missing chunk of evidence, had overturned Jinky's lies and Coltrane's posturings. Unbeknownst to Jamie, she had master-minded his appeal. The decision had been made for him. His penance would still be waking to death, every single day. But not waking to it here. This was it, he was getting out. He tried to breathe in slow.

'Can someone tell me what's happening please?'

The pile was shoved towards him. 'Just get in there and get changed.'

Alone, in the manky dog box, he stroked his thumb over stripy silk, brushed his cheeks deliberately with crisp white cotton as he pulled his still-buttoned shirt over his head. His thick fingers had not been able to undo all the buttons when he took it off before. Even his boxers were in the pile, still smelling of Persil and home. His tie flapping loose, he scooped the prison clothes from the floor, and went outside, dumping the soiled garments on the counter.

A form was put in front of him. 'Right, Worth. Sign for your property where the cross is.'

Old habits: always read what you're signing first. He read the page, saw **Prisoner Transfer** stamped along the top. Felt stupid crystals of hope melt, the leaden mantle return.

'Transfer? Where am I going?'

'Botany Bay,' laughed the warder, handing the form, and the plastic envelope that still contained Jamie's wallet and belt, to another guard.

'Don't you believe it, sunshine,' said the guard. 'We've no koala bears down there. Just plenty fresh air and farmyard animals.'

'Aye, all full of shite like you!'

Even as he was trying to work out where they were taking him, Jamie yearned to be part of the banter. Two other prisoners were waiting by the desk, one in brutal pinstripes and an overblown tie, his tooled leather shoes screaming money. The other, a small, scruffy ned with junkie jitters, nodded at Jamie. 'Alright, Big Man?'

Jamie looked away.

The warder holding all the plastic envelopes raised his arm, like he was heading up a wagon trail. 'Gentlemen, your chariot awaits.'

They weren't cuffed. Just led in single file to a minibus. An ordinary white one, no bars on the windows. Only difference was the seats; two rows along the length, facing into each other, rather than the standard two by two. Not a word was spoken until they were all safely inside. A second warder turned round and grinned at them from the driver's seat. 'Any of you boys smoke? If so, yous can have a fag now.'

'Gonny tap us one then?' asked the ned. 'I'm all out.'

'Excuse me,' said Pinstripe. 'Does the law not apply here at all? If smoking's banned in lorry cabins, then I'm pretty sure it must be illegal in a prison van too. And I don't particularly want the stink of nicotine all over my suit.'

'Ach, there's aye one,' said the driver, taking off his hat, rubbing his shiny pate. He flung the cap at Jamie's chair. 'Ho, Hotshot.'

Jamie bridled. Why 'Hotshot'? Did this man know him, know his story? 'You speaking to me?'

'Aye, cowboy. I am that.' The driver winked, raised his index finger at right angles to his thumb. 'Kiss, kiss, bang, bang.' Blew the top of his index finger, winked again. 'You get the final vote. Yea or nay tae fags?'

Jamie's hands gripped hard on the edge of his seat, wishing it was the baldy bugger's neck. He shrugged. 'I don't give a shit either way.'

'Well,' said the driver, lighting up two fags and passing one to the ned, 'I'll no tell if yous don't.'

'Bloody ridiculous,' muttered Pinstripe. He edged as far away as he could from the smoke.

'Cheers, officer,' grovelled the ned. 'So, where is it we're off to?'

'Deepest, darkest Dumfriesshire,' said the first warder, who was sitting with them in the back.

'Where the fuck's that?'

'Nearly as far south as Englandshire, pal. Loads of coos and sheep.'

'Fucksake. How will the old doll get doon there?'

The driver chortled. 'Does she no go south as a rule then?'

'What?'

'He means does she not perform,' said Pinstripe.

'Perform what? She's pure crap at singing.'

'*God.* He's implying your wife doesn't give you blow jobs.'

Junky-ned swayed a little in his seat. 'I don't get it.'

'Ah, classic.' The driver slapped his steering wheel, spinning wide out of the prison gate.

Terraces and trees, cars and lampposts, still real, still there, but with a tinge of freshness, like when you return from holiday and see your house once more. A mongrel running, grinning. Free to pee and sniff and lick. Two kids on bikes, giving them V signs. *The sky.* It was so broad. How could he have forgotten that already?

'That's exactly my point, buddy. Exactly my point.' The driver kept laughing for ages, too long, too loud, until he caught Jamie staring at him in the rear-view mirror. 'What's up with your face, Hotshot? Too soon for all this sex talk?'

The other guard tapped the driver on the shoulder. 'Ho, Smithy. Ease up, eh?'

'Ho, George-*ee*. *Shut* up, eh? Well, Hotshot – is it? Bring back bad memories of your recent abuse, does it? And you a cop and all. Nae wonder law and order's gone to the dogs, if yous canny even protect yourselves.'

'Oh – *you're* the one,' said Pinstripe. 'Bit of a cliché, isn't it? A man-sandwich in the showers?'

'Give it to me, baby,' sang the driver, at the same moment as Jamie lunged from his seat, grabbing Pinstripe by his thrice-knotted tie.

'You fucking say that again, and I'll have you.'

'That's enough.' The other warder pulled Jamie back into his seat.

'The only thing happened to me is that I beat the crap out two guys,' shouted Jamie. 'Single fucking handed.'

Pinstripe straightened his tie. 'Only I heard you were in the scud at the time.'

Jamie lurched, took another swing at him. This time, he struck gold. Or rather a pliant belly, fist sinking into a cushion of flab.

'Oh God!' Pinstripe doubled over, '. . . can't . . . breathe.'

'Right, George, just cuff the lot of them,' yelled the driver. 'I'm no having this. I've got things to see to.'

Jamie was first, arms twisted up his back. George unhooked a set of cuffs from his belt, ratcheted them on tight. 'It's a long drive to sit with them on, you stupid bastard,' he said. He took the driver's cuffs and secured the wee ned next, before moving on to Pinstripe, who was still writhing across two seats.

'Sit up and shut up, you big wanker.'

The ned nudged up against Jamie, speaking low. 'Cool your jets, Big Man, or they'll barrel us all back up the road.'

'Couldny gie a fuck.'

Blade-edged dead voice. How quickly did it happen, this transformation to hard man from scared wee boy? It was all an act, just self-preservation, but it felt very real. He could almost believe his shoulders had squared of their own accord.

'I heard you fucking broke Leo's jaw, by the way,' whispered the ned.

'Is that right?'

'Aye. I'm Brian.'

'James.'

Jamie made a point of looking out the window. He didn't want to get drawn into any exchange of pleasantries. Give away any details about his life, himself. It had started raining, that smirry drizzle Glasgow excelled at. Still shops and houses, paved streets and pedestrian crossings passing by. He'd have thought they'd have gone on to the motorway by now, to pick up the A74 for the journey southwards.

'Right troops,' said the driver. 'I've a quick homer I need to do. So yous lot all sit tight and play nice, okay?'

The van pulled up outside a row of tenements. Jamie reckoned they were round about Alexandra Parade, though it was hard to tell through the window. 'What kind of a homer?' asked George.

'To see a man about a dog. How? You got a problem with that?'

'No, no. Wire in, Smithy. I'll keep an eye on things here.'

The driver jumped out, left the engine running.

'Is that a good idea? Leaving the three of us, here with you?' Pinstripe was the right way up again. 'I mean, we could stage a breakout, or anything.'

George sniffed. His status may have been lower than Smithy's, but it was certainly higher than theirs. 'Yous are hardly criminal masterminds now, are you?'

'The big man here's a murderer, by the way,' piped up Brian. 'Fucking shooters, the works.'

'Shut up, you arse,' said Jamie. He craned his neck, trying to see where Smithy had gone. He'd put a civvie jacket on, over his uniform shirt and tie.

George tapped him on the knee. 'Ho, you. Keep your hands and eyes facing front where I can see them.'

Jamie swivelled round, raised his tethered arms high above his back. 'What d'you think I am? A contortionist?'

'Less of the cheek, you.'

Jamie could feel Brian press into him, snuggling up almost, like he was basking in the glow. He couldn't move away, his other side squashed up against the side of the van, his legs stretched out far enough to touch Pinstripe's pointed black shoes. Pinstripe's face was all sulky, like a wean being left out. He turned his shoulder away from Jamie, leaned towards Brian. 'I'm Peter.'

'Alright Peter? How you doing? What you in for then?'

'Embezzlement,' sighed Pinstripe. 'Some of my clients were sharper than they looked, sadly.'

'A rip-off lawyer?' Jamie shook his head. 'It's *you* that's the walking cliché, pal.'

'Right, girls. I said that's *enough*.'

Garthlock Prison looked like a berthed liner, or an Art Deco stately home. Fine squares of grey granite, ridged straight pillars and thin metal ironwork gates, all cast adrift in a sea of green acres; which were dotted with sheep and cows, right enough.

'Ah. Smell that country air.' The driver beamed at them all as he drew up outside the main door. 'Welcome home, folks.' Blew Jamie a kiss. 'Ladies first.'

Jamie rose from his seat. A tug at his jacket. 'Leave it, Big Man.'

'I'm just getting up.'

Jamie thought Brian had been sleeping. Clearly not. Maybe he just shut his eyes when he was recharging. He certainly seemed a bit sharper than before. Jamie pulled his sleeve free, stepped out of the bus. His legs and back ached from the two-hour journey. How would Cath ever get down here? She hated driving on twisty country roads.

'Excuse me,' he asked George. 'Will someone tell my wife I've been moved here?'

'Aye, if you want. Though most of the boys here are quite happy to escape the earbashings! One of the advantages of being so far from home, know? Now, out we get, gents. Matron will have supper on.'

Up the steps, and in through the portico. No butler waiting for them, just another couple of warders, with three baskets of clean clothing, soap, towels and shampoo. The air felt lighter, like there was ozone buzzing brighter ions here.

'Help yourselves, boys,' said one of the new warders. 'Your names are on the baskets.'

Peter picked up a bar of soap, sniffed it. 'Well, at least it's not carbolic.'

'Aye, and the towels cover your arse and all,' said Brian, unfolding one for inspection.

'Brian Finnegan?'

'Yes, officer.'

'Right Brian . . . assault and robbery . . . eighteen months. Och, you're only in for a shit and a shave. And you're on the methadone programme, I see?'

'Aye, that's right, sir. Where do I sign for my green juice?'

'We'll discuss that once you've seen the doc. Peter Grant?'

'Yes.'

'Embezzlement, eh? Well, we'll put you in charge of the Christmas Club then.' He looked over his specs at Jamie. 'And you must be James Worth?'

Jamie steeled himself for the comments.

'Okay, James. Straight to the hospital ward, please.'

There were only two levels to the main building. Reception, the dining hall and various offices were on the ground floor, plus the hospital ward, which was beside a shower block and a gymnasium. Jamie was taken straight through to see the doctor, a stooped man with thinning, slicked-back hair and thick black spectacles.

'Ah, Mr Worth, is it?'

'Yes, doctor.'

'That's fine, Mr Donald,' the doctor said to the warder. 'You can wait outside. Okay then, let's have a little look, shall we? I'm Dr McLay, by the way.'

Jamie began to unbuckle his belt.

'No, no, at your file, not you. I'm not going to embarrass you, son.'

Don't call me son. That's what my dad calls me, and I don't want him here.

'Don't need to examine you, eh? You're not concealing any pills or anything, are you?'

'No, sir.'

'Good man. Have a seat. You coping?'

Jamie sat on the edge of the examining couch. 'I suppose.'

'Sleeping?'

'Not really.'

'Eating well? I see here that you're a vegetarian. Since when?'

'Since . . . since May.'

'Okay. Well, you'll need to watch for iron deficiency. Plenty leafy greens, kale, that kind of stuff. But we grow lots of our own veg here. In fact, you should try and get a wee job in one of the labour teams – do you good. Lovely countryside round here, too.'

Jamie nodded. Wary. This felt like a timeshare presentation, not a medical.

'Now, it's been suggested that you might benefit from a degree of counselling. How would you feel about that?'

'Not my style, doctor.'

'Fine. I'm not going to push you. What I will say, though, is that you need some kind of an outlet. I imagine you're still getting flashbacks?'

Jamie shrugged. 'Sometimes.'

'Panic attacks? Anxiety? Constriction of airways?'

'A bit.'

The doctor nodded. 'Do you have a faith, Mr Worth?'

'I was brought up a Catholic. Why?'

'I find it helps. Particularly if you're trying to internalise what's happened to you. Never a good idea. Those men in here who can believe in something tend to fare a little better than the nihilists. We all need to have hope, Mr Worth.'

The warder came back into the surgery. 'Dr McLay, that's the governor ready to see him now.'

'Well, that all seems tickety-boo,' said the doctor. 'Away and get your audience with Himself.'

The warder took Jamie back towards the main entrance, turning off through an archway to a corridor of offices. Jamie was still carrying his basket of clothes. There was a new pair of plastic shoes on the top, what looked like a heavy jumper, a couple of T-shirts, jeans and underwear. Looked clean, too. He nudged the jeans over to check. Aye, four pairs of boxers, still in the packet.

'Nice togs, eh?' said the warder.

'How did you know what sizes we were?'

'Bar-L tells us. Yup, we know everything about you before you even get here – right down to your inside leg measurement. You don't have to wear that stuff, mind. You can wear your own clothes if you prefer.'

'Really?'

'Aye. Unless you're into plastic shoes that is. Okay, here we are. Governor's name is Mr Ethelridge, Ethel to his friends. Now, mind and curtsey when you go in.' He pressed a little buzzer on the door jamb. 'Prisoner to see you, sir. New arrival.'

'Come,' said a metallic twang through the speaker.

Ethelridge had his back to them when the warder opened the door. He stood with military bearing, hands clasped behind him, examining a row of books on the mantelpiece behind his desk. Soft putters and snaps sparked from the open fire, and the room was filled with the scent of cedar wood. An elegant room, all clubby leather and Landseer prints – designed for sipping whisky and smoking a pipe in.

Ting.

Jamie felt a little pulse of pleasure on seeing a clock just like his gran's.

Ethelridge spun smartly on his heel as they approached his desk, grey eyes sweeping up and down. Kind of guy you should salute.

'James Worth. So, you're the police officer that's been gracing all of our media headlines recently?'

'Ex-police officer, sir.'

'Well, ex- or no, you'll understand the importance of keeping proper order in any form of civilised community.'

Marching, pacing, all the time he spoke. Jamie didn't know whether he should keep staring straight ahead, or follow the governor as he patrolled around the room. *Follow the leader*, Eilidh loved to play it, in the garden, skipping around her dolls and bears. A sudden punch of self-pity, aching deeper than his kidneys.

'And I do, very much, see this as a community. Now, I'm not blind, Worth – or stupid. I know the sorts of things that go on in every jail. However, Garthlock is somewhat of an experimental prison. We're not an open jail, yet we practise many of the approaches and theories one would associate with such an establishment. Indeed, I believe we're far in advance of many of them in several aspects. "Respect earns Results": that's my motto. That and *Nemo Me Impune Lacessit*, of course.'

He stopped, dead, two inches from Jamie's face. Wide, black pores on his nose, little nostril bristles twitching. 'I'm nobody's patsy.'

'*Wha daur meddle wi me*, sir?'

'Indeed, Worth, indeed. My old regimental motto. Were you in the services?'

'No, sir.'

'Hmm.'

Ethelridge moved around his desk, sat on the padded leather chair behind it. 'You're very fortunate that you've arrived at Garthlock, Worth. Prisoners that come here are all strong candidates for rehabilitation; they tend either to be approaching release, or to have specific personal or custodial circumstances that require a more . . . considered approach than can be offered in mainstream prisons. Rigid, yet relaxed.'

He liked his alliteration, this man. The warder coughed. Was Jamie meant to say something? Offer his compliments on Ethelridge's vision? There were still locks on every door.

'I certainly noticed a different atmosphere when I arrived here, sir. Your staff seem – much less tense. Well, most of them.'

The governor smiled. 'You've seen Barlinnie, Worth. Boys working in places like that; it's as much a sentence for them as it is for the prisoners. You'll know all about pressure: the danger of being attacked, living on your nerves, existing in a powder keg every day. Brutal, isn't it?'

'Yes, sir.'

'But they're not all bad, even in the Bar-L. Some of my best men have come from there. One of them, Cunningham, has actually chosen to go back, to head up a new restorative justice unit.'

He paused, eyeballed Jamie.

'What is it, Worth?'

'Nothing, sir.'

'I detected something of a sardonic smile there, did I not?'

'I'm just a bit cynical about the benefits of getting a ned to say sorry like a nice boy, then thinking he'll see the error of his ways, and never offend again.'

'Takes a brave man to look his victim in the eye, and see the impact of what he's done. Or the victim's family, for that matter.'

Ethelridge never let his gaze leave Jamie's face. His stillness, after all the stalking that preceded it, was disconcerting. That was why Jamie felt uneasy. It was the staring, not the words – a spiel the governor probably fed every new arrival. Words couldn't burrow themselves inside you like pictures could. And if he was made to look at Sarah's father's face, then that would be another picture, to pile on top of the pictures of Cath's face and Eilidh's face and Daniel's face and his mother's face. And Sarah's face, that never moved.

There was no more room.

'Still, good man, Cunningham. I trust his judgement. Was him that put in an eloquent plea to get you moved here. So,' Ethelridge clapped his hands together, cracking the spell, 'arrangements while you're here. You'll have your own peter.'

'Peter, sir?'

'Cell. You're free to come and go within Columba wing, but will have no contact with prisoners outside until you've been properly assessed. In time, you may be moved into one of the other wings. And you will be here some time, Worth, longer than most of the men here. So, it's in your interests to co-operate with my officers, keep your nose clean, and set a good example to the rest of the inmates. Don't think you have anything to prove here – understand?'

'Yes, sir.'

'You'll have the opportunity to look at retraining. Do you have a trade, Worth?'

'Not any more, sir, no.'

Ethelridge nodded. 'Well, we'll allocate you somewhere menial to begin with. There's a pecking order for plum jobs, I'm afraid – tiresome, I know, but it's all some of these chaps have to strive towards.' He stood up again. 'I have no doubt that you are facing one of the biggest challenges of your life, Worth. We'll keep you busy, work you hard – the rest is up to you.'

'Yes, sir. Thank you.'

The warder led Jamie out. 'Right, let's get you up to your new hoose. We've four blocks, all named after saints. Your peter's in Columba.'

Instead of going back the way they came, they went further along the corridor, to an outside door. 'We'll nip across the quad. It's quicker.' As they walked across the courtyard Jamie saw two men, huddled in the far corner, in the shadow of a row of recycling skips. There were several different containers: a bottle bank, a paper bin, and one that smelled like compost as they got closer to it.

'Governor's right into being green. He's even talking about getting a wind turbine in. See up there, on that turrety thing.'

The warder was pointing upwards, looking in the opposite direction to the men, but Jamie was straining to hear what they were saying. You couldn't just eradicate sixteen years of sniffing out shite. There was never something right about two men huddled in the dark, shoulders slumped, voices low. Jamie could almost make out their voices. When they drew level, he could hear that it was the taller man speaking, the one with his back to Jamie.

'There you go, sunshine. Two new Nokias as requested. Fully charged and ready to roll.'

The other prisoner hopped from foot to foot, hand outstretched. He must have been able to see Jamie and the warder coming. Maybe it was all above board. Then Jamie clocked the prisoner's eyes, cloudy pupils filling the iris. And the hands. Track-marked trembling, reaching to grab at the package the first man held.

'Ah, ah. Not so quick. Cash on delivery, if you remember.' Suddenly, the first man's voice got louder, sterner. 'Right you. I'm confiscating these. You know you're no supposed to have them.' He slapped the prisoner's head. 'You fucking know that, Wilson.'

Turning his head round, he offered a carefully crafted look of surprise. 'Och, it's yourself, Ronnie. Just caught this wee scrote trying to do the dirty.'

It was Smithy, the driver that had brought them down.

'Aye, well, we'll leave you to it, Smithy,' said the warder. He kept right on walking, steering Jamie in front of him. Didn't even break his pace.

20

She should have killed her. Pressed her stringy windpipe hard, till her perfect, pale face turned purple. How dare Anna Cameron turn up at Cath's front door, a camel-coloured hyena come to pick over the bones? Spouting a load of crap too, all *ooh, I'm Anna, I'll sort you all out. There's been a miscarriage of justice, don't you know?* Did she not think Cath had explored that avenue already?

She'd met with Len Mackenzie two days after Jamie was jailed. A reluctant, hurried meeting on Len's part, but one that Cath insisted on. She didn't know if it was embarrassment at his failure to help them, or concern over who would be paying for the consultation that led to his clock-watching, arse-shuffling evasiveness.

'I mean, an appeal could cost thousands. You do realise your husband's not represented by the Federation any more, don't you?'

'Don't worry. I've asked Citizens' Advice about Legal Aid.'

'And there's the um, slight problem of having no further evidence to raise. Constable Robertson's original testimony was our only, rather slim piece of corroboration to back up Jamie's story. And, with that gone . . .' Another glance at his watch, a slight but careful pause, '. . . what fresh insight would we take to an appeal?'

'But why did Jinky change his statement? Surely that's worth checking out? Maybe Coltrane threatened him . . .'

'Have you heard the tape?'

'What tape?'

'Of what Jamie said to Constable Robertson the night before the trial?'

Cath rubbed her forehead. All those times she told him he was being stupid, that Philippa's phone was making the same noise, and they should move to one of those cable packages anyway. 'The bastards.' One more final turn of the screw. 'They bugged our phones?'

'No, no. Just advised Constable Robertson to switch on his tape recorder if Jamie ever phoned him.'

'And? What did Jamie say?'

'Along the lines of: "Remember to say what I told you".' Mackenzie poured himself a whisky. 'Not his best move. Would you care for one?'

'No.'

'Believe me, I quizzed Jamie, interrogated him after Robertson gave his evidence. Went over each separate point – and your husband grew more confused with every word, till, at the end, even he admitted he wasn't very sure what Coltrane had told them any more.'

Cath recalled the morning after the shooting. Recalled it. Ha. As if it were a dusty memory that didn't tear fresh at her head each morning. Saw clearly the state of Jamie when he came home that day: shivery, incoherent, unable to focus or make any sense. But that hadn't been because he was a murderer. She had rapped her two hands down on Mackenzie's desk, pointing them towards him, like an accusing prayer. 'Did you ever think he might have been in shock? It's not every day you get stabbed in the back.'

Mackenzie had reached across his expanse of leather blotter – another affectation, to match his inkwell and paperknife set in the shape of a vintage car – and patted Cath's right hand. 'Or maybe, hard as it is to believe, Constable Robertson *was* telling the truth. No matter what Coltrane is alleged to have told Jamie, the incontrovertible fact is that there *was* no gun in the flat.'

He'd sat back, folded his hands on his mauve silk belly. 'I mean, are you suggesting that, as well as lying about the information he gave Jamie at the scene, as well as intimidating Constable Robertson into committing perjury, Inspector Coltrane also managed to run inside the flat the moment after Sarah was shot, and steal *and* dispose of the alleged gun too? For what possible purpose, Mrs Worth?'

Oh, it was her Sunday name now, no more jolly, friendly Len'n'Cath. One pudgy finger smoothed his moustache, wiping one side, then the other. 'I think you have to accept that we gave it our best shot.'

'So, you're just saying I should give up?'

'Mrs Worth, seven years isn't that long a time. Maybe you should focus your energies on just getting you and your family through them. I know this is very hard for you—'

'But shut the door on your way out. It's okay, I get it. *Et tu, Mr Mackenzie*. I guess that's us officially a hopeless case then?'

'Mrs Worth, my door is always open. And, if any other material facts arise that could influence an appeal, I'd be more than happy to pick up the case again.'

And how was Cath supposed to obtain these 'material facts'? No one in the whole of Strathclyde Police, bar the doughty Jenny, would speak to her. Calls went unreturned, old friends would hurry by on the other side of the street. She'd seen Derek's wife last week in town, and the poor woman – a Sunday School teacher, a church elder and a stalwart of the Women's Guild, no less – had dived into Ann Summers rather than speak to Cath. For spite, Cath had stood engrossed for ages at the window display, just for the vicious pleasure of seeing Mary panic inside, twisting and turning and flicking her way through the scants and bras. She finally stopped at a red lace basque that near matched her face, whereupon Cath had rapped the window and waved at her, giving her the thumbs up before moving swiftly on. Of course there was something going on. Had Anna Cameron only just grasped that? Did the cow think she was some kind of guardian angel, come to give succour and sustenance to poor, forlorn Cath? And what was her agenda anyway? Guilt, or gloating? Or something else?

The washing machine bleeped to tell Cath that another load was done. She'd been washing all Jamie's T-shirts, plus his socks and pants, every pair, to take down to him. They were allowed to wear their own gear at Garthlock, he'd said. His new home from home, which she'd have to try and find this very afternoon, driving and reading her AA Autoroute directions all at the same time, instead of navigating comfortably from the passenger seat like she always did when they went somewhere new. Usually, Cath decided on the destination, picked somewhere by the sea, where they could take a picnic and huddle up on the sand. Kids shrieking at the waves, Jamie making castles for Eilidh to shell-scape and Daniel to crush.

Cath hadn't got a say on Garthlock. Didn't even know why Jamie had been sent there. Mrs Rennie had simply informed her he'd been transferred, sent her the details along with the last batch of leaflets. Before, Cath might have protested, or at least asked for an explanation. That was when she thought the world worked a certain way, that things happened for a reason; that you could influence decisions, see the logic in outcomes and be satisfied that your voice had been heard.

Cath's expectations had shrunk since then. Not just her expectations of life, or her friends or her future. Her faith was shrivelling too. Her nightly, angry rants at God had produced only benevolent silence, a yawn which she could choose to fill with hope or despair. Or with the simple practicalities of carrying on. She put the letter about Garthlock on the top of the laundry bag, so she didn't forget to take it. Better conditions than Barlinnie; visiting was permitted once a week, but it was hundreds of miles away, which meant a full day there and back, by the time you factored in the actual visit. There's a fun day out for all the family: let's go see Daddy and all the nice men in the jail. But Cath daren't take the kids. Not yet, not till she'd seen how he was and what the place was like inside. She opened the machine, tipped the washing into a basket. The breeze of hot air shrilled over her broken tooth, making it sing again.

Thumping Anna Cameron may have been puerile, but it was also cathartic. Close of chapter. Oh, it hurt still, it always would; a niggling, desolate pain, but Cath's energies had to be focused on the basics. Feeding the kids, trying to sleep, keeping Jamie sane. Avoiding the neighbours and the majority of the schoolgate mums, with their *schadenfreude* smuggled via sympathetic smiles. And the biggy: finding money. She took another look at Jamie's final payslip, lying scrunched on the table where she'd flung it that morning. Much less than she'd expected. They had deducted his rent allowance, and done some fiddling with holiday pay. Not fiddling, more like fraud. They had deducted the leave he'd put in for their holiday to Majorca, then said he 'owed' them for taking more annual leave days than he was entitled to pro rata for the year. Pettiest of all, they had deducted money for 'unreturned police property'. Most of Jamie's uniform was still at Stewart Street – Jenny had dealt with all that – but, according to this, a whistle, a set of epaulettes and his bloody plastic notebook cover were still missing. They were invoicing Jamie for the notebook that the DCI had seized. Unbelievable.

This was the organisation she'd been so proud to serve, that she'd defended at all costs whenever people slagged the police. Some rough edges, but a decent heart, was what she'd thought. But then, she'd never been on the receiving end before. There was also a letter from Police Welfare, advising her she could no longer take up their offer of an appointment with a guidance counsellor. Cath thought she might cut the letter into four neat squares and use it for toilet paper, along with the lovely *Prisoners and Their Families* leaflet that Mrs Rennie from Barlinnie had posted out. She didn't *want* to be a prisoner's family, or a single parent, or any other label she hadn't asked for. She didn't want to be putting packets back on the shelf because she couldn't afford them.

They had some savings in an ISA, which would cover the mortgage for the next couple of months; then, after that, nothing. Cath's parents had insisted she sell the house, come and stay with them. No way. That would give her mother the perfect opportunity to say *I told you so. That boy was never good enough for you.* On a daily, possibly hourly, basis. Sure, it would be tempered with: *It's okay pet, we'll look after you now.* Tempting, that offer of enfoldment in maternal arms. A blessed escape, but only for a moment, till you remembered the suffocating that went with it, as each last vestige of independence and pride became subsumed by someone else's desires. Cath understood why Eilidh sometimes fought off

Cath's help when she tried to do up her buttons, or write her own name. 'Leave me alone, Mummy. I can do it,' she'd tut. And, equally, Cath understood the sadness of standing by watching, knowing you could do a better job, but that you're no longer wanted. Still, you had to do it. Stand back, so the next generation could start from scratch all over again, making the same mistakes. Aye, human evolution was a glorious thing.

She wound Jamie's socks into matching pairs, wondering when she would do this again. The prison had its own laundry – Jamie said he was going to start working there soon. That was the only real option left to Cath, too. Either get a job or sign on. But what kind of a job? Precognition agent, security guard, store detective: those were the kinds of things most ex-cops did. Or go back to working in a bank, which is what she did before she joined the police. Yeah, she could just see it, the moment they ask why she wants the job: *well, my husband's just got life in jail you see . . . Oh, but I'm very trustworthy and reliable.*

Even if someone was mad enough to employ her, who would look after the kids? Her mother still worked, her sister was in Australia. Jamie's mum Doris wasn't coping so well since the trial. Watching the kids would either kill or cure her. Neither Doris nor Jamie's dad drove, so Cath would have to drop the kids off there each morning – then how would Eilidh get to school? More importantly, how would *they* feel, her babies? That was something Cath should never lose sight of, but she did, frequently, at the moment. She knew she did, those nights when she sobbed quietly and Eilidh crept in, snuggled down beside her, held her hand. And Cath let her, needing the comfort. Or those days when Cath was screaming at Daniel, who was only playing up because he didn't understand. Just sensed something was wrong and someone was missing. How would Cath getting a job help them? They lose their daddy, then their mum disappears too, coming home each evening to see them for a few brief hours, even more crabbit and knackered than she was before.

'Boo,' squealed Eilidh, jumping in the back door.

'Boo, you,' said Cath. 'That you put your bike away?'

'Uh-huh.'

'You ready to go to Gran's then?'

'Want to come with you.'

'Well, you can't. I told you; I'm going to a grown-up place.' Cath scrunched the last of the socks together, then zipped up the laundry bag, and put it on the table by the window.

'What's that?'

'Nothing.'

'What's in it?'

'Nothing.'

'Is so.' Eilidh crouched to the floor, waved a fallen sock triumphantly. 'Is Daddy's socks in there? Is Daddy coming home?'

'No, I'm just washing them, I promise. For when he comes home.'

Cath leaned out the back door. She knew the next question would be *When?* It looked like it was going to rain.

'Daniel. Time to come in, pet.'

Their garden was a fair size, but there were few nooks and crannies to it, just square lawn and some bushes around the edge. No real hiding places, and no sign of a little boy anywhere.

'Eilidh, where is he?'

She could hear the scrape of a chair leg, then a busy little grunt of effort.

'I putted him in the shed.'

'You did what?'

Eilidh had clambered on to a stool, and was munching on an apple from the bowl. 'You *telled* me not to let him go out the garden Mummy.'

'Yes, I know but – oh, for goodness sake, Eilidh. The shed's full of – och, where's the key, you naughty girl?'

'Am *not* naughty,' she yelled. 'Am good.'

'Eilidh, give me that key now, or so help me I'll smack your backside.'

'Ah posted it to Dan-pants,' she wailed, 'so he could come out when he wants. Am a *good* girl!'

'Posted it where? You tell me where this minute.' Cath was shouting as she ran down the garden path, Eilidh screaming after her: 'Unner the stupid chewy bit in the stinky door. I *hate* you!'

Next door's dog started barking in agreement, manky paws skittering on the fence between them.

'Shut up, you stupid mutt!'

They'd had to put the fence up to stop the dog crapping in their garden, or having sex with the kids' toys. He'd even had a go at eating their shed. The bottom of the door had been gnawed ragged, leaving lacy mouseholes along the bottom. But, the gap was just big enough for Cath to slide her hand under. As she did, a sturdy little boot stamped hard on her fingers

'Aye-ya!'

The dog barked even louder, possibly scenting blood. Daniel chuckled from inside. At least he wasn't having hysterics yet. Unlike his mother. Cath resisted the urge to swear, and used her best singsong voice instead. 'Daniel. It's Mummy. Would you like a sweetie?'

'Deah!'

'Okay, well, you need to give Mummy the key. Did Eilidh give you the key?'

'Deah!'

'Can you see it? Is it on the floor?'

'Deah!'

'Can Mummy have it then?'

'Deah!'

No movement.

'Honey, you need to push it back to me. Can you do that, clever boy? Can you post the key to Mummy? Push it under the door for me?'

Daniel's throaty laugh again. 'Nee pooh, Muma!'

'Okay, well, we'll do your pooh once you give me the key, darling.'

A scuffle, then a little silver key emerged from under the door.

Cath seized it before he could change his mind. Quickly, she undid the padlock. Daniel sat inside, surrounded by old oil cans and weedkiller and lethal garden tools. She snatched him up. 'Oh, clever boy, baby.'

'Muma. Done pooh-pooh.'

She tried counting to ten. Up to her elbows in crap again. 'Great. C'mon then, let's get you cleaned up.'

Cath lugged him outside, put him down while she locked the door. Immediately, Daniel scurried off.

'Hoi, you, come here!'

Too late, she tried to grab him, but her baby was sleekit, toddling fast and low, forcing her to give chase around the side, where she finally caught him.

Stopping dead. Staring in disbelief at the huge, blotchy, pupil-less eye someone had painted on her shed.

Voices through the wall. She didn't care who, just turned on her side and curled small as her uneasy body would bend. Nothing to eat, belly grumbling. Her gran had left again, taking all her father's drink. He had slapped them both, sending her brother's head through the window, and then gone out to the pub or the dogs.

She could make out one voice. It was her brother, nearly shouting. She got off the bed, moved towards her door.

'C'mon man. I'll pay you at the end of the week, I swear. I just need a wee charge the now, know?'

'You'll fucking pay me double then.'

'Nae sweat, man. Nae sweat.'

'I'm only doing this cos you're Trina's boy.'

'Appreciate it, man.'

'Mind, it's an expensive habit you're getting, son.'

The girl edged into the hall. Her brother's door was open, she could see him standing by his bed, legs jiggling like he was warming up for a run.

'Fuck aye, man, aye. Is that it? Nice. Aye, I'll need to start tanning houses at this rate.'

'You been in trouble before?' She couldn't see the other person, but his voice rumbled like a phlegmy train. She pictured him with fat wet lips.

'No really.'

'Well, there's easier ways of earning a crust for boys like you. You drive?'

'Aye. Nae licence but.'

The girl pushed the door slightly, trying to see who was there. But it swung too wide, leaving her open in the doorway. An older man sat on her brother's bed, fat arse indenting a starburst on the duvet. He smiled at the girl. 'Well, hello there, sleepy. Nice knicks.'

She pulled at her T-shirt, trying to cover her legs.

The man winked at her brother. 'Or you could always set your wee sister to work, eh?' he said. 'I mean, why keep a dog and bark?'

Cath told Jamie about the eye when she finally made it to Garthlock. It had been a horrendous drive; missed her turn-off twice, then it was all twisty roads and sheep for the last fifty minutes or so. Already she was thinking about how she'd get here in the winter, when the roads were iced and dark. You could hardly see where the road ended and the rocky verges began in broad daylight. Oh, but it was worth it, just to see him.

She decided on the way down not to tell him about Anna Cameron. Any talk of fighting for an appeal seemed to send him into a further depression, and a mention of Anna . . . Cath had no idea what reaction that would provoke.

This was their time, no one else's. Two weeks apart, same country, different universe. The prison insisted he had a fortnight to 'settle in' at Garthlock. No distractions, no visits. Only phone calls tying up the loose ends of both their lives, saving snippets for the end of the day, once the kids had gone to bed. Because Jamie wouldn't talk to them, no matter how much she begged.

'It'll just upset them Cath.'

But they're upset now.

She hadn't planned to say about the shed, but it all looked so clean and fresh here, out in the country. And Jamie looked less stressed. Still tired and drawn, but a bit more together. That should have made her happy, and it did, of course it did, but something bad in her wanted him to know.

'Side of the shed's been vandalised.'

'Same as on the front wall?'

Oh no, the front wall had been classy stuff. Day after Jamie had been charged, they'd woken up to *MUDRER* daubed in great red letters. Painted considerately on both sides of the wall, so it could be seen from the house and the street.

'No. This was an eye.'

'How d'you mean an eye?'

'A big human eye, with an eyebrow and a wee curly bit coming out the bottom. But all dark at the centre, no pupil.'

'Like on those boats we saw in Corfu?'

Cath thought for a moment. 'Exactly like that. Weird eh?'

'Just kids, I suppose.'

'Maybe, but it's a bit creepy. Like someone's been hiding there, watching us from the garden.'

'And who'd do that, Cath?'

He sounded terse, like she was bugging him with trivia.

'Same people that left flowers on my doorstep?'

'So that's bad, is it? Leaving someone flowers. Why can't you just think it was someone being nice for a change?'

'Oh, forget it.'

She hadn't driven all this way to argue with Jamie about a lot of nonsense. Cath took a mouthful of her coffee. Biscuits too; chocolate ones. Garthlock was very civilised. Night and day compared to Barlinnie. Visits were spread over two rooms: the old drawing room she could see through the archway, and this place, which she guessed might have been a billiard room at one time, with its vaulted ceiling and wooden beams. Of course, it wouldn't have had bars on the windows then, nor blue linoleum on the floor, giving every movement an institutionalised squeak. A little girl scampered past, running towards the outstretched arms of another prisoner.

'So.' Jamie drank his own coffee. 'What else has been happening?'

'Kids have been asking where you are again.'

'And?'

'I tell them you're working.'

He nodded.

'Jamie, please let me bring them here. Other folk do, and—'

'I've told you no. I don't want them here. It . . . it would just confuse them. And they'd get upset when they had to leave.'

'You mean *you'd* get upset.' Cath took his hand. 'Mrs Rennie said you refused any counselling at Barlinnie.'

'That's none of Mrs bloody Rennie's business.'

'Well, it is mine. What about here? What are they offering you?'

'Let's see . . . if I'm good, I'm going to get my own wee job washing other people's underwear; then, if I'm very good, I can get promoted from Columba block to Ninian.'

'And what happens in Ninian?'

'I'm officially off solitary and get to eat my dinner in the main hall. Woop-de-fucking-doo.'

'Jamie, I meant what support are they offering?'

He scowled at her. 'Let me deal with this my own way Cath. I don't need any support.'

'Is that right?'

She took her hand away.

'I don't mean from *you*. I mean do-gooders.'

A prisoner walked by, slapped Jamie on the back. 'Alright, Big Man? How's it hanging?'

'Aye. Fine.'

Cath waited till he'd left the room. 'Who was that?'

'Just a guy.'

'Who?'

'I don't know. He's called Brian.'

'So why'd he call you Big Man?'

'Och, that's just him.'

'Jesus. You're well in here, aren't you? Got a nickname already.' Jamie smirked, shook his head.

'What? What's so bloody funny?'

'You, Cath.'

'God, Jamie, I just don't want to see you go down to their level.'

His irises sparked brown to black. Just huge, wild pupils, giving Cath the evil eye, and it scared her. She looked away, down, grateful to see the laundry bag lying on the floor. 'Oh, I brought down more clean clothes. And this came through for you.' She unzipped the bag, took out his wage slip. 'Look at all the deductions they've taken off.'

'Hmm.'

He hadn't even read it.

'That's something we need to think about, Jamie.'

'What's that?'

'Money. We have none.'

'We've got savings.'

'Aye enough for two, maybe three months' mortgage, tops.'

'Well, what d'you want me to do Cath? I mean, honestly. What?'

That twist again. When did Jamie's face start to look so mean? All the softness shrunk away, just hard bone and bitterness. 'Put in extra shifts at the laundry? Jesus, I don't even know if you get paid in soap powder or fags.'

Cath rubbed her temple. Migraine explosions popping behind her eye, and she could feel tears threatening. 'I don't know. I'll need to get a job, I suppose, but even then; I'm not going to make your kind of salary. So. Should we sell the house?'

'It's up to you.'

'*Why* is it up to me? Why? I'm fed up having to decide everything myself. It's alright for you, tucked away all safe here. It's me that has to deal with everything!'

Words running away with her, those nasty secret thoughts never meant to see the light of day, firing out in furious bullets. She watched them pummel Jamie back in his chair, a recoil, from her, from his wife, the one person he should be desperate to touch. Folding in on himself, retreating, like before, to the safety of his own arms.

'Safe? Do you know why I was really moved here, Cath? Two guys tried to fuck me in the showers.'

A hard, sick, gutting in her bowels, while she tried not to be sick, or scream or run. Stay calm, sit nice – why had she done this? Pushed him to open a door to a world she didn't want to accept, had barely acknowledged her own terrors about, and now he was spilling out her most repulsive fears as facts. She leaned forwards, clutched his knees, which were all she could reach. 'Jamie . . . I didn't know . . . You never told me.' Wanting to cover his mouth in kisses, cover her ears.

'Are you okay?'

'No, I'm not okay, Cath.' He moved his legs away from her. 'I'm bloody shitting myself. I've had folk spit, piss, and probably shite in my food. I've had death threats near every day since I've been inside. Do you know they put razors in the soap, jump folk in the gym? I don't know how much I can take. Have you ever tried sleeping in a box that stinks of your own shit, listening to an old man crying, night after fucking night, with a bulb buzzing over-head cause you're not allowed to decide when to turn off your own bloody light?'

'Did they – did those men hurt you?'

Stop twisting your face like that, Jamie. It's me, Cath.

'It's alright Cath. I'm still virgo intacta, if that's what you're worrying about. Though I have heard it's a useful source of income if you're strapped for cash. Maybe I should give it some thought . . .'

'Stop it! Please, stop it.'

'Don't worry. Death before dishonour, that's my motto. Or, in my case: death *then* dishonour, eh?'

'Jamie, don't. Please.'

'*Now* do you understand why I don't want the kids here?'

'Yes. I'm sorry.'

Another half-hour of careful talking about the weather, then it was time to go. Jamie barely kissed her when she left, just a rigid, dry pressing of lip on lip, and a sudden, claw-tight gripping of her upper arms, before he was led away. Not passionate, but angry. She prodded at one of her arms as she was driving out of Garthlock's gates, guilt dolloping on guilt at the relief of escaping. It felt tender, probably bruising. It was like he was punishing Cath for him being there, but then he wouldn't let her do anything to help get him through it. Or get him out. If this was Jamie after a month in prison, what creature would come out in seven years?

The gate glided shut behind her. She noticed a woman standing at the verge outside the prison wall, sucking on a cigarette. Her nails were long and pearly, her belly slightly swollen. Cath knew her face from somewhere . . . that girl she'd talked to at Barlinnie. She wound down the window.

'Hi there. Stella, isn't it?'

'Aye?' Stella peered in the window, frowning.

'Cath. We met at Barlinnie last month.'

'Och, aye. The new lassie.'

'Aye, that's me. Look, can I give you a lift?'

Stella shook her head vigorously. 'Och, away, don't be daft. I'm just waiting on a taxi.'

'Where d'you stay?'

'Glasgow.'

'Well, that's where I'm going. Jump in.' Cath opened the passenger door. 'Please.'

'You sure?' All relieved smiles, now she knew it was for real.

'Yeah, no bother. You can help me navigate my way back.'

'Och, this is brilliant, so it is.' Stella climbed inside, pressing on her mobile phone. 'I'd best just cancel thon motor first. Don't want to noise up the only taxi company for miles around, eh?'

Cath waited until Stella had finished her call before driving off. 'You weren't really going to get a taxi all the way to Glasgow, were you?'

'Naw. I get the taxi into Kirkcudbright, then a bus to Dumfries. You can get a train there that takes you to Glasgow Central. Then a bus to my house in the Drum. Pure doddle, so it is.'

'Pure nightmare, more like.'

'Aye. Trains, planes and automobiles, eh? That's why I havny brought the weans. Still,' Stella fluffed up her hair in the sun-visor mirror, 'they'll gie you the cost back, so that's something.'

'Who's they?'

'You no on the Appies? Assisted Prison Visits Scheme?'

'No. Never heard of it.'

'Did you no get all the bumph off that woman Rennie?'

'Yeah, somewhere.'

'Well, read it then, doll. Mind, you've to be on Income Support, but. You on Income Support?'

'Um . . . no, not yet.'

'Fucksake, you must be rolling in it, eh?' Stella pursed up her lips, smoothed pink gloss all around. 'What was it your man did again? Great Train Robbery was it?'

'No.' Cath swerved around a couple of curious sheep. Too sharp, too fast. Nearly went over the edge of a gully.

'Shite, naw. Your man's just in for murder, isn't he? So what's he doing at Garthlock if he's a lifer? He canny be getting rehabbed already.'

'No, he's for . . . well, it's sort of a rehab, I suppose. And for his own protection.'

'Oh right. Team of bad bastards got it in for him?'

'Aye.'

'Who is it? My da's quite well connected, know?'

'It's kind of everyone.'

Stella snapped the lid back on her lipgloss. Cath could see her profile turn to take a closer look at who it was that was driving her.

'Your man that polis, then?'

'Aye.'

Silence for a while. Not the companionable kind, more the *who'll break first?* type. Cath had nothing more to say, and the whole stomach-churning road to distract her. Stella only had her seatbelt, which she kept pulling in and out. Swoosh of nylon, swoosh of nylon, swoosh of nylon, till Cath was frightened it would combust. A cough, a zip of handbag. Rustle of plastic bag.

'Want a sweetie?'

'No thanks.'

'I didny mean what I said about my da by the way. He's straight as a die, him.'

'Stella, Jamie *used* to be a cop. He's not now.'

'Aye, I know, but—'

'Can we just talk about something else? What about you? Why's your husband been moved?'

'Brian? Just struck lucky, I guess. He never gets kept in the

Bar-L that long, but they usually punt him somewhere more local. It's a funny place but, Garthlock. It's no low security, but it's totally laid back, isn't it?'

'I know. I felt I was having afternoon tea in some hotel.'

Stella laughed. 'Me and all. I was waiting for a frigging maid to hand me my coat there on they way out!'

'Maybe we could stay for dinner next time.'

'Aye, I've heard the food's cracking an all.' A sniff. 'Too bloody nice, if you ask me.'

'How d'you mean?' Cath changed gear as the car chugged up a hill. The road was single track at this point, only sporadic passing places dotted here and there. A lorry up ahead of her. Luckily, it was going the same direction as them, but what was she supposed to do if she met one coming this way? Breathe in?

'It just looks so bloody cosy, doesn't it?' said Stella. 'And here's me heading home to a one room and kitchen with damp on the walls. Feeding his weans, and praying the electric hasny been cut off again.'

She took a mint imperial out the bag, began to suck. 'Sorry I'm offloading onto you, doll, but it's nice to have someone new to talk to. All my pals have pure gied up on Brian. They canny be annoyed hearing me any more. And maybe they're right.' She crunched her sweetie. 'Och, I don't know. You get that sick of doing everything on your own, know? You canny blame us for getting a wee bit pissed off. I mean, what do we get? Work, worry and the weans, while they play snooker and get their dinners made for them.'

She swallowed. 'Sometimes, I wonder why I do it. I mean, my Brian, don't get me wrong, we've been together for yonks, but he's a face on him like a spaced-out boxer, and he's no exactly the sharpest tool in the box.'

'He must be doing something right.' Cath nodded at Stella's belly.

'Och aye, he's a randy wee bastard all right. We're brilliant together in the sack, but you canny spend your life in bed, can you?'

'True.'

'Mind, I seen a photie of your man in the *Daily Record*. Quite a looker, isn't he?'

'You think?'

'Oh aye. You'll need to introduce us next time I'm down.'

If I recognise him myself.

Cath indicated to join onto the dual carriageway. She wanted Jamie back. Her laughing, strong, brave husband, not this defeated, ugly stranger that she didn't think she could take.

21

Jamie had been counting down the minutes till Cath arrived, had seen her mad tangle of black skewed curls bounce by the window and felt his whole body shake with the wanting and the needing. So why had he spent all their precious time sneering and bristling, brushing off her every concern and question until he could see in her eyes that she wished she'd never come? And only then had he been satisfied, telling himself that she never wanted to come in the first place.

Don't go down to their level, Jamie.

Is that what she saw, when she looked at him? Broken souls, stripped of everything except their crime, which would chime and swing around them all the days of their lives. For that's all Jamie was now; a murderer and a criminal. All the other tags that had defined him were gone. He'd laughed at Cath once, years ago, when she'd tried to explain to him how it felt not to 'be' something. Oh, not in a nasty way – he'd rubbed her hair and told her she was still Cath and that was all that mattered, but still. How trite, how mean.

He pulled on the soft fleece she had laundered for him. It smelled of home and his babies' heads, a smell that gnawed at the empty space within him. Not even a father really. Not fit. Cath had put a picture of her and the kids in the bag, but he'd pinned it up inside his locker, so no one else could see it. He didn't want his family tainted. Some inmates had their whole life plastered on their walls, photos and cards, and paintings their weans had done. A silent scream to wake to every morning.

Look at me. I was someone, once.

Nobody in here need know anything about his family. He'd asked Cath to bring bog roll next time. And boot polish. They seemed to like it if you begged for the basics here. Jamie picked up the shoes Cath had brought him, gave them one final rub. He never wore trainers at home, and wasn't going to start with plastic shoes now.

He made his way down to breakfast. It was a week after Cath had visited, and this was his first day in Ninian, the first day that he hadn't eaten in his cell. It was a self-service affair, he'd been told, only on from half seven to half eight. Nearly that now. He'd left it late, because then there might be an empty table and he could sit on his own. Each block had its own association room, where the inmates congregated. Jamie had been in solitary since he arrived at Garthlock, so all he knew was that it was on the ground floor, one below his cell – and that he was in no rush to visit it. But all meals were taken together, in the main dining room in the old house.

After the rigidity of Barlinnie, it felt strange to be wandering down a flight of stairs without a uniformed accompaniment. Mind, there was nowhere else he could go, only this one single corridor, leading out into the enclosed courtyard. Colditz-walls on all four sides, only one door open across the yard. Nothing subtle here; you knew the door was open because the barred metal gate in front of the door was also open, clamped wide against the wall. Jamie crossed over, aware of a tiny whirr, bird-like, as the CCTV camera covering the courtyard swivelled its neck to record his passage.

A uniform stood inside the back entrance to the main house, hands clenched behind his back. Jamie wondered if Ethel had them all out at night, doing military drill.

'You're late, bud. Lucky if there's anything left.'

First the low bass of hundreds of male voices and the rumble of scraping chairs, then smells of bacon and toast beckoned him on, through to a set of double swing doors marked **Dining Hall**. They were heavy, probably fire doors, and he had to push them twice before they opened, a double-flapping that acted as a clapper-board. As Jamie entered, all conversation ceased, mouths clipped shut like snapped purses. Blobs of faces, merging into blurs. His eyes sought a place to go, saw food. Walked over to the servery, took a tray. Bowls of cereal, and a tin tray of toast. Some rubber eggs draped over shrivelled bacon and grease-leaking pink slabs of Lorne sausage.

He picked something up, not sure what, a melamine dish of something, put it on his tray. Trying not to hear the silence. Poured black liquid from a jug into a plastic beaker, spilling scalds on his wrist because it wouldn't stop bloody jerking. Like a puppet master was working him from on high. He needed juice, water, his throat was dry, couldn't see any, couldn't see a table that was free. All fours and sixes and a couple of twos. Chose a four, they'd all be busy talking. Except nobody was talking, just watching. He went to the nearest table, pulled out a chair. As one, the group rose from their seats, took their trays and left. He was aware of them all sitting down at the table next to him. And then the talking started, a normal hum that he could hide in and try to force hard food through parched lips.

'Oink, oink.' A snort in his ear. It was Smithy, that warder who had driven them down. 'No having any bacon for your brekkie then? Suppose it's just too much like cannibalism, eh?'

Jamie continued chewing his toast.

'That's right, Worth. Don't speak with your mouth full. Your mammy's brang you up well. Gied you a good sook at her udders every night, I'll bet.'

Crumbs tickling, making him want to cough. Bite down and chew. Bite down and chew.

'Bloody hell. You're nae fun this morning. Anyway, you've to report to the bathhouse after breakfast, get your working party detail.'

'Where's the bathhouse?'

'Aye, right enough, you're honking. Probably never heard of it, down in the sty.'

Jamie was aware other tables were watching their exchange. Smithy seemed equally aware, playing to the crowd. Voice growing louder, head sweeping around for approving glances.

Jamie placed the toast on his plate, looked up at Smithy. 'It was quite an easy question. Exactly how simple do I need to make it?'

He kept his face still, let his eyes widen, twitch a little, like they were wired to the moon. Quiet menace, it was a look he'd specialised in, quick switch from nice guy to Mr Psycho. Been his party piece at work:

Do your nutter face Jamie. Mind, the one you did at that rammy in Delmonica's? And he'd always oblige. Scared the shit out the probationers.

'*What* did you say?' Smithy's face up close, hissing last night's curry.

Again, the room grew still. That quietening, not quite silence this time, just a waiting, a slowing of sentences, a licking of lips. So what gallery was Jamie playing to? None that would give a toss, whoever came off worse. But something was sticking in his throat still. A stray crumb, pride? The very last shreds of any dignity? He swallowed it down, whatever it was, like a good boy.

'I said, could you tell me where the bathhouse is?'

Smithy shook his head. 'Please.'

'Please.'

'Go back to where the hospital wing is, and it's on your left.'

'Thank you.'

Jamie stood up. He was taller than Smithy, by at least a head, straight-shouldered where this guy was slumped. 'Can I get past then?'

But Smithy kept standing there, blocking his path. Was Jamie supposed to walk through him, over him? Wait until he'd got bored? He was playing a game of chess with an opponent so thick he'd think a pawn was something you ate with pink sauce. Then a prisoner wedged himself between them. He tapped Smithy's shoulder.

'Eh, Mr Smith. Have you got a delivery for me at all?'

'Keep your voice down, Douggins.' Smithy grabbed the prisoner's elbow, guided him away from Jamie's table. A bell rang somewhere, and the prisoners began to vacate the hall. Jamie took the chance to follow the crowd. If Smithy wanted to pursue this, then he could come and find him.

Most of the prisoners were going the same way, out the side door opposite where he came in, and along a corridor that nipped of antiseptic. Still, nobody spoke to him, or even looked his way. That suited him fine.

Jamie knew he'd get put in the laundry. It was where all the new guys went, a warder had told him: no skills required, no tempting fields to escape over, no sharp objects on which to impale yourself. Worst you could do was overdose on Daz.

'Worth? Turn left, and welcome to Laundry.'

Another clipboard, another face. Another turn, more faces. A heave of hot, soapy air, a mum-smell, not sour like men.

'Alright, boys,' said the warder who met him, 'this will be your place of work for the next few months. Mr Schwarzenegger here will show you the ropes. And make sure you get Mr Ethelridge's smalls whiter than white. I'm away for a wee sit-down. Break at eleven, okay Arnie?'

'Nae bother, sir,' said an elderly man, arms and legs crooked like a monkey's. 'Just you leave it to me.'

The laundry was warm and full of silver: Meccano-shelves and shiny washers and dryers, two tiers high just like a real laundromat. Couple of ironing presses in the corner, and a sweet, synthetic freshness from the open tubs of soap powder. There were five of them altogether: Jamie, Arnie, the old-timer who seemed to be delegating duties, a boy with a weasel face and sandy hair, that ned Brian from the Bar-L, and Pinstripe. Jamie hadn't recognised him, in his polo shirt and cords, all ready for a day in the country with the shooting party. He prepared himself for the jibes to begin. But, soon as the warder left the room, it was the young guy, not Pinstripe, that started.

'Pure stinks in here, eh? Bowfing pigshite, that's what it is.'

'Right, Ross,' said Arnie. 'You've been here a while now. I need you to show the new boys how they machines work. Get them sorting out the whites and the colours while I away and get the governor's laundry on.'

'Does he get his own special machine then?' laughed Pinstripe.

'Aye. Well, would you want your scants washed with all the skid-marked shite of the day if you were him?'

As Arnie shuffled off, the boy, Ross, raised his game a little. 'Canny wash out the stink of pigshite but, can you, boys?'

Brian and Pinstripe said nothing, just got on with sorting out the baskets of clothing. As Jamie walked past Ross to reach a tub of soap powder, the boy deliberately dug his elbow into Jamie's side. 'Fucking polis bastard. You're card's fucking marked, man.'

'Is that right?'

'Just leave it, son, eh?' said Brian. 'Ross, is it? Gonny show me where I put the soap stuff in?'

'Leave it? When we've got a fucking pig to play with? Haw, no way man. I fucking hate these cunts. He deserves to—'

'Ho, you, wide boy.' Arnie had a fair turn of pace on him, for a man with bow legs. He was over at Ross and had clipped his hand across the back of the boy's head before any of them realised he was there. 'Shut the fuck up, you hear me? There's nae fucking gangsters in my laundry, or you'll be back up the road quicker'n you can whistle. You understand?'

Immediately, the boy clammed up, skulking off to investigate a big pile of dirty linen.

'C'mere you to me.' Arnie took Jamie's arm, nudged him towards where the dryers were starting to churn. 'I don't gie a stuff what you did before you came in here, right? All of us did stuff we wurny proud of outside. But the polis have never done me a bad turn . . .'

'Well . . .' Jamie scratched his ear.

'Aye, well, apart fae the obvious. But I bloody hate thugs, so I do. And any trouble in my laundry reflects on *me*. So, you treat me right, and I'll do the same for you, okay?'

'Okay.'

It was almost funny. This aged, short, bendy-bandy man was offering him protection. A rosacea-cheeked nothing that you'd feel sorry for in the street, passing him by on the other side as he crooned at his bottle and made love to a lamppost. In here, though, in this room full of scum and whites and coloureds, Arnie was king. And in the gymnasium, some wee nyaff with a really loud whistle and a subtle fist was the boss, and in the canteen all the neds with their blunted knives would be jockeying for position too; last one in peels the potatoes. Everyone vying to be top dog of someone else: the drug dealers and armed robbers, sex offenders versus child molesters, commercial housebreakers who thought they were better than the domestic ones. Then the heroin addicts like Brian, who didn't know which way was up.

All these layers of dross that Jamie would have hoovered up and binned. Now, he had to define where he sat in the order of them all.

Outside. Please God, keep me outside.

Whatever else he was, old Arnie was a person, not a cartoon. Those bandy legs had once been muscly, the nose most likely reddened from hard knocks as much as from the drink. And he was offering Jamie something other than contempt. There was a good Scots phrase for men like him, crafted specially to fit the dour, malnourished stock of West Coast malehood: *He's wee, but he's game.*

'Aye, there's plenty others don't think like me, mind. You'll need to watch your back in here, son, and no just fae young scrotes like Ross here.'

'I know that.'

'Aye, well, I canny be seen to be too friendly, but I'll look out for you. If there's a problem, I'll let you know. No saying I can do much about it, but I'll let you know.'

'Thank you.'

Jamie held out his hand for the old man to shake.

'Away tae France, son. I'm just after telling you. I'm no your pal, pal. And I'll no be here forever; my time's nearly up. Now, go and get that big basket of ironing, and Ross'll show you how to work the press. And you . . .' he shouted at Ross. 'If you burn the man, I'll fucking pulp you, and pap you in the slurry for Ethel's coos.'

Next day at breakfast, the same routine. Jamie had been knacked last night. Five hours of hot, wet work, with forty-five minutes for lunch. A day of warped-wood tongs yanking dripping clothes from nonstop drums, shoulders aching at the sodden weight of fibres flooded double. Belching hot air and the buzzing vents, the perpetual drone of Radio Two, avoiding eyes, evading Ross. There was no system to their labours, just a guddle of dampness and baskets. More than once, Jamie had loaded a machine with stuff he was sure had just been dried. But it was his job only to be a mindless set of arms and shoulders. Bend and lift, bend and lift, all clammy with the slap of condensation as steam hit brick.

By the time they'd finished for the day, his neck and back were louping, hands all puckered and chafed. Then straight through for dinner. One by one, his workmates peeled off, gravitating to different tables, other groups. Even Pinstripe had some buddies to sit with. Jamie went to the servery, selected lasagne verdi for one. *Table by the window sir? Glass of wine?* Aye, he wished. All this restaurant served was rubber pasta, a plastic beaker of water and four men vacating the first table he went to, one stopping to carefully pick his nose and flick it in Jamie's dinner. He bit into his roll, just kept chewing until they'd gone.

Now he was in Ninian, Jamie didn't have to sit in solitary every night. After eating, the inmates were free to 'enjoy some recreation'. Jamie had been deemed fit to socialise; *he* had been assessed as okay to mingle with *them*.

'You've got the gym, ping pong, telly or the library,' a warder told him.

Aye, or more noising up and threats.

'Later on, you can maybe do a bit of supported study. How's your reading?'

'My reading's fine, thanks. I can do joined-up letters and all.'

Jamie chose his room, same as every other night. As he was crossing the courtyard again, he saw a figure hurrying towards him. Bloody Smithy. Jamie slowed down, knowing what was coming. His head was sore, his belly empty. Why not have his balls booted too? But Smithy marched right by him, hands in pockets, didn't even stop. It wasn't change of shift time, no sirens blaring for assistance, and dinner had been vile as usual, so why all the rush? Jamie watched him scurry to the other side of the courtyard, near the kitchens and the dining hall, then dart off to the left.

Instinctively, Jamie moved into the shadow of the wall. Knelt to tie his shoelace, head facing away from Smithy, but cocked low enough that he could see what was going on behind him. He saw Smithy glance around quickly, before unlocking the bin shed and slipping inside. Hell of a fuss to make about a rummage through the trash. Who knew? Maybe the guy got a hard-on from midgie raking. All Jamie cared about at that moment was lying on his bed and getting this pounding in his head to stop. It was like the washers and dryers were playing him a private encore, only with the sound turned up. Then he heard voices, saw two shapes coming round the corner.

'So, when have we to do it, Tai?'

'Disny matter.' He could hear another man laugh. 'Let's take our time and do it nice, eh? Make it drag on till we've scared so much shit out him that he'll be begging for the blade.'

'How?'

'Mair fun. Noise him up, gie him a few tasters. Any time, all the time. So he disny know who or when or how. But he still knows it's coming, know?'

'Like we're fucking haunting him, Tai?'

'Exactly that, boy.'

Jamie straightened, felt his body sway. Some poor bastard having a future torment planned. The two figures were walking back towards the dining hall. He could follow them, report them. Get chibbed by them. Ninian block was right in front of Jamie. He took his time, took some deep breaths, and went inside. Up one flight – avoiding going anywhere near the association room – and on to his room. He wouldn't call it a peter, wouldn't use any of their stupid patois. It had four walls and a bed: it was a bloody room.

He unlocked his door. Ethel's trust thing was bizarre, just a psychological trick. All doors locked automatically at night, and each corridor was sealed at either end. But you got your own key to make you feel like a big boy, and to stop the even bigger boys stealing stuff from your room. He locked the door on the other side, and flopped down on the bed.

By now, he was used to the curls of cinnamon-scented smoke creeping from under doors. But tonight, he'd only eaten his soup and a roll. He was starving, and the smell made him feel sick. He got up, stuffed his duvet along the bottom of the door, trying to keep the sweet sharpness of the dope at bay. The warders *must* smell it, surely? Every night, some mornings, yet no one appeared to bother their backside.

He was so hungry. Cath said she'd bring him more money, so he could buy stuff at the tuck shop. He'd probably be the only one. From what he could smell, most of the men in Ninian spent all their pocket money on tasty things to smoke rather than eat. God, for a big bag of cheese and onion and a pint of lager. His feet up on the couch, watching the football, head in Cath's lap and her in her slippers, stroking his hair. He closed his eyes and pretended he was there. Within minutes, he must have nodded off.

When he woke, it was morning. He felt cold and stiff, but rested. For the first time he could remember, he'd had no dreams, only sleep. He got up, washed, ready for another day of the same. And the same, and the same and the same. He stooped over the sink, watching the mirror man draw his safety razor around his chin. Rasp on his skin, scraping till it chewed. No more than he deserved. When Jamie was at school, they'd taken all the fourth-year boys to a seminary out at Cumbernauld. You were supposed to volunteer, but the priest had personally visited each of their mammies in advance, so refusal was not an option. A young priest there, not that much older than them, had shown them around. Kept a straight face the whole time too, as he extolled all the virtues of a monastic life to a bunch of sixteen year olds whose turbulent hormones, were, day and night, literally bursting their balls.

Jamie had noticed the priest was limping, had asked him what was wrong. Proudly (and perversely, thought Jamie's schoolboy self), the boy had raised his surplice to reveal a cilice, that crown of thorns around the thigh which zealots favoured; a taut barbed-wire band biting into the boy's flesh. With an actual buckle for adjusting the girth. These folk didn't strap their tortures on so tight in homage to the suffering of their Lord, Jamie realised now. It was in revulsion at themselves.

Today would be another day like yesterday. If he just thought of that one day, every day, got through that, and never thought of all the days and years ahead, then maybe he would survive. Only tomorrow would be different. Tomorrow Cath would come again, and this time, he'd try harder, think of some funny stories to tell her. Make them up.

Breakfast was more of the same too. He'd decided, before he went down, that he wouldn't even hesitate. Just grab a chair, start eating, and stuff the lot of them. No hush as he entered this time, only casual stares and sneers. As he left the servery, he saw Arnie, made for his table because it was nearest. When Jamie sat down with his tray, two of the men got up and left. But some stayed. Sat silent and glowering, but their backsides remained on their seats.

Find grace in tiny things.

Jamie began spooning up cornflakes. He wasn't going to starve because of them. Eventually, Arnie spoke. 'You're allowed mair than that. How not take some kidneys, or a wee bit of thon black pudding. It's rare.'

'No, I don't eat meat. I'm a vegetarian.'

First time he'd said it out loud. Made him sound like a smug-sandalled tree-hugger. They'd have ripped the pish right out him at work if he'd simpered *I'm a vegetarian*, Derek calling him Thumper, or Bugs or something daft, Jenny putting on a mincey voice, and Alex stuffing a sausage down his throat for the hell of it. Bunch of nutters, so they were. Used to have some great breakfasts together, nipping up to the Burnbank Hotel on the early shift, where old Rodney would 'see them right' and take them through the dining room to the curtained-off booth at the back, never complaining when all four of them bowled up together, even though there were already two beatmen there, munching on their kippers. That was the good old days, when even the sergeant would take the odd complimentary repast, always prefaced by the casual: 'Now, mind I'll be up by, later on.' Code for: *so you'd better be bloody well gone.*

Jamie scraped his spoon around the bowl. Proper china plates you got in the Burnbank too, served with that old-time respect for the status of constable. Years before Jamie's time, the cops used to collect the entire shift Christmas dinner from their beats; a bottle from each of their pubs, a couple of turkeys from the local butcher. Oh, they weren't greedy, it was only when you were backshift on Christmas Day that you scrounged the purvey. A fine tradition, shopkeepers had the stuff ready and waiting, were miffed if you favoured the Bradford's Christmas cake over the Gregg's one. Folk used to *like* the polis.

'So you're a vegetarian?' said Arnie. 'Is that right? Well, you should of had your porridge then, eh?'

They all started laughing.

'Aye,' another man chipped in, 'but, if you eat your porridge, it means you'll be coming back.'

'Then I'll no be eating any porridge.'

Already, Jamie was beginning to slur his words, slime up that glottal stop so he was talking like most of them. He used to do it all the time, modify his accent to suit the occasion. Good cops knew how to work their audience; clipped and deferential for the irate homeowner, outraged that some oik would steal their car from their leafy suburban driveway – *and what were the police going to do about it, exactly?*; pure broad-as-get-out for jollying up the piss-heads coming from the football stadium, getting them into their buses and out the bloody road. Soaking up the essence of what you needed to be, to get through and get on. He wouldn't do that here.

His dining companions were arguing amongst themselves. 'Naw, naw, it's just on your last day. You've got to eat porridge on your last day, so it means you'll no be coming back. Is that no it?'

'Fucked if I know. Tastes like wallpaper paste, any road.'

'Fucking sick, that's what it is.' A big, beardy man was scowling down at their table, his menacing face at odds with his Highland lilt. 'That pudding should stick in your bloody craw, Arnie West. Sitting eating with a frigging polis.'

'Away you and shag a sheep,' said Arnie. 'We're all Jock Tamson's bairns in here.'

'Well, it wouldna be me, you bloody turncoat. I'd bloody jab his eyes out with ma fork.'

'But you've only got a spoon,' laughed Arnie.

'Dinna mock me, Arnie West. You ton't know what you're doing.'

'You think you're so smart, big yin?'

'Aye, that I do. Smarter than the fool who would sup with a stinking polis.'

He lumbered off, staring back at Jamie like he'd 666 carved on his scalp.

'Ach, just ignore him,' said Arnie. 'They all boast, like to tell you how tough they are, how clever they are, but if they were that clever, they wouldny be in here.'

Arnie's mate slid a plate of toast across to Jamie. 'I'm Bomber, by the way.'

'I'm Jamie.' He nodded at the guy's grey blouson. 'Is the name because of the jacket?'

Bomber shook his head. 'No. Just the bombs.'

'James Worth?' called a warder from the door of the dining room.

Jamie raised his hand. 'That's me.'

As if the entire room didn't know.

'Come with me. You've got a visitor.'

Jamie got up, went towards the warder and the open door. Stamping, and a banging of spoons on plates followed him out.

'Piece of bloody nonsense this,' scowled the warder. 'No notification, inappropriate papers. Bloody UN? I mean, I know this place is a bit mad, but we're hardly a war zone. I suppose this has got something to do with you being a cop? Some secret file you didny hand over.'

'I'm sorry, I don't have a clue what you're talking about.'

'There's someone from the United Nations to see you.'

'You're joking.'

'No. Have you been asking for food parcels or something? Can I expect Amnesty bloody International tomorrow? Here, Tommy. Do you know anything about the UN coming here?'

The warder who was pinning a poster to the noticeboard turned around. 'Och aye, it's one of Ethel's mad . . .' He stopped when he saw Jamie. 'I mean, Mr Ethelridge is helping with some study they're doing into international prisoner welfare. Apparently we're a *model* of modernity.'

'Glad you told me. Oh well, there you go, Worth. You must've been specially selected.'

'Worth,' said the other warder, scribbling on a notepad. 'Right, that's one name for my list.'

'What list?' asked Jamie.

'You any good at painting? It's either that or singing.' The warder tapped the poster. 'Mr Ethelridge wants us to get a male voice choir together, for the commissioning of the new chapel.'

'No, I'm not into all that God stuff.'

'Right, well, painting then? There's a bit of a rush on to get the place finished, plus he's got some poncy artist coming down to do "an installation".'

'Aye, I can paint a bit, I suppose.'

'Consider yourself hired.'

'Och, I don't know, Tommy,' said Jamie's escort. 'How will he fit it in, what with all his humanitarian work for the UN?'

It might have been the disdain in the man's tone, or the lure of change in a sea of bland repetition, or some childish urge to be among prayers and incense, but Jamie found himself agreeing to it.

'Aye, alright then.'

'Great. Now I just need to find one more painter and an entire bloody choir. Easy.'

'Right, can we get a move on now, Worth?' The warder took him back towards the hospital area, then turned down a short corridor Jamie had never noticed before. He began to feel uneasy. The UN? Didn't sound very likely. Was Smithy waiting with a truncheon and a rubber hose? Or was this some sick joke, and the boys from Discipline had come back for more? What else could they take?

The warder opened a door marked 'Interview Room'. 'Okay, ma'am? That's Worth now.'

'That's fine. If you could just wait outside please. This interview is completely confidential.'

Her voice like clean water. Blonde hair swinging straight as her head turned and night-blue eyes met his, seeking, spinning lights and hope.

'Anna. What the hell are you doing here?'

22

He was still beautiful. Thin, haunted, with razor cuts all across his chin, but his eyes were intact, showing her his soul for one fleeting instant before the brown thickened like mud. She'd thought and thought about doing this, but, seeing him, now, she knew she was right.

'Anna.'

She could hardly hear him. Again. 'Anna.'

Anna held her finger to her lips. 'Don't call me that. I don't know if the screw's still outside.'

'Well, don't call him a screw, then. He doesn't like me already.'

He grinned.

She grinned.

'Why are we whispering?'

'Because they think I'm here to do a stupid questionnaire.'

'Why are you here?'

'To see you.'

'Why?'

She didn't answer.

Jamie reached out to touch her arm.

'I just want to check you're real.'

'Real as you are.'

'Aye well, that's debatable. None of this seems real, me included. Feels like I'm just empty skin, you know?'

'Been shite, eh?'

Too much, this desire to place his head on her breast and let him rest there. Not kissing, or touching, just lying with his weight upon her, taking the strain.

'You could say that.'

'But Jamie. What happened?'

He moved his hand away from hers, sat back.

'I shot a wee lassie. Stone dead. Murdered her in cold blood.'

'No you didn't.'

'How do you know? You weren't there.'

'I know what I've read in the papers; that it was a turn, and you thought she had a gun.'

'Yeah, well, she didn't.'

'But you thought she did. Coltrane told you she did.'

'Did he? At first, I thought he had, but now . . .' he looked away, 'now I don't know what I remember. Nobody else remembers him saying that, so maybe I imagined it. Maybe I *was* frothing at the mouth, desperate for my first kill—'

'Jamie, don't be stupid.'

'Look, I don't want to talk about this. Is you coming here some ruse to get me to go for counselling or something? I've told them I don't want to know.'

'Don't be daft. Nobody knows I'm here.'

'So why are you here?'

'I want to help you, Jamie.'

'How?'

'How as in "why" or how as in "how"?'

'Both.'

'"Why", because I know you're a good man. And I know I screwed up your life, and I'm sorry.'

He tried to interrupt, but she carried on. 'And "how", because I *do* believe you. But I need to check a few things first. Who was the fiscal that was working on your case?'

'Some prick called Millar. David, I think.'

'Right, well, I . . . I overheard Millar talking, and it sounded like there had been some pressure applied to make Jinky change his story.'

'Duh. You don't say. Coltrane would say black is white to save his own skin, and Millar's an ambitious wee shite, from what my brief told me. Must've been a real gold star for his CV, to crucify a cop.'

He was getting agitated, trembling hand constantly moving at his chin, rubbing at all the little scabs there.

'I mean, did you see some of the stuff they wrote in the papers? You'd think the polis were one big team of vigilantes, going tooled up to butcher people on a daily basis.' He shook his head, sniffed. 'I honestly thought I was trying to help folk. You know, doing my bit to protect society. Well, Anna . . .' He stopped picking at his chin, held his hands tight. Thumb still smoothing over his fingers, always moving, 'I'm seeing a different type of society now, and let me tell you, society is fucked. I'm probably best here, out the way.'

'Jamie,' she said gently, 'it's more than just Coltrane getting his shift to speak to stuff, or Millar wanting to gain a reputation. I got the impression that an ACC had been involved.'

'Jesus. I should be honoured I was that much of an embarrassment. I knew I'd been hung out to dry, but I didn't think the big guns were actively working against me.'

'You didn't? What about the controller's recordings going missing?'

He scratched the back of his hand. 'I know, but I reckoned that was probably Coltrane pulling in a favour. Or it could just have been the usual polis balls-up. Productions going missing? It's hardly MI5 stuff.'

He was going to make it bleed.

'Well, was there anything else unusual you can think of?'

His movements were jerky, yet he seemed so slow, like a child not quite engaged with the world around him. She was prising each word from him, hard-won. Anna didn't think he'd be sitting cracking his usual jokes, but she hadn't expected him to be so . . . withered. Left to rot with the scum you thought you'd locked up. It went against the grain of everything for which Anna had joined the police. How was doing this to Jamie upholding the law? He wasn't bad, or dangerous, or cruel. He'd made a mistake, and it was killing him.

Anna had never thought beyond the jailing of neds. She would arrest them, charge them, write up the case, send it to the Fiscal, and turn up for court. Never once had she considered what the accused might be doing in the interim, or what his wife was feeling, or if his kids were scared, or if he'd lost his job. And never, ever had she thought about asking why they'd done it in the first place. She would search for motive, yes, but reasons? How many other people in here were screaming at the unfairness of it all? Anna didn't want to think about that. She *had* to believe in the system, otherwise she couldn't be a cop. All this, Jamie, was just a blip, which she was going to put right.

'There's my notebook, I guess,' said Jamie.

'What about your notebook?'

'I took notes, right at the start of the turn, before things got too hairy. I wrote down exactly what Coltrane said to me. They say I deliberately destroyed it, because it would incriminate me. But I swear I didn't. That woman Armstrong took it, I saw her.'

'Armstrong?'

'Aye, DCI in G Division.'

'I know her,' said Anna. 'She used to work on the Accelerated Promotion Scheme. Bitch wouldn't let me on it.'

Jamie gave a wry smile. Its brief heat nudged her body, rousing memories of when it had been brighter, full above her, as she lay and they talked and planned out their world.

'Waste of time anyway,' he said. 'Coltrane was an AP man, and look how cool he was in a crisis.'

'Aye, but he's been clever enough to walk away from it.'

'True.'

'Did Armstrong get you to sign a production label?'

'Nah, I was too taken aback at getting my house turned to even ask.'

Anna ticked off the list on her fingers, like she was a schoolteacher making things crystal clear.

'Missing productions, nonexistent tapes, statements changed. Is Coltrane really so clever he could engineer all that on his own?'

Jamie thought a minute. 'See how you were saying about an ACC? Coltrane's uncle's an ACC, I think. I remember Jinky telling me.'

'D'you know which one?'

'Nope.'

He stretched away from the table, eyes flicking around the room.

'Sorry Jamie, am I boring you? It's just, you don't seem very interested.'

He shrugged.

'Look, I'm bloody trying to help you here.'

'Maybe I don't want you to.'

'For God's sake, why?'

'Cause I killed someone, Anna. I killed a kid who had as much right to live as you or I. I took away her life, and I can't ever bring her back. But at least in here, I'm not the worst. I don't have to look my wife in the eyes and know she sees a murderer. I don't have to see my kids grow up, and know that Sarah didn't.'

'So you're running away?'

'Aye, that's right, Anna. I'm running away. Got loads of places to run to. I'm a man who gets locked up in a wee box every night. If I'm good, I'm allowed to walk six times around the perimeter grounds before bedtime, and I have to ask permission to have a bloody visitor.' He narrowed his eyes. 'And I don't remember asking you.'

'That's not very friendly.'

'So, how *did* you get in?'

She'd got in thanks to Marla in New York. Anna had felt sore and ill after her visit to Cath, hadn't known what to do next. She'd gone expecting grateful thanks, maybe a cup of tea. Not a full-on belt across the jaw. After all this time, Anna had thought they'd got away with it. She didn't understand why Jamie would tell Cath *now*. Perhaps going to prison was like approaching death, made you want to tie up loose ends. It would have been nice if he'd warned Anna, though. What if Cath had kidnapped Alice, boiled her in a pot and sent back her collar? Anna knew what Jamie's response would be if she asked him, and she couldn't bear the snub.

It's between me and Cath, Anna. Nothing to do with you.

Did Jamie see *Anna* as a bunny boiler? Did he think she was sniffing around in the vain hope she could snare him back, writing faithfully to him like they do on death row, standing by a man whom nobody else wants? That wasn't what was in her mind when she'd called Marla. Her first thought, after leaving Cath's house, was to drive straight to Aitkenhead Road, where G Division's headquarters were, demand to see the super who'd led the investigation. Then she would go to Complaints and Discipline, and access all their files relating to Jamie, hunker down and burrow through everything until she found a trail that she could trace. How thorough was the original investigation? What did the forensic examination of the locus actually find? Why did Jinky change his story? Who were the other witnesses? What happened to the missing tapes? And why did Coltrane lie?

Well, that one was obvious – because he knew he'd made an arse of the whole operation, and he didn't want to take any of the blame. But she'd have to prove it first. Coltrane was clearly a clever man, well quoted with the senior management. If she blundered in, alleging conspiracy theories, all he would do was cover his tracks even more, and God knows who else would be helping him. She knew that before she did anything else, she had to get the facts straight from Jamie. And if Cath wasn't going to help her, then she'd have to do it herself. She hadn't *planned* to inveigle a meeting with Jamie; Cath had left her no other option. But she couldn't just turn up as a member of the public; they'd never let her in. And she certainly didn't want it known that Jamie had been visited by Anna Cameron from Strathclyde Police. Anna Cameron of the United Nations sounded so much better. Who was going to question that?

So, after the fist-shaped redness on her face had calmed down, and the David-shaped dent had firmed itself up, Anna dialled Marla's mobile number.

'Hi Marla. How're you doing? It's Anna Cameron here.'

'Hey kid, good to hear from you. How's things in bonnie Scotland?'

'Dreich.'

'Excuse me?'

'It means damp. Depressing, dismal, dull.'

'Dreek – I like it. Can you use it about your work as well as the weather?'

'Absolutely, but you've got to say it right: drrreechgh. Like you're coughing up some catarrh.'

'Oh, okay. Maybe I'll pass.'

'Listen, I was wondering if you could help me?'

'Sure, if I can.'

'Right, I know this is probably against all protocol, but is there any way you can make a call for me, pretend I'm doing a job for you?'

She could hear Marla laughing. 'Hey, you *shouldda* been a New Yorker, you know. No bullshit, no preamble . . .'

'Yeah, well, I'm an angry Glaswegian with an agenda – that's miles worse.'

'What's up?'

'I'm not sure. Yet. A friend of mine's in trouble, and I need to speak to him. But I kind of need to go incognito.'

'You working for Special Branch now?'

'No, look it's hard to explain. He's in prison, and I don't know who put him there.'

A click, a disapproving tut. She could picture Marla's scarlet lips chewing the end of her sleek, slimline specs. 'Bad idea, honey, fraternising with the criminal classes. It's the glamour of the bad boy, yeah?'

'No. There's nothing glamorous about this, believe me. He is – was – a cop. And I think someone's fitted him up. Or at least passed the buck, so he's the fall guy. Anyway, I remembered you lot were doing that study on worldwide prisoner welfare. All I'm asking is that you send the pro-forma letter to the governor of the prison, with me as the named contact. Then maybe follow it up with a call?'

Silence on the other end of the ocean.

'Please? Marla, you know I'm not into anything dodgy. I won't bring you into any disrepute. I just need to have a legitimate reason to get my foot in the door. I'll even do the stupid questionnaire for you if you want.'

'Programme's finished anyway.'

'Oh.'

'But . . . I guess I could say it was something we'd discussed before. If anyone asks, it could just be a clerical error the pro forma was sent out. And that would be it, okay? No follow-up phone call, no further involvement. If any shit hits the fan, you're on your own, honey.'

'Okay, fine.'

'Sheesh.' Marla was chewing her glasses again. 'He must be a real good friend.'

'Yeah, he is.'

'Okay. What prison and who's the governor?'

'Oh Marla, you're an absolute star.'

'Yeah, yeah – and we never had this conversation.'

There wasn't enough time to give Jamie the full explanation. Anna checked that the interview-room door was still closed. She'd only been given fifteen minutes with Jamie, and their time was nearly up.

'I got a friend to drop them a line, tell them I was acting on behalf of the UN Police and Justice Task Force.'

'Fancied a wee shot at being Walter Mitty did you?'

'No, I'd done a secondment with them already, so I had all the ID.'

'But why not just flash your warrant card?'

'Because I don't want the police to know I've been here.'

'Why?'

'I don't know who to trust yet.'

'Ach, that's just you all over, Anna.'

She smiled at him. 'Don't start trying to psychoanalyse me. I'm much better left as a closed book.'

'You think?' He looked so tired. 'So how's your life, Anna? Are you happy? With your job, with the way things are going?'

'Sometimes.'

As long as she didn't dream too high, she thought. If she could just stop getting carried away on one great crusade after another, believing hers was the only way, that she was unique, wonderful, bound to succeed. Because, every time, she would freeze with self-doubt when it didn't immediately all go to plan, then sink under the mass and mess of her own ambitions.

Until the next time.

'I'm an optimistic pessimist, I guess.'

'An opti – pissed.'

'Something like that.'

This was getting silly. They were grinning at each other again like two daft children. She needed to ask him more about the shooting itself; who else had been there, what had happened right after the event. But a grinding of the door handle signalled the end of their conversation.

'Time's up, I'm afraid, Ms Cameron.'

Anna stood up, nodded at the warder.

'No problem. We're just finishing here anyway. You've got my number, Mr Worth?'

'Have I?'

'I've already given you it.'

'Oh. So, you did.'

She held out her hand for Jamie to shake. 'Thanks very much for your co-operation.'

His hand in hers. Still Jamie, who could make her skin shiver and compress to nothing but begging nerves. He kept his voice low. 'Come back?'

'Of course I will. There'll be another, more detailed phase of the questionnaire to come. I'll keep you posted.'

Both holding on, his thumb pressing hard in her palm. If she could just smuggle him out, away from here. Wave some fake document that sprung the door, and they could drive off into a Mexican sunset. But she had to go, and he had to stay. Story of their lives.

'Thank you for having me, Mr Worth.'

'It was a pleasure, Ms Cameron.'

The warder led her out to the car park.

'So, what did he say then? Complaining about the food, I bet?'

'Something like that. Could you pass on my thanks to your governor for his co-operation?'

'Aye. Look, he'll probably want to see you. Dead keen on raising the prison's profile is Mr Ethelridge. If you hang on, I can—'

'I'm sorry, I'm on a really tight schedule at the moment. And my boss'll kill me if I'm late.' She tried to look flustered, which wasn't hard; the thought of a tête-à-tête with the prison governor made her desperate to get out of there.

'Maybe next time?' he said.

'Do my best. Thanks again.'

Anna got in the car and started up the engine. She glanced at her watch. Half three. It would take her at least two hours to get home, so she was bound to hit rush-hour traffic somewhere. She'd maybe stop and get some fish and chips for her and Alice's tea. She didn't want to waste time cooking; tonight was for going over everything Jamie had said today, noting it down and matching it with what she already knew. As she was reversing out the space, she saw another warder in her rear-view mirror. He was running towards her, waving a bit of paper.

'Ho, wait up there!' The warder banged his hand on the bonnet.

Shit. Anna cut the engine, rolled down the window.

'I've got that list you were looking for.' The guy was out of breath.

'Pardon?'

'On your letter, it asked for details of our minority ethnic prisoners, and any other prisoners that might be . . .' he checked the document he was holding, '". . . particularly marginalised or stigmatised in the prison environment".'

'Oh, gosh, that's right. I'd forgotten that.'

He frowned. 'Are you sure? Maybe I've got it wrong. I can check with Mr Ethelridge. He's got the original letter. This is just a note from him.'

'No, no, you're absolutely right. It's me. Got a head like a sieve sometimes.' Anna took the piece of paper, put it on the seat beside her. 'Thanks so much,' she smiled, 'you've been a great help, both of you.'

'Well, safe journey back.' He looked up at the thick scudding clouds. 'Looks like it's going to rain.'

She moved her car off quickly, before the warder ran and fetched his boss. Gave both warders the thumbs up as they opened the gate, a nice little wave as she drove away. Sometimes it paid to be blonde.

It was cold, late. The yellow streetlight shone through the girl's window, and she pretended it was sunshine, and outside was the beach; that running water was sea, not rain cascading from a broken gutter. She wound herself in the sheet, and it became a warm embrace that swaddled her. Or a shroud. Her father was away again, and another party boomed downstairs. Music thumping, laughter flaring. She had a test tomorrow; English, she was good at that, but she had to get to sleep. The sheets were all twisted, had been for days. Weeks maybe and why were people in her room? Four, five boys and her brother at the back, carrying a pink-flowered cup from the tea set that was her mum's.

'Haw, you. I've brung you a drink.'

She sat up, pulling her sheet close. 'What is it?'

'Mushrooms.' Everyone laughed, apart from her.

'They're magic.'

Little black floaters, boiled in funny yellow water. The liquid tasted sour, but she drank it down as he told her, even when it scalded her throat.

'Thank you,' she whispered.

His friends laughed again. She felt dizzy, must have sat up too quick. One boy began to rub her back. 'You no feeling too good, doll?'

She shook her head, felt worse. Then all the boys crowded around her, poking at her flesh, and she heard her brother shout: 'Don't touch what you canny afford!'

They smelled like her father, that angry tang of cheap brown alcohol. She saw her brother hold out the teacup for the round gold pounds that came chinkling in. Someone shouted, 'A pound a poke!'

'Fuck off man,' her brother slurred. 'Four quid each – and that's just your pay per view. It's fifteen a pop, and we're talking two max.' His hand on hers, patting it like when he helped her go on her bike. 'Nae shagging, but.' Then he tugged the curtain over, shuttering his face and muting the friendly yellow to black.

It was in her room, her room, and the bed had not been made.
Nobody made beds any more just lay in them they made her lie, they
made her lie and one spanned filthy hands across her petrified, wee-girl
nipples.

When the hurting started, she tried to fly through the sky to another
place, tried to remember her words for tomorrow.

But she could still feel blackness all around her.

Anna hadn't said 'don't tell Cath I was here' before she left. She
would leave it up to Jamie. But she'd keep Alice indoors for a
couple of days, just in case.

Work was turgid as ever; a community council meeting tonight,
and staff appraisals this afternoon. Anna had written a list of things
to do next. She wrote lists for pretty much everything. Not to
prevaricate, but to set out the parameters, and see where she was
going next. Lists on computers were best, because then you could
cut and paste as your priorities changed. But she wasn't leaving
anything on her computer this time, just scraps of paper that she'd
keep in her pocket. Finding Jamie's notebook was key, if it still
existed. DCI Armstrong would need a visit, certainly. And what
was the best way of getting to Coltrane? She'd have to be subtle, at
least at first. Her friend Elaine was the Personnel Manager in G
Division. She could ask her. Elaine was bound to be at her desk just
now, stuffing a sandwich in her face as she dealt with the latest
crisis: sergeant leaving his wife for the new probationer, dis-
gruntled cop suing the Chief Constable, complaints from Training
that G Division staff hadn't turned up on courses – there was
always some panic on with Elaine. Anna really liked her, she was a
great laugh, but she was always fire-fighting. If she'd just get
herself a bit more organised. Write some lists once in a while . . .

Anna didn't want to use the tie line. Hopefully, Elaine would
have her mobile switched on.

'Hi, Elaine? Anna.'

'Anna, you besom. Where've you been hiding? We were supposed to do lunch ages ago.'

'I know, I know. Can you talk just now?'

'Mmhmm. As usual, they've all buggered off and left me to hold the fort. Today of all days. Would you believe it? All the Three Group shift sergeants *and* the inspector have taken out a grievance against the SDO, and here's me—'

'Lainey, that's all very interesting, but will you shut up a minute?'

She snorted. 'Hope you're not on wanting a favour?'

'No, I'm wanting your professional advice.'

'Go on.'

'That guy Coltrane, the AP inspector. What's he really like?'

'Hmm. Off the record?'

'Definitely.'

'Bit of an arsehole. Very bumptious. Talks a good game, but doesn't really have much practical experience to back it up. I think his degree's in Mathematics and Politics or something. Should never be a cop in a million years.'

'Is he approachable, reasonable?'

'No way. He's a pompous wee prick. Thinks he's fireproof. Any faux pas he's made to date – and believe me, there's been a few – just get brushed under the carpet. I mind this time I—'

There she went, on another one of her disaster stories. Anna was getting impatient. 'Could you burst him easily?'

'Could you what?'

'Och, d'you not know any polis lingo yet? How long have you worked there? Could you make him confess to something? What would be the best way: softly, softly, butter him up? Or go in heavy with the questioning?'

'How the hell would I know? What's this all about?'

Anna hesitated. She hadn't really thought this conversation through. Elaine was a force support officer. Not so hidebound by misplaced loyalty, or any fear of reprisals that a cop might be silenced by. And Anna had to have someone on her side.

'Lainey, you remember that guy I told you about, years ago – the one that I used to work with?'

It had been one drunken night, on the second bottle of wine that she really shouldn't have ordered, that Anna had got all teary, and sniffed out the story. Well, part of it. She'd been sufficiently in charge of her tongue not to name any names.

'Oh, yes. Mr No Name. *The One*. What, has he finally left his wife?'

'No, no. I . . . God, this is maybe going to put you in a difficult position. Can I trust you, Lainey? Really trust you?'

'I'll take your secrets to the grave,' she croaked dramatically.

'It was Jamie Worth.'

'Who?'

'Cheers. Spoil my big denouement. James Worth? That cop that just got sent to prison? For the shooting? The one in *your* Division.'

'Oh, *him*. The one Coltrane gave evidence against? Oh, God. *Him?*'

'That's it, Elaine, you can do it. I can hear those rusty brain cogs whirring. But gonny keep your voice down?'

Even though she was alone in her office, Anna lowered her own voice. 'Elaine – I don't think Coltrane told the truth in court. I just want to get the chance to speak to him. You know, informally . . .'

'Oooh. I love a bit of intrigue, me. Hey – there's a pay-off in a couple of weeks. He'll probably be going to that.'

'Are you going?'

'How? Would you like to accompany me? It's the last Thursday of the month.'

'Oh, that would be very nice. Thank you for asking.'

Elaine giggled. 'This is quite exciting. So you want me to help get the lowdown straight from the horse's mouth? Find out what really happened?'

'Why? Do *you* think something's a bit iffy? What's the buzz in G Division about the shooting, then?'

'Och, just that "there's another Coltrane balls-up that Uncle Pete's sorted".'

'Uncle Pete?'

'Peter Wishart. ACC Community Safety.'

'*Ah*. So that's who his wire is. And no, I don't want you to help me get any lowdown, thank you. Just get me talking to him.'

'If you can. We'll need to get there sharp, though. He never hangs about long at these things. Thinks he's too good to mingle. The do's in town – I can pick you up about six, okay?'

'Brilliant. And Elaine, please don't say to anyone—'

'My lips are sealed.'

To her growing list, Anna added 'Pay-Off', police-speak for somebody's leaving do. Coltrane had an assistant chief constable watching his back. Several statements absolving him of all blame. No evidence to dispute that what he said was true. Walls on all sides, protecting him and keeping her out.

Anna's pen kept tracing the words in front of her.

Pay-Off. Pay-Off.

What was Jinky's pay-off? Jinky John Robertson; what made him sell his soul and turn on his neighbour? At some point, Anna would have to speak to him. As far as she knew, the guy was off long-term sick; suffering from a plague of locusts hopefully, or riddled with worms. But she'd deal with Coltrane first.

Above Jinky on the list was Forensics? It was crucial that Anna got her hands on the forensic report. If the girl did have a gun in the flat, then there had to be some evidence. There had to be a bloody gun. Could she have chucked it from the window, or down the stairwell as she was running out? How quickly did the police search the flat, when everyone was milling around the dying girl and Jamie? Could someone have nipped inside, removed the gun?

But why? Coltrane's actions struck Anna as those of someone out of his depth, desperately trying to save his skin when it all went wrong. If she believed Jamie – and she did, she did – then Coltrane was certainly lying through his back teeth, probably using his authority to cajole others into doing the same. But actively to hide a gun to frame Jamie, and wreak all this unnecessary havoc down on them all? Unlikely.

So, if not Coltrane, then who else? And how did they get in? Even with all the turmoil going on below, the flat would have been sealed off in minutes, ready for a detailed search as soon as it was practical. Loads of stripy tape, big polis on the door – that was how they did it.

Unless someone else had been in the flat with Sarah.

Anna took a mouthful of her coffee, swallowed it slow. It was too obvious. Someone must have considered that already, surely, the fact that Sarah hadn't been flailing wildly out the window for no reason. That someone else had been in there with her, possibly struggling with her – had been chasing her even, down the stairs and out. Only no one would have seen them, would they, all running to the front of the house as he – or she – scarpered out the back. Still clutching the gun.

She gulped the remains of her coffee, closed her eyes tight.

Calm down, girl. Don't get ahead of yourself.

Thought it once more. Wrote it carefully on her little bit of list-paper.

Someone else in flat with Sarah? Who? Check possibilities. Friend? Family?

She could spend days, months, chasing her tail, trying to access records, begging folk who didn't want to know for information and favours. But there was one person who could bring all this together. One man who already held all the evidence in a neatly boxed file, who would know of any convoluted links and conversations between police and prosecution.

David Millar.

She would have to see him again.

23

'Right boys, from the top again. Some of you are just not trying, and it's such a shame. This music could be really lovely if you just put in some effort.'

'Ooh-er. You heard the man, gie it some . . . uh . . . effort.'

The two pricks in the last row began gyrating their hips against the arses of the men in front.

'Fuck off, ya pervert.'

Ten of them in the choir, mostly new saps who'd been press-ganged into performing by Mr Ledbetter, a warder who would have been much happier with a career in musical theatre. Jamie wondered how he coped with the macho posturings of a place like this. Prison reminded him of his first weeks at primary school. Lesson one: any show of sensitivity or compassion will be seized upon as weakness. For wee boys to become big men, you must first reject all the softness and kindness you have learned at your mother's knee. Only in prison, failure to comply would earn you a scar for life, rather than your head being held down the lavvy.

Jamie had started work on painting the new chapel. At first it was simple stuff, gloss on woodwork, emulsioning walls. And then, with the arrival of a proper artist, they'd started putting the meat onto the bones. Ethelridge had an idea for a mural on one wall, and various illustrated alcoves and illuminating texts dotted around the rest of the space. Calvin, the artist, had sketched out his designs already, and Jamie and a guy called Donaldson were tasked with colouring them in. Basic washes, nothing fancy, but it meant each time Calvin came to Garthlock he could get right to work on filling in the detail. The mural was a graceful angel, curving over towards a single rose. Ethelridge's inspirational phrase of choice for this one was: *From thorns come beauty.* Aye, well, not in this place.

Ledbetter tapped his little stick against the lectern.

'Will you all *please* try to all start at the same time? On the count of three: now watch my baton.'

'Bet he says that to all the boys.'

As was the way, the bad lads doing their own subjective commentary stood at the back; two bears with the magnificent names of Tyrone Patrick Fergusson and Ally McInally. Both had the casually bored, defiant faces of those that thought they owned the place, but the bearded one, Tyrone, could actually sing a bit, so Ledbetter seemed to tolerate him. Jamie could detect a trace of something in their accents, Highland, or Irish, that reminded him of the boys up at Townhead. He wondered how his team were getting on. Had Derek stuck to the training schedule? You had to keep on top of them, keep giving them new challenges, or they'd just get bored and drift away. Jamie had already let them down, he didn't want someone else to.

Next to Tyrone, Brian yawned. He'd volunteered gladly for the choir, declaring he *couldny take another day of boiling water scorching my bloody skin.* This from a man with hot sears of trackmarks up both arms, and the habitual limp of a used-up user with few places left to jag.

'I'm off the smack, but. Straight up,' he'd promised Arnie, who'd warned them all on day one that, if he found any drugs in his laundry, he'd put them, and their owner, into one of the spin dryers. 'I promised the wife I'd go to they classes.'

'That's only cause they gie you methadone,' said Ross.

'Naw, that's bullshit. I'm gonny do it this time. We've a new wean coming, and I want to be clean. Everyone can find a million excuses to go on it, but they canny find one to stay off.'

'Aye, just you wait till you start pure rattling, and someone lights up a wee half-gramme of kit.'

Arnie had closed the conversation with a: 'No in my laundry they willny.'

But Brian was right. Anything was better than the laundry. You didn't feel safe there, in among its heat and noise and confusion.

Not anywhere really; Jamie felt constant threat in every part of Garthlock, lurking thicker and darker than its siege walls. But the laundry was just . . . chaotic. Elemental water and fire, and Jamie was glad to be away from it for a while. Though he'd already got it organised far better in a few weeks than old Arnie had done in years. It was simple really. He'd just asked the screws for some coloured baskets. Brown for dirty, blue for clean and wet, red for clean and dry, green for ironed and ready to go. Operating to a system meant the work was done in half the time, each of them responsible for their own area. It was why he and Brian had both been allowed time off for extra-curricular activities – they were getting through double the amount of work than they had done in the past.

'We're way ahead of schedule anyway,' the warder had said. 'Good idea of yours, Worth. They baskets.'

'Wasn't my idea. Arnie thought, now there were more of us in the laundry, that it'd be easier.'

'Whatever, it's working. But not all your ideas are so clever, Worth, so just be careful, eh?'

'I'm not with you.'

'No, but you were with Ross Durward yesterday, weren't you? When he slipped?'

Despite Arnie's warnings, despite Jamie trying to ignore him, Ross had never let up. Every time he came in to the laundry, he would have a wee rap at Jamie's chest – not a punch, more a prod with angry fingers. He'd say nothing, just jab in passing like a vicious gnat, until Jamie could take it no longer. So he'd decked him. Just as silently, grabbing his irritating index finger and twisting the boy's hand to force him to the ground. After a moment holding him face down on the soapy linoleum, Jamie had let him up and on his way. Ross had kept out of his way all that day and the next.

'You were a lucky boy yesterday,' said the warder. 'That's all. Just watch it if you want to go back to the laundry after all this painting business.'

'I had to defend myself.'

But the man pretended not to hear.

Jamie hadn't realised it at first, but being in the laundry gave you a little power, and any power was worth preserving. Prisoners' personal clothes only got washed after all the linens and uniforms had been done. This was a barter they could use in the laundry – he'd already seen inmates approach Arnie, looking for 'a wee favour'. Invariably, if Arnie liked them, he'd say *aye*, ask no favours in return. They needed to exploit these opportunities more, use them as leverage for . . . och, more on your plate at dinnertime, or something. Jamie had plenty of ideas to improve life in the laundry. At the moment, everything went in the wash in one big rag-bag bundle. No effort was made to keep items separate and return them to their owners. Men would literally end up sharing uniforms, and so would keep refusing them, sending them back, requesting new clothes, without stains and holes. If each prisoner had their own individual sheets, underwear, pillows, shirts and stuff numbered and with their name on them, and they organised each wash a floor at a time, each House with different laundry days, it would cut their working week still further, and would probably save the prison service some money. He'd mention it to Arnie; didn't want anyone to think he was trying to gain Brownie points. Although Arnie didn't have long to go before his parole came up.

Jamie shivered. Now he was plotting the Machiavellian overthrow of the poor old laundry man. He wasn't, he wasn't. Reorganising the laundry just made sense. As a cop, it was second nature to make quick, practical decisions on a daily basis. Just because they tried to infantilise you in here, binding your hands and lopping off your dick, didn't mean they could switch off your mind. If anything, the fewer stimuli he was presented with, the more his brain was racing; full of grand schemes and omnipresent threats, suspicious acts and tiny nonsenses.

And nightmares. The chapel hadn't been consecrated yet, it was still all dustsheets and dirt, builders' scaffolding lying crisscrossed in the corner, them painting around the choristers. But Jamie tried to imagine it holy, a vortex exorcising all the badness from its midst, just by dint of intentions. Could God see him better in here, know he was trying? It was hard, maintaining all this bluster and hubris. Keeping it tight, never letting anything slip. Jamie no longer knew what was a façade, and what was really him. It never mattered before, when you had your family and your job, your mates and all your stuff. And every name that followed you through life, shaping the you that might never quite match up, with the you you kept inside. All the people he'd ever been: policeman, good guy, daddy, smartarse, joker, scared wee boy. Adulterer.

He was least proud of that one. Anna visiting him had been wonderful, mind. Like catching a glimpse of a film star or a speeding yacht. A distant, luxurious commodity that he could never have – and the unattainability made it all the more thrilling. Not window-shopping, not yearning, just appreciation of a beautiful thing. Not that he could choose Anna now, even if he wanted to. But he didn't, he truly didn't, and that was the best thing of all. Freedom to love Cath, no ghosts in the shadows whispering what-might-have-beens. He knew it as soon as he touched Anna. Warm flesh, nice perfume. Unremarkable. Just human. It was good of Anna to come and see him, nice of her to think she could help. Loyalty was a quality he seemed to inspire in very few people. But Cath was everything to him. Her forgiveness, her strength – he could never repay that, could only be grateful. And pray that she never gave up.

'Watch out, boys!' yelled a voice from above, as a metal rivet fell crashing to the floor. As one, they all looked up, to see, not God, but the dirt-smeared face of one of the builders, booming down at them through the wooden ceiling.

'Oh look,' said Brian. 'There's a trap door up in the roof.'

'Excellent. Maybe we can tunnel out up the way.'

'Indeed you will not,' scolded Ledbetter. 'That there is going to be the *pièce de résistance* of the whole show . . . I mean service.'

'How d'you mean, sir?' asked Jamie, glad of a break from them practising scales.

'See at the end of the anthem? *In This Place*? The one we're kicking off with – that none of this lot can get the bloody melody for?'

'Aye.'

'Well, just as we hit the final note, those doors are going to open, and a great big ebony cross is going to drop right down, transforming this,' he paused, painting inverted commas in the air, ' "nondescript hall" into a "holy shrine of worship". That's what Mr E wants anyway – if they ever get the bloody pulley to work.'

The cross at Billy Wong's funeral had been a simple one, placed discreetly on the altar. This sounded like a Las Vegas monstrosity.

'Is that not, I don't know – a bit disrespectful?' said Jamie.

'Not at all. It'll be very tastefully done. And a bit of drama never hurt anyone. Even God himself wasn't averse to a wee bolt of lightning now and then. Anyway, it's all multicultural you know, depending on what service is being held here. We've a Star of David too. Plastic, mind, but it's all painted gold. And one of those crescent moons.'

'What about Satanists, Mr Ledbetter? Can we swivel the cross-thingy upside down?' asked Ally.

'Aye, that's your favourite position, isn't it, bawbag?'

'Right,' sighed Ledbetter, 'I don't know about you lot, but I've had enough. You'd better all practise hard for tomorrow otherwise I can't see us being ready in time. We've still got three hymns to learn – pitch-perfect, mind. And Mr Ethelridge wanted a descant during the anthem.' He sighed again. 'Do any of you even know what that means?'

'Is it like an ordinary cunt, sir?' asked Tyrone.

'Just go. Any more nonsense and you'll all be back to your work parties. Worth, Donaldson, you may as well go too, and I can get locked up.'

It was still half an hour till dinner. Maybe Ledbetter hadn't noticed. Jamie had run out of paint anyway. No point in opening another pot now. He quite liked how these twining – thistles was it? – were turning out. Jamie had added a couple of extra leaves around the edges; it gave it a bit more balance. And his were just as good as old Calvin's. He wrapped up his brushes, and left with the rest of the prisoners.

'Excellent. Just in time for *Countdown*,' said one of the escaping choristers.

'That's a loada shite, so it is,' said Brian. 'I canny understand it.'

'Naw, it's great. I watch all the quizzes, me. Keeps my brain ticking over, know? Stops me fae going out of my mind.'

Tyrone barged between Jamie and Brian. 'What about you, pigshite? What do you watch, eh?' As he spoke, he placed his hand on Brian's shoulder, moving him gently away from the group.

'*The* fucking *Bill*,' honked Ally, taking Brian's place. '*Miami Vice*. Naw, naw, man,' he was doubled over, creasing himself with laughter, 'Garthlock Five-O. You know? Like *Hawaii Five-0*, but without the surf-dudes!' As he said it, his hand shot out, striking Jamie hard in the belly.

'Jesus. What was that for?' Jamie gasped, clutching his gut. Tears of surprise smarting, smudging the shapes around him.

'Cause you were fucking there, ya bastard.'

'Woah, woah, easy. Ledbetter's looking over,' said a voice he didn't recognise. 'Hold him up till we get outside.'

They all shuffled out the half-finished chapel. Jamie wrenched free from the arm that was guiding him. 'Get your fucking hands off me.'

'I was only trying to help you, Big Man.'

He thought at first it was Brian holding him, but it was one of the other singers, a young housebreaker from Tollcross. He noticed Brian had fallen back, was whispering with Tyrone, hands in pocket, neither looking directly at the other. Jamie sensed a deal being done. He kept his head down, hands on knees like he was still winded.

The open availability of drugs in the prison had shocked him at first. He'd read all about it in the papers – hadn't everyone? – but it was so barefaced, the warders turning a blind eye to packages hurled over fences, folk hunched in their rooms, chopping and rolling, sniffing and blowing. Huddles in the courtyard, pinprick eyes, rival factions having turf wars. It was barely masked at all; folk passing eccies, jellies, Valium around the dining table like they were sweeties.

It made him think of when he worked down the Drag. The problems there were so insurmountable that you could barely keep a lid on it. Over a thousand prostitutes, feeding their weans and veins. How could you possibly contain that? But if the lassies kept themselves to themselves, didn't hassle passersby, then he couldn't see what the problem was. That was probably the thinking here. They might get the odd sudden spat of aggression, fits of paranoia, but mostly, untrammelled drug abuse provided the Garthlock warders with quietly spaced, self-medicated morons, who gave no trouble if they were left alone. They weren't getting this one, though. Cath had told him about Brian's wife. Sparky lassie called Stella, living on the breadline. Jamie snapped up straight, thrust his hand into Ally's chest, sending him flying.

'Woops, mind that floor, pal. You might break your neck. Here Brian,' he called over, 'we could nip back and give Arnie a hand with the deliveries. Save him wheeling all the carts around himself.'

'You're alright Big Man. I've a wee message I need to be doing.'

'What kind of a wee message?'

'It's fuck all to do with you, pigshite.' Ally launched himself at Jamie, knocking him into the wall.

'Ho, ho, now watch the man,' said Tyrone, coming over. 'Any more of that nonsense and you'll be getting sent up the road to the Big Hoose, Alistair. And what would I dae without my other half?' He smiled at Jamie. 'Purely platonic mind, Big Man. Though I do like a bit of variety once in a while.'

'But how come we're no . . .'

Tyrone gripped Ally either side of his polo shirt lapels. 'Shut the fuck up, Alistair. Naw, on you go, Brian. We'll see you later.' Tyrone linked his arm through Ally's, and sailed off up the corridor.

'Good on you, Big Man,' muttered the *Countdown* fan. 'They tossers think they own the place.'

'Right Brian, c'mon,' said Jamie.

'Fucksake, Worth. You're no ma maw,' he grunted, pushing past to catch up with Hinge and Brackett.

The inmates were allowed to walk around the grounds in the evening, so long as they'd been behaving. It was only a copse of ancient apple trees, some plots of vegetables and a gravel path, looping in a sprawled-out figure of eight, but you could hear the animals lowing in the sheds beyond the kitchen compound, catch a whiff of dung that wasn't human. And from the top of the rise behind the old house, if you turned your face away from the high brick wall and waves of twisted wire behind you and looked west, you could see miles of patchwork green. Suddenly, the world just opened up, the sense of freedom fleeting, but intense. Jamie usually walked around on his own, but tonight, old Arnie had followed him out after dinner.

'You don't mind, do you? It's just, I know some folk like their ain space.'

'No, it's fine. Free country and all that.'

Arnie raised a quizzical brow, then laughed. 'Aye. Free as a bird, me.'

They walked side by side, enjoying the crunch of the stones, the brittling of leaves cutting crisp flutters across the changing light. Everything dying back, yet the trees were at their brightest. Soon, each russet flare would tumble to the ground, clagging the gravel with taupey mulch. A quiet scuffle as a bird hopped onto a branch, began to preen and twitter. It made Jamie think of Ledbetter. He let the air fill his sinuses, slide in across his palate. It smelled sharp, fresh as quick-snapped rhubarb, its pointed breeze promising winter. He could feel almond shapes of cold beneath the hollows of his eyes, striping his cheekbones in invisible war paint. A huge, low sun struck pink under his lids, lashes flickering like the leaves. Way down below, across the fields, a farmer worked his dog, its black and white flashing in zigzags, bounding, circling.

'I canny be annoyed with all the crap that lot watch on the telly,' said Arnie. 'Rather no watch it at all. It just reminds you of what you canny have.'

'I know. Sometimes I find myself watching kids' TV, because I know my wee girl will be watching at the same time.'

'What age is she?'

'Five going on fifteen.'

Jamie didn't want to talk about Eilidh. 'Anyway, you'll no have to put up with the blaring tellies for long. You're getting out soon, aren't you?'

Arnie drew air deep into his lungs. 'Aye.'

'Don't sound so pleased.'

'Naw, naw. Don't get me wrong. There's been times I've been scared I'll be carted out of this place in a box. Imagine that – if Garthlock was the last place you saw on this earth?'

The bird was in full throat now, sweet breakings of music near higher than you could hear, trilled over and over to the bleeding sun.

'Truth is son, I'm feart.'

'Of what?'

'Everything. Last time I went on a bus, we had clippies.' Arnie took a hanky out his pocket. 'You'll no even mind what they are – conductors, you know? How will I know what to do when I get on?'

'You'll not have to do anything. Pensioners get on for free now.'

'Is that right? Well, fancy.' Arnie shook the hanky, then burrowed it around his nose. As he blew into it, the bird took flight, wheeling down towards the fields. 'The wife never telt me.'

'The wife? You kept that quiet, you dark horse. Well, just think what else you'll have to look forward to.'

Arnie shook his head. 'Och, away. I'm too old for all that nonsense.'

How had he stood it, growing old in this place? Seeing your faculties fade, your desire turn to apathy, as the world passed further out of reach. All that time wasted, slipping by in routines and meals and visits.

'I bet you'll be surprised.'

Arnie stared at his shoes. 'Son, it's been that long since I did more than kiss her goodbye. We're more like brother and sister now. And she's got used to me no being around. What if I get on her nerves, under her feet all day? She looks after our Sheila's wee ones some days.' There was a catch in his voice. 'I've got grand-weans I've never even seen.'

He blew his nose again. 'You're doing alright though, son. You keep your own standards – that's good. Keep your cool too. I've seen plenty macho-men lying howling and greeting. Most of them canny handle it here unless they take drugs.'

'I know,' said Jamie. 'I'm a bit worried about Brian—'

Sudden rustling ahead of them, as a figure stepped out from behind a tree. 'Evening, pigshite. I think I owe you a fucking kicking.'

It was Ross. The boy was shaking. It was pathetic. He lunged at Jamie, but was too slow to make much impact. Jamie feinted to the side, then caught Ross's waist as he fell forward, pushing him on to soft grass. As he lay there, Arnie swung a kick at the boy's crotch. He rolled over, groaning, until Jamie lifted him up by the scruff of his neck.

'And . . . here we are again.' Jamie leaned Ross against the tree he had been hiding in. 'Look, can we get one thing straight? I *was* a cop, not now. I was put in here by the polis, just the same as you. And I'm not the slightest bit interested in fighting. So, you ignore me, and I'll ignore you.'

Arnie kicked Ross on the shin. 'And you can find yourself another job and all.'

'Fuck off, old man. I'm no working in your stinking laundry any more anyway.'

'Too right you're no, ya cheeky bastard.'

Arnie began to chase after him.

'Hold up, Linford.' Jamie jogged to catch Arnie's arm. 'Let him go; he's no worth it.'

'He's a bad wee bastard, but. Got in with a bad crowd.'

'You mean there's a good one here? Look, you need a seat, pal.' He led Arnie over to a nearby tree stump.

They sat a while, watching the light fade. It was getting cold. Jamie twisted round to look behind. Darkness came rapidly in the countryside, the sky halving as a door slammed shut in the east. There, it was sudden night, no streetlights to temper the shadows, while the west still shone with bruised daylight. Jamie shivered in his thin fleece. He'd bought it to go hillwalking – got the entire shift to scale Ben Nevis. One of the best days out he'd ever had. They'd borrowed the SPRA minibus, loaded up with beer and sandwiches, and just hiked and hiked and hiked. No one would admit to burning thighs and side-ripping breath. The only time they stopped was to take in views of black crags and purple bracken. And for more beer. Then, at the top, standing knee-deep in perfect snow, scanning boundless cities of white steeples. And sliding back down on their arses through the snow, Jamie's trousers tearing on a boulder. Dinner in a hotel at Fort William, then the quiet yawns and banter of the journey home. They raised enough to get new strips for each boy in the Townhead team. They'd all promised they'd go back, do it every year. But they never had.

Jamie would probably never see those views again. And he'd left his camera in the minibus.

'Think I'll head in. You coming? It's nearly lockdown.'

'Naw. I'm gonny sit here a while, get my breath,' Arnie smiled. 'The spirit's still willing, you know?'

'That I do.'

Jamie left him there, walked down to the greying bulk below. Arnie would freeze his bollocks off if he wasn't careful. But he couldn't stay out much longer. It would soon be lights out. A belch of warm air met him as he opened the door to Ninian. There was baying from the association hall.

Football on tonight, someone had said at dinner. But what was the point of watching just the first half of the match? He would phone Cath, then go straight to his peter. He meant his room.

There were payphones at the rear of the hallway. Jamie stopped to check his pockets for change. Felt a bump as someone careered into the back of him, then something struck his foot.

'Ach, shit. Watch where you're going, you.' It was Smithy. He was scrabbling on the ground, looking for whatever it was that had dropped.

Jamie could see what had hit him. A mobile phone, lying beneath the radiator. Motorola, same make as the ones Smith had bundled in his hand. Smith's other hand clutched a polythene bag, which Jamie could see was full of sweeties. Smartie tubes and packs of Poppets. Jamie rested the tip of his toe against the phone.

'Evening, Mr Smith. That's a lot of phones you've got there. All they sweeties too. Are we having a party?'

'You being a smart-arse, Worth? Where did that phone go?'

'This one?'

Jamie kicked the phone gently, so it slid across to Smithy. He stooped to retrieve it, dropping another phone as he did so. This one hit the ground hard, its back flying off. 'Fucksake,' muttered Smithy, scooping it up and stuffing it in his pocket. He rubbed his foot back and forward across the ground, like he was wiping a dirty mark.

'Where you been anyway?'

'Just out for a walk.'

'*Just out for a walk*,' Smithy mimicked. 'In the grounds?'

'No, on the moon.'

'Right. Get in here.' Smithy turned the handle of the caretaker's office.

'What for?'

'Spot check.'

'For what?'

'For drugs, Worth. That's the only reason folk go wandering around the grounds at this time of night. Doing your Easter bunny hunt were you? Someone leave you a pressie earlier?'

'You know that's a load of bollocks, Mr Smith. I don't take drugs.'

'You might sell them, but.'

'How? Frightened I eat up some of your profit?'

'What did you say?'

Jamie wiped his foot across the linoleum, just as Smithy had done. 'Bit gritty this floor, isn't it? As if someone's spilled something powdery?'

Smithy opened the office door wide. 'Get your fucking arse in there now.'

But the room was already occupied. A scrum of three men: two big, one small were playing Twister on the floor. Twister prison-style, though no one had their cocks out yet. Just as well, because the smallest one didn't want to play.

Jamie felt sick, remembering the showers at Barlinnie, the hot wet vileness of the degradation, and he tried to get past Smithy to stop it. Smithy shot his arm across the doorway.

'Stay back, Worth,' he hissed. 'I'll deal with this.'

It was dark in the room, but Jamie recognised one of the bigger men. Tyrone.

He was crushing the wee guy's face to the floor.

'Now, you hold still, man, and you'll soon be in seventh heaven.'

'I fucking telt you,' he screamed. 'I don't want to go back on the smack. For fucksake, I only wanted some weed.'

'Nae money in weed, son.'

Jamie could see what they were doing now. They were sticking a needle into Brian's arm.

'Stop them, you bastard. Stop them,' he yelled.

'Walk away, Worth,' said Smithy, closing the door. 'Just walk away.'

He shoved Jamie into the hallway, locked the door. Jamie waited for him to get on his radio, call for assistance. Instead, he stood sentry with folded arms.

'You total fucking bastard.'

Jamie took a run back. If he hit the door hard enough, it might burst open. It was only a caretaker's cupboard. He tensed his body, powering up inside. Too late, he saw Smithy's baton, hanging high above before it cracked him on the head. Heard ringing in his ears, Smithy's wheezing follow-through.

'You assault a prison officer and you're scooped, pal. Plus, young Brian's begging for it really. Now, do like I say and crawl away.'

24

David Millar's flat was in the West End of Glasgow, in a beautiful sandstone terrace on Great Western Road. Full of noisy traffic, but the compensations of lofty ceilings and elegant cornicing were obvious. Anna could see inside from the street. What looked like the lounge; wine-red walls, with the picture rail stripped to natural oak. She'd been standing there a while, had worked out which flat was his from the nameplate on the intercom. Two up left. *Millar.* But she hadn't gone in yet. You got a better view from back across the road.

From there, where she waited now, she could see a painting. Some kind of abstract in oils, lots of scarlet and burnt orange. The kind of furious colours she hated. There was a strange, darting light trembling from what she guessed must be the mantelpiece. *Candles.* So there was definitely someone in. Was he in there alone, though? Lolling on the couch watching the telly, with his hand comfortably nestled down his joggers? Bag of peanuts and a bottle of beer? Hardly the picture of a Diptyque man. Or was he seducing some beautiful lawyer, serving up asparagus hollandaise and a dollop of Cocteau Twins?

Anna, who would ever get their kit off to that? Apart from you?

David wasn't that subtle. Okay then, a dollop of Barry White. Anna shook the rain from her hair, moved deeper into the overhang of the building behind her. This sandstone row was a quirky mix of palatial townhouses and scabby bedsits, ethnic art shops and greasy chippies, before Great Western intersected with Byres Road. From there, the uniform arches of the Grosvenor Hotel stretched pale and long down one side, while the dark, verdant rustlings of the Botanic Gardens claimed the other. Man-made and Mother Nature, squaring up to one another for a century or more; both growing blacker with each passing year's traffic fumes. Old Mr Wajerski had lived not far from here.

The rain was falling faster, little stabbing jags that nipped her eyes and nose.

Come on, doll. Just get in and get it done. Either that or walk away.

Anna buttoned up her coat. Stepped out, weaving through the buses and taxis, dodging two students on one bike, and walked up the steps to David's intercom. She pushed the silver square beside his name.

A moment, a click. 'Hello?'

'Court document for David Millar.'

'Come on up.'

He pressed the buzzer to unlock the door. Inside, the close smelled of fresh paint and money, hoovered doormats and expensive orchids. A wrought-iron staircase wound elegantly around and up, past burnished brass doorknobs and crackle-glazed tiles. Anna walked more slowly the higher she climbed. Above her, she could hear the scratch of a lock, an echoing creak as hinges shifted. David was waiting at his open door, head turned back to keep an eye on the telly.

'Just put it—'

He looked up. 'Anna!' Seized her hand, pulled her inside. 'Anna Cameron! You're all wet.'

'I know.'

She'd spent ages on her hair, straightening and polishing, and now it was all lank clumps.

'God, it's good to see you.'

'You too.'

'But why are you here?'

'I'll go if you want.'

'No. No, I bloody don't want. You've no idea how many times I've wanted to open the door and see you standing there. But I didn't think . . . I didn't think you wanted to know me any more. Shit. Anna.' He stroked her fringe back from her brow. 'Anna. Come in, sit down. Can I get you a coffee? Wine? A towel?'

He led Anna into his gory lounge. It was actually quite nice; only the back wall was red. She could smell garlic, saw the remains of something pasta-ish in a bowl on a tray. Chunky white candles – man candles – stood either end of the mantelpiece. And the wooden floor was just like hers at home. Except real wood, not laminate. Water splashed from her sexy boots as she clipped in like a circus pony, white patches swelling over the beige. The suede was ruined.

'No. Yes. And no. Just hang my coat up somewhere to dry, will you?'

'So you're stopping then?'

'Might be. Depends what wine you have. If it's Chardonnay, I'm walking.'

'What about a pretentious wee Beaujolais?'

'Go on then. I'd expect nothing less from you.'

This was too comfortable. David switched off the telly, took her coat away. She could hear him clinking in the kitchen, homely sounds of sharing and preparing . . . and she wasn't really here to see him. Or to enjoy this. Anna closed the door over slightly and looked around the room, searching for – what was it again? *A nice oak chest that my auntie left me.* She doubted if he really did keep all his important stuff there, but it was worth a try. And if not, well . . . getting him onside would still be a good move. There was a bureau in the corner, but it had the crazy gnarling of a walnut veneer. Clear glass Habitat console, very nice – had the same one herself in the hall – and a bookshelf. That was it, apart from two couches, a chair, and the low table with the remains of David's dinner on top. Which, when she looked closer, was not a table, but a large chest. No legs, just squat and mellow, with a hinged top and two deep drawers, each with their own keyhole.

David returned with two clear goblets and an open bottle. He poured her a drink, then flopped back onto a black leather couch.

'Sit down then.'

She sat on the armchair facing him, next to the warmth of the radiator. Took her boots off to feel her socks. Her feet were soaking.

'Cat socks. Nice.'

A mistress of seduction. She had meant to put on stockings, but nylon itched like hell under wet jeans, and it was too bloody cold to wear a skirt.

'D'you like them? I've got other ones with wee bells on the back.'

'Seriously?'

'Yeah. And buttons.'

She peeled off the damp socks and draped them over the radiator.

David watched her, smiling. 'Just make yourself at home.'

'Okay.'

Anna curled her feet up onto the seat.

'So.'

'So.'

'Am I forgiven?'

She shifted her position. Sat up straighter, hugged her knees into her chest. 'Do you deserve to be?'

'I was only doing my job, Anna, same as you do, every day. There was nothing *personal* against the guy—'

'I don't want to go there.'

That sounded too brusque. She tried again.

'But I'm sorry I overreacted. It was just a bit of a shock, you know? Like . . . when you're little and you find out your best friend's run off to play with someone else. And then you find out they were making fun of you.'

'Am I your best friend then?'

'No, I didn't mean that . . .'

Why was she reverting to baby talk, all cooried up like a five-year-old in her jammies? What happened to the: *you have to understand I'm a police officer, David. And when I see a fellow officer being treated vindictively, see another legal professional gleaning some pleasure from his downfall, it makes me furious.* No, let's make googly eyes and start sniffing about playground tormentors. She'd be stuffing her thumb in her mouth next.

'But a good friend, maybe?' he said.

'Maybe.'

'A very, very good friend? A dear friend? A close, personal friend?'

She chucked a cushion at him. 'Shut up.'

'Police brutality!'

'Summary justice.' Anna raised her glass to him, took a swig of wine.

'*Are* we friends then?'

'I guess.'

He smiled at her again, a deep, warm glow that you could climb right into. The skin around his eyes crinkled. His face was more swarthy than she remembered. It suited him.

'You been away somewhere? You've got a tan.'

'How? D'you want to see my white bits?'

He was so much like Anna. *I was only doing my job.* Wasn't that her patented get-out clause for pretty much everything? Not calling her mother, or cancelling dates. Shafting some poor sod who believed her when she said that confession was good for the soul. Kicking lying scrotes in the kidneys, sitting stony-faced as a widow broke her heart, deliberately closing her ears to the pleas of some desperate junkie as she huckled them into a cell.

It's my job. I was only doing my job. Say it once, and all is forgiven. Then you can move on, no hard feelings.

'So tell me, Anna Cameron. What have you been up to since our lovely lunch?'

'This and that.'

'Uh-huh. Okay, end of that conversation. What about our buds at the UN? Have you been in touch with any of them?'

'Have you? What about *Pee*-lar?'

His lips twitched. 'Pilar? Why – d'you not like Pilar?'

'Do you?'

'What's not to like? She's gorgeous: Spanish, raven-haired – and I think she had the hots for me.'

'Really? Well, I think Rutger had the hots for me.'

David snorted, red wine gushing down his chin. 'Oh, Anna, you kill me. So,' his accent switched to staccato German, 'you vant me to grow a big bushy moustache. Jah?'

'You leave Rutger alone. He's cuddly. Like a big woolly bear.'

'I'm cuddly.'

'No you're not.'

He pouted. Rubbed a wine-soaked finger on his bottom lip. God, even when he was being camp he was sexy.

'And how's the Gorbals?'

'It's not Gorbals, it's Easterhouse.'

Why could he not remember where she worked? And why did she care that he couldn't? The wine hit Anna's empty stomach, acid splashes in her throat.

'What is it? You look like you're going to bubble.'

'M'not.'

David opened his arms wide. 'Come here, you.'

She shook her head. Picked at wet fingernails, stripping pink from the quick.

'Well, I'll come to you, then.'

David got down, shuffled over on his knees. He looked ridiculous, like a designer-clad Munchkin. 'While I'm down here – will you marry me?'

This had to start somewhere. In response, she kissed the top of his head, lingering longer than she meant to. He smelled so clean. She rubbed her cheek across his hair and then he held her, wrapping his arms around her legs. His face was in her lap, breath burning at the hollow dip of her thighs. Sliding his hands up, over her legs. Under her T-shirt.

'This is wet,' he whispered.

'Take it off, then.'

'You can see in here from the street you know.'

'Is that right?'

'Uh-huh,' he said tugging with his teeth at the hem of her T-shirt.

'You're crap at this.'

She took it off herself, flung it over to the couch. One shoulder caught in a swirl of cold air, the other still hot from the heater.

'Mmm. Nice clean, white bra. No cats?'

'No cats.'

He pulled at the zip of her jeans. 'Pants?'

'No cats.'

She raised her bum off the seat to help him. He eased off her jeans, but one leg stuck at her foot.

'Why can't you wear a skirt, like normal girls?'

'And why can't you be slick, like normal boys?'

And then there was no more talking. Just his lips, his hands on her. His shirt still on, undone, guiding her down on top of him, his cheek against hers, rough on smooth. Slowly, unravelling, bodies fitting, barely moving to the digging juts of his hips as she crouched, breasts splayed soft, astride him. Time and motion, tiny motions, on and on and on till she was swaying and kneading and the curling tease was building like a whirlpool flowing upwards and it hit her, barely moving.

Licking could heal, if done gently. Some people did it to be nice, she had heard. Mother animals lapped faces to keep their babies clean. More pictures came into the girl's mind, of hungry mouths and gaping holes, of sweated dirt and blood, all cold and full of promised hurts. She knew enough to recognise the bitter smell of evil. It was here, in this high-up room her brother had brought her to.

'I've brung you a wee sample, Tai. This is Helga.'

Again, he licked his lips. 'Helga? Is that no German?'

'Aye, well, it's something like that. Disny speak a word of English. You canny touch the merchandise, but.'

And the man had laughed, a croaky breathing grunt. 'Is that right? Come you here to me, hen.'

These men, these men. She kept her eyes shut, like the last time. Chanting nursery rhymes in her head and she was Humpty Dumpty and she was falling down and she was Little Bo Peep and she had lost . . . she had lost.

Then his thumb was pushing past her lips, his stink a flavour on her tongue and she felt his rasping breath, telling her to strip.

David's arm was heavy on her chest. Anna gently lifted it, raised her head from the pillow, trying to see the clock. *4.00 a.m.* She lay back down. David didn't snore, exactly, more twitched like a grumpy rabbit. Quite sweet, the way his lip curled on each fricative sigh. She'd thought this through, she had; for the last six hours, as they'd dozed and talked and touched and dozed. Now he was sleeping deeply, and she must have been too, for a while. Until he sighed into her face. Her head was dopey, sinuses tight. If he discovered her wandering, she would say she was going for a drink of water.

Quiet as she could, she slipped one foot, then the other, on to the floor, then slid from the bed. Bent low, she felt her way around the unfamiliar room, as if being small would make less noise. Baby steps, her thighs chafing together, sticky-dirty. Silky duvet corners, a wrinkled bump – his toe. She pulled her hand back, as from fire, but David snuffled on, probably dreaming of giant carrots. Anna shuffled sideways out of the door, and into the hall. Stairwell light shone through coloured glass above the front door, and she could see enough here not to stumble. Through to the lounge, to that table. It was much clearer in here; David had left the curtains wide. Outside, black bulks and streetlights, the odd brightness of a bus trundling by. Her nipples stroked by moonlight . . .

Her, standing stark naked in full view of Great Western Road.

She crouched down again, crabwalking to the table in the centre of the room. Knelt down to try the drawers. The first one opened easily, but it was only full of bills, Chinese carry-out menus, some coasters with pictures of . . . she turned it the right way round – Paris. The second drawer was locked. Of course it was. So where would he keep the key? She checked the console table, the bureau. Nothing. Then she remembered. Last night, when they were going to bed . . .

When they were going to bed . . . it sounded so domesticated. *You put the milk bottles out, darling, I'll feed the cat.*

Anyway, when David was locking the front door, he'd gone into the kitchen with the keys, and come back without them. Anna crept back into the hall, into the kitchen. Cool vinyl on her feet, slightly tacky. And his bin smelled. David should get a cleaner.

Sure enough, by the cooker, several bunches of keys hung on a spoon-shaped rack, with a little motto painted on the wood.

My kitchen is clean enough to be healthy, and dirty enough to be happy.

Car keys, door keys, gym swipe card and wristband. She lifted a little knot of – window keys possibly? Same shape, same size. And, beneath them, tied together on a string, two dull gold keys. They looked old, seemed small enough. She carried them back to the table, slotted one in. It turned, two turns, then the drawer glided open. This looked more like it; clear plastic folders, each labelled according to their contents. The top one said: **Photos**.

Poking out the side was a black and white shot of a fat little boy on a beach, brandishing his spade at the camera. She guessed it was David when he was wee.

A sudden noise in the hall made her drop the folder. It was the skiffle of slippered feet. And she was thinking, he wears *slippers*, as she jumped up, tits bouncing off in all directions, leaning left, leaning right, finally settling on standing, arms folded, staring out the window. As you do.

'Hey, you. What's up?'

'Oh, hi,' she said, turning round nice and casual. Shit. She'd left the drawer open. Her gaze shot back to the window, like an ostrich diving head first into sand. 'I . . .'

Did I mention I was a naturist, David? Moon-bathing is really good for the skin.

'. . . I couldn't sleep.'

He came up behind her, pressed his stomach to her spine. 'Did I not tire you out, then?'

'I've just got too much to think about. My mind's running overtime.'

'You know that wee man down there can see your fanny.'

'*David*. We're in the shadows here anyway.'

Damp goosebumps prickled as she realised her body was on display. Not her face, it was hidden, David kissing at her neck, spreading hands on her belly, her breasts. But the wee man would see him touching her body, see her pubic bone sharp against the streetlight, yet never know her face. It chilled and thrilled her, David's fingers finding their way in and the man would see that too as her knees buckled forward, thrusting her wider to the world.

She opened her eyes.

'What wee man?'

There was no one there.

David bit her ear. 'Come back to bed.'

'I'm not sleepy.' She turned to look at him, his hair all up in spikes, bare chest above stripy PJs. The drawer behind him lying open still.

'Who said I was going to let you sleep?' he said, tailing off into a yawn. 'Oh, excuse me. That was sexy, eh?' he grinned, heavy lids half-covering his eyes. 'D'you see my tonsils there?'

'Yup. That's me officially seen every bit of you now. Look, on you go back to bed, get some sleep.'

'Will you come back soon?'

'In a while. I'll maybe have a drink of something.'

'More wine? You've some thirst on you, lady.'

If she had more wine, she wouldn't be able to drive. 'Nah . . . maybe . . .'

What would take the longest time to make? 'Have you got any hot chocolate?'

'Think so. Want me to sort you some?'

'No, I'll do it.'

'Well, don't be long. Some of us have got work in the morning.' He yawned again. 'I think there's a tin of Cadbury's behind the coffee.'

'Great.' She smiled. 'Thanks.'

'Don't stay up too late.'

'I won't.'

Anna waited five, ten minutes, squatting on the floor, her shoulders sweating and shivering. Listening until she could hear his breathing deepen. Her clothes were still on the couch. She pulled at her T-shirt, which smelled of David's aftershave, stuck it on. Back to the drawer, quickly flicking through the files. *Case* against Jackson, Crown versus Arlington, a thank-you notelet. Anna held it close to her eyes. It was from a girl . . . no, it was from a complainer. Another case David had been working on.

It won't ever take away what he did to me. But, thanks to you, at least I know he's been locked up.

She didn't read any more. Eyes on the door, eyes on the drawer. Where was it, where was it? What if David hadn't kept it? Jamie's case was done and dusted, so maybe his file wasn't here. But it was still recent – was this it? She scooped up the second last file.

Case against Worth

Yes.

Anna stuffed all the other files away, locked the drawer. She dragged on her pants and jeans, then crept to get her coat from the kitchen. Carefully, she replaced the keys on the rack, picked up the housekeys to unlock the front door. She'd worry about how to return the file later.

Okay. Keys, file, coat . . . shoes . . . where had she left her shoes . . . ? This was the bit on TV where the baddie would wake up, just as the heroine thought she'd made it and was making for the door . . . but she couldn't run in her bare feet . . . ah, there they were, under the heater in the lounge. As she was cramming her feet into her boots, she heard David cough in his sleep.

He's not a baddie. *Nasty little sneak-thief, Anna.*

There were pens and a memo pad on the console table. She'd leave him a note. But what could she say that was honest? She chewed the pen. Blotchy black Biro ink, her epitaph for David.

This is too hard. A. ✗

Anna propped the note against the pen-pot, then let herself out. Keys rattling goodbye as they dropped back through the letterbox.

She sped through city streets, skirting street-sweepers and milkfloats. As soon as she got home, none of this would have happened. And she could get to work on the file that was whispering excitedly. *Work.* It was five a.m. In two hours, she was meant to be at her real work. She'd phone in sick or something. Nothing on today that was more important than this. Plus, what if

David discovered the file had gone, came to seize it back before she'd read it? Why would he, though? Everything was left the way she found it.

Apart from him, perhaps.

Alice greeted her with a *chirrup*, demanding to know where she'd been.

'None of your beeswax, madam. Now, out you go and catch an early bird. Or worm, or something.'

Alice licked her paw, wiped it coyly above one eye. Stretched, then sauntered out, only when it suited *her*.

'And don't bring any dead things back in here, lady.'

Anna put the kettle on, laid the file on her kitchen table. She'd shower later. Deliberately, she unplugged her landline, switched her mobile off, just in case. Because what would she say, if he phoned and asked her why?

The file had the official police case at the front. She'd read that pile of shite later. What she wanted to look at first were the bits and bobs the court never saw: records of missing evidence, witnesses not called. And David's own notes, which she found in a separate plastic sleeve at the back. She opened them out. Fantastic. A work of art and science combined. David was a list man like her, but his were not prosaic numbered rows like Anna churned out. David wrote in the sprouting broccoli curlicues and squiggles of mind maps.

<u>*Witnesses for:*</u>

A whole list of names, including all the investigations team and, of course, Coltrane.

<u>*Neutrals:*</u>
Tactical firearm instructor
Nightshift super
Miss Maxwell (neighbour below)

<u>*Witnesses against:*</u>
Accused
Constable Robertson*

Jinky *had* been down as one of the good guys. But why the asterisk?

Constable Callum Grant

There was a pen line scored through this final name. Who was he, anyway? Anna had never heard his name before. She flicked through the police case to find Grant's witness statement.

Was on uniform foot patrol when received a call to attend . . blah, blah - where I was told by the divisional controller that a young girl, whom I now know to be the deceased Sarah Brisbane, had been seen allegedly <u>*brandishing a firearm*</u>

A dribble of coffee slurped from her mug. This guy was corroborating what Jamie had said.

So why was there a line through his name? Anna checked further back, then forwards, through the sheaf of papers. David might like his fancy bubbles, but he wasn't very organised with the filing. Eventually, she found a copy list of witnesses. This one had an additional scribble by Grant's name.

Will not appear. Soul and conscience – in hospital undergoing back op (essential – disc herniation resulting in severe sciatica.)

A copy of the soul and conscience certificate was attached, signed by Grant's GP. Perfect timing. So what about Miss Maxwell then? She was the old lady Constable Grant had mentioned in his statement.

Miss Maxwell traumatised following this incident, and various other antisocial behaviour problems in area. Moved down south to stay with sister. Excused attending by reason of age – statement inconclusive in any case.

Right, what were you saying Miss Maxwell?

The police came and asked me if I'd heard any noise from the flat above. I told them there's always comings and goings there, but tonight had been particularly bad – shouting and banging and all sorts. While I was talking to the policeman, there was a really loud crack like a gun or a firework going off, and he told me to stay inside.

What was inconclusive about that? The lady had heard a bang she thought could be gunfire.

Another bubble with:

Police Balls-Ups!!!

*Recordings of radio traffic **missing**. How? Report from Airwaves been requested.*

*Worth's notebook: **missing** (NB he alleges taken by DCI Armstrong)*

To do: Interview Armstrong

ACC Wish insists full statements from controller et al be rewritten retrospectively, in light of missing tapes. Advised him this not possible.

PS – bloody Armstrong woman is a nutter!!

Fucking Billings overruled. Have asked for this instruction in writing.

David had signed and date-stamped this insert. Then, what looked like a late addition. He hadn't even bothered with the bubble this time, just a hurried arrow.

Accused's call to witness Robertson during trial – can use as leverage?

And, in a separate bubble all of its own: *Forensics???*

Why were there so many question marks? Anna searched for the Forensics Report.

Full Ballistic report – Billings has.

Forensics. Incomplete Again! – speak to Prof Borges. Again!!

No trace of any bullets/casings found in flat. Have asked for confirmation that wrecked furniture in flat was fully examined prior to disposal. Possibility of bullet lodging in wood? No confirmation received – lab techs currently on strike.

Two casings found in Gryffe Street approx one and a half metres from position of PC Worth. This would be commensurate with the two bullets fired by him.

***CROSSMATCH** Residue from both casings match residue from PC Worth's gun.*

Bullets: One bullet recovered from Sarah Brisbane during PM. One bullet recovered from spot close to broken chair on pavement – approx 50 metres from where Sarah Brisbane fell.

CROSSMATCH? *Still awaiting confirmation that rifling on both match rifling in PC Worth's gun.*

Sarah Brisbane: Gunshot residue found on deceased's hands, face and chest (point of entry). Crossmatched with PC Worth's weapon and forensic samples taken from him. **MATCH.**

PC James Worth: Gunshot residue found on accused's face and right hand. Crossmatched with gunshot residue found on deceased. **MATCH.**

Potential powder mark on wall of kitchen at Gryffe Street (between cooker and kitchen window). Tests inconclusive – area could have been used to strike matches on (roughened brick).

<u>*Failure to crossmatch*</u> *potential powdermark with either PC Worth or PC Robertson's firearms. Had this been done, would either:*

eliminate search for any other firearm OR

suggest AFO had fired further shots into house OR

suggest possibility of presence of another gun in house <u>AT SOME RECENT POINT</u>

NB – Father has criminal convictions (Gerard Brisbane). Check son (Craig Brisbane) – no trace. Check associates?

This last was overwritten with:

*Billings & ACC say waste of time + **bad PR** – not family being investigated, is Worth.*

No trace for the son. Did that mean he wasn't on record, or that they couldn't find him? Anna would need to find out more regarding Craig Brisbane. She remembered seeing him on TV that night the story broke, all indignation and despair. Yet she couldn't once recall seeing him in any photos or footage taken after the trial. Had he even been called as a witness?

Back to the police case. Craig Brisbane wasn't listed anywhere. She finally found mention of him in a document paper-clipped onto a copy list of productions.

<u>Notes about the Brisbane family</u> (fao Family Liaison Officer)
Dawn – unlikely to be welcomed with open arms here! Deceased resided with father Gerard Brisbane, SCRO number: xxx. Older brother Craig Brisbane seems to spend his time between family

home and Manchester, where he was living at time of shooting. Has since returned to Glasgow to be with his father, but states will be returning south soon, as girlfriend expecting baby. Can be contacted c/o French at 14 Lillybank Crescent, Manchester.

Both father and brother reluctant to talk about mother, Catriona (née Clarkson). Story seems to be she left family home following a dispute with Gerard clan when Sarah was approx 5–7 (Gerard Brisbane cannot remember when!!) and has subsequently died. Confirmed this with registrar's office: Catriona Clarkson or Brisbane d 6 June 2002. Cause of death – drugs overdose.

Gran Betty Brisbane, who is mother of Gerard, is extremely vociferous, but appears to have limited contact with any of them. Minor convictions for D & I , Breach etc – bit of a fighter in her day! Contact via Paisley Police Office – no fixed abode, but you'll find her there most Saturday nights apparently!)

Good Luck!

They sounded like a lovely bunch. Good on Sarah and her brother for not following in the Brisbane family footsteps. The boy probably just couldn't face staying in Glasgow with his sister gone. But maybe he could shed a bit more light on all the 'comings and goings' at his father's house that Miss Maxwell referred to. Gerard hadn't long got out of jail before Sarah died. Who knew how many of his dodgy friends had called in to see him. And any one of them could have something to do with the missing gun. Anna was now convinced that someone had been there with Sarah the night she died.

She yawned, began to put the papers back into the file. There was another document she'd missed, folded up in a corner. It looked like a medical form, for BUPA. She was about to disregard it when she noticed the name at the bottom: Coltrane.

He'd appended his signature after filling in the 'Reasons for Referral' box:

He is in continual and increasing pain, which severely limits his concentration and capabilities. I therefore firmly believe that

Constable Grant would benefit from immediate medical inter-vention, paid for by the Force, to allow him to carry out his duties fully.

It was Coltrane who'd recommended Grant be put forward for a back operation – directly before Jamie's trial. That couldn't be a coincidence. He'd done it deliberately, to get Grant out the way. No doubt helped by Uncle Pete.

Anna needed to let this all settle. Her own concentration and capabilities were starting to wane, and she had to be clear on what she was doing next. It was seven a.m. She could either go into work late and snooze at her desk, or call in sick, and go to bed with a breakfast of . . . hmm. She looked at the rack . . . Côte du Rhone.

A little card fell from the plastic sleeve containing David's notes. It looped once, flapped to the rug. Anna leaned over to get it. It was a photo of her, beaming outside the toy shop in Times Square. Arms akimbo, eyes red in the dark, and a huge great grin on her face. Looking so damn happy.

She shoved the photo back in the envelope, poured herself a pint of wine, and pressed the remote. Played Skunk Anansie's *Hedon-ism* full blast on the stereo, over and over until her neighbour from up the stairs banged like thunder through the ceiling.

25

Two messages winking when Cath had come in last night, but she'd been too tired and dispirited to listen to them. An excursion to Jamie's parents' house was never a barrel of laughs, from the very first time she'd been taken to meet them, and spent the afternoon at the bingo with Doris and Auntie Bessie, whilst Jamie and his dad got puggled in the pub. When the boys tottered back, Jamie's pinkly pissed dad had conned her, by being at his most effusive, never-to-be-repeated best. Mostly, for all the years she had known him since, he'd let his wife do the talking. All of it. And she'd been on good form yesterday.

Doris meant well. She was a good soul, but she and Cath had little in common save Jamie. He'd been their bulwark and their common ground, and without him, Cath and Doris splashed rudderless. It was difficult too, to ignore the reproach dripping in Doris's eyes whenever Cath went round. It may have been the ever-lengthening gaps between visits, but she sensed it was more than that. Each time they spoke, Doris would always ask 'What's happening now?' or 'Any news?', as if Cath could control the currents. Not once did Doris ask how Cath was coping, or offer to help, or cuddle her grandchildren when they came, and Cath would seethe her tea through throbbing teeth, then notice Doris's hand shake as she lifted her cup, and be filled with shame. What if it was Daniel that had been ripped away from Cath, and every-thing she knew of him thereafter was mediated through some reluctant filter? Jamie was her *son*. So Cath kept trying; going to Doris with chocolates and a chirpy smile, and coming home drained and angry at she didn't know what.

The door rattled. Must be the postman, the paper was already here. Cath scooped up the mail, did it quick, like taking medicine. Two brown ones: bills, a couple of circulars. White with livid red – that would be a final demand. It went in the bin first. She was going to have to do something soon, shake her head out of the sand. Her body, her brain were perpetually cold, that same lethargic dampness you get from wet jeans against your legs, but she was *trying*. On Friday, she'd gone to the social security office: the Burroo. Cath never, never wanted to go there again. Standing in a queue of the hopeless, the hurt and the professional hustlers, her name proclaimed out loud, her business discussed in public. Enunciating her problems through a plastic window, studded molten-yellow with fag burns.

'If your husband's in jail,' boomed the clerk, 'then you're due income support. You'll need to fill in a claim form.'

'And what . . . what about my mortgage?' She'd lowered her voice, embarrassed to admit she owned a house. The woman at the next counter was in the middle of begging for a crisis loan for kids' school shoes.

'You can get your interest paid after a year.'

'But what about now?'

'You've just got to let the arrears build up.'

'Will they not throw me out before then, though?'

The clerk shrugged. 'You'll need to speak to your mortgage company.'

'And my council tax?'

Cath had written a list, so she wouldn't forget all the things she had to ask.

'Need to speak to the council. They'll give you a form. Any council tax benefit will be means-tested, so they'll take all your income and capital into account anyway. But you'll get something, if you're on income support. You'll be claiming as a lone parent.'

'But I'm married.'

'But your man's not here, is he? So, in the eyes of the DWP, you're on your own. You'll probably get free dental care too, school dinners, stuff like that.'

Take it Cath. You've paid your taxes. She could feed the kids *and* get her front tooth fixed. Have it filed to a pointy fang, then veneered all better with sparkling porcelain. Only then, the rest of her teeth would look dirty by comparison, and she'd have to get them falsified too. It might look nice, but it wouldn't be her. Sometimes, the pain of that ragged edge was comforting. An angry sharpness that reminded her of a life before, when a chipped front tooth was the worst that could happen.

Cath lifted the letters out of the bin. What was least urgent? She'd deal with that first. Day-old messages, then bills, then people. She poured herself a cup of tea from her Cheshire cat teapot, and clicked the answer machine.

'Alright doll? Jenny here, just checking in. You're probably on Doris-duty. Just wanted to remind you that we're off tomorrow. Catriona can't wait; bloody Mickey Mouse is all I've heard for the last week. Anyway, I wasn't joking about you guys moving in with me. The kids all get on great, and we've got the room, so long as you don't mind the cat creeping up on your bed at night. And it would mean I could dump my horrible child minder. You'd be doing me a really big favour. So. Please think about it, and I'll call you when we get back. Cheers, me dear – and take care, yeah?'

Typical Jenny, offering solutions, not charity. But whether Cath lived with her or moved back to her mother's, the end result would be the same. Giving up her house meant giving up on Jamie.

The Cheshire cat teapot beamed at her; fat face so chuffed with its lot.

She pushed it away. 'Shut it, ginger.'

Time for message two. All Cath got at first was a muffled sob, then a burst of broad Glaswegian.

'Catherine. I'm no gonny go to Garthlock this week, so thanks, but no thanks to the lift. Look – ' there was a pause while Stella swallowed – 'you might as well know, I won't be going again. Me and Brian. That's it. Finito. Wee shite's let me down once too often, and I'm no having it.'

What sounded like a gargle of something liquid came next, then another sniff. 'So, fuck him. Fuck the lot of them. Good luck to you, hen. Keep in touch, eh?'

Poor Stella. That could be Cath in a couple of years, struggling to cut loose the albatross dragging her down. Should she phone her back? What point would there be in prolonging contact? What point was there in anything, really? Cath's hands were burning, pressing hard against her scalding mug. The impotent rage she'd experienced when Eilidh was a baby had galloped back these last few months, drumming faster and closer with every dull-shock day that whispered:

This might never get any better.

It was easy to love the world when it loved you back. But when the world turned hostile, it was equally, scarily, simple to slip from love to hate; not just of your lot, but of other people's fortune. And then, fast-biting at hate's heels, came the urge to destroy that fortune, to burst it wide open with the pain that was yours and trash everything that was beautiful and good, because it was not yours. It was probably why housebreakers crapped on their victim's couches. Why part of her thought it served Stella right, for being so bloody loyal. Every day, Cath had to fight this anger, for her family, her sanity. She wondered if her first depression had been a trial, a warning of what was to come, because now that she knew the signs, she could keep from plunging under; tiny swimming kicks one day against the next, keep breathing, keep on finding the light.

She turned to the appointments section. Tuesday was jobs day in the *Herald*, and there had to be something that she could do. What was she good at? Scowling – well, there was always working in local government. Cleaning up shite and snotters, and refereeing fights. Bar work, then? How about shouting? She was excellent at that. Did they still have town criers? She drank her tea, circled a few possibilities, and waited for the rain to stop. And then, when her cup was finally empty, she turned to the bills.

One hand reached automatically for a strand of her hair, winding it around her finger, until a little bristly tip nestled in her mouth. The final demand was for electricity. Surely the dole would pay for that? They wouldn't see kids without heat and light. Would they? Phone bill. Was that considered an essential? She'd need to check. The other brown one wasn't a bill; it was stamped **HMP Garthlock**. Puzzled, Cath ripped it open. Inside was a hand-written letter. From Jamie. She closed it back over, her stomach folding like the paper. People only wrote when they had bad news, things they couldn't say to your face. But it had begun *Dear Cath* – she'd seen that bit. *Dear* meant love, you wouldn't say it . . . yes you would. Everyone said it, on every letter that was ever written. *Oh, for God's sake Catherine, it's from your husband.*

Exactly. She checked her cup. Still empty. Put it down. Opened the letter.

Dear Cath,

I know. This is weird, me writing to you when I phone most nights. But I wanted to talk to you, properly, the way we used to. If I write, it feels like you're here beside me. Just you and me – no screws, no noise, no inmates.

I want to tell you I miss you, Cath. I miss your breath on my neck at night. I miss bringing you tea and us arguing about stuff on the news, and seeing you buy a new dress then sneak it into the wardrobe. I miss you nagging me about using the washing basket and your macaroni cheese and Eilidh drawing me pictures and the smell of Daniel's head. Most of all, I just miss you.

And I'm so, so sorry. I can never keep saying how sorry I am for hurting you. Before, when I was stupid and confused and weak and selfish, and now, when I've left you to cope on your own. I keep letting you down, yet you never give up on me.

Please Cath. Don't ever give up on me.

Sometimes, I can hear you in my head, actual conversations that we've never had.

Did you know that you're my lodestar? You always showed me which way was right, and I don't have that any more. I see things happen in here, wrong things, and I look the other way. Aiding and abetting by acting in concert. Do you remember learning that at Tulliallan? So I'm as bad as the rest of them, like you said I

*would be. But I'm praying not to be. I know, me praying – my
mum would be chuffed! Don't tell her though – I don't know if it's
to you or God or a big black hole in the sky, and I hardly do it,
only in bed, at night, when there's nothing to pin your mind to. It
helps, a bit. It's more like I'm recounting my life – tiny things that
seem so big now. Please don't show anyone this letter. They'll
think I'm mad (or suicidal) and I swear I'm not. I just need you to
be my confessional for a wee while. Is that okay?*

*They're switching the lights off now. I love you, and I'll see you
soon. Kiss my babies for me. Try and get Eilidh to read the first
few lines of 'Nothing' with you. She was getting really good at
recognising the words. But you have to do the funny sad voice, or
she'll make you read it again!*

I love you, Catherine.

Your James. xxx

Cath laid the paper flat on the table and watched her tears mingle
with the ink; words that Jamie had chosen carefully, crafted into
perfect sense, becoming feathered smudges, and she wiped them
away. All those years, praying for Jamie to pray. She didn't know
what she believed any more. Maybe God *was* there, in the dark
margins. Omnipresent, omniscient but unable to intervene. Absorbing all the anguish of the world, as pained and powerless as she
was for Jamie. He had given them all this, all the world and free will
too, and could only watch in pity as they scattered and scurried
and sobbed. Maybe that's exactly what God was: a great, sad
sponge that mopped your tears, and took the weight you couldn't
bear.

'Mum-mee!' screeched Eilidh from her room. 'Is it morning
yet?'

Cath jumped, glanced at the kitchen clock. *Shit.* It was ten to
nine. They were going to be late for school. She ran upstairs two at
a time. How could she be late when she'd been awake since six?
Eilidh was normally great at getting herself up and dressed. She'd
been a bit off-colour yesterday though, very quiet when she came
home from school, then not eating much at her gran's. Though

who'd want seconds at the house of Our Doris of the Perpetual Mince Patty? With extra gristle.

'Quick, quick. Up you get.'

'Are we late?' Big scared eyes beneath moptop hair.

'Just a wee bit. If we skip breakfast, and brushing teeth, we can still make it. I'll change Daniel after.'

'But I'll get a row if I'm late.' Eilidh's lips were trembling. 'Mrs Harrison says—'

'I don't care what Mrs Harrison says. Just get up and get your uniform on, please.'

'Please don't make me go, Mummy.' Eilidh began to cry.

Cath sat on the edge of the bed. 'Look, Mummy will come in with you. I'll tell the teacher it was my fault.'

'Don't make me go.'

'What is it? Have you got a sore tummy again?'

'No.'

'Well, what is it then? Why don't you want to go to school?'

'Nobody will play with me,' she sobbed.

'Oh darling, why?'

''Cause I hitted Gelly with my ruler.'

Cath tried not to laugh. 'Why did you do that? I thought you liked Angela.'

Eilidh shook her head. 'I hate her. I hate her more'n Dan-pants.'

'No, you love Daniel, Eilidh.'

'But I *hate* her.' Eilidh stared up at Cath, fists clenched tight into her Polly Pocket duvet.

'Why do you hate Angela then?'

If this was a delaying tactic, it was working. On Eilidh's bedside clock, Winnie-the-Pooh waved his big paw at the twelve. The honeypot was dead on nine. They were never going to make school now.

Eilidh's voice was barely audible. 'She said my daddy was very, very bad, and that's why he can't come home.' She leaned closer to Cath, like she was telling a secret. 'Mummy – she said my daddy deaded someone.'

'Oh, sweetness.'

Keep the world away from my children. Let me craft them a safe place, where it is always sunny and good people smile. I'll patch it up and keep it tight and I'll know it's not true, but let them believe it. Please.

'Daddy did do something bad, but he didn't mean to. It was an accident.'

'*Did* he make a wee girl dead?'

'Eilidh, it's really important that you listen to Mummy. Somebody died, but it *wasn't* your daddy's fault. Your daddy was trying to help.' Cath groped for the right words. 'You know that time when you were trying to make me breakfast and you broke the plates?'

'Uh huh.'

'Well, you were trying to do something good then, weren't you?'

'Yes.'

'And remember how Mummy shouted at you, even though it was an accident. Even though you said you were sorry.'

'*And* you smacked my bum—'

'I know. I know I did, and I'm awful sorry. But that's like Daddy. You know how he's a policeman, and policemen help people?'

'Yes, like when they came to show us their horses, and the big one poohed and Mrs Harrison made them pick it up . . .'

'That's right. Well, Daddy was trying to help this girl who was upset. She wasn't a wee girl, she was a big girl, and she was so upset that Daddy thought she was going to hurt people, because someone told him she had a great big gun. So he had to go and get a great big gun to try and stop her.'

'And he banged her with his gun?'

'Yes.'

For a long moment, Eilidh said nothing. Her hands, still clutching the covers, got closer and closer to her mouth, until her right index was crooked over her nose. Her thumb slipped slowly into her mouth. She'd not done that since she was a toddler.

'Was that not good?'

'He thought it was, baby. But then the other people said she didn't have a gun, so Daddy got into trouble.'

Eilidh sat bolt upright. 'But it wasn't his fault!'

'No, it wasn't.'

All of a sudden, she began to wail. 'I want my daddy. I want my daddy.'

'Ssh, ssh.' Cath covered her daughter's hair in kisses, rocking her and holding fast the chubby arms that were fighting her away. 'Ssh, ssh, baby girl.' Determined, strong, but so was Cath. 'Sssh now. He's fine, he's just in a special place.'

'I . . . want . . . my . . . daddy,' she screamed. Eilidh was inconsolable, her hair soaked with sweat and tears. Cath raised her head to the side, trying to get a breath that wasn't filled with hair. She started crying too. What had she done? But she couldn't keep lying to Eilidh.

'Daah—aah-dee.'

'I'll take you to Daddy, I promise.'

Eventually, Eilidh's whole little body went limp, clinging on to Cath, fast heartbeats echoed on both their breasts.

'Ssh, darling, ssh. I'll take you to him.'

'You promise?' she panted.

'I promise.'

A cry from next door told her Daniel was awake. Once he started, nothing would stop him but cuddles and a big bowl of Weetabix. Cath untangled Eilidh's arms from her neck. 'Okay baby. I need you to lie down for a minute and I'll go and get Dan.'

'Don't leave me Mummy.'

'I'm not leaving you. I'm just going to get Dan-pants and then we'll all have a snuggle.'

Daniel's yells grew louder. He was always starving when he woke up.

'Look, you don't have to go to school, okay? We'll have a snuggle-day and stay in our jammies.'

'Oh-kay,' Eilidh snuffled.

As fast as she could, Cath dashed into Daniel's room and plucked him from his cot.

'C'mon big boy. We're having a duvet day.'

Daniel grinned, slapping her joyfully with sticky fingers as they bounced from the room. She felt like a little child, running from hidden monsters. Could feel them panting rancid heat, but they couldn't get her if she made it back to bed. Bed was safe, with its huge big covers.

Eilidh was lying quietly when Cath returned, her pale, crumpled face passive. The set of her jaw broke Cath's heart. She was holding a tiny doll.

'Budge up, missus. Oh, that's pretty. Can Mummy see?'

It was a crude wooden peg doll; red wool strands for hair, pipe-cleaner arms, and a chequered square wound round for a dress. Strange, straight lifeless lines for the eyes and mouth.

'Where did you get that?'

'The fairies left it. Ooh,' Eilidh sat up excitedly, 'maybe it's from Daddy!'

'The fairies?'

'Like your tooths. The fairies put it on my pillow.'

Sick seeping ice-chips to splinter Cath's ribs.

'When?'

'Last night I 'pose. I finded it when I went to bed. Her's Rosie.'

Cath began to shake. Clutching her children, trying so hard to stop it.

Someone had been in their house. The someone who had left that posy, who'd been drawing symbols on her wall, her shed.

They'd crept in to her daughter's room and left an omen on her pillow.

26

'You're the last person I ever want to see, you realise that?'

'I know.'

'But I'm totally, shitting-myself scared, and there's no one else that can help me. The one cop I trust is Jenny, and she's not here. That's the only reason I phoned you.'

'I know.'

'And don't expect me to say thank you, or be grateful, because you frigging owe me, Anna Cameron.'

'I know I do.'

'Right, well, come in then.'

'Thank you.'

Anna wiped her feet and stepped into Cath's home. Cath stood like Mother Courage, gaunt and proud and blankly terrified, one child on her hip, the other clamped to her leg. No, that was wrong. Courage was bent solely on her own survival, even at the expense of her children. Anna felt a twist of envy as she recognised Cath would never do that.

'How are you?' Anna's throat was tight as she spoke. Jamie's eyes drilled out at her from Eilidh's face. Their baby would have had those eyes, would have gripped Anna as unconditionally as Eilidh owned her mother. Their baby would be a teenager now, all stomping moods and pleas for cash and rich decades of love and memories. If she'd let it.

'Cut the crap Anna. What are you going to do to help us?'

Anna opened the canvas bag she carried. 'I brought a CCTV unit. It's not great – it can't be linked up to anywhere, but at least you can record stuff, play it back for proof. And it means you can keep an eye on what's going on outside, without leaving the house.'

Cath nodded. 'Fine. What else?'

'Well, we need to think about who might be doing this.'

'Duh.'

'Can I sit down maybe, go over things with you?'

'If you want.'

They moved into the lounge. The coffee table was littered with kids' drawings, skinny stick men and houses and big blue skies.

'Eilidh, why don't you go and put a DVD on?' said Cath.

Silently, Eilidh acquiesced, seizing her brother's hand.

'Go into the living room, okay? Mummy'll be through in a minute and I'll get you some crisps.'

Anna took out a notebook, shifted some of the pictures aside, so she could lean on the table.

'Here,' said Cath, 'give them to me. Eilidh's been going mad doing pictures for her dad.'

The drawing on the top of the pile was of a house, with three stick people outside, and a big, smiling sun shining on them. The sun's eyes were brown, and Eilidh had scrawled 'Daddy' coming out like rays. Cath put the pictures on her knee.

'So. Where do we start?'

'Let's make a list. Have you got any ideas who might be doing this?'

'Anyone? We're not exactly popular round here. Murderers' families rarely are.'

'Okay. Let's think about nasty neighbours then. Possible for the vandalism, but not likely for the other stuff, yeah? You said flowers were the first thing. Why do you think they weren't just from a well-wisher?'

'No name, and it was heather. You know, lucky white heather, the day after Jamie's jailed. Like someone was really saying "get it up you".'

'Polis, d'you think? Someone being snidey?'

Lucky white heather was a common quip in the police, like saying Sod's law, or tough shit when something went wrong.

Cath shrugged. 'It's possible. You'd be amazed how quick folk are to kick you when you're down.'

'What about the most obvious suggestion? Someone from Sarah Brisbane's family? Trying to frighten you.'

'That's what's scaring me the most. But, from what I gather, they're a bunch of heidbangers. This all seems too subtle. I mean, leaving a peg doll in a kiddie's bed?'

'A peg doll? I thought you said a package on the phone?'

'No, a peg doll.'

Cath had been semi-hysterical when she'd called, and it had been difficult to make out everything she was saying.

'Have you still got it? Can I see it?'

'Yeah, it's here.' Cath went to the sideboard, lifted up a Tupperware box. 'I've hardly touched it.' She reddened slightly. 'I didn't know – can you get fingerprints from wood? Never got beyond parking tickets and shoplifters me.'

'I don't know either. If I'd wanted to be a detective, I'd have had a personality bypass and a desiccated liver put in.'

Cath smiled. 'Don't you hate the way the CID swan around—'

'Like wearing a suit from Slater's gives you magical powers? Aye.'

'Look, do you want a tea or something?'

'Nah, I'm fine. Thanks, though.'

Cath handed her the box. Instantly, as she looked inside, Anna thought of Dlia Bejko. At the UN conference, she'd held a doll just like this, as she'd spoken of her sister. Red hair and sad, shut eyes.

'Cath, did Jamie ever talk to you about trafficking? You know, girls, women. Was he ever involved in turning a brothel?'

'Not that I know of. Why?'

'It's just – I've seen one of these before. They're not really dolls, they're symbols. I heard this girl talk, when I was working in America. Her sister went missing. They were Albanians. The family could never prove it, but they reckoned she'd been taken by traffickers. It had happened to several other girls from the same area.'

'And they never found her?'

'No. But she always carried a wee peg doll with her, with a piece of her sister's scarf wrapped round. It was a custom, she said, in their country, to make little dolls like this. You know, as a memorial. If they had no one to bury.'

'Are you telling me my daughter's going to be trafficked?'

The pile of drawings on Cath's lap slid slowly to the carpet.

'Oh, no. God, no Cath, I'm sorry. I don't mean that at all. I don't think it's been meant that way.' She held the doll up. 'Look at the hair for one – Eilidh's hair isn't red, it's black. They always make them like the person they represent.'

'So what does it mean?'

'I don't know yet. And you say it was lying on Eilidh's pillow?'

'So she says.'

'She couldn't have just picked it up outside somewhere?'

'She could, I guess, but why would she lie?'

'Was there any sign of a break-in?'

'None. I unlocked the front door last night, when I got home from my mother-in-law's. And I checked the back door this morning – obviously. Once I'd calmed down a bit.'

'That would be after you spoke to me then?'

'Probably. Did I just scream down the phone like a banshee?'

'Pretty much.'

Anna turned the peg doll over, but it was still only wood and wool. No cipher, no hidden scroll, just a little limbo-doll. 'Can I see Eilidh's room?'

'As long as you ignore the mess.'

Cath led her upstairs, to a pink palace where unicorns pranced on one wall, and a nest of teddies and dolls stared beadily from fluffy rugs. The hopper window was open, soft grass and damp smells blowing the curtains in wide billows above the bed. Anna looked outside. The window faced the back garden, with its high fence and hedges. She unlocked the main window, leaned out a little further. There was a tall wooden gate at the side of the house. 'Does that gate lead round the front?'

'Yes. We sometimes lock it, but only if we're going on holiday. I take the bins out that way.'

'And d'you normally lock this window?'

'That one, yes. Not the top one. Eilidh likes to sleep with it open.'

Below Eilidh's window, the kitchen extension jutted out into the garden, making an L-shape around the paved patio. The kitchen roof was flat, with a dip for drainage around the edges. Anna hung on with one hand to the inside of Eilidh's windowsill, reached down as far as she could with the other. Her hand rubbed stone, then tubed curves of plastic – a gutter overflow, that ran down the wall, skirting past the flat roof, and on to the drain beneath.

A low voice behind her. 'Did she fall or was she pushed?'

Anna pulled herself back up. Not funny. 'Cath, I reckon someone could climb up here – if they were light and agile enough. There's a drainpipe running from the flat roof. If you pulled your big bin over, climbed up on that—'

'Then scrambled from the kitchen roof to here – you think that's how they got in?'

'I don't think they got in at all. Look where Eilidh's bed is: right under the window. All someone would have to do is drop the doll in the open hopper, and it would land directly on her bed.'

Cath fingered her daughter's pillow. 'And if they could do that, they could drop anything. Next time it could be a knife or—'

'Why though? Why warn you first if they were going to do something like that?'

'I don't know, Anna. I don't make assumptions about anything much these days.'

'I honestly don't think they meant to hurt her. Look, why not try the CCTV for a few nights – and keep the windows locked and the kids in with you. If it is the same person, we want them to come back.'

'Do we?'

'Well, if this all began since Jamie got the jail, it might be a lead to helping him. And I promise, I'll keep my mobile on day and night. Just phone me if anything happens.'

Cath walked away from the bed, arms crossed tight. Her shoulders were rounded, her body all hunched in on itself like it was under siege. Anna wished she could give her a hug.

'Alright.' Cath stopped at her daughter's bookshelf. She was straightening a row of bright paperbacks. 'Show me how this camera-thingy works then.'

'I've not read the instructions yet.'

'Brilliant.'

Anna slipped the sheet of A4 from her bag, and folded it into her pocket. Cath would never miss one of Eilidh's drawings, and everyone said the pen was mightier than the sword. She checked the address. Paisley was a part of the world she'd never much had cause to visit, even though it was just a few miles from the city. She saw enough drug dealers in Glasgow. But the estate Jinky Robertson lived on was very nice: swanky houses and four by fours. He was still off sick, so he'd better be in. Anna didn't have much time before her shift started, and it never looked good if she arrived after her troops. All – what was it – three of them today, that were mustering. Three cops to cover a huge swathe of one of the biggest, busiest, baddest chunks of Glasgow, chasing their tails and getting short shrift for their troubles. Trying to batter through all the ensuing paperwork at their piecebreak, fighting to get on the voicebank, and recorrecting reports that the typists hadn't heard right, and resubmitting them, and trying to call complainers who were never in, and if you didn't get them this week that was you on nights and then you'd never write off the CR. When Anna had been a beatman, you'd be mustering anything up to twenty cops on each shift, with foot patrols neighbouring up in pairs, the way it should be for protection and corroboration and just . . . well, two heads were always better than one. No way could you hold every piece of ever-changing legislation you'd ever learned inside a single brain. No wonder half her shift were off with stress.

As was Mr Robertson. Hell slap it into him. She'd start off gently and see where that got her. Anna got out her warrant card, knocked on the door. A dog barked inside, then, after a minute or so, a rock-hard blonde with incompatibly dark eyebrows answered.

'Yes?'

'Good morning. I'm Inspector Anna Cameron. Is John in?'

'He's in the bath.'

'That's fine, I'll wait.'

Oh will you? said the eyebrows. Anna stepped over the threshold, forcing the woman to move aside.

'In here?' said Anna, gesturing to the front room.

The blonde's extra-long nails drummed on the door she was still, futilely, guarding. You could take someone's eye out with those nails.

'I'll go and see how long he'll be.'

Anna sat on one of the leather couches. Was her house as cold as this one? It was all done in similar colours, off-white and taupe. Very sterile. What they needed was a nice bright picture above the fireplace. Like David's. She rested her chin in her hands. David. One word with many nuances. First it was a happy uplift, then, quickly, it became a rapid heartbeat. Now, when she thought of 'David', the word dropped like bricks. He'd only phoned once, but it was a tirade. Anna had sat by the answering machine listening to every word, unable to pick up the phone.

'Anna, what are you trying to do with me? You're totally messing with my head. You lose the plot at me for no reason, won't speak to me for weeks, then you turn up here out of the blue, screw my brains out, and piss off into the night again. Oh yes, but this time you leave a note. So that's okay then. And what do you mean *It's too hard,* anyway? Of course it's hard. Life is hard, Anna. But that doesn't mean you have to put up these insane barriers against anything that might make you happy. And I could have made you happy, Anna . . . Anna – are you there, listening to all this?'

Anna had flinched at that. Could he see her? Did he know her that well?

'Anna? Please?' A long exhalation, like his breath could blow her away. 'Okay then. The only other thing I can say is goodbye, Anna. I hope you find what you're looking for. From someone.'

That buzz of the receiver going down. She could still hear it; the swansong of a life-support machine flatlining. DO NOT RESUSCITATE writ large above her head.

'Inspector?'

John Robertson had come into the room without her noticing. Excellent, he was still in his bathrobe. That was one layer peeled away already. Nothing like near nudity for racking up your vulnerability.

'Ah, John. Take a seat.'

That's right, in your own house. There's a good boy.

She smiled. She was a *real* blonde. 'So, how are you feeling, John? Still finding it a bit hard going?'

He frowned. 'Aye, well. No so bad. Sorry, Inspector, are you from Personnel? Only, my line's in for this month – I'd someone out to see me last week.'

'No, John, I'm here to talk about Jamie Worth.'

He blanched, a horrid yellow wash that really did make him look sick.

'You see, we're just going over all the statements again, and I wanted to have a wee chat with you. Oops,' Anna pretended to cover her eyes, 'I'd stop that jiggling if I were you.'

Jinky's legs were shaking so hard, his robe had loosened at the waist.

'Shit. God, I'm sorry ma'am – I'll go—'

'No, it's fine. Just relax. Obviously, we'll be speaking to everyone involved – including Inspector Coltrane.'

'Uh huh?'

'But I thought it would be best to see you first. Give you the best possible chance to make this right, before Coltrane's arse is exposed and you go down with him.' She laughed, shook her head. 'God, that's a terrible line isn't it? Makes you think of, I don't know. What might happen in jail . . . ugh. Sorry. Just ignore me.'

'Inspector, I don't know what you mean.'

'Look, I can understand if Coltrane pressurised you, John.' Anna crossed her legs. 'Senior officer, well connected. And a right smooth talker. I bet he finds it dead easy to confuse folk. But, let's be honest here. He's just an AP guy, streaking through the ranks while the rest of us are out there grafting. You and me, Jinky – we're real cops. We know what matters, out on the street.

I mean, if you can't trust your neighbour, who can you trust? Ever again?'

Jinky said nothing. He was fumbling with his dressing-gown cord, his face yellow patched with puce.

'D'you know where I've just been, John?'

'No ma'am.'

She put Eilidh's drawing on the arm of the couch, so Jinky could see it. 'I've been at Jamie Worth's house. Look what his wee girl's been drawing for him. See, that's her, her mummy and her baby brother. And that's their house. Mind, it won't be their house much longer. Poor Cath's completely skint – they stopped his wages the day he went to jail.'

'I know,' he croaked. 'Poor sod. I . . . I've been meaning to phone Cath.'

'She's probably going to end up in a DHSS hostel, her and the kids. Still, it's better than what's happening to Jamie. His wife tells me they tried to rape him. Held him down on the—'

'Stop it, please.' Jinky had his hands over his ears, tears pumping over his mottled cheeks. 'I canny take this.'

'Then *you* fucking stop it, Robertson.'

Anna stood, towering over him like an avenging angel. God, she was *good*. 'Be a bloody man and tell me the truth. Why did you change your statement?'

'Because Coltrane told me to,' he blurted. Great bubbles coming out his pockmarked nose. 'He said we'd both fucked up – me and Jamie. That we'd both end up getting done. But that he could give me a chance to save myself. Only, I canny live with . . .' He hugged himself, legs going like he was sitting on a washing machine. 'You've got to understand – look around you. This house, my life. I'm no a fool. I know why the wife stays with me. I lose my job, lose my status – and I'm nothing. I canny risk losing her.'

'Did Coltrane tell you both that Sarah Brisbane had a gun?'

'Aye.'

She could just make out the words from inside his hands.

'Did he tell you to lie about it under oath?'

'Aye.'

Anna picked up Eilidh's drawing, put it back in her bag. Jinky was watching her. Blood-swirled eyes and thickened lids. 'Ma'am? What happens now?'

She'd no wish to crucify this guy further. And all she had was his word against Coltrane's. Who would she take her suspicions to anyway, with Uncle Pete lurking in the background? No, she needed to build a stronger case first, see if Coltrane would admit to anything, find Jamie's notebook, the tapes. Find that gun.

'Nothing for the moment,' she said. 'Let me speak to Coltrane first.'

Jinky rubbed his eyes. 'It's not him you need to burst, ma'am – it's that woman Armstrong.'

'Armstrong? The DCI in Jamie's case?'

'Aye. Fucking cow.'

'But how's she involved? Surely it's Coltrane that's been misdirecting this whole investigation?'

'Ma'am, the pair of them are doing a line. It's her been protecting her boyfriend's back all along.'

The girl sat on the embankment by the railway line. It was warmer there than the cold grey of her father's house, with its spattered walls and deep-grained shames. Gentle rain reached down to stroke her, but it couldn't reach inside. She closed her eyes, drifting. Maybe the whole world would have been like this, if air hadn't split from land and sea. Swishing formless empty safe. Neither hot nor cold, for they were subjective and she was not. No longer subject, nor object, nor predicate. See – she knew all this, even when they thought she wasn't listening. The teachers had called it parsing, and she liked the crispness of the sound. Liked the act of giving meaning to meaning too, of dissecting words into yet more words – and would do it, with the newspapers that lined her floor. But never at school where people would see.

The girl had not been back, not since that minister came to assembly. He'd talked of sin, and being honest, and saying that you were sorry. How that guaranteed you'd enter heaven, no matter what you'd done. And she'd shouted out that he was talking shite, then Mr Wesley marched her straight outside and told her to go to the headie. But it was only being honest.

She liked to imagine her own funeral. All those schoolgirls who snivelled and clutched outside the crematorium. Strange, buckled faces that had never even spoken to her, and now she was the most popular she would ever be, yet she would feel nothing. Because there was nothing left to feel. Literally nothing; they would burn her crisp and dry, and the smells of spilled fat and dustiness were the last she would ever know. Did it hurt? the girl wondered. She lay down on the tracks beside where she pretended her mother's ghost was. Tried to ask her. But she was gone.

By the embankment, a dog is crouching. It is mean and wiry, and slevers from a grey tongue.

27

'What's going on?'

A brace of prison officers was marching some poor unfortunate past Jamie's room.

'I never done nothing,' the prisoner was shouting. 'It's no mine, I never fucking seen it afore.'

Several of the other inmates, Jamie included, had heads craned out their doors, gawping like old women in a close. Jamie listened to the buzz around him.

'It's that Ross Durward . . . aye, they done a random search . . . one of the screws found a knife in his locker.'

'Is that right? Daft bastard. What'll happen to him now?'

'Straight back to the Bar-L for starters.'

'Stupid cunt.'

Ross's legs were last to take their leave of his former roommates. Struggling all the while, he was not for shifting. Eventually the warders caught him under an armpit each, dragging him backwards through the fire doors and out into the stairwell.

Briefly, Ninian held its collective breath. Then the babble began, louder than before, all relieved it wasn't them. Where Barlinnie had dog boxes and despair, Garthlock had pillows and privileges.

'Fuck it, I'm gonny ask for his room,' said one of the guys nearest to Jamie. 'It's the one with two windows on the corner.'

'No you fucking arny,' said another. 'I've been here longer than you, ya tosser.'

'Ho, hold up. How come you get to decide then?' opined a third. 'You're just a frigging bag-heid.'

'Woah, cool your jets there, pal . . .'

'Naw, you fucking—'

The prisoner next to Jamie tugged his sleeve. 'Ho, Big Man. What do *you* think?'

'I think it's no who's *been* here the longest that should get it, but who's *gonny* be here the longest.'

There was a moment while they all digested what he'd said, heads pecking like hens.

'Aye, right enough.'

'Aye, fair dos, I'm no here much longer any road.'

'So, who would that be? Big Tam?'

'Aye – naw – Swally Simpson. Ho Swally, it's you, in't it? You'll be here till fucking Kingdom Come.'

'Ach, they'd never gie it to me any road,' said Swally glumly. 'They screws fucking hate Blue Noses.'

Though he was in for two separate murders, Swally had also done a bit of gun-running for the UDA in his time, and the warders who allocated room swaps in Ninian were both fervent Celtic supporters.

'How don't you ask them, Big Man?'

'Why me?'

'You talk their lingo.'

Jamie looked at Swally. He reminded Jamie of Gollum from *Lord of the Rings*. 'You wanting a swap then?'

'Oh aye, Big Man, that would be magic.'

'Right, I'll ask, but I canny promise anything.'

Excitement over, the inmates drifted back to their rooms. Jamie clocked old Arnie, leaning against the door jamb of his peter. A vague smugness played around his grizzled lips.

'What was all that about then? With Ross, I mean.'

'How would I know, son?'

'A knife, eh? D'you think someone planted it there?'

'Now, why would somebody want to do that? To a nice boy like our Ross?'

Jamie moved a little closer to him. 'I hope you didny do it on my account.'

'Do what?' The old man blinked. 'All I'm doing right now is getting ready to pack my bags and get the hell out of this place. You were right, son. I canny get by being bitter for what's past. That's no my style, never has been. Being bitter sends folk mad. So, I'm planning out what I'm gonny do instead.'

'And what's that?'

'Have a fucking giant, slap-up meal. Friday tea time, I'll have gravy dripping all down my chin!'

Jamie laughed.

'Seriously. I canny wait for the wife's stew. Used to be a braw wee cook, so she did. Here, come on in while I sort my socks out.'

This was the first time Jamie had been in another prisoner's cell. It was nothing like his. Arnie's room was covered in pictures of Scotland, all the touristy bits. Every inch of wall plastered with lochs and mountains, a smattering of castles, golden eagles and proud red deer.

'Like my calendars, son? The wife sends me one every year. I don't like throwing out all they nice photos when they're done, but. Look at that yin. Aonach Mor. May 2001. Beautiful, in't it?'

'Can I ask you something, Arnie?'

'Aye.'

'What was it you were in for?'

Jamie had never asked any of the inmates that since he'd arrived.

Arnie wiped his nose with the back of his hand. Liver spots blotched between the dip of his knuckles.

'Armed robbery. Aye. Seventeen-year stretch this time.'

'And . . . did you use it? The shooter, I mean.'

Arnie tapped the side of his nose. 'Ask me no secrets, and I'll tell you no lies. That was well done, by the way.'

'What was?'

'Way you handled that mob. Slick.'

'Like the way you just changed the subject?'

What was this now? Nearly the end of November? For the first three months in prison, Jamie felt he'd just been finding his feet. Keeping his head down, trying to survive. In truth, he'd probably been in shock. But the growing realisation he was actually more intelligent, more streetwise, and had had more chances than most of the other prisoners, meant he wasn't so scared any more. There was no option inside but to use your head. Fists too, if required, but that gave him no pleasure. You saw some of them, though, begging for a fight. Any release from the unbearable anger and the need to punch and belt and leather into something. Someone. Either that, or numb the noise with smoke and needles.

'You know some of they lads out there are feart from you?' said Arnie.

'How? All I've done is kept myself to myself.'

'Aye, but that's just it. You're an unknown quantity, son. They canny get the measure of you.'

'I canny get the measure of myself sometimes, Arnie.'

Arnie opened up his locker. 'Look, they're wary of you, but they're no watching your back, you know? And I'm no gonny be here after Friday.'

'And?'

'James, see thon Ross – he's the young cousin of some loony-tune called Mad-eye Murray. You know him?'

The nutter from Barlinnie, who jumped him the first day.

'Aye.'

'Total bunkernut. But he's a dangerous one. Like an octopus. Arms everywhere, know what I mean? Anyway, I was thinking, what with me for the off, I think you should dump the laundry. Go back to that painting shite.'

'You been talking to Ledbetter?'

After Brian . . . after Jamie had washed his hands, and washed his hands, he'd locked himself in a cubicle. Couldn't get the image out his mind. The three of them, writhing, Brian looking up at him, wild dead eyes like Sarah Brisbane. Jesus. Exactly like Sarah. Hollow, no hope, but with something of the spirit lingering. Just for an instant; one last, brief plea before it fled. How could he be in the same room as them all after that? For the last week, Jamie had been back to scrubbing smalls. He told Ledbetter all the paint fumes were making him feel sick.

'But the mural. Who's going to finish it, Worth?' Ledbetter had said. 'Calvin can only commit to one more day, and, quite frankly, Donaldson is as much use with a paintbrush as my hamster is.'

'Ach, just emulsion it over. It was crap anyway.'

But Ledbetter hadn't painted over it yet, not according to *Countdown*-boy. 'Daft prick's been trying to get Donaldson to do it all. It's pathetic. He's no nearly as good as you, Big Man.'

Jamie hadn't been that good either. But he was missing it, his wall. Missed pasting swirls of thick colour like comets over concrete, shaping and making dimensions and form. It was his idea to alter the wording on the mural too. Ledbetter had agreed it sounded better, and Calvin didn't care, as long as the font in which it was painted was suitably ornate. 'I'll speak to Mr Ethelridge, Worth,' Ledbetter had told him. 'I think he'll like the change. Says more about surviving this place, doesn't it?'

He probably hadn't bothered though, now that Jamie had jacked it in.

Jamie felt an elbow in his side.

'Ho! You listening to me?' said Arnie. 'I said I think you should go back to the chapel, I mean. Just for the next wee while. It's better supervised than the laundry.'

'Maybe so, but I don't get hassle off Tyrone and his girlfriend in the laundry.'

Jamie hadn't let on to Arnie what had happened with Brian. Because the next question was bound to be: *so what did you do then?* He'd given him the same paint fumes nonsense.

'You know that saying. Keep your enemies close.' Arnie dumped a load of clothes on his bed. 'Here, gonny fold they T-shirts up, son?'

'Why d'you say the next wee while? Is something going down? Have you heard something?'

'No exactly.' Arnie walked quietly to his door, clicked it tight shut. 'No me, a mate of mine. You know, Bomber?'

'Aye.'

'Well, right, I don't want to panic you Jamie, but he overheard Tyrone and a couple of the other lads talking about how they could use the big steam press – "just stick his head under it and pure clamp it shut" was what one of them said.'

All the moisture in Jamie's mouth freeze-dried. He pressed the roof of his mouth, rubbing his tongue to make saliva.

'Were they definitely talking about me, though?'

'He couldny be sure. But it was just after you and McInally had had that set-to outside the chapel. And Bomber said one of them said something about roast pork and all.'

Dust down his throat, pushing at his palate.

'Now, I've heard that Tyrone's for the off soon . . .'

'How d'you mean?'

'Never you mind. There's bigger boys than Tyrone in this shitehole, you know. If you can just keep tabs on him for a wee while longer, but keep your heid down too, know what I mean? And where better than the chapel: loads of folk about, and no boiling oil. What's he gonny do in there? Beat you with a hymn book?'

Arnie took the pile of folded T-shirts from Jamie and put them in his suitcase.

'But why?' said Jamie. 'Does Tyrone work for Mad-eye?'

'Fuck knows. Boys like Tyrone go wherever the gold is. Now don't start looking like someone's stole your scone. It's probably a total load of shite but, well . . . I thought you should know.'

'Thanks Arnie. I appreciate it. But, see what you said about Tyrone being for the off – don't you be doing anything stupid, please.'

'Look son, I like you, but I'm no a sap. I'm getting out of here, and I'm no giving a toss about fuck-all else.'

Ledbetter was delighted to see Jamie. All the other painting had been done, the boring stuff, so it meant Jamie could concentrate on finishing the mural.

'Mr Ethelridge will be so pleased, Worth. You might have noticed,' he waved over the lettering at the top, which had been changed, but now read *Find peace in tiny things*, 'I had to get Donaldson to step in to fill the breach. Mr Ethelridge was very concerned this wouldn't be finished in time for the opening.' He rested his arm around Jamie's shoulder. 'Would have been a bit of a black mark against you, actually. You and me both.'

'Well, if Mr Ethelridge is happy, then I'm happy.'

'That's the spirit. Och, and it's a lovely day too.' Ledbetter clapped his hands together, three sharp bursts. 'Right boys, from the top. Are you ready?'

As the men sang, Jamie lost himself in his painting. It took him back to secondary school, sheep skulls, huge windows, a hundred brushes crammed in rows of scrubbed pickled-onion jars. Stacey Bell in front of him, winging silver thread around rows of nails, Miss Anderson's perfume as she leaned over, charcoal transforming scrawl to sense in a few deft strokes. 'There. That's super, James. First class. Have you ever thought about art school?'

But art school was for fannies.

Only, imagine. Days spent spreading light and colour, building layers of rough and smooth, reworking, crafting. Creating something bigger than yourself, opening out and reaching up to scrape blue sky. To make new sky, new realities only hidden in your head.

To not be here. To not have done.

To not.

A trickle of paint ran down his wrist. Jamie shook his hand, then positioned himself so his brush was over Donaldson's shaky calligraphy. First, he washed blue over the lettering, blending the edges to fit in with the rest of the sky. It wasn't as if the right words were hard to remember:

Find grace in tiny things.

That was what he wanted, what was on his mum's daft poster. Grace, not peace. Peace implied acceptance, a wiping of hands, then a sighing out of *ah, all done*. Finito. Whereas grace was more about mercy. An undeserved mercy perhaps, but all the better for helping you endure. One coat was enough to smudge it all away. Once it was dry, he'd repaint the letters. After that, all that was left was to finish off the angel's wings. Calvin had painted her face in, but she seemed too literal to Jamie. This angel was earthbound, no translucence to her skin. Looked like a Barbie doll, or a man in drag. Mind, it was hard, in here, to do otherwise, with Garthlock's dearth of female faces. Unless Calvin had modelled it on Aggie in the canteen.

There was a break in the singing.

'Here, Mr Ledbetter. Correct me if I'm wrong, but does that shitey angel over there no remind you of a blow-up doll?'

Jamie could feel Tyrone's eyes on him, but he wouldn't look round. Wouldn't give him the satisfaction. Razor-sense on his shoulder blades ever since Tyrone had walked into the room. Tyrone was no longer a beardy joke, a punter of drugs and a bully, but a man who, for whatever reason, wanted him dead.

'Well, personally, I don't have too much knowledge of such things,' said Ledbetter. The arsehole was laughing too, that pathetic, ingratiating can-I-be-in-your-gang? kind of way. Jamie pushed his brush into silvery blue. Used the paint to tick each loop of feather, detailing plumage from chalky white. Slow, methodical, the rhythm of the brush like the beat of birds, just him and his arm on the up and the down, and the egg-delicate hues of inside a shell. But it was still too . . . flat. There was a pot of opaque glaze he'd noticed by the chancel steps. Calvin had been using it to make a marble effect of opals and moonshine on the wooden balustrade. If Jamie thinned it with turps and just barely, barely, eased the sticky liquid in feather-strokes of light . . . the wings would flit and hint at life.

He stood back. Just like that.

No more singing. He hadn't even noticed the inmates leave. Ledbetter was alone, clearing up. 'That you done, Worth? Oh, very nice. Very nice indeed.' He came over for a closer look. 'Lovely. Don't suppose you fancy giving the old singa-longa-Jesus a shot too, do you? Now that you've finished?'

'Absolutely not, Mr Ledbetter. Not unless you want your nice new windows to crack.'

'Shame. Now that Brian's dropped out, we could really do with another pair of lungs.'

Ledbetter was something else. Brian had hardly dropped out, as if it were a conscious choice. Tuned out, perhaps. Spaced out – any fool could see him shambling about the place and know. Yet no one seemed to care.

'You know why Brian canny string two notes together any more, sir?'

Ledbetter blanked him.

'I said, you know why that is? Because your favourite two choirboys have been pumping him full of free heroin. Now why would they do that?'

Ledbetter started folding up the music stands. 'Right Worth, that's enough.'

'Have you ever thought about where they would be getting all this heroin from anyway? Enough surplus just to give it away. Have you got any theories on that, sir?'

'I gave up on theories a long time ago, Worth. I just come in and do my job.'

'My theory is that it's an investment. One wee freebie and that's you hooked. A kind of business plan, when you think about it.'

Jamie's brush was waving wildly.

'Okay, Worth, I think we'll just call it a day, eh? You're getting paint all over the floor.'

'Ah, but the brains behind the operation, creating the supply to create the demand. What would you do, Mr Ledbetter, if you thought you knew who it was?'

'Honestly?'

'Honestly.'

'I'd keep well out their way and not be a hero.' Ledbetter zipped up his music case. 'Heroes don't last long in here. Right, put the lid back on that pot, I'll need to lock up now.'

Jamie flung the brush deep into another open pot, great splodges of red bursting on his angel.

'Fine, let it dry up. It's your funeral. And I'll let Mr Ethelridge know the reason why the angel's got measles while I'm at it.'

'You do that, sir.'

Jamie pushed past him, reached for a turps-soaked rag to wipe his hands.

'Worth,' called Ledbetter.

'What?'

'There's a staff meeting next week. I reckon they'll be putting you in charge of the laundry.'

'Is that right? Well, I'm honoured.'

'You should be, you've only been here five minutes. So I wouldn't be making any waves if I were you. Or starting any vendettas. And I'd think carefully about who you choose to work with you, too.'

'What planet are you on, Mr Ledbetter? *Nae* bugger wants to work with me.'

Jamie walked out of the chapel. Decided to head over to Ninian, not the dining hall. Dinner time would be nearly over, but he wasn't hungry. He needed to speak to Cath, and, once the fed and watered hordes descended, you could wait an hour to get a phone. But both phones in Ninian's hallway were free when he got there. He scrunched inside the little plastic hood that supposedly afforded you privacy, and dialled home. You never went straight through; a pre-recorded message prefaced every call, warning the recipient that they were about to receive a phone call from a Scottish prison. One day, Eilidh would pick up the phone, and that would be that.

'Hey, Cath. It's me.'

'Hi, darling. You're early tonight.'

'Yeah, just had a quick bite.'

'What did you have?'

She asked that most evenings, as if by charting his food intake she could share in his day.

'Eh, just beans on toast.'

'That'll not fill you up. You'll be hungry later on.'

'I'll be fine.'

He waited. Waited for her to know that he needed her hands on his head and for just the right words to pour unbidden through the receiver; that echo-linking lifeline.

'I got your letter.'

'Good.'

'It was lovely, Jamie. That bit, about hearing me talk in your head? I hear you too, sometimes. Least, I think I do. Either that or I'm going mad.'

'You didn't think *I* was mad then, to send it?'

'*No*. It made me cry.'

'You're not supposed to tell me that. You're meant to be Mrs Positive.'

'No, cry in a good way. It made me all ooze up with love. I went and got one of your jumpers out the drawer. Just sniffed it for ages.'

'Perv.'

'No, that would be if it was your pants. Oops . . . hi there, honey.'

He could hear a rustle, then Cath going, 'It's Daddy, yes.'

'Cath? Cath, what are you doing?'

'It's alright Jamie. She knows where you are.'

'What? Why did you tell her? I told you not—'

'Yeah, well, someone else got there first. But she's fine. She knows her daddy's a good man . . . what, darling? Sorry: the bestest daddy in the world. Jamie, Eilidh needs to speak to you.'

'No way. Cath, please don't put her—'

'Daddy? DADDY! Is it *you*?'

An exquisite kick, a love-sharp slap; burbling baby cadences bringing beauty clean into purgatory.

He breathed her name. 'Eilidh.'

'DADDY! DADDY. It *is* Daddy, Mummy!'

'I know it is, pet lamb. Tell him what you told me.'

'Daddy?'

'Yes.'

'Daddy, I love you the mostest in the whole world. And you've not been a bad boy, you've been a good boy. A very good boy, cause you were trying to help that lady, and I told Gelly that, and then I told my teacher, in my news book, how my Daddy was very brave—'

The phone slid down his face, wet with silent sobbing.

Faintly, he could hear Cath calling him. 'Jamie! Jamie, are you still there?'

'Uh huh.'

'Speak to Eilidh then. Don't let her think you're upset,' she hissed.

He wiped his eyes, tried to clear the thickness in his throat. 'Hey, baby. That was lovely what you said. Thank you.'

'When can me'n'Dan-pants come and see you, Daddy?'

'Oh, I don't know. I'm quite far away here. But, hey, it's your birthday soon, isn't it? What will we get you?'

'Not havin it.'

'But if you don't have a birthday you won't get any presents.'

'Don't care. Am staying wee till you come home.'

The little plastic bubble crushed down hard on all the air, pressing his sides, his spleen. Apart, invisible; sounds from inside his Kevlar helmet, the rush of inner ear, dull thuds outside his body. His daughter not denying him.

Suddenly, the weight lifted.

'Eilidh. What if you had your birthday where Daddy is? Would you like that?'

'*Yeah!*'

'Okay, well, put Mummy back on and we'll try and sort something out. Alright?'

'Alright, Daddy. Is you going to bed now?'

'Soon, darling.'

'Night, night.'

'Sleep tight.'

'Don' letta bugs bite!' squealed Eilidh. 'If ae bite, squeeze 'em tight . . .'

'And they won't come back tomorrow night! Bye bye, darling.'

'Bye, Daddy. Love you.'

He wasn't a bad man. He'd made her, this creature of joy and infinite knowledge, who, in turn, made his heart feel full and sound.

Cath came back on the line. 'You okay? Did I do the right thing?'

'Yes. Thank you, wise woman.'

'Well, I am right about almost everything, you know. Sooner you bow to my superior intellect, the better.'

'I said to Eilidh she could come down. There's a kind of open day this Friday. It's just before her birthday. What if I got passes for that? I can only get two though, I think.'

'Oh, Jamie, that would be fantastic. Eilidh'll be so excited. I can get my mum to watch Dan. Oh – he was dry this morning! Slept right through the night and no accidents.'

'That's brilliant.'

No nappies would make life easier for Cath. Another stage in his family's life complete. Fleetingly, he wondered who was going to teach his son to pee standing up. Or show him how to play football.

'Jamie, that other stuff you said in your letter, about seeing wrong things happen. D'you want to talk about it?'

He didn't really want to tell her anything. But her voice was stroking him open, so calm, so measured. Cath was his safe place. She knew all there was to know of him, yet she still loved him. Cath would know what he should do.

'It's not an "it" really. It's loads of things. For starters, there's this guy Tyrone—'

The hall door swung open, and several inmates clattered inside. Feeding time must be over. And, thank God, it stopped him. What could Cath do anyway? Just more worry-fuel for her widow pyre.

'Look Cath, it's getting a bit busy in here, and my phonecard's nearly done.'

'Okay. We'll talk when I come down. All I can say is, whatever it is you're worried about: you do what you've got to, to survive in there. But remember, you've got to survive *inside* too. In your soul.'

'Yeah. I know.'

'And you won't be in prison forever, Jamie. You've got to live with yourself afterwards too.'

'I know. Look, how's things with you? How's the money holding out?'

'Yeah, fine. Everything's fine.'

The phone started to bleep. 'That's my credit done. I'd better go. Love you, wife.'

'Love you, husband.'

She was right. Prison stripped you bare, but it also stripped you back to basics. And gave you nothing but time to think about those elementals. Jamie could deal with anything now.

Not could, would.

Mr Ethelridge never left Garthlock before dinner was served. Frequently, he would dine with the inmates, either as a shredded remnant of standing shoulder to shoulder with his men, or to prove the food wasn't quite as shite as everyone said. If Jamie hurried, he might still catch him.

When he got to the governor's rooms, a warder was just switching off the lights in the outer office. Not just any warder – Smithy. The very man Jamie was going to fire in to Ethelridge.

'Excuse me. Is it possible to see the governor, please?'

'Why?'

'It's a personal matter.'

'Fancy a wee greet on Ethel's shoulder?'

'Something like that.'

'Is it the wife? Been up the dancing on a shag-a-thon? Don't worry, they all do it.'

'Even yours?'

'Worth, Worth, Worth. When will you ever learn it's no a good idea to wind me up?'

'About the same time you realise that about me. If Mr Ethelridge isn't here, then I want to make an appointment.'

'Aye, aye. No problem.'

'I mean it. In his diary, please.'

Jamie slid the big black book over to Smithy. The diary was sacrosanct. Mr Ethelridge was a stickler for order and officialdom, punctuality and paperwork. But also, for honour amongst thieves. If he made a commitment to see an inmate, and it was in 'The Diary', then it was widely recognised he wouldn't renege or reschedule. Might send you away with a flea in your ear for whatever nonsense you were spouting, but he would dignify you with an audience at least.

'Oh dear,' said Smithy. 'Diary's very full. He's tied up until after the chapel opening service.'

'Fine. Put me in as soon as possible after then.'

'Sure I can't help?'

'I doubt it.'

Smithy scribbled something in the book. 'That's you then. Quarter-past two, next Monday.'

'Let me see.'

It read: *Mary had a little lamb.* In pencil. Jamie handed him a pen.

'Now do it properly.'

The two men stared at one another. Both realising there was nobody else there. Smithy clicked the pen, then wrote: *Worth 2.15.*

'Satisfied?'

'Thank you.'

Jamie left the office, walked back across the quadrangle to Ninian. He was sure Smithy was watching him from the governor's windows. So sure, he set his shoulders firm and slowed to a stroll. A group of guys in trackie bottoms jogged past him.

'Ho, Big Man. Fancy a game of footie?' Countdown was running on the spot, clearly taking his warm-up seriously.

First time Jamie had tried to play, no one would pass him the ball. Until he scored a cracker of a goal, and then they all capitulated. And then, he no longer wanted to play.

'Nah. Cheers anyway, but I'm just gonny catch a bit of telly.'

He hoped there might be news on, but the goggle-boxers were drinking in some crappy soap repeat, all Australian accents and buffed, bronzed blondes. No point trying to change it; people got very protective of their programmes. He'd seen two armed robbers come to blows over *Emmerdale.*

Jamie sat beside a group playing cards. For once, the spill of voices and warmth of meaty breath felt comforting, like cow flanks in a byre. Until he picked up on the men's conversation. Two old hands, both early twenties at most, were initiating a new arrival into prison protocol and procedure.

'Aye, but fuck that. You can get done for a bit of blaw far easier than smack. Know how they gie us all spot checks?'

'Aye.'

'Well, see after you've had a wee burn, they canny find nae heroin in your pish at all. All you need to do is drink loads of water.

Pure washes it out or something. But they cannabis traces last for yonks.'

'Fucking twenty-eight days,' said his buddy.

'Aye. So it's safer just to go straight for the hard stuff, man.'

Jamie stood up. He would just go to his room. The hallway was empty when he went out. It felt eerie, full of dusky dimness. Then he realised the stairwell was in darkness; the corridor lights had not yet come on. Still, he knew his way by now. One hand groping for the stair rail, he felt his way upward. God, he was getting unfit. He had to start going to the gym. It was easier to see at the top, blue safety lights shining from the floor, as if he was on an aeroplane. He unlocked his door, pushed it forward. But it didn't move. Tried again, turning the key backwards. This time, it opened. As if it hadn't been locked the first time.

A figure was sitting on his bed. Tyrone.

'What are you doing here? You don't stay in this block – you're not allowed in Ninian.'

Tyrone stretched, stood up. 'Didn't you know? I'm getting old Arnie's room when he goes. Mr Smith's worried about you, see. He says I've to drop in and keep you company any time I can.'

'Fuck off out of here, Fergusson. Before I rip your fucking head off.'

'That's no very friendly, is it?'

Tyrone began to prowl around the room, Jamie moving all the time to keep him in sight. Tyrone picked up a photo of Cath from the dresser.

'That the wife? Nice jugs. Bit chunky, but. She a pig too?'

'Put that photo down.'

'Where is it she stays again? Wester Bumblefuck or somewhere, in't it?'

'I said, put it down.'

'Nae worries, pal.' Tyrone opened his hand, letting the picture drop. As it hit the ground, the frame broke.

'You bastard.' Jamie swiped the photo from the floor. A splinter of wood had slashed Cath's smile.

'Oops!'

Tyrone moved behind him. Jamie realised how vulnerable he was, but he stayed stock still. Let him make the first move.

'Aye, bit of a porker, eh? But I'd still gie her one.' One soft hand on Jamie's shoulder, delivering a gentle knead. 'Or get someone else to,' he whispered. 'See ya, *Big* Man.'

Tyrone let the door swing wide as he went out. It hung in a howl, a great dark gape through which there may have been voices and movement. But Jamie could register nothing.

28

Walnut doors slid in a sensual curve. Soft burr of a black velvet curtain, smoothed aside by a besuited, shaded matador. Anna glided inside, wishing she'd worn a black mantilla.

'Wow,' said Elaine.

Two massive wrought-iron candelabra dripped flickering light beyond. The bar's interior was Glasgow-fabulous: a see-you-Jimmy bling, contrived to take your breath away. Limestone staircase coiling to another level, hourglass balustrades, wrought-iron sconces. Thick carved tables with chairs like mediaeval thrones. Gold jars of towering lilies, waxing and waning in the perfumed heat. In one corner, a pianist was hitting just the right note: discreetly classy, by the way. Scores of sleek thirty-something girls with comfortable men, not posing at all, just choosing not to sit. And, dominating the little raised platform along one side, a rabble of loud, pished, tapas-munching misfits. *Someone call the polis.* No, that was the polis. Obviously.

'Can you see Coltrane?' whispered Elaine.

'No, but I can wait. He's not the only person I want to speak to, anyway.'

Anna had clocked Nikki Armstrong, holding court at the biggest of the tables. One of the saddest sights Anna knew was that of a past-it policewoman on the piss. Or worse still, on the pull. It wasn't clear if that was Armstrong's intent; perhaps she too was awaiting Coltrane's arrival, and this was just a warm-up. Young DCs flanked her on all four sides, slurping their pints and ogling their gaffer's pushed-up breasts, which she'd brought out specially for the occasion. All front and no substance; you could tell by the knobbles of her collarbone, the stringy nothingness of her neck, that those spilling tits were really loose triangles. How could she? A professional woman in her mid-forties, thinking it was okay to don a tight (bursting out of its half-done buttons, in fact) satin blouse and white skinny jeans for a work night out. Necking a beer straight out the bottle. Anna had seen it so often, from the youngest female probationers in micro-minis – which they'd jail folk for wearing out on the street – to women like Armstrong, who should know better. Being surrounded by sobriety and uniforms in your career surely didn't mean you had to compensate so overtly out of hours.

Anna felt suddenly nervous. Not at all sure how to play this. Confessions were rarely as simple as the one she'd extracted from Jinky. He'd been a gift, a big pus-bag of blubbery remorse, just waiting to erupt. But Coltrane and Armstrong, they had more at stake. Coltrane in particular.

Anna had convinced herself Armstrong would be the weakest link. Nothing but a hackitt has-been, desperate to retain her toy boy's attention. A woman who would do anything, anything to keep him sweet between the sheets. Anna could crack her nae bother. She had to, for Jamie's sake. If she messed up here, with Armstrong and Coltrane, then it was over for Jamie. Totally. As soon as Coltrane knew Anna was on to him, he'd set a forest fire to destroy any lingering traces of what had really happened. She could guess how his mind would work: slash, shred and shame everyone and everything, as long as he was still standing at the end of it all. It was what Anna would do herself.

But the sight of DCI Armstrong, all dolled up in her glad rags, invited back the creeping fear that Armstrong was just as dangerous. What did Anna think she was doing here? Confronting a woman who thought she was in her prime. Queen of the Hill, surrounded by her acolytes, and supremely confident in her ability to stay on top. Bold and brash enough to wear cerise satin and match her boys pint for pint.

'Here, gie's your jacket and I'll grab us some seats. Mine's a white wine spritzer, by the way,' said Elaine. Anna handed over her brown leather jacket, pulled her top down over the back of her jeans. Not tight, just fitted. And Lycra helped them keep their shape longer anyway. It made sense. The bar was crowded, but Anna managed to catch a waiter's eye. She always did. If you stood still long enough and held your stare, they couldn't really avoid you.

'Any chance you could bring us some drinks when you have a sec?'

'Sure madam, no problem.'

She smiled, gave him the order, and went to sit with Elaine.

'Hello gorgeous, what's your name?'

Beery breath in her face, flabby arm around her shoulder.

'My name's Grumpy Cow, and I've got a black belt in karate.'

'Oooh. Feisty – I like it.'

The guy's mate nudged him. Anna knew that black crew cut well. It was young Alex from A Division. 'Hello Inspector, how you doing? Long time no see.'

'Inspector?' slurred his pal. 'Aw shit. I'm away for a pish. 'Scuse me.'

'I'm doing great Alex. You?'

'Aye, brilliant actually. I've got engaged.'

'Excellent. That you finished sowing all your wild oats then?'

He grinned. There was a sudden crashing rattle, and both their heads turned to see his buddy bending unsteadily towards the mock-limestone floor, lifting shards of glass into the air, and shooing people out of the way. A waiter with a tray of drinks had clearly come between the drunk man and the bogs.

'You better go and help your mate, Alex. We'll catch up later.'

Anna recognised another couple of faces in the crowd, but it was Armstrong she wanted to get at. Almost immediately, she saw her chance. A gale of laughter, then Armstrong swung out of her seat, gallantly assisted by one of her whelps. From the rear, she could have been twenty as she shimmied towards *Señoritas*.

Anna tapped Elaine's shoulder. 'Back in a minute.'

Two cubicles in the ladies, both occupied. Anna stood at the mirror, pretending to sort her hair. She'd not even had a sniff of alcohol, and already her cheeks were flushed. Childish splotches that only accentuated the sallow shadows beneath her eyes. Baby Jane on a bad day. She put her middle finger to where cheekbone met temple, pulling up the skin till the sagging disappeared and Anna came back.

A cubicle opened. Two young girls came out. That was something else that annoyed her: why did so many women go to the toilet in pairs? If the boys can pee in front of each other, so can we? It wasn't like they had that familiar coke-sniff to excuse their togetherness. Left without washing their hands too. Manky cows. Next to emerge was Armstrong.

Anna nodded at her.

'Alright? It's bedlam out there, eh?'

Armstrong frowned, went to the washbasin.

'I'm Anna, Anna Cameron. Work in the East?'

'I know who you are.'

Shit. Anna was crap at small talk at the best of times. She didn't get the ebb and flow of chitchat, it was like a foreign language. Marla was right: You have something to say, you say it. And what she had to say was: *did you fit up Jamie Worth?*

'Oh, yeah, we met at that AP interview, didn't we?'

Armstrong wiped her hands on a paper towel. 'Hmm. Probably not your best performance.'

Aw, fuck it.

'And what about yours?'

'I'm not with you, dear.'

Anna waited until the woman in the last cubicle had left. As she did, Anna stood in front of the door, leaning her body weight against it so no one else could come in.

'You know. The one where you lie to save your boyfriend's skin. Deliberately falsify an investigation and send an innocent man to jail.'

She folded her arms.

Ooh, dead tough, Anna. But it was more to keep Armstrong from her vitals, and keep herself from falling apart. 'James Worth? Ring any bells?'

Armstrong unzipped her bag. 'I'm sorry, did I miss something?' She puckered up at the mirror for another layer of lipstick.

'I just want to hear the truth. It's not too late to make this right, Nikki. I know all about it, what really happened. I know you were trying to help Coltrane; but at what cost?'

Armstrong shouldered her bag and moved towards the door. 'Let me past.'

'I know what Coltrane made you do. Have you got Jamie's notebook? Did Coltrane ask you to hide it for him? What about the recordings? Did Coltrane get you to erase the tapes of the radio traffic?'

Armstrong tried to reach for the door handle. It was made of crystal, carved like a futuristic control panel. But it was just a knob. Her hand went nowhere near. Did she think there were two of them? The woman really was quite pissed.

'Modern technology,' said Anna. 'Such a bugger when it disny work, eh?'

She blocked Armstrong's way. 'You were one of the senior investigators. It would've been dead easy to access them.'

'Inspector, why the fuck are we still having this conversation? I find your tone very offensive. If you have any evidence to substantiate any of this shite, I suggest you go ahead and report it. Otherwise, piss off out my road.'

'Just think about Jamie for a minute. Please. You've met him. He's a good guy, a cop like you and me, and he's dying in there. Lost his job, lost his future. And he'll probably lose his mind. Help me get him out, please Nikki.'

'You really are a sap, aren't you? Nobody's interested in Jamie Worth. He's yesterday's news. Our job is to feed the beast. As long as someone pays, the punters are happy. Happens all the fucking time, you know that, I know that. Nobody gave a shit when Worth went down.'

'But it isn't *right*. What about justice?'

Armstrong looked her up and down, like Anna was wearing a clown suit. 'How long you been a cop for? Fuck *justice*! It's survival of the fittest. Ian Coltrane's going places—'

' "*And I'm going with him*".' Anna tried to mimic the woman's gruff voice. 'So you speak in stereotypes as well as act like one?'

Armstrong bared her teeth. 'At least I'm getting my hole out this, doll. What's in it for you?' Not a smile; that grimace could never be fathomed as anything benign. 'A few major barriers to happy-ever-after that I can see. One, your boyfriend's married; two, he'll be in the pokey till his pubes are old and grey; and three, I've heard he takes it up the arse now, anyway.'

Flat of Anna's hand faster than her brain, tart tongue sharper than her wits.

'Fuck you, you washed-up old cow.'

She saw her hand push through air, impact on the bony angle above Armstrong's breasts, saw flesh quiver as Armstrong stuttered backwards. It must have stung, smarting palm, yet she never felt a thing. Just shaking, heat-seeking rage. They stood. Stared. Armstrong's incredulity manifesting as panting, hyenic laughter.

'Ooh. Ooh, that's classic.' She smeared a hand across her collarbone. One of the chicken fillets inside her bra had slipped, making her all lopsided. 'Absolutely classic. I'm gonny have your job for this, doll.'

'Your word against mine.' Anna sounded like a defiant schoolgirl. Squealing *I'm not scared of you*, as she burst into tears and ran for her life.

'Oh, I think you'll find there are at least three other lassies who were in here. Saw it all.' Armstrong shook her head. 'Oh, you are so fucked, Cameron. Didn't you know? Getting folk to speak to stuff – it's what I do best. You really think you're smarter than me?'

She'd lost it, she'd bloody lost it. That key in Anna's back, spun tighter than it should. Steel wires singing . . . straining . . . snapping. And she was off, speeding on spite and stress and certainty.

'The fiscal's investigating you, you know.'

Momentarily, Armstrong's eyes widened.

'Yep. Going back over every case you ever did, digging and picking till he scrapes up enough shite to bury you.'

'Well, he'll have a bloody hard job, cause I'm fireproof.'

'Not if Coltrane fires you in, you're not. And that's what he's doing, right now. That's why he's not here. He's in an interview room at the Sheriff Court, and he's spilling his guts and he's shafting you sideways. We've found the gun, you see, the one Coltrane said was never there, and right about now, he'll be telling them where you hid Jamie's notebook—'

Anna was flying now, lush lies becoming truth as they sprung from imagination to oration. In that moment of utterance, she believed them. True, all true. It was just that the time was wrong.

A glint of dribble on Armstrong's sharp chin. 'And how can he do that, you fucking heidcase?'

'Coltrane will do anything, Nikki. Don't you understand? He'll give them anything to save his skin; even you.'

'Well, he'll no be giving them the frigging notebook – cause I fucking torched it,' she yelled, staggering backwards against a sink. There was a lull as Armstrong steadied herself, wiped her nose. Then blinked. A single, sober second.

Anna put her hand to the side of her head, like she was fiddling with an earpiece. 'Roger. Thank you, and goodnight. Well, it's been a pleasure chatting to you, Chief Inspector Armstrong.'

'Woah. Wait up you . . .' Armstrong made to seize Anna's T-shirt. 'You wearing a bloody wire?'

'DCI *Armstrong*. No way am I smart enough to think of that.'

'You fucking are, you cow.' She tore at Anna's clothes, struggling to force scratchy nails inside the cotton.

'You're wasting your time. It's all gone straight to a voicebank anyway.'

'Jesus God. Fucking, fucking, fuck. What are you trying to do to me?'

'Can I suggest you have an early night to yourself? Someone from the Fiscal's office will be round to see you first thing in the morning. This has gone *way* beyond the polis now.'

She untangled Armstrong's hand from her top. Would Armstrong notice Anna's fingers were shaking as fast as hers?

'Why don't you plan out what you're going to say to them,

Nikki? Try and salvage something from the mess Coltrane's put you in.'

She left Armstrong leaning against the vanity unit, and forced her legs to shift outside. From the throng, she saw Elaine, waving at her. Anna's head was thumping, hangover-hard. What in God's name had she said all that for? Was she devoid of all rationality? All she'd done was warn Coltrane, and wind Armstrong up. And prove that she, Anna, had delusions of being an M15 agent. Once Armstrong was sober, she'd deny she'd ever mentioned the notebook. Particularly when there was no taped confession to prove it. Oh, why the hell hadn't Anna thought about doing that for real? Even a wee dictaphone stuffed down her knickers would have done. And that bollocks about the Fiscal's office? The last place Anna could look for help was the Fiscal's office.

Although. Anna tried to think clearly. Nothing about any of this actually suggested David had deliberately helped Coltrane and Armstrong. Been swayed perhaps, leant-on or seduced by the promise of greater things to be less diligent than he might but . . . maybe David would listen to her.

Aye. Right.

Hi David. Darling. Mmm, nice suit. Anyway, you know how I shagged you, so I could break in and steal your private papers, so I could help get my ex-boyfriend out of jail, by proving that your shoddy casework had helped facilitate a miscarriage of justice against him, and that you were possibly as corrupt as some of the protagonists? Well, any chance of helping me out here? For old time's sake?

'Anna, Anna, your mobile's been ringing and ringing.'

Elaine appeared in front of her, holding Anna's silver phone. 'There it goes again.'

'Hello?'

'Thank God! Where the hell have you been?' a woman whispered.

'Cath? Cath, what is it?'

'There's someone here.' Cath's voice was very faint. 'They're in the garden, behind the shed.'

'Can you see who it is?'

'No, the CCTV picture's really fuzzy. I can just see movement.'

'Right. I'll be with you in ten minutes, max. Lainey, got to go. Phone you, okay?' Anna started running for the door. 'Just keep inside Cath, and keep watching them.'

'Ten minutes? They'll be long gone in ten minutes, and then we'll never know who it was. Stuff that. I'm going outside.'

'No! Don't Cath. Dial 999. Tell them there's someone trying to break in. Cath? Cath, can you hear me?'

The line went dead as Anna clattered into the street. She tried to flag down a taxi, but none would stop. She should have brought her car. What bloody use was she to Cath; an emergency response that came by public transport?

'Excuse me, sorry. Strathclyde Police. I'm commandeering this taxi.'

'Are you fuck,' said the boy in front of whom she'd just barged.

'I fucking am. Now move.' Anna jumped inside the Black Hack. 'Sorry about this, driver. Get me to Westerton Mains as fast as you can.'

'Polis you said? What's up?'

'Can't say, pal. Don't worry, you'll get your fare. You'll get double if we can make it in under ten.'

'Aye, well, mind there's a boundary charge and all.'

'Just drive, eh?'

Anna opened her phone to try Cath again, but it rang before she could hit the number.

'Cath?'

'Inspector Cameron?'

'Yes, who's this?'

'It's Constable Deans. Group One at E Division, ma'am. We've just had a message come in for you, from Greater Manchester Police.'

'And?'

'Message says . . . "re your enquiry to contact one Craig Brisbane: there's no trace of that address".'

*　　*　　*

The girl still has blood on her fingers, warm fur beneath her nails where she had to press so hard.

He is laughing at her, curling hands like pleading paws and hopping, making rabbit teeth.

How could he, how could she?

Was he sorry?

'Say you're sorry. Say you're sorry. Say you're sorry. Say you're sorry!'

She is screaming, hot metal in her hand, then in his. Twisting, slippery like a fish. It smells like caves. She had hidden the gun in the cistern and the dank water is running up her arms and it is dirty! Dirty! Don't touch, her mummy says, wiping her fingers on a towel. It is on the beach, it was a rockpool, and he'd taken her to touch the jaggy flowers . . . She tries to get back to the start . . . he was little once and kind. Would reach out his hand to help her. Does he think about that? She does. All the time, in her mind. Only her mind, for that is all she is now. It is her mind that is making her hands work. Making them tear and spin silver and reach and grab. Now she has it, she has the gun and there are people outside and she will show them, show them, what he has. What he is. She can see one hand above a shoulder. A single finger reaching high . . . it curves, it looks like hers, yet everything is thick, dark ink and smashing rooms and glass that bleeds and that face, that face . . .

Her hands are cut, but they are limpets, they are strong. Not strong enough though. Not strong enough to hold on and pull and blast his face away. He twists her wrist until the prize is his. And he says he will kill her and she is running and running and the stairs are so slippery and he will kill her.

Thick black outside, a coated, furred air of weight and slow shades. Cath hid behind her kitchen blind, standing in shadow as the once-familiar contours of her garden bled and rose into monsters and tidal waves that would beat down, and smash her house, and carry off her children. The police would take even longer to get here than Anna. And exactly what superhuman powers of strength and perception did Anna Cameron have, that she was worth waiting for?

You couldn't make out a thing on her rubbish CCTV – that's why Cath had crept down here, in the dark. All she knew was that a person, or people, were behind her shed, dipping and lurching as they painted some new obscenity there. Who was Anna to tell Cath what to do? It was Cath's home being defiled, her kids being stalked as they slept. Her husband that needed saving.

Her husband. Cath's. Who would fight tigers for her.

Without taking her eyes from the bobbing shadow behind her shed, she reached for the draining board. There in the cutlery rack was the knife she'd used to chop courgettes earlier. A flashing Sabatier that made her wrist flick like a chef's. Cold flinch as she touched the heavy steel, then the warmer smoothness of the handle. She drew it nearer, still peering into night. Suddenly, she was aware of only stillness. The movement of shadows had stopped.

Her babies were tucked upstairs, their windows shut and locked. Help was on its way. Cath wasn't going to be cornered like a rat. She inched sideways to the back door, clicked the key round slowly, prising up the handle as quietly as she could. Opened the door a fraction, steeling herself for an onslaught.

Nothing.

A metallic thunk, then a scuffle at the side gate. She'd locked that too; they were trying to get away.

'I SEE YOU!' she yelled, running out towards the noise. Going over the top, sheer fear that was almost exhilarating as she screeched and waved her knife above her head. Just her and her limbs, all loose and powerful, pounding, pounding, her teeth jarring.

Nothing scarier than a mental burd. A backhanded compliment years ago, shouted in the middle of a pub fight. Her plunging spinning and shrieking into the mêlée, baton swinging like a flail.

And it worked this time too.

'You bloody stay where you are,' she roared, grabbing on to the leg that was disappearing over the top of her wall. She tugged, he pulled, she twisted, he fell. Hard on the ground, a little crumple of clothes.

Very little.

Cath knelt down, turned him over.

It was just a boy. No more than twelve or thirteen, thin, tight face, huge eyes fixed slightly to the left of her.

'Don't hurt me, missus,' he whimpered. 'I'm sorry.'

She realised she was still wielding her kitchen knife.

'You on your own?'

'Yes,' he snivelled. 'I promise.'

Cath put the knife down.

'Right, stand up.' She pulled the child to his feet. 'Have you hurt yourself?'

'No. M'okay.' But he seemed to be limping.

'Come on into the light where I can see you.'

Cath helped the boy into the kitchen, switched on the light.

'Hey, I know you. Where have I seen you before?'

'Mr Worth's football team, missus.'

'That's right. Barney, isn't it?'

'Benji.'

Cath sat at the kitchen table. Little buzzy head-nips biting at her brain. After the high, the comedown. 'Is it you that's been doing all these horrible things to me, Benji?'

'They're no horrible, I was trying to help you.'

'Help me? How?'

Out in the hall, the doorbell rang. She was frightened Benji would bolt. But if it rang again, it would wake the kids, and then she could start a bloody crèche in her kitchen.

'Right you, sit there. Don't you move a muscle, you hear me?'

She nipped into the hall, and let Anna in.

'Cath, I got here as—'

'Chill. All sorted. Check out my tormentor,' she said, leading Anna straight back to the kitchen.

'A juvey!'

'Yup. This is Benji, and he was just about to tell me what the hell he's been playing at.'

'Honest – I was only trying to look out for yous.'

'By making me think some loony was out to get us?'

'Naw. When Mr Worth got sent . . . I wanted to tell . . . I wanted . . . the flowers were just cause I was sorry.'

He began to cry again, scouring at his face. The embarrassed, angry tears of a little boy trying to be big. Cath wanted to fetch him a glass of milk, but she held out.

'Is that right? And what about the graffiti?'

'I didny do nothing, I swear.'

'Not even the eye?'

'Aye, I done *that*. But that wisny graffiti, missus, it was to keep bad things away fae here. Berta telt me what to draw. See, I knew yous would be on your own—'

'And was it Berta that put you up to this?' snapped Anna.

'Naw, nobody knows I've been coming up here. She just telt me how to do an evil eye hingy. But I never said what it was for.'

'So who's Berta?'

'Just a wumman at the camp.'

Anna raised an eyebrow.

'He lives on the Townhead travellers' site.'

'So you know him?'

'Not really, but Jamie did.'

'That's what I'm trying to fucking say,' blurted Benji. 'I was only—'

Cath smacked her hand down on the table in front of him. 'Ho, you. Less of the language.'

'See, I could maybe believe you about the flowers and the eye painting,' said Anna, leaning close. 'But what about that wee peg doll? You left that too, didn't you?'

'Aye. I just thought it would cheer the wean up.'

'Now, that's a lot of shite, and you know it. Those dollies aren't for playing with, they're for remembering. Remembering dead folk.'

'Naw, naw, I just took one fae Berta's van, I promise.'

'So Berta's got more of these has she?'

'Aye, a few.'

'Right sunshine, you and me are going to pay a visit to Berta, I think.'

'Eh, what about me?' said Cath. 'This concerns me too.'

'Yeah, but . . . you've got the kids and everything. Let me take care of it.'

'No way. Having children doesn't mean you can't function as a sentient human being.'

'I didn't say it did. But this doll thing's got nothing to do with you and Jamie anyway. It's a whole other investigation.'

'Stop telling me what to do, Anna.'

'Ho, Mrs Worth. Who is that wumman anyway?'

'She's a police officer.'

'Aw fuck. Aw, no way. Please don't bring the polis to the site. Ma papo'll kill me.'

Cath touched the child's back. 'Benji, it's alright. You're not going to get into any trouble.'

'Wee bit premature to be promising that, Cath. There's a fair chance Benji's going to get into a whole *load* of trouble, specially if he doesn't co-operate with us.'

'Och, shut up Anna and stop frightening him. He's just a kid. Now give me five minutes till I go and ask my pal if she'll babysit, and then we'll go. You got your car?'

'Eh, no.'

'Then how were you planning on getting there if I didn't come?'

'Hadn't really thought about it.'

'Exactly.'

The travellers' camp lolled in the shadow of the M8, bright flashes above it as traffic sped, dark patches below where dogs growled. It had the desolate air of a run-down council estate, but on wheels. Chaotic clusters of vans and cars, some intact, many in pieces or propped up on bricks. Distant tips of fag-light, canisters of gas lying loose on their sides, water hoses dripping into murky troughs of mud. Still some kids up, though it was late. Four little ones, the smallest in just a vest, being dragged by a huge Alsatian on a chain.

A woman emerged from the wagon nearest to the gate. Silently, she watched them park the car and get out.

'So, your grandpa's the boss, Benji?'

'Aye.'

'Well, you better take us there first.'

As they passed the first wagon, the woman sniffed. 'Gavver.'

'What did she say?'

'Och, just ignore them. They're all tinks at the front. We don't talk to them.'

'So, you're not all the one family?' asked Anna.

'No *way*. We're Roma. Proper gypsies. Council just stuffs us in with all the tinks, but. *And* they new-age nutters, sometimes.'

He stopped outside a gleaming caravan. Cream and chrome with Venetian blinds. And longer than the width of Cath's house.

'Do I have to come in?'

Anna pushed him forwards. 'Yup.'

Benji knocked on the door.

'Who are your friends, Benjamin?' came a low voice from inside.

'Eh, they're polis, Papo.'

'Again?' The door opened. 'Yes?'

Anna positioned herself in front of Cath. 'Mr – um?'

'Thomas. Just Thomas.'

She held out her warrant card. 'Thomas, my name is Anna Cameron. I'm afraid we caught your grandson vandalising this lady's house.'

'Is that true, Benjamin?'

'Aye, but—'

The old man pulled him inside. 'I will deal with this.' He made to shut the door, but Anna was already up the step. 'That's not all, sir. We need to speak to a lady I believe you have on your site. A woman called Berta?'

'There is no one of that name here.'

'You sure, sir?'

He closed the door.

'Thomas,' said Anna, 'if necessary, I will get a warrant to search every inch of this site – and who knows what we might turn up if I do that.'

'You do whatever you think is right.'

Anna frowned at Cath. 'So much for frigging courtesy. We should've got Benji to take us straight to Berta's van.'

'Let me try.'

Cath stepped up to the door. 'Thomas. Please don't punish Benji for what he did. He was trying to protect me, by painting symbols around my house. You see, he knew my husband. Constable Worth?'

She waited a moment, not sure what to say next. Then the door clicked open, and Thomas's white head reappeared.

'You're James Worth's wife? The football man?'

'I am.'

'He shouldn't be where he is.'

'I agree. And it's very difficult for me, being on my own. I get scared. I worry about things too much now. You see, Benji also brought this to my house. To give to my little girl.' She offered up the tiny doll. 'But Inspector Cameron here, she believes this is more than just a peg doll. Have you ever seen one of these before, sir?'

A phut of air through his nose. 'Long time ago. Not here.'

'Benji only meant to be kind, Thomas. We understand that absolutely, and there's no way that he's in any trouble. But, we have to investigate this, now we've seen it. It looks so new you see, not an old memory at all. You understand?'

'Inspector, if we'd lost one of our women, I would know.'

'Yes, but would you tell *us*, Thomas?' snipped Anna, hard elbows at Cath's back.

'*Anna*. Please excuse my colleague. She didn't mean to be so rude. We just need to talk to Berta, Thomas. That's where Benji said he got the doll. I'm sure it's nothing, just a little souvenir she's made. To sell, maybe.'

Thomas turned the doll in his hand. 'We wouldn't sell one of these. Berta wouldn't. Absolutely not. Benjamin,' he called over his shoulder, 'come with me.'

Berta's van was tucked away at the back of the site, behind the toilet block and hard up against a soil and scree embankment. It was tiny compared to Thomas's; a mess of patched metal and corrugated iron, with an old-fashioned stable door that split in two. Thomas barked some foreign phrase, and an elderly woman, wrapped in a shawl, keeked out the top half of the door. In the grimy grey-dark, she was just a swathe of folds; until her head turned towards them. Two brilliant, sparkling eyes scuttled over Cath like darting scarabs, seeking a way to burrow in.

'Come inside,' said Thomas.

The caravan stank of damp and tobacco. Berta flapped an end of her shawl over a chair, and gestured to Cath to sit. Hunched by the stove was a young girl, with thick red hair tied beneath a scarf. Her eyes were puffy and Cath noticed she picked constantly at her nails; same way Cath worried at that chip on her tooth.

'This is Monika,' said Thomas. 'She is Berta's niece.'

Cath smiled. 'Hi Monika.'

'She speaks little English. Neither does Berta. They are from Albania.'

'I see.' Anna stayed standing beside Thomas. 'Is that where you're all from? Originally?'

'We are Roma, Inspector. The countries we move through don't claim us. Now, what do you want to ask her, and I'll translate?'

'Can you ask Berta why she has this doll, please?'

Thomas took the doll from his pocket and placed it on Berta's lap.

Monika clicked her tongue, two, three times sharply, hands up to her face.

But Berta didn't move, didn't acknowledge the object. Instead, she leaned towards Cath and took her hand.

'*Udovica.*'

Her eyes were moist, her rough fingers working Cath's flesh, finding her palm. She traced the long curve that ran from Cath's wrist to above her thumb. The rubbing made Cath tingle.

'Berta!'

Thomas shouted some guttural words, and she dropped Cath's hand. Then, she began to talk, pointing and smiling like a lovely old gran.

'She says these dolls are like her children.'

'Ask her how many others she has.'

At first, Berta shook her head, but Thomas was insistent. He stood over her, finger flipping back and forth each time he spoke, like he was conducting an orchestra. She sighed, thumped her old hands down onto her open knees and pushed herself from her stool. Five stumpy fingers were splayed under Anna's nose.

'I take it she has five?'

'*Va. Pandz,*' said Berta. She shambled to a cupboard and took out four other dolls. Proffered them to Cath like flowers in a bunch. Each one was distinctly different; black wool hair, brown wool hair, purple scarf, silver shawl. But all with the same, shut faces of black straight lines.

'Berta has no children of her own,' said Thomas.

'Yes, but do they represent real people? The one Thomas is holding for example, it has red hair, just like Monika here. And look, the scarves are very similar too.' Anna looked directly at Berta. 'Is this one Monika?'

At the sound of her name, Monika made to go to the door, but Thomas stopped her. He too was looking at the doll, and then at her. Once more, he began to shout at Berta, a fast stream of invective and hand waving. Berta stamped and yelled back, but not quite as aggressively. Thomas was snarling, arms poised as if to strike her. '*Hovavno!*'

'Excuse me!' Anna shouted. 'Could someone tell me what is going on?'

Benji had a cushion held to his face. Wee soul.

'Benji. What does *hovavno* mean?'

'It means liar,' said Thomas. 'This woman has betrayed my trust. And she has brought danger to this camp. You were right, Mrs Worth. These dolls *are* symbols; but not of the missing. These are of the *found.*'

'I'm sorry?'

'Berta has made these in memory of the women she has saved. She says she has been helping girls like Monika.' Spinning his signet ring, round and round, big circle on slender finger. 'To escape from slavers, men who sell them. She has been letting them hide here for a time – *pretending* they are family – then makes them melt away with other travellers.'

A short while ago, Cath had been snug in her house, watching *Newsnight Review*. Then, iced grass crisping her knees as she held a strange child on her lawn. Then careering through the city, creeping into a camp. Swept inside a crystal ball. Now she was sailing on a slave ship that should be centuries out of date. And everyone was yelling.

'But why are you so angry? Is that not a good thing she's done?'

'Not when she puts my people at risk. And not without my blessing. You can do what you like with her, Inspector. I don't want them, either of them. Come on, Benjamin. You will not see Berta again.'

Both Berta and Monika were crying. Benji squeezed Berta's hand as he passed, then stopped. He looked so worried. Did he have a mum? Cath hadn't heard one mentioned. Maybe Berta was the one who looked after him. Monika was shivering, her hand cupped upwards, eyes moving from Anna to Thomas and back again. One broken soul careering like a pinball to the next encounter that would buffet her on.

Don't hurt her Anna.

'But Papo. I think Berta is brave. What will happen to her if we throw her out?'

'That is not our concern.'

'Papo, what will happen to Monika? What if the bad men come back for her?' Benji gasped. 'Monika! Do you know where the bad men are? Maybe we could catch them?'

'That's a very good question,' said Anna. 'Thomas, would you ask Monika if she knows where she was held? Please? There may be other women still there. Little girls even – I've seen it before.'

Thomas spoke rapid-fire to Monika, never looking at her face. At last, she bowed to his pressure, her tears thick as her tongue.

'*Va, va.*'

Haltingly, fidgeting with her nails, her face, Monika told her tale. A couple of times, Thomas shook his head, and, once, he caught his breath in hard, glancing quickly at Cath. She was still unnerved by Berta's palm stroking, and this old man's troubled stare made her even more uncomfortable. She shouldn't be here, playing at cops and robbers. She didn't get paid for that any more. Home was where she belonged, with her children, not floating loose in a world of transience and misery. Cath had her own world full of that already. She didn't need someone else's pain piled on top of her own.

When Monika had finished, Thomas took over. 'She says it was a high house; I think she means like a skyscraper. But she also says she has seen the man that took her again. He was on the television.'

'Someone famous?'

'No. She saw him on the news. Crying when his sister was shot.'

Why was Anna staring at her like that?

'By a policeman. Mrs Worth, I think the man she's talking about is the brother of the girl your husband shot.'

'No.'

'That is what I believe.' He opened his hands, palms out. 'If you find this man, you may find more about your slave traders. Now, Inspector, it is late, my grandson is tired.'

It felt like the glass keeping her from Jamie was shattering, and Cath could see his face, clear and desperate as Monika's; they couldn't leave now. She needed time to piece these jagged parts. Her husband was somehow connected to this grief? It made no sense. What more did Monika know; had she met Sarah Brisbane? She'd met the brother certainly: a brothel keeper, not a hapless boy at all. But it didn't alter the fact that Jamie had killed Sarah. Did it alter anything? Cold confusion, but she couldn't let this girl, Monika, drift away. Why was Anna guiding her towards the door? Why were she and Thomas just talking? Cath listened to their parallel conversation as she plucked and worried at a thousand fragments.

Anna was shaking Thomas's hand. 'Thank you for your help. We'll use the information you've given us to trace the man Monika told us about. Can you tell Monika she's very brave, please? Berta too.'

'I will. Will Monika be returned to Albania?'

'I'll do my very best to make sure that doesn't happen.'

'Fine. I'll allow them to stay here in the meantime. But only if they agree to do exactly what I tell them. I want no one else to know about . . . all this.'

'Shall we walk Benji back to his van then? While you're talking to the women? It's on our way out.'

'Yes, thank you.'

Spiky night-air. Cath realised she was outside, being led further from Monika, who shared some tenuous connection with Jamie, and who would surely evaporate into never-been, the instant they left the site.

'Anna, what are you doing? We need to go back and get that girl.'

'Just a minute, Cath.'

Anna hauled Benji in front of them both. 'You knew exactly what you were doing when you brought us here, didn't you? Stop picking your nose.'

Benji wiped his finger down the back of his jeans.

'Kind of, miss.' He looked at Cath. 'I promise, but: they flowers and the evil eye were true. I just wanted to make you feel better, Mrs Worth. But . . . I don't want Papo to hear.'

'Okay, walk while you talk. But it better be good.'

He waited until they had walked a little further from Berta's van. 'I knew Berta knew something about that lassie's brother; I heard her and Monika yabbering. They think I canny understand them, but I can pick up enough to get by.'

'I bet you can,' said Anna. 'Go on.'

'We were watching the telly, and it came on the news, when Mr Worth had, you know. Anyway, the lassie what got shot's big brother came on, kidding he was greeting, and Monika pure jumped up. She started yelling at the telly and Berta had to slap her face. They sent me out after that, but I was eariewigging outside. Berta's van's crap; nae insulation. See ours, we've got a big—'

'Okay Benji, just keep telling us the story.'

'I heard her say that *that* was the man what hurt her. She was pure roaring and greeting, something about *phen*. How he was so evil that he'd hurt his own *phen*.'

'What's a "*phen*"?'

'I think it means "girl". Or maybe "sister". It was raining, and they were talking dead fast. But what I definitely heard her say was that he'd a "*pistol'i*", miss. And I know for sure that means "gun". Berta talks about "*pistol'i*" when we go after rabbits. So, if he had a gun, and he'd been hurting other lassies, I knew he was a right bad bastard. I knew it was him what kilt her, Mrs Worth. Right away, I knew it. That lassie's big brother, no your man at all.'

Benji looked so fierce. It had been a long time since Cath had seen such loyal devotion to her husband. She wanted to kiss his angry wee face. If only it had been true. But. Her skin scented change before her mind did, each pore opening. The boy had a gun. If the boy had a gun . . . could? Could what? Could Jamie have imagined that he'd pulled the trigger and seen Sarah fly backwards? That vicious image he woke to, wept to, drank to? Her pulse slowed back to drumbeat pace.

'Why didn't you just go to the police if you thought all this? You could have talked to Jenny, surely.'

'But my papo disny know Berta's been helping these lassies get away. I didny want him to know that I did.' He scuffed his foot along the ground. 'He's meant to be in charge of everything here. But I thought if I gied you one of they dolls this time, and then I was gonny—'

'There's more?'

'Oh, aye. I thought if I gied you clues . . . well, I knew you were a polis, Mrs Worth. And you could do something about it and get Jamie out too. I didny want to get Berta into trouble, or Monika. She'll no get sent back, will she, miss?'

'No,' said Anna. 'I promise.'

'Anyway, next I was gonny leave you a photie of him and his van.'

'You're joking?'

'Naw. I took it on my moby, see? I just didny know how to get it printed off. Look.'

They peered at the tiny screen. 'Craig Brisbane,' said Anna.

It was the man who had grinned at Cath in court.

'That guy's a total cunt, miss.'

'Benji!'

'He is, but. Monika telt Berta what he made her do.' Benji's scowl threatened to drip fresh tears.

'You're right.' Cath gave the boy a hug. A brief one, but not brief enough, judging by his horrified expression. 'He is. On you go.'

'I heard all these things Monika was saying, about how they'd brung her to England to work in a shop—'

'Do you know where in England?'

'Manchester I think? Anyway, she said this man, the one she'd seen on the telly, had came in a big white van and took her and another couple of lassies up to here. And then she said what happened.' He grew quiet. 'Monika's only fifteen.'

They were back at Thomas's van. Cath had that sensation of being padded again; a ragdoll stuffed with stockings, held by her hair and being thwacked against the tight-packed thigh of the precocious little girl who ran with her. There, but not. Aware, but mute; her big cloth tongue sewn in too tight.

'Coming in?' asked Benji.

'Long as you keep talking.'

Anna had her arch face on, the one that knew exactly where it was going. Fine. Cath let herself be carried.

'Aye, but if Papo comes back . . .'

'We'll go. I promise.'

They all sat down, Anna and Benji trying to outspeed each other.

'So, how did you get the photo?'

'Monika does so know where the lassies were taken. You know they high flats up at Sighthill?'

'Aye.'

'Up there.'

Sighthill was full of asylum seekers. Glasgow had taken in hundreds of them in recent years, unleashing multicoloured misunderstandings and rainbows of sectarianism that no amount of community fun days could quell. Cath's church was involved in a project at Sighthill, providing starter packs of towels and crockery for families who had fled their homeland with literally nothing. Piled high in prefurnished boxes, and spoon-fed with food vouchers, these new Glaswegians were easy pickings for any disaffected local, already floundering in their own dirty sinks. So sadly, shamefully, the grateful refugees quickly reverted back to scared, pulling their scarves tighter around their heads, and looking forward to a life of isolation in this, the 'Friendly City'. How easy it must have been to hide a few more desperate foreign-looking women there.

'I minded what the bastard looked like, so I just hung about till I seen him one day. And I snapped him!'

'Benji, you are quite possibly the cleverest boy I have ever met,' said Anna. 'Any chance you can remember exactly where the flats were?'

'Aye. They big ones in the Red Road. I seen what block he came out of too. It's a kind of brown one – all the rest are grey.'

'*You* are a total star, young man. Okay, you hang fire there and I'll go and make a couple of phone calls.'

Anna left Cath and Benji alone. Off on a mission, not even deigning to tell Cath who, what or why. She felt like a sleepy-husked fossil. Old to her bones and afraid to wake.

'How come she looks at you like you're shit one minute, then she's all pure *who's a clever boy* the next?'

'That's just Anna, Benji. You know the White Witch in Narnia?'

'Where's that?'

'Never mind. Here, you look shivery. Is it not way past your bedtime?'

'I don't have a bedtime.'

'Well, put that blanket over you.'

She passed him the plaid blanket folded behind her on the couch.

'Ta. So, *was* it him that killed her, Mrs Worth? The brother? Was I right? Is that what that poliswoman's finding out the now?'

'No Benji. It's a nice idea, but Jamie did shoot Sarah Brisbane. They proved it, with science and graphs and stuff.'

'But no on purpose.'

'No. Not on purpose. And if you're right about her brother having a gun, that could help him. So, so much.'

But she wouldn't get excited about it. Not yet. It was easier to stay dull and safe, than set yourself up to be eviscerated again.

'Good.' He wrapped the blanket tight around his shoulders.

'Benji. How come you knew I used to be a cop?'

'Mr Worth telt me. He talked about you all the time, like you were a pure doll. Not that you're no, I mean . . .' The boy blinked.

'I'd quit while I was ahead if I was you.'

He grinned, a sleepy smile, and lay sideways, his legs swinging over the arm of the chair.

Tin on tin as the van door slammed against the wall. 'Right,' said Anna. 'It's out of our hands now.'

'What is? Who were you speaking to?'

'A girl I know at the UN that deals with this kind of thing. We can't just go charging in, in case they've got tabs on this gang already. She's going to pass it on to a contact at the SCDEA.'

'Drugs Enforcement?'

'Nah, they deal with all this kind of cross-border crime now. Though there might well be drugs involved too.'

'But you told her about the gun. About Jamie?'

'Don't worry. They know it's urgent.'

'So, what do we do now?'

'Nothing at the moment. We've just got to hope they find a gun. And, if they do, then we've got to hope that forensics can find some prints on it.'

'Craig Brisbane's?'

'Aye, but, ideally Sarah's too. See, my theory is that Craig was in the house with Sarah, the night she was shot. I think they had some kind of a fight, a tussle over the gun maybe, and it went off. That's what the neighbours heard. There's marks near the cooker that could indicate a gun being fired inside.'

A black-red glowing ember, kicked out as the ash pit in Cath's stomach churned. 'And Sarah ran outside to get away from her brother? Leaving him and the gun to disappear? The gun everyone bar Jamie denied was there?'

'Exactly. But Cath, even with the gun, there's still a lot to prove.'

'I know, I know. But, God, it's something.'

What was it that stupid poster at Doris's said? Something about being happy with small things? She'd kidded Jamie it referred to his willy.

'Best thing you can do is go home, get some rest, and I'll phone you first thing in the morning, alright?'

'I guess.' Cath was exhausted, drained, and she wanted her own children. Needed smooth small foreheads to draw her cheek along, and a night of peace and space. Wanted, *needed* someone else to do the graft. This wasn't her world any more. Jamie was.

Please God, let it be true.

She patted Benji's forehead. 'Right, sleepyhead. We're going to go now.'

'Okay.'

'Thank you, by the way, for painting on my wall.'

'Nae probs.'

'Something else you can maybe do for me. When Berta took my hand, she said "*udovica*". What does that mean?'

'Oh,' he closed his eyes. 'I dunno.' Stretched his mouth in that little kid-on yawn Eilidh did, when she was feigning sleep.

'Yes you do,' Cath cajoled. 'Go on, what was it?'

He raised an eyelid.

'It means widow.'

29

Anna had dreamed about him after she got back from the camp. Little sleep and lots of wine, laced with spider graphs and mind maps and all the things she'd learned of him. His hands scooping a heart to frame her head, his face on hers, push of paper-lips rubbing fire. She had felt his warm body fitting round and through like water fills space. So sure, when she woke to bells, that he'd be there.

'Anna. It's David. And, before you hang up, I'm phoning about business.'

'David. No, I wasn't going to hang up.'

'We can't talk on the phone. I need you to meet me.'

'When?'

'Now. Soon as you can. I'm busy this afternoon. Meet me at Candleriggs. And bring every single scrap of any intelligence you've gathered on James Worth.'

'What?'

Had Armstrong contacted David right enough? Anna felt that way you do waking up after a bender. Slow, mud-moving dread for something you're not quite sure of. Then, drip, by drip, it comes trickling back, until the whole cringing picture of what you did floods large and lurid over your head, and you want to dive under your own dark rock. Crawl beneath and never surface.

'Just do it, Anna.'

David was waiting for her inside the old market. Candleriggs was a great, cobbled hangar, tucked away in the Merchant City. Anna had gone there once or twice when she was little. Her mum never approved, thought it 'a dreadful guddle', but all Anna could remember was her dad's safe hand steering her through crowds, bright paintboxes of enamel pots and pans, stallholders shouldering crockery towers and juggling with mugs. Ducking as bales of towels were thrown over the heads of the folk gathered for the banter and the bargains. Now it rang to piped music and clinking cups, the stalls torn down for zinc-lined bars and trendy restaurants. Another chunk of Glasgow gentrified. No industry, no banks, no shipyards, no soul. But plenty of chilled white wine and penthouse flats.

'Hi.'

David was wrapped in a big black coat, insulation against the face-hurting cold of a West Coast winter. The folds of fabric made his face look leaner. Pinched almost.

'David. I'm so sorry—'

'Save it, Anna. I don't have time. I've had a call about the Worth case. Several, in fact. Funny thing was, when I went to dig out my file, it wasn't there.'

They still had the old cobbles in Candleriggs. Smooth grey humps which had rubbed the feet of thousands. David was wearing beautiful tan shoes.

'David . . . I want to explain.'

'Not interested. But I know you are. So, I thought you'd want to know; they've recovered a gun from a flat in Sighthill, which might be connected with the Brisbane killing. I've asked forensics to look again at the evidence they took from the Brisbane flat. I understand you've been doing your own wee investigation. Got a lovely wake-up call from ACC Wishart at 4 a.m.'

'What did he say?'

'That doesn't matter. What his nephew says will though, depending what we put to him. So, what have you got?'

Anna handed over the file she was carrying. 'It's all in there. It's pretty clear to me that Coltrane's a lying shite, and that what Jamie said in his statement is true. You'll want to interview DCI Armstrong too. She thinks she's already on tape confessing to burning Jamie's notebook, so you might want to string that out a bit.'

Without a word, he took the file. His own file, with her additions.

'Did they get *him* at Sighthill? Sarah's brother?'

'Yes, he was there.'

'And?'

'Investigations are ongoing.'

'David, don't.'

He stared straight at her. 'Craig Brisbane is a cocky wee psycho. Seems he's been working as a delivery driver for a trafficking ring. They specialise in East European girls; the younger the better. Gets a real kick out of it when the girls start to cry apparently.'

'But he's got no pre cons.'

'I know. That's how these people work. They use clean skins where they can. Clean skins, nomads, illegal immigrants, so there's no paper trail, and no criminal network that can lead back to them. That's why they sheltered Craig Brisbane after his sister was shot too. They knew he'd fucked up, but if they cut him loose, he was just more likely to say something stupid, draw attention to himself.'

'Like on his one and only TV appearance?'

'Exactly. After that, it made sense for the trafficking gang to keep him close, but totally off the radar. Otherwise, Craig Brisbane opens his big mouth, leads to more background checks, to little girls, guns, grooming, trafficking gangs—'

'Grooming? He was grooming his own sister?'

'Possibly. There were certainly issues about lewd and libidinous practices towards other younger kids when Craig was at primary school – which none of Strathclyde's finest bothered to check, of course.'

'You said the gang kept him off the radar. But he was seen in court during the trial.'

David shrugged. 'Like I said, Craig Brisbane's a psycho.'

'What about the father?'

'Don't think he was involved at all. Apart from laying a fertile seedbed in which to grow a fucked-up son.'

'And Coltrane? You don't think he's implicated?'

'Jesus, Anna. Coltrane's not a gang master, if that's what you're asking. I think he's just an arsehole who panicked when you guys couldn't find a gun.'

'That's what I thought too. Just Jamie's tough shit he fell between the gaps.'

There must be air conditioning on somewhere, or a vent, because this one thin strand of her hair kept flapping back and forth across her eyes. Like she was viewing David through slatted blinds.

'David. Did you . . . see, at first, I thought you were involved too. You know, what you said . . .'

'That in your special file too? *Check out David's credentials*? No, you already did that.' Tips of two white teeth, working on his lip. 'Expertly. Anything else you want to tell me?'

'I also spoke to Jinky Robertson. He admits Coltrane told him to lie. Oh, and the brother's alibi in Manchester doesn't check out. No trace of the address he gave.'

David shook his head. 'Been pretty thorough, haven't you? *Worth*.' He smiled. 'Was he?'

'Was he what?'

'Worth it? I take it he's somebody special?'

'He was.'

David tugged at his tie, loosening the knot slightly. Long shadow of stubbled neck, vertical slice of bone. Anna had kissed her way along those curves. Beneath all those clothes, she knew him better than anyone else walking through this place. Despite his rancour, despite her shame, it turned her on. It was what she loved about uniforms; their hard-edged authority and impositions of dominance, but underneath, underneath was all soft and compliant and she *knew* that.

'Look. I'm going to tell you something else too, Anna. I don't know if it's just more bullshit and bravado, but, as I was leaving him, Brisbane said, "Cunt'll be deid by now anyway." I asked him what he meant, but he just went "tie-tie", and gave me a total psycho stare.'

'Was he talking about Jamie?'

'Can't think who else. I'm sure it's a lot of shite, but, you might want to say to the family. Are you in touch with them?'

'Yeah. With his wife.'

'*Cosy*. Well, flag it up, just in case. I'm sure it's nothing. As a cop he'll be at risk all the time, so Garthlock will be watching his back anyway.'

'I'm not so sure. He's been attacked a few – well, you'll know. It was in your file.'

'Yes.'

She followed David's gaze up to the ceiling. That was where the draught was coming from. She could see big turbines twirling recycled air. In and out and round about, full of germs and dust and spittle. A huge net of fairy lights was strung in front, as if their delicate bulbs could mask the bulky workings behind. Other, coloured, lights swung in sparkling strings above the bars and restaurants. It reminded Anna of New York. She was aware of David, watching her.

'You said he said "tie-tie". You mean "ta-ta", like cheerio?'

'No, it was definitely "tie-tie". But he was waving, like you would at a kid.'

'And after that? Did Brisbane say anything else at all?'

'Nah. Wee tosser kidded on he was sleeping.'

'I take it you didn't get any kind of a confession out of him about what happened to Sarah?'

'Not yet. That's up to the SCDEA. It's a Chief Superintendent Stevens in charge. Know him?'

'No.'

'Yeah, well I couldn't tell what they were going to bargain with. Either use the threat of implication in his sister's death to get more on the trafficking gang, or say they'll extricate him from the trafficking charges, and get Craig to spill his guts on what he did to his sister.'

'Why not both?'

'That's not how it works Anna, you know that.'

'Okay, well tell them to treat Brisbane as a cop killer. Maybe that'll help them "decide".'

She must be getting louder; people were turning round to look at her. 'Tell your Stevens guy to do that, because Brisbane's as good as bloody murdered Jamie.'

'Calm down. Hopefully, Worth'll not be in there much longer.'

'Really? D'you mean that? Is there enough already d'you think? To get him out on appeal?'

'I'll see what I can do, okay? I know for a fact the original trial judge wasn't happy with the evidence we led. If I 'fess up that we might have "overlooked" a few issues . . . well . . . but it won't happen immediately. And you'll need to get in touch with Worth's lawyer. Obviously, we'll pass all the material facts on to him as we get them.'

'Thank you.'

Without thinking, Anna dipped her face into his, kissed him on the brow.

Stiff shock, both jerking back. Him swallowing, swallowing, her trying to find a phrase.

'I . . . I need to go and read this,' he said, cardboard file across his coat.

'Oh. Okay.'

He walked some paces. Turned. Raised the case file. 'You know, Anna. If you'd wanted the file, you only had to ask.'

Then he left her quickly, a dark arrow, diagonal through the exit. She wished it was David she had been dreaming of.

Old Arnie left Garthlock that morning. At breakfast, took his porridge like a man, then scraped back his chair and went, 'That's me, then.'

'That you, is it?' replied Bomber.

'Aye.'

'Take it easy, pal.'

'You and all.' The old man nodded to the table. All the faces he'd sat with for umpteen years. 'Boys.' Then he strode to the door, a hundred-spoon salute crescendoing in pursuit. A swing of wood and metal, and Arnie was no more.

'Is that it?' said Jamie.

Bomber shovelled more cornflakes in his mouth. 'What did you think, you arse? We all stand with hankies, waving him off on the train?'

Tea with no milk, no sugar. The tang of teeth staining tannin, served with a twist of loneliness. Jamie drained his mug, got up.

'That you off to get ready?'

'What for?'

'Your fucking daft church thing. It's the day.'

'Aye, but I'm not doing anything in it. The wife's coming down for the sideshows and that.'

'You're gonny go to the service, but? We're all going. You get tea and sausage rolls after. And I heard Ethel was for giving you a gold star.'

'Aye, and a big colouring book and all.'

'Naw, naw, one of they scrapbooks the lassies used to have, mind? With all they wee pictures of glittery angels.' Bomber half rose from his seat, hands in a pyramid of prayer, eyes flickering. 'La, la, la. My name's Angel-a, and I paint *lovely* fairy pictures.'

'Piss off.'

On the way up to his room, someone called out *Big Man*. Jamie didn't turn around. What if it was Tyrone? Just like him to have moved in already. Arnie's bed still crumpled, his panorama of Scotland not yet torn down. Sleep would be difficult after tonight. How could Jamie close down every safeguard, knowing that man snored a few rooms away? And today? Jamie still had to get through that, this church service, his family milling around afterwards. Little Eilidh running into his arms, God, he hurt from wanting that, but if that man *touched* them. If he even looked at them, Jamie would rip Tyrone's eyes from his sockets and force them down his filth-filled throat. Stomach-clenching, hard-packed hate; this wasn't good. He had to calm down, get some perspective. He would try to speak to Ethelridge today. Monday was a lifetime away.

'Ho. Big Man.'

It was Brian.

'Don't call me Big Man.'

'Sorry, Bi—'

'Jamie. My name's Jamie.'

'Fair dos, Big J. Listen, can I talk to you? In private, like?'

Brian could be part of the threat too. Initiated into Tyrone's gang, kept biddable and primed with regular free gifts. Even so, Jamie could blow on him and he'd fall over.

'What is it?'

'I canny talk here. Gonny let us in your peter? Just for a minute.'

There was no one else around that Jamie could see.

'No. We can talk here.'

Brian turned his head left and right, like he was checking for someone. Jamie resisted copying him. As Brian put his hand inside his shirt, Jamie tightened his fingers into fists, ready to strike at whatever came out. A knife, a needle? Or this tattered piece of paper with writing on.

'You alright Big J? You look pure sweaty.'

'I'm fine.'

Brian passed him the letter. 'Got this fae the wife.'

'Good for you.'

'Eh, gonny read it for us, Big Man?'

Jamie shoved it back at him. 'Read it yourself. I'm no interested in your love life.'

Brian scratched the back of his head. 'I canny.'

Jamie smoothed the paper, ashamed. Small, mean man that he'd become. Brian swayed before him, neck bowed, his yellowed fingers never still.

'No that many, any road. All they words thegither, they just get jumbled up.'

'But, why don't you go to the literacy classes?'

'Cause I'm no a fucking spazzy.' He spoke quieter. 'Nobody knows.'

'Not even your wife?'

'Well, how the fuck would she be writing me a letter, then?'

'Fair point.'

'I can write my name and that, and I can do numbers. But I canny understand pure big sprawls like that. Anyway, she's never wrote me before.'

Jamie pictured Brian at school, keen wee ginger-boy, all freckles and gumsy smile. Then struggling. Not growing so big, being last for the team. Hand up in class, maybe asking once or twice. Thirty-odd other voices louder, more persistent. Him at home, the slap when he interrupted. Then running to keep up. Nobody waiting for him. Eventually, running away; join a team, rule the scheme. Drugs and dosh and a bit of respect. Bugger books and learning.

'So?'

'So?'

'Please? Can you . . . ?'

'Oh, sure. Sorry pal.'

Jamie read the letter, to himself at first.

Brian,

I meant what I said on the phone. You and me are finished. I'm not wasting any more time on you. All you do is steal and lie and smoke yourself stupid and leave me with the weans. I've lisened to all your promises for years, and you'll never change. I love you, but I cant do this any more. I told you to choose me or the drugs, and youv made your choice. Ill tell your mum when the weans born and she can bring you a picture. But thats it. Im not coming back down and you cant come here when you get out. Have a nice life.

Stella

'Is it about our fight? We'd a wee bit of a barney.'

'Aye, aye.'

'So, what's the moaning cow saying now?'

Brian tried to roll his eyes, but as each one lived its life in perpetual, independent motion, that was outwith his control. Jamie knew what he meant though. Knew also what he really meant, because Brian's hands were very still for once, one clamped firm on top of the other, holding on tight as he could.

'She's saying that she's still really pissed off with you, and she's not going to come to Garthlock for a while. She needs to cool off. And she wants you to keep your promise to stay off the drugs.'

Brian's face flushed. 'Fucksake. What are they like eh? You sure that's all, but? There's nothing wrong with the wean? I mean, it's no that long till she drops.'

'No, no everyone's fine. But she's pretty angry with you, pal. Look, d'you want me to ask Cath to give her a bell?'

'Aye, would you mate? That would be brilliant. I've tried phoning the house, but nobody's been answering. Phew.' He blew air into his fringe. 'A letter. I was pure shitting myself there. Heavy stuff, man. But, aye. I can do that. Chuck the drugs. I'm gonny, I have. Tell your Cath to tell her that, will you?'

'I will.'

'Cheers, pal. Right, I'll away. Any blaw? Naw? It was a *joke*, Big Man, a joke. Nae offence, eh?'

As Brian stoated off, Countdown came charging up the stairs. 'Ho! Jamie, Jamie! Someone's painted over your angel.'

'Och, they wee red splashes? That was me. I'm scunnered with the whole thing. Anyway, *Calvin* can sort it when he gets here.'

'They're no *wee* splashes, pal. Some tosser's pure painted her face out. Big red splatter like she's been malkied with a tomato. Calvin's coming down for the service, but he'll no be here in time to do her full fizzog. Ethel's doing his dinger. He says you've to come and sort it now.'

Eilidh wouldn't stop crying. Cath had tried her with Calpol, Smarties and the offer of an early birthday present, but the same monotone, migraine-pitched wail persisted. Daniel was careering around in the scud, she'd been waiting heart-in-mouth for Anna Cameron to call, but she hadn't, her mother was suggesting an old sock around Eilidh's throat might help – she could nip home and get one of Father's – and the clock kept telling her how late she was. And now someone was at the door.

Speak of the Devil. Wearing TK Maxx, not Prada, in all her favoured shades of sludge and custard.

'Anna! I thought you said you were phoning me?'

'Sorry for breathing. I've been busy actually, helping your husband.'

'That what you call it now?'

'Oh, for God's sake.'

'Sorry, I'm just a bit uptight. We're supposed to be going to a family day at Garthlock. Should have left by now, but I think Eilidh's got chickenpox – it's been doing the rounds at school. And she's desperate to see her daddy.'

'Darling, she'll be fine.' Cath's mum sailed into view. 'I've told you, leave her with Dan and I. We'll have a super time, won't we, munchkins?'

'I want to go to Daddy's castle,' screamed Eilidh. Her cheeks were puffed and scarlet, a few Rice Krispie blisters scabbing around her ears and chin.

'No, Mum, really. I should stay.'

'Catherine, all that man has to look forward to is counting the hours till you appear. Sorry if that sounds melodramatic, dear,' she said to Anna, 'but it's true. He adores my girl. Can't live without her.'

Steady Mother. She'll think I've briefed you. No, Anna, my mother is not as subtle as that. If she thought for a minute you were my competition, she'd have sliced your flesh clean with her tongue, and would now be gnawing on your ribs.

Anna smiled. 'Look, Cath, why don't I go with you? If you've a spare visitor pass now Eilidh's not going, I could fill you in on the way – and ask a few more questions . . .'

Her mum's perfectly proportioned – and only very slightly lifted – nose never missed a trick. 'Questions?'

Once her mum thought there might be some developments in Jamie's case, Cath would have to give her hourly updates, Doris too, and this might all come to nothing. Anna was still doing her cheesy smile routine. Julia Roberts, without the warmth.

'Anna's a policewoman, Mum. She's doing a dissertation on prisons, aren't you?'

'Eh? Oh, yes. Prisons. Can't get enough of them.' Anna looked expectantly at Cath.

Take Anna along for the ride? When the prize was two extra hours with Jamie? Not in a million years. Anna's fake grin was growing increasingly annoying. 'I've got quite a lot to tell you, Cath.'

'What about dear?' asked her mother.

'Oh, just the latest scandal, Mum. Anna's a terrible gossip.'

The old clock in the lounge clonked twelve. There was some kind of opening ceremony, Jamie had said. If she didn't go now, they might not let her in. Cath kissed the top of Eilidh's hot head, then passed her to her mum.

'Mum, are you sure you'll cope with the kids?'

'How do you think I managed with you and your sister, dear?'

'Mama!' sobbed Eilidh.

'Ssh you, Eilidh-girl, don't you scream,' crooned her grandma. 'Cause we're going to have ice cream.'

'Cream?'

'Uh-huh. And chocolate.'

'Dan-pants too?' she croaked.

'Oh yes, but you'll get more.'

'Right . . . well . . . oh, just come on Anna. Hurry up though, cause I'm late.' Cath threw Anna the car keys. 'I just need to get my bag. You go open up. But I'm driving.'

'Catherine darling . . .' said her mum.

What now? What bloody lecture am I getting next? Your room's all made up, you know. Anytime you want to come home. Or: Have you thought about divorce yet Catherine? Your father plays tennis with a very good lawyer.

'What?'

'Tell James we love him. Very much.'

On the way down, Cath tried to concentrate on the road, the route, the clock, as Anna explained everything the fiscal had told her. Promises, promises, it all seemed too good, but the fluttering, sputtering little sliver of light wouldn't go out.

Please God, let this all be true. Make it happen, and I'll never ask for anything ever again.

'So you went straight to the Procurator Fiscal?'

'Best to go straight to the top. What you'll need to do now is get Jamie's lawyer to liaise with him.'

'D'you think we should tell Jamie all this yet?'

'What do you think?'

'I think he needs every grain of hope he can get. Anna . . .'

Cath turned to catch the profile of this iced-blonde impassive creature whose lips she would like to shred with scissors because they had touched her husband.

'Thank you.'

Anna kept staring ahead. 'One other thing. Does "tie-tie" mean anything to you?'

'Nope.'

'You may as well know. Main reason I wanted to come to the prison actually. David, the PF, says Brisbane made a suggestion, just a suggestion mind, that someone might be out to get Jamie. On Brisbane's behalf.'

'Who?'

'Brisbane didn't say. Just smirked and said "tie-tie". I don't even know if it's a name or a joke or what. They'll keep working on him, don't worry, but I thought I could maybe do a bit of digging down at the prison, see if I get any clues.'

'*Tie-tie.* A tie? Jamie works in the laundry?'

'Has he had any hassle there before?'

'Some ned called Ross, but he's away from Garthlock now.'

'Any other names he's mentioned?'

'Eh . . . old boy called Arnie, Countdown, whoever he is . . . that Brian, oh, and the other day he talked about . . .'

This guy Tyrone.

'Anna, any way you can do a PNC check? Or phone the office and get someone to do one for you?'

'Yeah. Why?'

'Right, the brother has no pre cons you said?'

'None.'

'Okay, cross-reference the father, Gerard Brisbane, and see if he has any known associates listed by the name of Tyrone. Not sure if it's a Christian name or surname. Then find out if this Tyrone is currently residing at HMP Garthlock.'

Jamie never liked her face anyway. There must be some other art connoisseur in Garthlock who agreed that Calvin had got it wrong.

Angels weren't prosaic creatures of the earth. They were ephemeral light and air, shades who caught prayers and reflections. An imagined someone to watch over you. So, it was only right to imagine the face. It didn't take long to paint it over. Jamie used the same glazes he'd done on the wings, hinting at her face in abstract shimmers. He could picture her in candlelight, not that they'd be allowed, but flame would cast movement and depth to the angel's face, like she was under golden water.

The chapel was empty, waiting. Air fluting in thin veils. All the debris and dustsheets had been packed away, everyone gone to get ready. He savoured the total silence. You were never truly alone in jail. His angel smiled at him, the meekest flicker that could be anyone and everyone but was Catherine and was his mother and was Eilidh, and then it turned darker, shining Anna, shining Sarah.

Then grabbing from behind, a flash of fist as a deft, heavy arm struck his skull. Men seizing his wrists, feet kicking him. Bound his limbs, stuffed rags into his mouth. Lifting him up, up, till he almost touched his angel, then carrying him off.

'Your time has come, you pigshit bastard.'

It was Tyrone who held his arms and head, Ally at his feet. Like rushing on a trolley through hospital corridors, Jamie tried to track his way by lightshades and ceilings and colours of walls. He didn't know where they were taking him, but it seemed to be up. Black rafters, another punch to the side of his head. They dropped him on some wooden floorboards, and his tongue spilled free.

'Jesus Christ! Why are you doing this?'

''Cause you killed that lassie Sarah.'

'*God*. I know I did. But you've killed two people. So what does that make you?'

'Aye, but Sarah was my mate's wee girl, so she was. And this is my present to Brizzers. His boy asked us to do this for him, and it's a fucking honour.'

Jamie's body began to convulse as they slipped a noose around his neck. Uncontrollable spasms, speeding rhythms with his desperate heartbeat. They were really going to do this. No joke, no eleventh-hour reprieve. He was going to be throttled till his eyes burst, and his neck snapped from his spine.

'Please, don't do this,' he begged. 'I've got a wee girl too. And a boy. It's not their fault.'

'Never is, pigshite.' Tyrone pulled the cord a little tighter. Jamie shut his eyes. Waited for his life to end. One last gasp to hold his breath, as if he could store the reserves.

'Right, that's us Ally. Gie's a minute, and you can untie his hands.'

Jamie didn't understand. Were they done with him? Scare the shit out him, then let him go?

'You just gonny leave me here?'

Tyrone grinned. 'Naw pal. We reckoned you should go out in style. We're gonny gie you the trip of a lifetime first.'

He grabbed Jamie's right arm, yanked up his sleeve. As Tyrone began to tap on Jamie's vein, Ally moved round in front of him, a silver pencil in his hand. Not a pencil. Clear glass, some liquid spurting. It was a syringe.

'This way, you'll be so out the game we can undo you and leave you lying here.'

'Then it'll look like you done it yourself,' chirped Ally.

'Aye. Pure sin, so it was.' Tyrone shook his head. 'Just couldny hack the guilt.'

Jamie felt a tug, then a burning deep heat as they tied some kind of ligature around his upper arm. He tried to twist his legs up, to kick the syringe from Tyrone's hand, but Ally threw his dead-weight over Jamie's legs and stomach, crushing and crushing till the tingling went numb. A sudden stabbing in his elbow fold and molten death was coursing in his blood and he was worrying about AIDS but he was going to die anyway and Cath would never know he'd never meant it never meant any of it as all feeling slipped away and he was rushing up a tunnel and all he could see was Cath. She had no legs, just her face and arms, and she was holding two bundles . . . they were moving . . . his babies and they were receding, backwards, spiralling faster and faster down to the colours that were rising. Curly red wisp smoke bursting blood vessels into shapes speeding light and dark patches, dark winning over light, his body heavy, flying.

Gone.

When Cath and Anna arrived at Garthlock, there was barely room to park.

Anna insisted they were taken straight to Mr Ethelridge's office. Used her warrant card this time, thrusting it like a back-stage pass. It no longer mattered who knew she was here. She chose her words carefully. 'We've discovered the gun that was alleged by Mr Worth to be in Sarah Brisbane's flat. It's currently undergoing forensic examination to confirm that she did indeed have possession of it. Furthermore, Sarah Brisbane's brother has been detained for questioning with regard to his involvement in concealing the weapon, and in various other criminal activities. As a result of these new developments, the Crown Office has advised that James Worth will be given leave to appeal his conviction, and will be released from prison pending that appeal. You'll be receiving official notification to that effect first thing Monday morning.'

Fingers tightly crossed behind her back. Her mobile reception had given out before she was able to phone David. But it lasted long enough for the E Division controller to phone her back with a crossmatch. Not one, but two known associates of Gerard Brisbane, both currently at Garthlock.

'Well, it's not often I'm actually glad, but that's jolly good news,' said Ethelridge. 'Decent chap, Worth. If he'd been a squaddie . . .'

'However, we've also received information in the interim that requires me to speak urgently to Tyrone Fergusson and Alistair McInally.'

'Why so?'

'Both men are associates of Gerard Brisbane, Sarah's father, and of his son Craig. We have reason to believe they may be involved in a plot to harm Mr Worth.'

Ethelridge scratched his moustache. 'Can't this wait until after the service? They're just about to start the anthem. I know it sounds unlikely, but both men are singing in the choir. Tyrone is a passable baritone actually.'

'They're both definitely there? Now, as we speak?'

'Absolutely. They won't be going anywhere either; the chapel is totally enclosed, and we have increased security on due to the number of outside visitors joining us. We've even got a television crew in,' he said proudly.

Anna turned to Cath. 'What do *you* want to do?'

'I don't care about them right now. I just want to see Jamie.'

'Very well,' said Anna. 'We'll just see Mr Worth then, while we're waiting.'

'He'll be in the church too. They're just about to start the service. Which is where I'm meant to be now.'

Cath looked puzzled. 'Are you sure Jamie's there? He never goes to church.'

'Absolutely. He's actually been involved in painting part of our new mural. Is that not why you're here, Mrs Worth?'

'He just said it was a family day, that's all. Never said anything about doing a painting.'

'A lot of the men don't pass on every detail of their lives here. But yes, Mrs Worth, I can assure you he will be in church. Particularly as I'll be mentioning him and the other *artistes* in my speech.'

'Can you just check he's definitely there?' said Cath. 'Please?'

The governor tutted, picked up his walkie-talkie.

'Ethelridge to Ledbetter.'

'Sir, where are you? The natives are getting restless.'

'Ledbetter, is James Worth there?'

'No sir. Calvin was just looking for him. He's not very happy, sir.'

'Calvin?'

'The artist, sir.'

'Oh yes.'

'Complaining that his mural's been tampered with. Actually, I think it looks rather nice. Very *glowy*—'

'*Worth*, Ledbetter?'

'Oh, yes. Calvin says Worth has gone to the sick bay. Apparently he was feeling sick. Look have we to delay this any longer? Reverend Watson has a funeral in half an hour.'

'No, no. Carry on. I'll be with you shortly, once I've shown my visitors out.'

He put his walkie-talkie back on the desk. 'Hmm. No, seems he's not there after all. He's in the hospital wing.'

'Why?'

Cath darted forward, like the word 'hospital' was an unseen springboard.

'Dicky tummy, I believe.'

'Can you take us there, then?' said Anna.

'Look dear, I haven't got time to—'

'Mr Ethelridge, I don't think you realise how serious this might be.'

'Inspector, I have a prison to run. Now, you're very welcome to come and enjoy the service with the rest of us. I can assure you Mr Worth will be perfectly safe until we get back, whereupon I shall convey you, and your good wishes for his wellbeing, to him.'

'Mr Ethelridge, I'm instructing you to take us immediately to your hospital wing. You seem to be incapable of ensuring even the *location* of your prisoners, let alone their welfare, and—'

Cath laid a hand on her arm.

'Mr Ethelridge, please. My husband may be in immediate danger, and he shouldn't even be here. You know that now.'

'Not officially I don't.'

'Please just let me see him. What if he's been poisoned or something?'

'I hardly think that's likely.'

'You say the press are here already, Mr Ethelridge?' said Anna. 'Terrible shame if they're on hand to film the governor being marched off to a police car. Charged with obstruction, breach of the peace . . .'

'There's absolutely no need to adopt that tone, young woman.'

A horrible, honking yowl. Dear God, Cath had started greeting. Still as weak and weepy as she was three years ago. Bloody woman should have stayed on her happy pills.

'Oh, please take us. Please. Just to put my mind at rest.'

'Oh, very well, the hospital's on our way anyway. And then I really must get on.'

They left the office, Mr Ethelridge taking long, loping strides way out in front. He could get a job in the Ministry for Funny Walks when this posting was over. Cath bumped against her as they jog-trotted in his wake.

'Jesus, Anna. I can't believe you threatened the governor with a breach.'

'And I can't believe you turned on the bloody waterworks.'

That steady, sour smell of antiseptic told Anna they were getting close, but when Ethelridge ushered them through an elegant panelled door, she thought he'd made a mistake. The hospital wing looked like a library. On entering the reception office, instead of glass cabinets full of phials and potions, tall bookshelves lined three of the four walls. Piles of books and magazines were crammed in precariously on top of one another. One of the walls of shelves was empty, the contents all heaped on the floor. At a small desk in the middle of the room sat an apple-munching nurse. Her desklamp shone on a test-tube vase holding a single flower. When she saw the governor, the nurse hid the apple beneath the glossy magazine she was reading and rose slowly from her seat. The scene was far too bucolic and serene; Anna wanted urgency and action. It was a hospital, for God's sake. Lives to save, woman, lives to save. At the very least, she could have been mopping Jamie's brow, helping make up a foursome around his bed. This was going to be strange, her and Cath and Jamie, grouped in an awkward isosceles.

'Nurse Rodgers. I thought I told you to get these books sorted out.'

'That's what I *was* doing, sir.'

Ethelridge prodded one of the towers with his toe. 'Not very successfully. Anyway. Can you take us to see James Worth?'

'Who?'

'Worth. Came here a short while ago, complaining of a stomach ache?'

'No Mr Ethelridge. He never reported here. I've had O'Hare with a septic toe, but that's been the lot. No one called Worth.'

All the urgency you want now, girl.

Can you feel it, that plummeting belly-pit ticking of time running out, and you running ragged; Cath running on empty as her face folds in fear?

How about that, Anna Cameron? So what you gonny do now? Quick, girl. Think, girl. The buck stops with you.

'Governor, we need to find him. *Now.*'

'Right, I'll get a prison-wide lookout broadcast for him. Don't you worry, Mrs Worth. I can guarantee he'll still be in the prison.'

Ethelridge flung open the door, a tiny breeze shooting past Anna's face. Ruffling the papers on the nurse's desk, knocking over the test tube. It spilled out its single bud, a little river puddling onto *Hello!*

'Oh, damn.'

The nurse lifted up her magazine, shook the drops of water from the face of a toothy bride. The happy couple were posed beside a country church, weather-vaned spire wrapped garishly with white streamers.

'Come on, Cath,' shouted Anna. 'Let's go. We'll start in his room. What block is it?'

Cath didn't move. She was staring at the puckered page of the magazine, pale hands pressed against her mouth. Eyes darting, desperate.

'He's in the chapel,' said Cath.

'How do you know that?' Ethelridge's impatient fingers were drumming on the doorframe.

'I just know. Please, we've got to be quick.'

They ran back down the oaken corridor, Ethelridge shouting in his walkie-talkie, Cath only whispering, *It'll be okay,* over and over as she fled past Anna, feet flying with some power that Anna did not possess. Anna could hear deep bass singing, feel it boom and bloom, resounding through floorboards, jarring her shins.

Jesus Christ is risen, and is here . . .

They crashed through the double doors of the chapel as the choir proclaimed their climax.

In this place.

On the word 'place', the curtain above the chancel peeled back, as two leaves parted in the panelled ceiling above. There was an intake of breath as the mechanism jammed, something long and black dangling at the opening of the gap. With a grinding noise the machinery shuddered, then the hanging object dropped into place.

A long, thin darkness, no outstretched spar. Not a cross.

But a body.

Swinging tick-tock in time with silent seconds of disbelief. Twirling as it turned, back of head, front of face. Heads and tails, heads and tails. Stopped at tails. Jamie's head turned to face the wall.

Then urgent yelling, and a broken breath. Anna reached out, tried to catch her, as Cath fell to her knees.

Somewhere, a little girl runs barefoot along a beach, soft sand-skliff against her soles. The warm graininess is a revelation, a grit that is pleasant and can mould to your shape. Her brother is sprinting in his plastic sandals, streaming seaweed in glossed hanks of green, her tottering in his wake until he goes too fast and she can see him no longer. One foot catches in a tumble, her knees sink and she squeals.

It is not meant, simply blurted. She looks up, sharp, at her father, who is not angry. Her mother waves to her from the water and she runs, runs to that horizon, with the wind at her back, and a million searing rays painting ribbons in the sky. Shock of cold against hot skin, slaps that tickle and buoy, and she kicks up sea like a comet tail, her mother's soft hand in hers.

Afterwards they go for chips, laughing on the bus home, until she folds, salty, sated, into slumber. Gentle crooning curves its notes around her, and supports her like a lap.

It is a day that will stay with her for life.

The Last

This would be the last time Jamie ever walked out of these doors. He kept telling himself that, though nothing was guaranteed.

But the facts were there. They'd found the gun, found Sarah's prints still on it. The brother had told them how he'd panicked, fled the house. So keen was he to uncoil himself from the trafficking ring that he would have signed a confession in blood. Anna said Coltrane had been suspended, pending investigation. And Armstrong was off sick. Not that they mattered any more.

'You okay there?'

Cath was holding his arm, helping him down the stairs. They'd thought at first his neck was broken. He'd been unable to move, lying in the hospital wing for days until the swelling settled. A neurosurgeon had come to see him, paid for by the polis. If he'd known that at the time, he'd have told the man to piss off. They had scanned him, manipulated him. Discovered only torn ligaments and a damaged vertebra. Thank God for dodgy builders. The cantilever had never worked right, the weight of Jamie's leaden body unbalancing it further, so it stuttered and inched its load, rather than dramatically firing it into the waiting air.

He was face to face with his angel as he fell, swore he saw wings outstretched, flurried feather and fur. Felt fur, yes, as he slid to oblivion. Cool, soft on his brow, then he woke to Catherine's hair, strewn thick and shining on his pillow. And now, today, they had let him out on appeal. He was coming home. A day so distant as to be dead, crushed away with the memory of other foolish things like hope and trust and purpose, but other times so close he could almost smell the freesias on the hall table, Dan's nappies in the bin.

'Will we go straight home, Jamie? Do you want me to stop at the chemist's first?'

Do you want me to stop? Stop this segment of his life and frame it, block it high on a canvas as an 'other', not part of him? These months, this year were all woven in his fabric now, each skittered stitch tied tight as the sutures on his cheek. And, when they dissolved, he'd still be held together by the work they'd done.

Work.

What would he be now, apart from free? Would they take him back, would he want to go?

James Worth was a policeman. And he was ever proud of that.

But he'd grown too far, too fast. Like Daniel, whom Cath said had stretched so much. Would he recognise his daddy? Eilidh did, when she visited him in hospital. Ran straight to his face and kissed it fiercely, sweet salve on every cell.

'No, I don't need anything. Doctor gave me enough painkillers to choke a horse.'

They drove with just the radio between them, Cath flicking tracks to find his favourites, but it didn't matter, because he slept most of the way home. Took no leave, bade no goodbyes. Apart from the bits and pieces Cath had brought down, he carried only what he came in with. His suit, his watch, his good shoes and his mobile. When he switched it on, it still had charge. All these things, just as he left them. He slept so sound, it was like he'd never slept before. If he wanted, he could stop the car. Could turn down the music, could kiss his wife.

'Stop the car, Cath.'

'What is it? D'you feel sick? We're nearly home now, honey.'

'Just stop the car.'

'Um, okay. Give me a minute.' Cath looked around her. 'There's a bit further on we could stop, actually.' She drove on for a couple of streets, then clicked on the indicator and pulled into the side.

'What is it? You feeling alright?'

Light is glowing from inside her veins. Each knot of bone is new, the sheen on her skin soft and never-seen. He touches the flat of his palm to her cheek, afraid, enraged, now grabbing at her face. Chiselled, pared rawness that is only love; pure, deep, beating love that terrifies, striking him, gulping in her breath and her breathing into him hot and panicked, trying to enter and patch and meld and own and make it all whole. And it hurts. It hurts so hard he thinks he'll never breathe again. And all around is happy crying, childish hysterics blowing away the badness.

'I only ever wanted you, Cath.'

'I know.' She kissed him, kept kissing him.

They had pulled up by the River Cart. A playpark across the road, kids scrambling on the climbing frame. Rows of sandstone tenements, each hiding someone's home. The bachelor man, with his meal-for-one. A frantic mum with her grizzling baby, wondering why no one comes near. An old lady with her cats, all sharing buttered cod. A family, with a dad and a brother; the mum is gone, the little girl is sitting in her room. Her anorak is too small, but she wears it anyway.

'Is this Gryffe Street, Cath?'

'Mm-hm.'

'Did you mean to come this way?'

She wiped her eyes with her sleeve. 'Let's go for a walk.'

'No . . .'

'Come on. Just a wee one.'

Big steps, little steps. Don't step on the cracks. They stopped outside the Brisbane flat. Cath held him steady. Held him still.

'It was here, wasn't it?'

'Yes.'

This piece of concrete, on which children had chalked hop-scotch squares. Sarah's hair all splayed in puddles, and the sky-punching pummels of bullets and pain.

'I cradled her, you know. When she was lying on the ground. I put my arm beneath her head, but they pulled me away. I kept thinking; what if it was Eilidh? What if it was Eilidh and nobody stayed with her, and I don't *know* that Cath, nobody told me if someone stayed with her. They put me in a car and took her in the ambulance, but they were just holding onto the stretcher. Nobody was holding her hand.'

'But you did.'

Cath was crying again. Wide gapes of scars gasping open after fifteen years together.

'I'm sorry Cath. I'm so sorry I lost you. I lost me, too.'

Standing there, on the precipice, wondering and being so sure. Jamie felt his wife speak, chords reverberating inside his chest.

'Just hold me.'

His finger around her mouth, the soft, padded pressure of her perfect lips. Pushing her head back, to see her face.

'You are beautiful, Cath. Do you know that?'

Smiles through broken sobs. 'Daft bugger.'

His skin snagging, her flinching. 'God, your tooth. I'm sorry, I forgot.'

'It's okay. Doesn't hurt so much now.'

A ridiculous trill of trumpets as his phone shrilled in his pocket.

'See?' said Cath. 'Word's got out. That's you back on the social circuit already.'

He took out his phone. It was a text. From Anna Cameron.
Everything ok? Call me.

'Who is it?'

Jamie pressed delete. 'No one.'

He scuffed his sole on the dust. This would be the last time he came here. And he turned, with his wife, to go home.

THE END

SOPHIE HANNAH

The Other Half Lives

Why would anyone confess to the murder of someone who isn't dead?

Ruth Bussey knows what it means to be in the wrong and to be wronged. She once did something she regrets, and her punishment nearly destroyed her. Now Ruth is rebuilding her life, and has found a love she doesn't believe she deserves: Aidan Seed. Aidan is also troubled by a past he hates to talk about, until one day he decides he must confide in Ruth. He tells her that years ago he killed someone: a woman called Mary Trelease.

Ruth is confused. She's certain she's heard the name before, and when she realises why it sounds familiar, her fear and confusion deepen – because the Mary Trelease that Ruth knows is very much alive ...

'This utterly gripping thriller should establish her as one of the great unmissables of this genre - intelligent, classy and with a wonderfully Gothic imagination' *The Times*

HODDER